The Secret
Child

ALSO BY KERRY FISHER

The School Gate Survival Guide
The Island Escape
After the Lie
The Silent Wife

The Secret Child

KERRY FISHER

Bookouture

Published by Bookouture in 2017
An imprint of StoryFire Ltd.
Carmelite House
50 Victoria Embankment
London EC4Y 0DZ
www.bookouture.com

ISBN: 978-1-78681-308-4
eBook ISBN: 978-1-78681-307-7

For Cam, and all the other teenage sons out there
who probably have no idea just how much they are loved

PROLOGUE

8 February 2013

Six weeks. That's all I had with you. Forty-two days. Time we throw away carelessly, wishing the days away, to Christmas, to a holiday, to the end of, to the beginning of, to when we think we'll be happy. But those precious weeks formed the rest of my life, the moments I had to breathe you in, to draw you deep into my heart, to have enough of you to sustain me forever.

If you asked me now what I was doing during six weeks in the summer last year, five years ago, a decade ago, I'd have to hazard a guess – Danny and I on a week's holiday in the Isle of Wight? A trip to the garden centre? An afternoon in the park with my granddaughter?

But those six weeks in 1968. I remember every day. Or I think I do. The rational part of my brain knows that's unlikely. But the emotional imprint on my heart is certain. You arrived at three in the morning on Thursday 13 June. I remember reaching midnight and being glad that you wouldn't be a 'Wednesday's child, full of woe'. It still broke my heart that you'd be a Thursday's child with 'far to go'. Far away from me. My stomach twisted every time I thought about it. The nuns repeated the mantra, 'A baby needs two parents. If you really love your baby, you'll give him away. You'd be a bad mother. You'll get over it; move on with your life. You can't offer the baby what another family can.'

One nun, Sister Patricia, leaned over me when I was in labour, her lips tight and thin as though they lacked the elasticity to expand into a smile. 'Your pain is God's punishment for your sin.'

The rebellious bit of me wanted to burst out with, 'My last baby was far more painful and she was born within a marriage.' But not toeing the line is what had brought me here in the first place. And I'd promised my mother – trying to make amends for my disgrace – that I'd pretend to be young and unmarried, barely wise enough in the ways of the world to understand how I'd got pregnant in the first place. Bit late to be pulling the whole 'I didn't realise I could get pregnant standing up' trick with a two-year-old daughter at home.

But I wasn't going to give those nuns the satisfaction of seeing me squirm in pain. They didn't know you were my second baby and I already knew the truth about childbirth. This time I wasn't bumbling along expecting it to be 'like bad period pain' as my mother had assured me when Louise was born.

I forced myself not to think about Mum and how I'd let her down, news of this pregnancy following shortly after Dad had died, everything about her already frayed and leaden from the shock of losing him. But now wasn't the moment to think about that. I had forever to sift through the folly that led me here. As the nuns – who'd clearly skipped the scriptures about forgiveness – shoved my feet into stirrups, I sang to myself, silently in my head, to distract me. I don't know why I chose a hymn, 'Amazing Grace', when religion – if that was what this was – disgusted me. Still, those lovely words calmed me, eased your arrival into the world. As soon as you popped out, they tried to take you off to the nursery, but I made such a fuss, screaming and struggling, that they brought a Moses basket and let you sleep next to me.

Sister Patricia's face screwed up like an old paper bag when she saw I'd won. 'Don't think you're going to get special treatment. Tomorrow he goes to the night nursery.'

There was some tiny comfort in the fact that I knew, beyond a shadow of a doubt, that my baby would never be going to the night nursery. The nuns' need to enforce a rule would never match my need to keep you close. As soon as they'd gone, I picked you up and cuddled you. Really looked at you, trying to make sure I'd print your little face on my memory forever. The dimple in your chin. That perfect nose twitching with every breath. Your long lashes fanned out on your cheeks, still red and wrinkled as though you were a bit overcooked. Your eyes fluttering about underneath eyelids criss-crossed with tiny blue veins. They'd bandaged my breasts to stop my milk coming in, but I could feel them, heavy and full. I ripped the bandages off. That was one area where nobody, not even the mother who'd give you a much better life later on, could outdo me. Unlike Louise, who'd been a difficult baby to latch on, never quite getting the right position, you were soon sucking away, making little murmurs of satisfaction. Just for a moment, I could imagine sitting propped up with you on my pillows back home, Louise toddling about fetching your nappies, finding your dummy. Then I'd think about Danny, on the other side of the world, and imagine him walking through the door to discover me sitting there with a baby.

A baby that couldn't possibly be his.

When Sister Patricia and her little posse of crows came to fetch you the next day to whisk you off to the nursery, I refused, tucking myself around you and holding her off as her bony fingers tried to claw you away. Eventually an older nun, Sister Domenica, ran in to see what was going on. She touched my arm, her fingers cool and gentle.

'Let him go, Paula. It will be easier this way.' The kindness in her voice almost robbed the fight within me.

I shivered despite the warm air blowing in from the garden. 'I will give him up. I will. But let him stay with me until then. Just until then. I'm feeding him myself.'

She shook her head. 'You're making it much harder for yourself, child. Put him on a bottle.' Sister Patricia stood behind her, her face bemused as though maternal love was an indulgence, a vanity.

I tensed, defiance coursing through me, anchoring my feet, feeling the muscles in my stomach protest.

Sister Domenica sighed. 'If that's what you want.'

Then, as quickly as she'd arrived, she turned on her heel, with a sharp, 'Out you come,' to the other nuns. And they never tried to take you away from me again.

Until that day.

Sometimes you'd sleep with your eyes half-open as though you knew you needed to be on guard, as though you knew already that I couldn't be relied on, couldn't be trusted to keep you safe. Every night I'd stay awake as long as I could, terrified to sleep in case you'd gone when I woke. I tried to formulate a plan to keep you, going round and round with every impossible option, counting down the weeks, then the days, closing my ears to the screams from the floor above of the other poor girls in labour.

I couldn't ignore what was coming.

The day I had to sign a form consenting to the necessary vaccinations 'whilst in the care of prospective adoptive parents… until the Adoption Order is granted' nearly finished me off. I wouldn't be there to hold you tight, to reassure you that the pain in your chubby little thigh was for your own good. I wouldn't be there to press on the plaster, to cuddle you until you stopped crying.

I'd stare out of the window, my heart beating with dread, as almost every day, a different girl would walk to the office at the end of garden, head low over a bundle in a blanket. I'd watch and wait, knowing I didn't want to see but unable to tear myself away. After ten minutes, sometimes twenty, never longer, the girl would reappear, arms empty. Some of the girls would rush away quickly, their feet echoing on the crazy paving, as though they were being chased. Some would emerge head down, stumbling back towards the home, with the unsteady gait of a drunk. Others walked head high, dry-eyed, a tightly laced corset of numbness holding them in.

Whoever said time goes more quickly as you get older was wrong. I was twenty-two then and those six weeks raced by, a shoal of fish in the shadow of a shark. In comparison, the forty-five years since then have scraped along, out of kilter like a buckled bicycle wheel. I'm sixty-seven today and I don't feel like celebrating. It's just another birthday without you.

I still miss you, little one.

PART ONE

SUSIE

CHAPTER ONE
24 July 1968

The day before I gave you up, my mother came to visit for the first time. I hadn't expected to see her until I returned home to collect Louise. She'd been looking after her in my absence. Or, as it felt like to me, my banishment, sent away before anyone spotted the bump, first to hide at Mum's sister's, my Aunt Margaret's in Brighton, then to the hell that was the Mother and Baby home in London.

I tried to imagine Mum's face when she set eyes upon you for the first time: she couldn't help but love you like I did. I'd dressed you in a little white suit, with a knitted jacket I'd made during the afternoons when I'd finished all my chores. Your eyes were alert, flicking about, making sense of your surroundings.

Or maybe you were just watchful, sensing that no good was heading your way. You would be intelligent, strong and capable, I was sure of that. I carried you down the corridor, stopping to commiserate with the girl who was on her hands and knees scrubbing the floor. That had been my job before I gave birth. Her back would be killing her with the effort of keeping her balance with the weight of her bump hanging down. I scanned the corridor for any sign of the nuns milling about, then I offered her my free hand. 'Here, stand up for a minute and stretch your back. You'll find it helps.'

I pulled her up. She had the brightest ginger hair I'd ever seen. 'A proper carrot top', my mother would have said. Her head was a mass of tight corkscrews that stood out at jaunty angles. I bet the nuns picked on her. Hair that didn't look repentant would be reason enough. For a second, though, I was jealous of her. Her baby would most likely have ginger hair, *which would easily be spotted* in a crowd, whereas I'd be doomed to scanning the population for dark-haired males forever more. Would I even recognise you if you were standing next to me in five years' time, let alone twenty?

She stood up, pressing her hands into the small of her back. 'Those bloody nuns are bitches, aren't they? I'd like to see them down on their knees with their backsides in the air scrubbing these floors,' she said, in a voice that was far too loud, reverberating down the hallway.

'Shhhh. You'll get us in trouble.'

She laughed; a big throaty cackle. 'What, more trouble than we're in already? I can't imagine what that would look like. You from round here?'

I shook my head. 'South coast.' I glanced round guiltily. We weren't supposed to exchange personal information.

'Don't tell me, Plymouth? Portsmouth?'

'Portsmouth,' I whispered.

'Me too. Every other girl in here is from somewhere with a naval base. Them sailors have obviously been having a right old time on their leave. Think there's been a rush of women "visiting their cousins".'

Despite worrying a nun would come flapping round the corner and send me off to the laundry as a punishment for daring to laugh, I wanted to hug this girl and cling to her, the only one I'd met so far who wasn't slinking about looking as though she was braced for a blow.

I smiled, her bravado rubbing off on me. 'I'm "helping my aunt with a bad back". I'll let you know what trouble looks like. My mum's downstairs.'

Her smile faded a little. 'My mum can't visit. My dad won't let her.'

There was only one meagre upside to my dad dropping dead from a heart attack the previous year. I hadn't had to witness his disappointment that the daughter he'd handed to Danny on that chilly March day three years earlier – 'You take care of her, she's very special' – had done what no wife should ever do.

I shifted you in my arms. Most of all I'd let you down, allowed everyone to see you as a burden, an inconvenience to be hidden away, to lie about, to dismiss. I'd probably never get the chance to explain, but I hoped you were absorbing my love into every cell of your little body, storing it up for sustenance in later life.

'What's your name, anyway? I'm Elizabeth. Lizzy.'

I didn't know and didn't ask if that was her real name. 'Paula. Have you got long?' I asked, nodding at her swollen belly.

'Not quite sure when I fell pregnant. Might be two weeks to go, might be another month. Haven't exactly spelt it out to the sisters but it wasn't a one-off. Never been able to resist a uniform.'

I had to admire her spirit. Half the girls in here acted like it had been an immaculate conception. She was so matter-of-fact, as though there was a bit of her that regretted falling pregnant so soon, before she'd had chance to really enjoy herself. I still felt ashamed of how I'd ended up in here, even though clearly there wasn't much point in pretending I hadn't had sex.

She leaned over and peered at you. 'Let's have a proper look at him, then. Handsome boy. He's got eyes just like yours.'

I took so much comfort in that. That you'd have a part of me no one would ever be able to change. That no matter how you grew, what they clothed you in, how they cut your hair, there'd be one bit of your mother you'd carry with you forever.

Lizzy lowered her voice. 'It's not today for you, is it?'

I shook my head, the word tomorrow too big, too real, too terrifying to squeeze out. The sound of a nun's sandal smacking along the corridor signalled the end of our conversation before I had to force out an answer.

I walked on, looking round to see Lizzy stick her tongue out behind the nun's back. Louis Armstrong's 'What a Wonderful World' was playing in the distance. My brain tried to take refuge in the thought that whoever had switched on the radio would be for the high jump. But a greater, weightier hope obliterated that superficial sanctuary: maybe, just maybe, my mother had turned up to tell me that she'd found a solution; that she couldn't bear to see her grandson live his life with complete strangers. But even in my wildest, most optimistic imaginings I couldn't come up with a single scenario that would mean my husband wouldn't have to know what I'd done. My heart jolted as I imagined the hurt on Danny's face, grappling to understand why I'd already broken my vows. I couldn't disagree with my mother when I'd steeled myself to tell her my 'happy' news: 'It's the wives who are supposed to worry about what their husbands are up to, not the other way round.'

For a minute, the thought of losing Danny made me pause, clinging onto the banister until the fear passed. My mother wouldn't hear of me telling him the truth. 'Don't throw away your future. Do it for Louise, if not for yourself. This is the best way, the only way. Even a good man like Danny isn't going to take on some other man's child. Not in these circumstances. You owe it to the daughter you've already got to put this behind you and never breathe a word to anyone. I can't afford to keep you and Louise if he puts you on the streets, not now your dad's gone.'

I knew she was right. But the price of keeping silent was so unbearably high.

Sister Patricia appeared at the bottom of the oak staircase, a vulture gorging on other people's tragedies. 'Let's hope your mother can see sense.'

You curled your hand tightly around my little finger. A boy with great instincts. I pushed past Sister Patricia and into the reception room, feeling the drop in temperature in that gloomy space, cold even on a sunny July day. I pulled you closer to me as I shivered in my thin summer dress, one I'd worn pre-pregnancy. My appetite had gone and you were such a hungry baby. The other girls were jealous that the weight had already dropped off me. 'What's your secret then, Paula? You got some clever diet pills?'

The soreness every time you clamped your little mouth onto my breasts was almost a source of joy. I loved feeding you, those moments when no one could tell me I needed to be doing something else, when it was just you and me, cocooned together. I'd cried when the nuns forced me to put you on a bottle, ten days before you were leaving me. 'You've got to get him ready for his new life. His mother needs to be able to feed him on the way home.' I couldn't imagine what she'd look like, who she'd be.

I was your mother.

My own mother sat in a brown leather armchair, a thin shaft of sunshine settling on the purple and pink squares of her blouse, the only bit of colour in the room among the sludgy paintings of Jesus on the cross and wooden crucifixes. My eyes scanned her face as though peering at a portrait of a distant ancestor, trying to identify family traits. Widowhood and a wayward daughter had robbed her of her softness, of her plump face that had always held the promise of welcome, of refuge. Everything about her was pinched and rigid, a framework to exist in rather than a life to embrace.

She gave a little cry and jumped to her feet, locking her hands to her side in case they betrayed her by reaching out for you. Nothing like the memory I had of Mum and Dad jostling through the ward door to get the first glimpse of Louise in the hospital, all jolly banter and 'she's got my chin' jokes. Mum's demeanour today couldn't have been further from the industrial-scale knitting of shawls and bootees that accompanied my first pregnancy.

She walked towards me. 'Susie,' she said, as though her throat was clogged with emotion she dared not set free. It was so odd hearing my real name again after all this time answering to 'Paula'. I felt as though she was speaking to someone else. Which she was. I'd never just be Susie, Louise's mum, Danny's wife again. Her hands jerked upwards, then fell back down. I forced myself to remember that she was not the enemy, just a woman between a rock and a hard place who would, in other circumstances, have sung you lullabies, soothed you when no one else could, paraded you about the neighbourhood for all to see and admire.

Not secreted us away here.

She studied your face for ages, her lips twitching, trying to put her words in the right order.

'Louise is missing you.'

I nodded. My heart was so full of grief for you, I could barely recall what it felt like to love a child without a time limit. You had eighteen hours and thirteen minutes left of me. Louise still had a lifetime.

Mum rushed to fill the silence. 'I got Aunt Margaret to send all the letters you'd written to Danny. One about every week or so, like you said. These are the ones you've had back.' She unclasped her handbag and drew out a sheaf of blue airmail letters, with their Singapore postmarks. I dreaded reading that he was returning early, that I'd have no time to adjust to my old life

'You hang onto them, Mum. I'll read them when I get home.'

In less than twenty-four hours, I'd be giving you away forever. I had the rest of my life to work through the madness of trying to conceal another man's baby from my husband.

Mum tucked a piece of hair under her headscarf. 'Have you still got your bus and train fares?'

'Yes.' It seemed impossible that tomorrow I'd pack the few belongings I had, walk out of those big iron gates, then catch the bus to Victoria for the train back to Portsmouth, as though I'd done nothing more significant than gone on a day trip to the Big Smoke.

'Don't forget I've told everyone you've been giving my sister a hand to run her greengrocer's in Brighton while she's had a bad back. Even Eileen next door thinks you're wonderful for helping out.' Mum nearly smiled as though she believed her own story.

Then she sat up straight, the words appearing to drain out of her.

Nothing like the mother of the bride, twittering with excitement that her daughter was marrying a petty officer in the navy, patting Danny's uniform and saying, 'Doesn't he look smart?' over and over again. I was only bloody nineteen. My whole family made it sound as though the plainest girl in the whole of the British Isles had been sitting gathering a thick layer of dust until someone way better than I should have expected had rescued me. Aunt Margaret was the worst: 'Isn't our Susie lucky marrying such a handsome chap? And moving straight into a house of her own. Me and Bert rented for years till we had our own place. Hope she's going to make a good wife. Men like him don't come along every day.'

I doubted that Danny considered himself lucky, with both his parents dying before he was sixteen, even if he did end up with his own house. Thankfully Dad raised his eyebrows and said in my ear, 'He's the lucky one, love. If he doesn't look after you, I'll be after him with my shotgun.'

I'd laughed and said, 'You haven't got a shotgun.'

He'd looked me straight in the eye and said, 'Not yet, I haven't. Let's hope I don't need one.' He'd winked. But there was something comforting about knowing that, at least to my father, the most important person was still me.

Aunt Margaret had looked as if the milk had curdled in her tea every morning I was staying with her. As my bump grew, she tutted every time she looked at it until I barely left my room, the little click of her tongue searing another layer of shame into me. But in the end, I had to be grateful; she'd helped me out.

A bell rang. One of the many. So much to say. But none of it would be any use.

Mum shifted in her seat, her eyes pleading for understanding. 'If Danny throws you out, I couldn't afford to keep you, Susie. Not with Louise as well. It's been enough of a struggle since your dad died. And most of my savings went on paying for your place here, away from Portsmouth…' Her voice dropped to a whisper. 'I had to bribe that social worker to sort somewhere, to say you weren't married.'

Her eyes glistened.

'Danny's a good man, a good provider. He doesn't need to know anything of this.'

'I know that, Mum. I love him.' The truth of those three words would have ripped me apart if I'd had any room left for grieving.

She paused, not quite meeting my eye.

'You didn't tell the baby's father, did you?'

'What do you think? I'm not completely stupid.'

Her face sagged with relief.

'There's only you, me and Margaret that knows. You need to let go of this little one now. You don't want to find yourself all washed up with two babies on your own. You've got to think of Louise. She's done nothing wrong.'

I couldn't imagine going home, picking her up, smelling that sweet scent of her soft skin. My baby, but not this baby. Yet I'd be there tomorrow. Without the angles of you in my arms, the comforting pad of your bottom in the crook of my elbow, your wispy hair soft against my arm. Maybe holding Louise would fill the space left by you. I didn't want to insult you by hoping that was possible.

Mum stood to leave. She couldn't help but tickle you under the chin. You gripped her finger and her eyes filled.

I held my breath, still hoping for a miracle that would allow me to keep you. Family was everything to Mum.

'It's for the best, Susie. It gives him a chance at a better life. Breaks my heart too, you know.'

I hugged you to me and walked out. I surprised Sister Patricia who was hovering outside the door. Her eyes narrowed, giving her the appearance of a sly cat, the sort that would purr loudly while preparing to claw your hand to shreds. 'Everything all right, Paula? Cheer up. Once you leave here, you can forget this ever happened.'

I stalked past her without even stopping to respond.

Eighteen hours, six minutes.

I didn't *want* to forget how much I loved you.

CHAPTER TWO

October 1968

I couldn't face going to meet Danny's ship, jostling among all the other wives, craning for the first glimpse of his dark hair and kind face. I sent a message with one of my friends that Louise was ill and I'd see him back at the house. Normally, I'd have rushed to the dockyard to be right at the front, jittery with impatience, in a hurry to get home, to separate him from his mates, the shouts of 'See you later, Danny boy!', the camaraderie that had replaced us, his little family, in the fifteen months he'd been away. I'd be longing for the time when he'd whisk me round the living room singing along to Engelbert Humperdinck, Tom Jones and The Beach Boys. Some of the wives half-dreaded their husbands' return, resenting the curbs on their freedom. Others moaned about the extra work – 'Jesus, all that having to cook a proper dinner every night – no more nipping out to the chippy – and that's before he starts trying to get his leg over!'

But I usually loved Danny coming home and getting to know him all over again. We'd dance round each other, a bit shy, to begin with. He wasn't a man to chase me up the stairs and start ripping my blouse off. Last time he'd been home, when Louise had finally flaked out, exhausted by Danny swooping her up into the air and swinging her round, he'd put out a hand to me: 'Will you run me a bath while I get changed?' We both knew that we'd end up in bed. Of course we would. We were married and young.

But I still felt awkward, oddly nervous of him seeing me naked, of disappointing him, of not living up to the love and longing in his letters: 'Dragging myself through these last few weeks. Can't believe how slowly the time is going. Think about you all the time.' In the end, he'd made me get into the bath with him, soaping my back, running his hands over every inch of my skin until the miles and months between us shrank back down into something manageable. And within a few days, it was as though he'd never been away.

How simple that seemed now. Of course I'd always worried whether he'd still find me attractive, whether I'd match the expectations he'd held in his mind all the time he'd been at sea. Whether he'd feel bored with just us for company, without the banter on the ship, the boisterous camaraderie to carry him through the days. Fretted that I wouldn't make the most of the time he was home, anxious about how soon he would be leaving again. Those worries seemed miniscule now compared with whether he'd notice I'd had a baby while he was sailing the South China Sea.

Now he'd be home in a few hours, the plan I'd hatched with Mum to keep the baby a secret suddenly seemed insane. Ever since 'I Love You Because You Understand Me' had played at the dance hall and Danny had put his hand out to me – 'Will you do me the honour?' – it had become our anthem. We did understand each other. We didn't need to lie. I wasn't one of those wives who splurged the housekeeping on a new blouse then waved away questions with the words, 'This old thing, I've had it ages.'

I wrote to Danny and told him when I'd been out with my friends. He'd write back: 'Glad you're not too lonely. Must admit to being a bit jealous though. Don't let any other men turn your head… You and Louise are my life!' I'd smiled when I read that.

I danced with other men when they asked but never more than twice, three times at a push if they were really good on their feet. I hated sitting out any song with a rhythm. Persistent admirers got frustrated. 'How can you say you don't feel like dancing? You can't keep your hands and feet still.' But even if they persuaded me, I never looked at any of them the way I looked at Danny.

When he'd arrived back in Portsmouth in June 1967 after several weeks in Scotland at the end of his last commission, Louise was fourteen months old and had learnt to say, 'Dada', to Danny's great delight. With a month of glorious leave stretching ahead of us, we'd soon got back into our rhythm of going dancing every Saturday night, leaving my parents to babysit. Dad had waved us out of the door, 'Go and enjoy yourselves, make the most of being young.' I felt like the golden couple on the block when Danny twirled me around to 'A Little Bit Me, A Little Bit You', his feet light, my skirt swirling. The very first Saturday we'd gone out, the band had asked for volunteers to sing the chorus to 'What Becomes of the Broken Hearted?' on stage.

'Only people who can sing, please, we don't want to empty the hall.'

Danny had nudged me. 'Go on, Susie.'

I resisted, hovering between plucking up the courage and sitting down at the side of the hall, but Danny pushed me to the front. The group's lead singer, Rob, knelt down on the edge of the stage and thrust the microphone at me. 'What's your name? And you reckon you can sing? Shall we try her?' A big roar went up. He sang the opening lyrics, then held the mic to me. When I'd sung the next couple of lines, he sat back on his heels. 'We weren't expecting that, were we, folks?' And suddenly, several hands were lifting me up onto stage. I kept my eyes on Danny, who was grinning as though I was top of the bill at the Albert Hall, rather than belting out the chorus at a dance hall that smelt of Players No 6 and stale beer.

And for the next couple of weeks at the dance, Rob looked over at some point in the evening and beckoned me up to join them. Danny didn't seem to mind: he'd dance with his friends' wives and girlfriends who were queuing up to take their turn with the jive king. I'd make a big show of hugging Danny before I went up, a two-way declaration of ownership. Whenever I was singing a love song, my eyes would lock onto his and for a moment or two everyone else would fade onto the sidelines and we'd be in our own little bubble. The next day over Sunday lunch, Danny would tell Mum and Dad which songs I'd performed and get me to sing snippets for them. Dad would make jokes about Danny being careful I didn't disappear off with the Beatles, but Mum would keep butting in, 'Any more cabbage? Yorkshires? Come on, Danny, a strapping lad like you, some more potatoes?' I knew when we went out to the kitchen to fetch the crumble, she'd reiterate her top tips for keeping 'a good man like Danny' – as though he didn't need to so much as crook his little finger to hang onto me. 'Make sure he feels the most important thing in your world. Don't let all that singing go to your head.'

I'd be irritable when she said things like that, but the truth was, when I was up there sharing a mic at the front of the stage, I did feel like a star on *Top of the Pops*. I wasn't just boring old Suzanne Duarte from Portsmouth, who spent half her life waiting for a letter from Danny to plop through the letter box and the other half counting down the days with excitement or dread, depending on whether he was arriving or leaving. When I looked down onto everyone swaying along to 'The Green Green Grass of Home' or going wild to 'Good Vibrations', I felt as though I was someone in my own right, not just a navy wife and mother. Secretly I fancied myself as the new Cilla Black. I'd even had my hair cut into a pixie style, though when Danny said, 'You look like Cilla!' I'd told him not to be daft and that the hairdresser hadn't listened to what I wanted when I'd asked for a trim.

Then, at the beginning of July, when I was already in bits about Danny leaving for the longest commission he'd had to date, Dad died. It would have been his forty-sixth birthday a few days later. But instead of singing, 'For He's a Jolly Good Fellow' and toasting him with Babycham, Mum pressed Dad's pocket watch into my hand and bought steak for dinner, with Louise in a highchair where Dad should have been. And a week later, when his shaving brush still sat on the bathroom sink and the scent of Acqua di Parma hadn't yet disappeared from their bedroom, I waved Danny off to sea on his new ship for fifteen months.

My usual response to people who sat snivelling in an armchair – 'They just need to find a bit of backbone' – came back to haunt me. I realised grief couldn't be herded into a neat little channel and corralled into a pen. That frailty, that inaction I'd once disdained, enveloped me. The only thing that made me get out of bed in the morning was the sound of Louise crying in her bedroom. And sometimes, I'd lie there listening to her thumping the bars, the months before Danny came home stretching ahead like a dark labyrinth I wasn't sure of navigating alone. Then I'd think of Mum, who'd never paid a bill by herself, never organised a coal delivery, never so much as changed a light bulb on her own, but who was still putting one foot in front of the other. 'I'll manage, love. I'll have to.' With a wave of shame, I'd drag myself through to lift Louise out of her cot.

And within a few short weeks, Mum was insistent I should resume my social life. 'It'll take your mind off things. It's not good for Louise to have a mother moping about. Dad wouldn't want you to and neither would Danny. I'll look after Louise. She'll be company for me. You get yourself off to the cinema with the other wives.'

But of course, the other wives wanted to dance. The band wanted me to sing.

I should have known better.

CHAPTER THREE

October 1968

I couldn't settle, waiting for Danny to walk in the door. Louise picked up on my mood and whined around my legs. I'd been up since six. Horse, stable door, bolted and all that, but I was going to try to be a better wife. I'd vacuumed everywhere and even got the polisher out on the parquet floor. My mum would have been proud of me. She was always joking, 'You keep on at her, Danny. My Susie's not much for housework.'

But I'd been lazy when I'd lived at home, more interested in singing into a hairbrush and plucking my eyebrows than helping Mum fuss about with her soda crystals to 'make sure our whites didn't go as grey as Eileen's next door'. Now though, I'd had plenty of practice in the Mother and Baby home. Fear that the nuns would throw a bucket of dirty water over a floor I'd just mopped or screw up a bundle of laundry I'd spent the morning folding had made me take time over things I didn't find important. I'd become adept at spotting dust, straightening towels, shining up the windows with newspaper and vinegar. My ironing was still hopeless because when the nuns weren't looking, I'd swapped chores with Maria, an Irish girl, who enjoyed it.

I picked up Louise, smoothing her eyebrows and kissing her head. She slipped off my knee and fetched her book. She turned to her favourite page, the one with the picture of a boy and a girl sitting in the kitchen with their mum and dad and a fluffy kitten in a basket on the floor. We could never be that family now. Sometimes when I looked at her Janet and John books with the serene mother potting up pretty plants and bathing a cut knee, I wanted to throw myself onto the settee and howl until the house shook. I wasn't that mother. I was a mother who'd lain in a hot bath until my skin was puce. I'd drunk gin until I was sick. It was only thinking about Louise screaming in her bedroom while I lay contorted and broken in the hall that had stopped me throwing myself down the stairs.

And you, you gorgeous boy, you'd hung on in there, refusing to leave me, demanding your chance at life. Then one day you were kicking inside me, fluttering a hello and, despite everything, I felt a flicker of excitement. Madness really. But who could resist a new life, a future yet to be foretold? I had to stop myself brooding about your dad. Whether he'd have regretted that night, when we were all giddy from the applause and foot-stamping following the band's final set. When I'd waved to the other navy wives from the stage and mouthed, 'I'll get a lift home.'

Best not to think about it.

Now I could never be the perfect mother of Louise's books, that mythical creature with her patient smile and soft hands, while everything inside me felt hollow and frightened. If Louise so much as scrabbled at a page in her book, pointing one of her chubby little fingers to John on a swing, despair would overwhelm me. I'd never take you to the park. Never take the crusts to feed the ducks.

Never hear you call me 'Mama'.

It would be a long time before I sang on stage again. I felt guilty if I even hummed along to the radio, allowing myself to feel carefree, to forget what I'd done. I'd immediately rush through to find Louise. Get out the paints. Bake some jam tarts. Play dollies in the garden, wheeling her little pram about. Anything that meant I was concentrating on her, not thinking about you.

And right now, four months after you were born, I had to do what the nuns said – I had to forget about you. Or I'd give myself away and all of this would have been for nothing.

Dusk was falling by the time I saw a dark shadow come to a halt outside our front door. I had all the lights off so that I'd see Danny but he wouldn't be able to see us through the net curtains.

I picked up Louise to hide behind. 'Daddy's home!'

I threw open the door and for the first time since I'd realised I was pregnant, something eased in me, the sound of his voice wrapping itself round all my sores.

He threw his kit over the threshold. 'How are my girls?'

The first thing that struck me was that he didn't sound disappointed in me. No hint of that flat tone my mother had, no slight undercurrent in his words. I'd expected it though. It seemed impossible this huge thing had happened and he was just breezing back into my world, with nothing more on his mind than how much Louise had grown. No reproach. No barrier.

He pulled us into a hug, his mouth searching for mine. Louise reached up and pushed her hand in between our faces. Danny pulled away, laughing. 'So little daughter of mine, feisty like your mother, eh? I thought you were poorly?'

I looked away. 'She had a temperature this morning. I didn't want her to catch a chill waiting for you on the dockside.'

'It's bitter out there. She needs to stay in the warm, don't you, my sweetheart?' he said, reaching out for her.

Louise started to cry.

Danny frowned. 'She doesn't recognise me.'

'She was only fifteen months when she saw you last. Give her time. She'll come round.'

I cuddled her and patted her back until she was calm, feeling a shameful satisfaction that I could still soothe my daughter better than Danny. I sat her on the rug with her Tiny Tears doll. Just looking at Louise putting the dummy in its mouth, adjusting the bib, made me want to cry. I swallowed and forced my face into a smile, watching Danny studying her, shaking his head.

'Wow. She's grown so much. It's like I've come home to a completely different person.'

'I'm still the same, though.' I hoped he couldn't hear the reedy thread of the lie.

He took me in his arms. 'Like the hair,' he said, rubbing his cheek against my head. 'You look thinner.'

I stiffened. 'It's all the running around after Louise. She never stops now she's walking, up, down, up, down. And I haven't been cooking so much since you've been away.' Before he could comment, I rushed on with, 'It's so odd though. I've lost weight but my stomach's still a bit fat.' I tried to make a joke. 'Guess I'll never look like I did before I had Louise.'

'You're beautiful. Absolutely beautiful.' He glanced over his shoulder at Louise. 'Think I'd better have a shower.' He looked away. 'A cold one.'

Panic fluttered in my stomach. I'd have to have sex with him. What if I felt different to him? I forced myself to calm down. Even if I wasn't as he remembered, would his next thought really be 'My wife had a baby while I was away and forgot to tell me?' No one in their right mind would jump to that conclusion.

I took his jacket. 'I'll put the kettle on.'

I went through to the kitchen and ran the tap, putting my wrists under the cold water, waiting for my heart to slow down. I heard Danny chattering to Louise, telling her that he'd just come back from a big boat and now he was going to see her every day for weeks and weeks.

All those days ahead of me, when I'd have to watch what I said.

Lie.

Deceive.

And grieve.

CHAPTER FOUR

June 1976.

It was usually sunny on your birthday. I told myself it was a good sign; that the gods were smiling on you, evidence that you were lucky in life. And this year, 1976, was no exception. The sun was beating down from early morning. Thankfully, even though it was a Sunday, there'd been a drama at the factory where Danny had been working since he'd left the navy five years earlier and they'd called him in. Mum had taken Louise to church, 'It's not right she's being brought up as a heathen.' And I was free to carry out my annual ritual.

I dropped the latch on the front door, pulled down the ladder to the attic and clambered up. I paused at the top to gather myself, then stepped into the dusty confines. I dug under the bits of old carpet, the windbreak and the tent Louise loved sleeping in with her friends in the garden. My hands found the chest I kept locked, immediately relaxing at the touch of the smooth wood. I hesitated before turning the key. Tried to recall the sensation of your weight in my arms, the throaty murmur you did just before you dropped off to sleep. With a sense of pain so familiar it was almost pleasurable, I pushed open the lid. I tucked in a Helicopter Pilot Action Man, next to the seven other presents. I hoped it wouldn't be too young for you, but that's what Gina across the road had bought for her son who was the same age. Perhaps you'd be a helicopter pilot one day. You'd definitely be clever enough.

And there, under the light of the bare attic bulb, with my back against the rafters, I wrote on the card with the '8' badge. I put what I always put: *I'm thinking of you today. I love you. I hope you're happy. I hope you are having a lovely life. I'm sorry I couldn't be a good mother to you but I never wanted to give you away. Love your (other) Mum xxxx.* You were about four when I started putting your 'other' Mum. The woman who had adopted you would have put in all the hard work by then, all the disturbed nights, the fevers, the teething. She'd also have had the first smile, the first steps, the first word. It was selfish, but I hoped you said anything other than Mama first.

I closed the envelope and put it on the pile with the other seven.

I always bought a card with a badge and a number. I wanted you to be sure I knew exactly how many years had passed. A whole eight years now. Eight years when I'd become increasingly desperate for another baby to fill the void you'd left behind. When Louise was born, I'd felt exhausted, frustrated by how long it took us to leave the house, by the buckets of nappies soaking in the bathroom, by her waking up and crying every time I sat down with a cup of coffee. Feed, change, bathe, repeat. And worse when Danny was away and the evenings dragged on, unless Mum popped round or one of the navy wives took pity on me.

But I wouldn't have felt like that with you.

When I was in that dreadful home – how I hoped Sister Patricia had met a sticky end slipping on a big green bar of Fairy soap in the laundry – I loved it when you woke up in the night. I'd take you to the window. 'Look, that's the moon. And those stars over there, see the line with the bucket on the end, that's the Big Dipper. Wherever you end up in the world, make sure you look out for the North Star, that really bright one up there. If you tell yourself we can both see it, I'll never really be far away.'

I pulled out a nappy. I'd hidden it in my case on the last morning at the home. With my finger, I traced my other name, the one the nuns had made us embroider in red silk in the corner of the terry towelling nappies. Paula. A name from another life.

In my mind, of course, you were still a helpless newborn. But now you'd have your own personality, your own fears and strengths. Would you be boisterous? Studious? Small and slender like me? Or tall and chunky like him?

I moved towards the final part of my routine, the bit I saved until last. I both dreaded and welcomed the agony of it. It was the proof I wasn't such a despicable person that I'd given you away and skipped off into the sunset without a backwards glance. My hands found the tissue paper, worn and soft through folding and unfolding. I pulled the corners back to reveal the one black and white Polaroid I had of you, slipped into my hand by Sister Domenica as I opened the doors to that home for the last time, blundering out into the street, my arms still straining to curve around your shape. I couldn't comprehend that for the passers-by with their shopping trolleys, their dogs, their briefcases, it was an unremarkable Thursday in July. I'm not sure I even thanked her. She'd always repeated I should forget about you. I never understood why she'd given it to me, but I was certain of one thing: it had saved my sanity. Chubby, bright-eyed evidence absolute that you had existed, despite the fact you'd never been spoken about in years. Except once, back in April this year, when Mum had found me in tears after my irregular period had arrived after a taunting absence of several months. Just when I'd begun to hope. She patted my hand and said, 'It's strange how you fell so easily with that other one but can't seem to get pregnant now.'

She had no idea that some days my whole body ached, physically burned with the desire to talk about 'that other one', to speculate on where you were now, what you might be doing. I wouldn't care we didn't know the truth, I just wanted to say your name out loud, speak about a world you might be living in with the only other person I knew who'd ever seen you.

But as always, I'd sucked down my rage, resigning myself to keeping quiet again to make up for my mistake.

One mistake on one occasion.

I stopped myself yelling, 'If you hadn't spent all that bloody money on bribing the social worker and paying for that Gestapo Mother and Baby home, I could have gone to live with you if Danny chucked me out.' Instead, I'd feigned a migraine and escaped upstairs to lie down.

By the time Danny had come in from his shift on the presses, there was a fountain of emotions within me, bubbling about, looking for a weakness to breach. He found me forcing a reluctant Louise to play Scrabble at the kitchen table. Between berating her for being stupid for missing double word scores and triple letters, I was ranting, 'You don't want to end up like me, stuck at home with no skills. You need to make something of your life.'

Danny had quietly taken the letters out of her hand as I stabbed at spaces on the board – 'Look! What could you put there? Think!' – and led her into the lounge.

He'd come back and stood behind me, massaging my shoulders. 'She's only ten. Let her watch some telly now. She's worked hard at school all day. She needs to have some rest.'

'I want her to do well. She's all we've got.'

He sighed. 'I know.'

All these years he'd championed me, supported me, told me he was happy with his two girls, 'My big one and my little one', that it didn't matter whether we had another child. But I'd become obsessed with having another baby, convinced it was the only way I could move forwards. Every time he was home on leave, I'd badger him to have sex until there was no pleasure in it for either of us.

The last time he'd left for a long commission in the West Indies when Louise was three and a half, I'd become hysterical. I knew it would be at least another year before getting pregnant would even be a possibility. I sobbed into his chest. 'I need a husband. Louise needs a father! There's no point in being married when you spend most of your life on the other side of the world!'

He'd tried to comfort me. 'Once Louise starts school and you can get a job, the time will fly past. I'll be back before you know it.'

But in the end, five years ago, Danny gave into my pleading and left the navy when the twelve years he'd signed on for were up. For a few months, I felt more optimistic than I had in ages, convinced I'd fall pregnant now he was home all the time. But none of it made any difference. All I managed was to make him as dissatisfied as me. He'd slump in after work, shaking his head. 'God knows how people put up with the clatter of those bloody printing presses, day in, day out. There's not a breath of fresh air in the whole flaming factory.'

He missed the excitement of going to sea. When his navy mates were on shore leave, he'd disappear off for a drink with them, regaling me with stories from his old ship when he returned. 'You'll never guess what Bobby did to a landing craft in Singapore?'

I'd turn away, unable to stand the wistful tone of his voice, finally snapping, 'Isn't it time they grew up?'

But the moments of antagonism I felt towards Danny were nothing compared with the searing hatred I directed towards myself. Pregnant when I shouldn't have been and barren as a windswept moor thereafter.

I looked down at your face one last time.

Danny would be home soon.

I put my lips to your photo, tucked it back into the tissue paper and locked the chest.

I'd see you in another year.

CHAPTER FIVE.
April 1977

The weekend before the 11+ results and allocation of grammar school places came out, I couldn't settle to anything. Louise sat curled up on the couch reading *Fab 208*, her dark hair falling over her face, chewing her lip in concentration as she soaked up details of all the pop stars she loved.

Every now and then, my nerves about the results would get the better of me: 'So you think it might be your maths that let you down?'

She'd be all irritable at being disturbed, 'It was really hard. But everyone found it difficult.'

I wandered about, telling myself that even if she didn't get into the grammar, it wouldn't be the end of the world. But for me it would. I couldn't let those nuns be right, that I was a bad mother and both my children would have had more opportunities with another family. I didn't want Louise ending up like me, grateful for a job serving tea and sandwiches at the café on the corner three days a week. Every time I asked her what she wanted to do, she'd say, 'I want to be like Agnetha from Abba'.

'Don't be silly. Ordinary people like us don't become pop stars.' And she'd shrug, her face closing up.

Today I stood bleaching cloths in the kitchen, desperately wanting to ask her more questions, questions I'd already asked when she did the exam ages ago. I moved on to dusting the collection of Whimsies on the windowsill. Hedgehog, fawn, dog.

My mind drifted to whether you would have grown up with a pet. I pictured you running around a big garden, throwing a stick for a spaniel puppy. I hoped your parents had read to you every night, taken you to the library to choose new books every week, not just let you sit in front of the telly after school. That you really had ended up with the better life the nuns promised.

I trailed back into the lounge, hovering by the couch. Louise looked up exasperated. I had to know. 'Do you think you got more than three quarters of the questions right?'

'I don't know! I did my best, all right? Stop going on about it!'

She snatched up her magazine and stormed upstairs, just as Danny came through the door.

'What's all that about?' he asked, as music blasted out onto the landing.

I turned away, so he couldn't see my face. 'I was just asking her if she was worried about the results next week.'

Danny sighed. 'I didn't pass the 11+ and neither did you. My life hasn't been a disaster. She'll be fine. I don't know why you're so obsessed with it.'

'I'm not *obsessed* with it. I want her to have opportunities. The days of women expecting to be rescued by a handsome prince are over. What have I done with my life? Got married and now I spend my time saying, "One sugar or two?" and running down to the bank to get change for the till.' I ignored the hurt that flashed over Danny's face, raging on, 'Louise is bright enough to be a teacher. She could go to university.'

At the word 'university', Danny's eyebrows shot up. He knew better than to contradict me though. As if he was talking to a dimwit, he said, 'Perhaps she could, but even if she gets into the grammar, we probably shouldn't start shouting about her going to university. We don't want everyone to think we're getting above ourselves.'

'What is actually wrong with wanting to better yourself? With earning enough money so that you get choices in life? It's always people like us who have to put up with being told what to do so that we don't end up on the streets.'

Danny did what he always did these days, he went silent. And his silence lit the bonfire of my unhappiness.

'If I had my time again, I'd have worked hard at school, made something of myself. I was top of my class in English. But Mum was forever telling me to put my books away and rest my brain. She just wanted me to find a rich husband. What did I know about the world, getting married at nineteen, a baby at twenty?'

Danny looked at me, shaking his head slowly as though he was struggling to recognise me. I barely recognised myself, the girl who spent hours perfecting her liquid eyeliner, loved to jive, always ready to see the funny side of everything. The woman who'd race to open the door as soon as I heard Danny's key in the lock, who'd run him a bath and sit on the loo, filling him in on all the gossip from the mess, watching his face take on an expression of mock-disapproval before he burst out laughing.

'I've done my best, Susie. We're not millionaires, but we've got a nice house. I'm still glad I married you, too young or not. Even if you aren't.'

I wanted to explain I was still the woman he married, still the woman who loved him, but that I was stuck. Or worse, not stuck, but drifting away, unable to be who I was before because of this great, gaping hole that only another baby could fill.

'But if you feel so trapped, why do you want another baby?' he asked.

My voice came out in a shout. 'Because I've made my bed and that's all that's open to me now, being a mother. And I can't even do that properly.'

My eyes filled as Danny walked away from me before I could get going on my usual rant: 'How is it fair that stupid Linda across the road has managed to have five kids who never have a bath from one week to the next, always covered in lice, and I can't even get pregnant with one? I just don't understand it.'

As soon as I went back into the kitchen, I heard him go upstairs, his voice low and calm against Louise's shrill, indignant one. I shut the door, turning on the radio, stuck in familiar territory of recognising I'd gone over the top, knowing that they were having to firefight the flames of my insecurities without understanding why I cared so much, why everything had to be just so, why my daughter had to be better than everyone else.

My instructions, 'Make sure you say please and thank you, ask to get down from the table, don't forget to wash your hands before tea,' followed her on every visit to a friend's house. I'd feel offended if the mother didn't comment on how polite she was, hovering on the doorstep for longer than necessary. I pitied those girls who came round for tea in old hand-me-downs, ugly jumbo cords two sizes too big, anoraks with sleeves too long.

'You spoil that girl,' Danny said whenever I turned up with yet another smock top or pair of dungarees for Louise.

'At least my daughter won't look like no one loves her.'

I sat in the kitchen, stirring my coffee, scratching the spoon on the bottom of the Denby. I wanted to join them in the lounge where they'd come down to watch *New Faces*. Danny and Louise were arguing over each entertainer: 'Seven for performance.'

'No way! No more than a five for content.'

Despite my sulk, I couldn't help smiling as Louise sang along to every song, her sweet voice powerful for her years. Danny encouraged her: 'You should go on there, Lou. You've got star quality.'

Eventually, he came to call me through. 'Come on, babe. Come and join us.'

I made a show of reluctantly switching off the radio, thanking my lucky stars I'd married such a kind man. I wished so much that I could talk about you to him. Or to anyone. That I could acknowledge your existence. And my loss.

Just the other day, Eileen next door to Mum had been poking her nosy snout over the wall in the backyard, fog-horning away so the whole terrace heard. 'You decided to have just the one, then, Susie? S'pose there's a bit too much of a gap with your Louise to have another one now.'

Normally, I'd force myself to joke that Lou was quite enough for me, but that day she caught me off guard. 'Number two hasn't come along.'

'You could always adopt. Plenty of young girls get caught in the family way, be glad to give their baby to a nice couple like you.'

Mum started bustling about unpegging the washing from the line with short, jabbing movements as though even mentioning the word 'adoption' might send my secret ricocheting down the road. She flung the laundry basket on the floor. 'You never know what you're getting with adoption, do you? Who the parents were? You could end up sticking your head into a whole lot of trouble.'

I stared at her open-mouthed. It was only Eileen beaking about that stopped me raging at her. I couldn't bear to think my son's new grandparents might have voiced the same opinions. But Mum, Mum should know better. Sometimes I think she was so desperate to pretend it hadn't happened, so good at lying, that she actually forgot.

But I wouldn't forget. When I died I was convinced they'd open me up and find your name engraved in the deepest corner of my heart.

Danny paused just before we went through into the lounge. In a quiet voice, he said, 'I wish I could make you happy, Susie.'

I leaned into him, dropping my head onto his shoulder.

He pulled me to him, closing his eyes and burying his face in my hair. 'I do love you, you know,' he said.

'I know you do. I know.' I couldn't say it back. Not any more. I couldn't talk about love after what I'd done, couldn't get the words out. People who loved weren't supposed to lie. I kissed him gently on the lips, running my fingers through his hair. 'Am I still your sunshine?'

He'd always started his letters home with 'Darling sunshine'. I'd teased him about it, but he'd been so earnest. 'Honestly, when I'm on the ship, I lie in my hammock and think of you, imagine us dancing around the lounge, you singing your heart out. Whatever day I'm having, it cheers me up.'

How long ago that seemed.

Danny smiled. 'You can be a bit cloudy sometimes, but you'll always be *my* sunshine. Come on, let's go and see if any of this lot on *New Faces* can sing as well as you.'

The next morning, Danny insisted on us all taking a trip along the coast to East Wittering, to get out of the house, 'get some fresh air in our lungs'.

Apart from one moment when a boy about your age was playing French cricket with his father on the beach, I managed to concentrate on the family I was with, not the person I wasn't.

I imagined the other families looking over at us, watching us playing Swingball, searching for shells and skimming stones. Maybe they'd be thinking what a happy little trio we were. How could they possibly know that my praise 'Good hit, Louise!' felt forced? That my laugh sounded harsh and hollow to my ears? That when I held Danny's hand, stood with him to watch the sun on the sea, gave him a heart-shaped pebble I'd found, I felt as though I was playing a part?

I almost felt more relaxed when Monday – results day for the grammar – rolled around, and with it, the possibility that I'd have to face the truth – I had turned out to be a hopeless mother. But then the image of Sister Patricia came into my mind, her mouth sneering, as though if she didn't whisk away my son and deliver him into the eager arms of his adoptive parents, he might get contaminated with my badness. I hoped – would even have prayed if she hadn't turned me off religion forever – I'd prove her wrong.

I was up at 5.30 a.m., watching for the post, even though I knew it wouldn't be there much before seven. I couldn't settle to anything. I was like a child waiting for a turn on a pogo stick in the playground. I wound the grandfather clock in the hallway. I polished Louise's school shoes, which made me think of my dad. In my mind's eye, he was spreading out the newspaper and settling himself at the kitchen table with his brushes, polish and rags – 'You can always judge a man by his shoes'. I'd never appreciated his quiet thoughtfulness, his ability, so like Danny, now I thought of it, to smooth over troubled waters. I wished I could talk to him. But I still wouldn't have told him what happened.

The rattle of the letter box burst into my thoughts. I hadn't hung around for the post like this since Danny went back to the navy six weeks after I first met him. How naïve that joy over a Singapore stamp seemed now. I skidded down the hallway to see one official-looking letter on the rush mat. Now it was here, I wasn't sure I had the courage to open it. If I'd been able to explain to Danny the pressure I'd put myself under over this one result, he'd have put his hand up to my face and said, 'Jesus, Susie. Are you sure you want her to go to the grammar? Most of the kids round here will go to the secondary modern. She'll be the odd one out.'

The truth was, though, she was already the odd one out. I didn't let her disappear off on her bike for the whole day like the rest of the kids, not since that poor girl had been kidnapped and found dead in a drain shaft. All the time Louise was out on the green, I'd keep making excuses to go out and check on her. 'I thought you might be thirsty, I've brought you all some squash.'

'I was sure I heard a scream. Is everyone okay?' 'Did I tell you to come in for tea at six?' I never liked to see her climbing trees or turning cartwheels. I dreaded the idea of taking her battered and bruised to have an arm plastered or a cut stitched up, the doctors raising their eyebrows as though I could somehow have prevented it if I hadn't been sloppy and inattentive. I had to get her through life in one piece.

I wished I could be more like Danny and be satisfied with her just being happy. He was probably only half-joking when he said, 'Anyway, all a girl really needs is a wonderful husband.' And then he'd get that cheeky look on his face and tell Louise, 'Your mum thought all her Christmases had come at once when she married me.' He'd pause. 'She was right, of course.' And I'd cuff him and, just for a minute, we'd be that couple again.

My fingers could barely gather the co-ordination to rip open the envelope. I took a deep breath and pulled the letter out, to see the words, 'It is our pleasure to offer a place to Louise Duarte at Shorefield Grammar School for Girls from 4 September 1977.'

It was ironic that the first words that flew out of my mouth were 'Thank god'.

CHAPTER SIX
June 1977

The seventh of June 1977 was a celebration and not just for Elizabeth II. The Silver Jubilee had delivered an extra day off work for Danny and a holiday from school for Louise. Despite it being less than a week to your birthday, I couldn't help but feel carried along with the party atmosphere. Bunting hung right across the green in the middle of our cul-de-sac. Mum had arrived at mine early doors with a couple of loaves of Sunblest, a jar of fish paste and some sandwich spread, plus a Union Jack plastic bowler hat she wasn't taking off for a second. 'Getting in the swing of it all. Won't be another jubilee till the golden one and that's not for twenty-five years. Might be dead by then.'

As usual when someone mentioned a date in the future, I did a mental calculation of how old you'd be. Nearly thirty-four. A grown man.

I promised myself I wouldn't think about you any more today, that I'd focus on the child I did have. Louise was in a beauty pageant and was desperate to win. I'd plaited her hair and pinned it up on top of her head. I'd bought her a long dress and some silver sparkly sandals. She loved the noise they made on the parquet floor, clacking up and down. Danny and I were sporting Jubilee T-shirts. He'd had to persuade me into mine because it was a bit tight around the chest and I was worried about looking tarty. 'You'd look classy in an old coal sack. Gorgeous you are.'

Outside, one of the neighbours was on a megaphone. 'Show your patriotism; make sure you dress in red, white and blue! Come and collect a Jubilee poster from my good helpers here to stick on your front window!' Rod Stewart crooned along on the radio, the commentator was fizzing with excitement about the Queen's gold state coach and Danny had already opened his first beer. He took a big swig before picking up the mallet to go and bang in some stakes by the lamp posts for yet more bunting.

'You'd better go easy on the beer or we'll be down the hospital with broken fingers, not cheering you on in the tug of war.'

'Don't forget I was a navy lad, Susie. Take more than a couple of cans of Double Diamond to get me in my cups.' He kissed me on the head and waltzed out. Mum glanced up from spreading the butter cream onto her butterfly cakes. One of those bloody looks that meant I hadn't quite behaved like a dutiful wife.

Danny put his hand on my arm as Louise was hoisted up onto the float between the Pearly King and Queen. The Pearly King – Kevin who unblocked drains for a living in real life – took the megaphone. He was the sort that loved to pause on every word for dramatic effect even when he was only talking about U-bends. We all stuck our fingers in our ears as the megaphone squealed. 'On this da-aay, the Queen's Silver Jubilee ninetee-een-sevent-yyy-seven, I proclaim Louise Duarte, eleven years old, Eastney district's official beauty que-eeeen!' He placed a red, white and blue crown on her head and she looked for us in the crowd. I shouted her name, waving my Union Jack, thinking how much she was like Danny. The same thick, dark eyebrows, that reserved manner of pausing to make eye contact with people, assessing her welcome before she'd break into a smile. At her age, I'd been far more outgoing, 'precocious' my mum always said.

It was good that she was more like Danny. That bit we'd got right. It might stop her making my mistakes.

The megaphone whistled again. The Pearly King announced the winner in the next age group: Sarah Blacklock, eight years old. She could have been Bonnie Langford's double with her bright ginger ringlets and broderie anglaise dress. Danny turned to me, 'She's a pretty little thing, isn't she?' and clapped loudly. Then he tapped me on the nose, saying, 'Of course our daughter is the most beautiful, you daft thing.' He knew me so well.

Then the marching band came round the corner, a huge net of Jubilee balloons was released and the float rumbled forward with Louise and that other little girl laughing and pretending to wave like the queen.

I watched the boys playing football on the green, forbidding myself to do my usual trick of working out which ones would be about your age. I shouted support for the men in the running race, flares and cardigans flapping as they ran towards the finish line ribbon with all the determination of the athletes on *Superstars*. Beer bellies came into their own in the tug of war as the whole street cheered on fathers, grandfathers and teenage boys as though we were rooting for Geoff Capes himself.

I headed towards Danny and the winning tug of war team with a big jug of iced squash. Half of them looked like the exertion and the heat might do for them.

Louise skipped over to me. 'This is Sarah, she's been on the float with me.' Danny was right. She really was a striking child with her ginger ringlets.

Just as I was pouring them some orange squash, Sarah waved to her mother, who was walking towards us pushing a baby in a pram with a red-haired boy riding on the bar. I braced myself for a stab of jealousy and ploughed on, smiling and saying, 'Aren't we lucky to have such beautiful girls? And look at this bonny pair. They're gorgeous.'

I'd become so good at making my voice light and jolly. Sarah's mum laughed and said, 'Right handful they are. Already had three and wasn't planning to have any more after Carl here, but then this little babba popped along, an unexpected bonus.'

I felt myself withdraw: I hated women who talked about getting pregnant so easily, as though they were somehow the smug epitome of womanhood, the fertile greenhouse of motherhood.

But before I could retreat from the conversation with a bland smile and 'I must go and find my husband', I recognised a prickle of unease, that split second when the mind grapples with something that's not quite right, without being able to pull the notion into sharp enough focus to identify. And then it hit me, bringing a floodwater of fear. She no longer had the waif-like cheekbones of nine years ago. Her upper arms strained against the short sleeves of her dress, her freckles stretching over jowly cheeks. She was puffing with the exertion of pushing the pram over the grass. A fatter, wrinklier version. But definitely her.

At the same time, she did a double take and said in a low, conspiratorial voice, 'Paula?'

'I'm not called Paula! You've got the wrong person.' I grabbed Louise by her upper arm, ignoring her protests, not caring that her squash was spilling down her dress. I marched towards Danny, narrowly avoiding a collision with two boys crammed onto one Chopper. I kept craning my head round to check that she wasn't following me. But she was leaning into her pram, lifting the baby onto her hip. Only Sarah was staring after us, a frown pleating her forehead.

By the time we'd reached Danny, Louise was in tears.

'Hey, what's upsetting my beauty queen?'

Louise was sobbing. 'Mum spilt orange on my new dress. She was running away from Sarah's mum.'

I unleashed my panic, harsh and vindictive, on Louise. 'Don't be stupid. I wasn't running away from anyone. I wanted to give

Daddy a cold drink before he keels over. I didn't want to get stuck chatting to her. Look how hot and sweaty he is after the tug of war.'

Louise sniffed. 'Why did you get so angry that she called you Paula?'

I nearly shouted. 'She didn't call me Paula!'

'She did.'

My words tumbled out of me, angry, vicious. 'You're hearing things. Better take you to the doctors and get your ears syringed.'

Louise's face crumpled again.

'For god's sake.' I could feel the hiccups of fear in my chest and tried to breathe deeply and quietly. I knelt down. 'I'm sorry, sweetheart. Really sorry. Granddad died at this time of year and I always worry that it was because of the heat. I shouldn't have shouted. Don't worry about the dress. It'll wash out.'

Danny looked at me and shook his head. There was something resigned about him, something wary. His eyes flicked over my shoulder, looking for an escape route to take Louise out of the storm, in a gesture that was so familiar to me now. He put his arm round her. 'Mum will sort it out. Don't worry. Shall we go and see if we can find some pork pie? Build my strength up again for the egg and spoon race? And you can tell me about your time on the float. Did you go through the town centre?'

And with that, hand-in-hand, they wandered off, leaving me scanning the crowd for Lizzy.

If that was even her name.

I kept my eye on where she was, choosing a seat at the far end of the trestle tables, well away from her. Every now and then, she'd catch my eye. I didn't want to look at her, but I couldn't help it. Four kids. I burned with envy. One of the sons was taller than Sarah. I did a quick calculation. If Sarah was eight, and the other one was older, she must have got pregnant nearly as soon as she left the Mother and Baby home.

Then another thought struck me, so painful I felt a cramp in my stomach. Maybe she didn't give her baby away. Maybe at the last minute she found a way to keep him. Perhaps she'd only had three more after the first one.

At one point, I saw Mum joking with her as she took round a tray of cheese and pineapple sticks. She'd be smiling on the other side of her face if she knew who she was. I couldn't relax, couldn't join in with the other women laughing as their kids stuffed their mouths with cream crackers in a competition to see who could eat the most without having a drink. I never fitted in. Everywhere I looked, mothers were so comfortable in their role: supervising the welly-throwing competition, taking part in the sack races, running in and out of the skipping rope, chanting 'Farmer wants a wife'.

I wasn't a real mother. I was a woman who gave her baby away. A mother without her child. Not someone who deserved to have children screaming with delight at Grandmother's Footsteps or to do the three-legged race with another mother who'd rather die than come home from hospital without her newborn.

And now there was someone here, less than a hundred yards away, who knew that about me. The one person who could whip the veil off my pretence. A wick of panic sat waiting to ignite in my stomach.

If only these people knew who I was. These husbands dodging jets of Watneys spurting from party kegs, doing tricks with coins and matches, and yes, casting a lecherous eye over me. 'Better tell my Lynne how you stay so trim. Or is it all that "exercise" you get with that husband of yours?'

More than one woman asked me what my secret was. 'You been doing the SlimFast diet? Or that Cabbage Soup one?' I wanted to shake them, shout in their face until saliva flew out of my mouth that I didn't care about being thin, that I'd waddle about like a penguin if it meant I could have another baby.

Louise begged me to join in the skipping, but I shook my head. 'Sorry, love, I'm not feeling that great. A bit queasy. Too much sun, I think.' It was true that I felt sick. Every time someone spoke to me, I had to force myself to respond. My brain was paralysed, frozen in fear. Eventually, Louise gave up asking and sat quietly, picking at a fairy cake. I'd spoilt her day.

Danny was excessively jolly to compensate for his stand-offish wife. 'Come and have some wine!' 'Here, let me get you a seat.' Then he'd rush around pouring out the Black Tower, flicking his lighter as soon as a cigarette appeared, joining in the doom and gloom over Portsmouth FC's financial predicaments and relegation.

The other women found me stuck-up. I hardly ever accepted invitations to their coffee mornings. I used to, when I still thought that with a bit of practice, I could go back to my old life. But the pregnancy announcements – 'We've got an extra special Christmas present arriving this year!' – would lead to me rushing off home, throwing out any excuse I could think of. Even worse was when mums would thrust their newborns at me. 'Go on, Susie, you have a hold, see if it makes you broody.' It was easier to stay at home.

Danny kept looking over at me, trying to include me in the conversation with 'Isn't that right, Susie?' and 'I'm always saying that to Susie.' But as soon as I could, I'd sink back into my seat, pretending to be watching the boys playing tag behind Lizzy but trying to work out if the son could possibly be the one she was carrying at the home. In the end, I couldn't stand it any more. I told Danny I was just popping back home to the toilet.

He nodded. 'Don't forget you're in *Opportunity Knocks* with Louise at four.'

I glanced at Louise, licking hundreds and thousands off her finger. 'Would you rather do it on your own? You look just like

Marie Osmond, pet. You'd probably get more votes without me,' I said, wondering how on earth I'd get a note out through the terror closing my throat.

But Louise wasn't having any of it. 'Mum. It's a duet. That's why we chose "I'm Leaving It All Up To You". Otherwise I'd have practised "Oh, Lori".' Her face clouded over.

Danny frowned. 'Don't let her down now, Susie. I love seeing you sing. You don't do it nearly enough. I can't remember the last time you entertained us all.'

I couldn't see a way to wriggle out of it without putting more of a dampener on the day than I had already.

'Back in a sec,' I said, heading along the green to home. Great waves of nausea were washing over me. Suddenly I couldn't wait to collapse on my couch for a few minutes, far away from everything in my present.

And my past.

CHAPTER SEVEN

June 1977

Even if it was the Queen's Silver Jubilee, I couldn't remember why I'd agreed to sing. It was over nine years since I'd picked up a microphone in public. My stomach was rattling and rolling with nerves. Louise and I sat through three little girls and a mumbled rendition of 'Halfway Down the Stairs', with Louise whispering, 'We should beat them, Mum.' Next on was the girl from the checkout at Budgens mooning over Olivia Newton-John's 'Sam', followed by our window cleaner, who only served to underline why 'Lucille' had buggered off.

Louise didn't seem at all nervous. And as soon as the music started, the opening melody called me in and I felt a rush of joy, of unfiltered pleasure, as my voice dipped and soared, looping itself around the lyrics with an easy familiarity, as though I was exercising a muscle that hadn't wasted away but instead had been sitting there all that time, primed for action when needed. But my real delight was watching the chatter along the green die away as Louise sang Marie Osmond's lines into the crowd. Everyone turned to listen. Eyes widened, mouths gaped. 'She's good' formed on people's lips. When she finished, a roar went up, with people banging on the tables with fists and spoons. A feeling I struggled to identify rose within me. Elation? Relief mixed with pride? Whatever it was, *my* daughter, *my* child, was the one people were looking at and praising, with me basking in reflected glory.

I was aware of Lizzy in the throng, of her swaying to the music with a little boy on her hip of the shadows of the past swooping around me. But I hoped she'd grant me this moment, one of the few times when I was sure I hadn't failed. That I'd been enough.

It wouldn't take long before she looked at Louise and puzzled at the fact that she'd won the senior beauty contest. She'd sieve her memory for recollections of the events of nine years ago and come up with the compere's words, the *eleven*-year-old Louise Duarte. And realise that there was a piece of the jigsaw missing.

The compere took the microphone now and said, 'I think we've found the new Karen Carpenter. You heard it here first, folks.'

And then he hugged Louise, his fat slobbery lips making contact with her cheek. I saw her flinch, then smile politely and say thank you. Well brought up as always.

For the second time that day, I grabbed her arm and marched her away.

I kept a close eye on where Lizzy was, ready to refute all knowledge of her if she dared to speak to me. As the evening wore on, she made no attempt to come over and the hard knot of fear started to loosen. Danny bumped into an ex-navy colleague, and ended up having a whisky for old time's sake. Then a bottle of Tawny port appeared from somewhere. I hardly ever drank – the odd sip of wine, an occasional Bacardi and Coke – but tonight someone had started with the crème de menthe frappés and the thought of blocking it all out, plunging into an oblivion I no longer allowed myself, was too tempting. Danny kept topping up my glass. 'Nice to see you getting in the swing of things.'

Mum appeared with the ice bucket. ''Bout time you let your hair down a bit,' she said, clapping as I joined in with Danny's attempts to imitate Tom Jones. Just for a moment, I was young and invincible again.

It was only when the crowd started to thin out and the throng of people acting as a buffer between us and Lizzy dwindled that I woke Louise from where she'd curled up on a picnic blanket.

'Come on, Danny, time to make tracks. We need to get this one home.' With a Silver Jubilee tie hanging round his neck above a T-shirt with a silhouette of the Queen, he put his arm round me – whether to protect me or for support, I wasn't quite sure – but I relaxed into him, feeling closer to him than I had for ages.

As we got into bed later that evening, he reached for me, hands exploring my body and I melted into him. As he worked his way upwards, he said, 'You been doing exercises? Your breasts feel much bigger.'

'Am I getting fat?'

He pulled me to him, slurring slightly. 'Only you could take offence at that. I love you how you are, you know that.' And even my alcohol-fuddled mind recognised that as the truth.

I let myself be led, let him take control, just gave myself up to him without holding anything back until we drifted off, satiated and satisfied into sleep.

It wasn't until the next morning when my breasts were throbbing in time with my head that a little kernel of realisation started to unfurl within me. I stood sideways in the bathroom mirror. I'd always been skinny, scrawny even. But there was no ignoring the tautness of the skin over my stomach, the unmistakable outline of a tiny bump. I'd thought it was middle-aged spread and had stopped eating potatoes.

I stood there, both hands on my stomach, studying my face in the mirror for signs that I was different, a mother-to-be again, nearly a decade after I gave you away. Joyful disbelief competed with the other memories of me standing in this very bathroom, tears trapped in a gully between my cheek and the tiles as I took in the reality that I was carrying another man's baby. I patted my abdomen and promised that I wouldn't let this baby down.

Danny banged on the bathroom door to see if I was all right. I let him in, putting a finger to my lips so Louise didn't hear.

I pointed to my stomach. I hardly dare whisper the words. 'I think I'm pregnant.'

Danny stood frozen for a second. 'Are you sure?' The emotion on his face, the mottling of pure delight, surprised me. It was as though my distress at not being able to conceive had forced him to downplay his disappointment, to stop us both from going under. He let his head fall onto my shoulder and in a half-laugh, half-sob, said, 'You clever thing.'

'What do you hope it is?' I asked.

Danny just laughed, wrinkling his nose at me. 'I know you too well for that game, wife of mine. I'd like a healthy baby. That's it. Let's just be happy with that, if we're lucky enough to be granted that a second time.'

I hugged him tightly.

He eased me off him, 'Careful, don't squash the poor little bean.'

I buried my face in his shoulder, hoping that your new father would have taken the same good care of you, right from the start. That he'd have been so much better than your real dad.

I'd only seen your father once since I'd given you away, a few months afterwards, coming out of the posh hotel on the seafront that he'd taken me to. I spotted him before he saw me, that muscly frame loping along, his arms swinging with a graceful rhythm as though the dance hall music was still echoing in his ears. I'd crossed over the road to avoid coming face-to-face with him. The time for polite pleasantries was long gone. I knew he'd seen me by the way his pace faltered, his Doc Marten hovering a couple of inches above the pavement before he decided to carry on forwards. He'd put his head down, that mop of chestnut brown hair glinting in the autumn sunshine, those eyes that drew me in and made me take leave of my senses cast down to the floor.

It was probably for the best, though for one mad moment, I considered darting between the buses and planting myself in front of him, forcing him to acknowledge that what had happened between us couldn't just be brushed away into a convenient pile like fag butts after a party. In the end though, I sat on the steps of the post office, folded over and sobbing until all the feelings I'd trapped so deeply inside me emptied out into the atmosphere, allowing me a temporary release until they bubbled up again like a mountain spring.

I forced myself to think about the here and now. I breathed in Danny. Deliberately filled my lungs with that scent of him, soaking up the solid feel of him. He was muttering away, 'I can't believe it, after all this time, a new baby for our family, it doesn't get much better than this.'

And in that moment, I thought he was right.

CHAPTER EIGHT
August 1977

Every time I had a bit of indigestion or wind, I assumed it was a sign I was about to miscarry. When that looked unlikely, I switched to fretting that the baby would be stillborn or disabled. But Danny refused to spend a second worrying, joyous from the outset. He'd have put an announcement in the evening paper if I'd let him.

I forbade Danny to tell anyone until I was five months pregnant. His secret-keeping was worse than England's chances of winning the world cup again. I hoped to God he never committed a murder because he'd have been wiggling his eyebrows whenever he walked past the shed containing the corpse. Every time he passed me, he was humming 'Daddy Cool'. He kept singing 'Isn't She Lovely?' in front of Mum to make me laugh, but fear that I didn't deserve another baby meant I couldn't share his delight. Which frankly put me into the category of 'women who were never bloody satisfied'.

He'd had years of me crossing my fingers as four weeks stretched into six or seven, before, inevitably, I stormed out of the bathroom in tears. 'I really thought I was pregnant this time.' Danny would stand in the doorway, not knowing how to ease my disappointment until I snapped at him to 'Go and find something to do!' Louise removed herself from the firing line, marching upstairs the second she got in from school. She'd almost stopped bringing friends home after one girl had knocked a bottle of purple nail varnish over her bedroom carpet. I'd just come out of the bathroom having discovered that the only thing my future held was another packet of Dr Whites. And Louise's friend had copped the full force of my disappointment. So much so that the girl had run home crying while I'd stood on the front step shouting at her to come back, that we were having butterscotch Angel Delight for tea, in a scene that could have been straight out of the *Two Ronnies*.

Danny had popped round to the friend's house to smooth things over later that evening, but the damage was done. After that, whenever I said, 'Why don't you invite Jane over? Or Karen?' Louise would shake her head.

'I need to practise the piano.' 'I've got too much homework to do. I don't want to be the dunce at the grammar in September.' And I stood by, impotent, shot in the foot by my own words.

The huge cloud of delight of my imaginings, my great, belated blossoming as the whole family focused on the happy event of another baby – needless to say – bore little relation to reality. When I was finally confident enough to tell everyone, we took Louise to the Wimpy as a treat to mark the occasion. We blurted out the 'exciting news' over chocolate milkshakes. She pulled a face. 'A baby? I thought you were going to tell me that you'd got tickets to see Showaddywaddy at the Hammersmith Apollo.'

Unusually for Danny, he was more irritated than me. He'd been telling me for weeks how happy he thought Louise would be, that she'd always wanted a brother or sister. But I last remembered her saying that when she was about seven. Danny sank back in his chair, sucking at his straw. He pursed his lips, doing that thing I'd never mastered – distancing himself from the reaction he'd hoped for in order to understand the reaction he'd got. His face was deflated, all the energy drained away.

He stretched out his hand to cover Louise's. She didn't pull away. 'No one will ever take your place, if that's what you're worried about.'

The way her eyes flicked down told me Danny was on the money. I should have been the one to reassure her. But I never seemed to find the words he did.

I persuaded Danny to let me tell Mum on her own in case the news brought a fresh wave of grief that my dad wouldn't be around to see his new grandchild. In reality, I was frightened the news might make her blurt out something about you, muddling up your birth with Louise's, making a mistake about the age gap or any of the hundred ways that the secret we'd fought so hard to keep might break the bank of silence containing it for nine years. In the event, Mum's reaction was one of astonishment that I was pregnant at the grand old age of thirty-one. 'Are you sure?' she asked, as though Danny and I should have given up having sex years ago. 'Aren't you a bit old now to be starting all over again?'

'It wasn't exactly how I had planned it, as you know.'

The cloud of the past hung between us, like someone you're trying to hide from in a crowded room but who pops up right next to you every time you go in search of a drink.

She smiled. 'Wonder if it will be a boy?'

I wanted to scream that another son could never make things okay. I knew her face would darken as though she couldn't bear to hear your name. I forced myself to believe it was because of her complicity, in case we could have done something differently.

In case I could have kept my son.

But deep down I knew she was just ashamed of me. The thought made me braver than normal. It allowed me to articulate the thoughts that still crept in at three in the morning, parking themselves on my pillow and sucking away any notion of sleep. I'd study Danny's face, the gentle curve of his lips, listen to his breathing, the breathing of a man who had never wanted much from his life, just his wife to be happy, his daughter to be safe and his new baby to be healthy.

'Even if it is a boy, it won't replace him. I still loved him, Mum.' I could hear the defiance in my voice, the gauntlet in my words, goading Mum to come out with it, say what she really meant. That I'd been lucky to get away with having another man's baby without my husband finding out.

Mum frowned as though I was being silly, as though it was slightly unreasonable I even remembered I'd had you after all this time. 'Best not to think about that other baby. You've got this lovely little one to look forward to. I'd better get knitting.'

Best not to think about that other baby. Those words acted like a blowtorch on the feelings I'd trapped, angry and impotent, like a wasp under a glass for so long. And getting pregnant again, having the proof – as if I needed it – that a baby was so precious, so irreplaceable, had lifted the lid off that angry seething mass.

'Best not to think about that other baby? How can I *not* think about him? I gave him away with the nuns telling me it was the best thing I could do, then afterwards everyone acted as though I'd done something absolutely awful, so bloody bad that I couldn't speak about it to my own mother. I've never even been able to say his name in front of you. Well, here you go now. Edward, Edward, Edward, Edward!'

I watched as Mum melted in front of my eyes. The woman who never cried in front of me after Dad died, always greeting me with a chirpy 'hello' and a bright smile at odds with her red-rimmed eyes whenever I popped by. Who started taking in ironing in the evenings to make ends meet, shrugging her shoulders and saying, 'I like to be useful.' Who squashed a little henhouse into her backyard, handing me a couple of eggs 'for Louise' whenever I went round.

Mum slumped into the armchair, shrinking away from me as though my truths were too painful after so many years of deceits. For this baby, Mum would be flipping through her pattern book for the perfect blanket, bending over her crochet hook until the light was too dim. No one had even marked your birth with a silly silver Christening mug or a teaspoon to tarnish away in a cupboard. Things that were only important if your arrival in the world was dismissed as a disaster to recover from, rather than a glorious miracle to celebrate.

But as I stood in front of Mum, sadness, rage and frustration seething for an outlet, I felt the new baby move inside me, bringing to the fore all the fear of ten years earlier. When I couldn't pretend I hadn't had a period because I hadn't bothered to eat properly while Danny was at sea. When I could no longer convince myself my little pot belly was normal, that the muscle tone had gone to buggery after I'd had Louise. That my sore, heavy breasts were hormonal, an indication that my period – the one I hadn't had for several months – was due. I could no longer ignore the signs that meant I was carrying a baby.

Belonging to a man I should never have sat under the stars with.

I raged on. 'You'd have loved it if I'd just popped him out, slugged back the sugary tea Sister Domenica gave me, hopped on my train and never thought about him again, wouldn't you?'

With great restraint, Mum said, 'It wasn't me who caused the problem, Susie. I just did my best to help you solve it.' She looked at the floor. 'I'm sorry. I thought with time you'd get over it and you had Louise to think of.'

Bless my mum. Sorry. Such a powerful word when offered up with no agenda. My anger softened, then withered. 'It's me who should be sorry.' Sorry I'd dismissed her reservations about me 'jaunting off' to the dance hall when Danny was at sea. Sorry I'd messed up so spectacularly before we'd even finished paying for the wedding rings. Sorry she'd had to lie to Danny, the man she considered the son she'd never had. Yet she'd never blamed me, never asked for details of just how stupid I'd been. And thankfully, I'd never had to tell her.

Her face softened. 'I thought it would be easier if we didn't keep talking about him.'

I nodded, recognising that not speaking about soul-crushing loss was how people of her war generation managed to get dressed in the mornings. Mothers lost sons they'd loved for eighteen years, ghosts of their boys reflected in the faces of the husbands who survived, sitting at dinner night after night, the table pushed against the wall where a chair should have been. Her own brother, Fred, had been killed in France, nineteen years old, blown up by a mine. But these women didn't fall apart; they swallowed their grief, fixing their eyes on the future, not allowing themselves to luxuriate in their loss. At least not openly. There was always someone worse off.

Mum never talked about Fred, never looked for pity. It was just how it was. So it was no wonder she thought giving away a baby at six weeks didn't merit much airtime. My eyes filled.

She looked up at me. 'Come and have a hug, pet. It's all going to be fine.'

And there, at the age of thirty-one, I rocked and wept on my mother's knee, tears dripping onto her tan stockings until she pulled a handkerchief I recognised as my father's out of her sleeve and dabbed my face. They were never rich, but I bet she'd hoped for more in old age than eking out coal in the winter, unpicking Dad's jumpers to reuse the wool, finely chopping cauliflower leaves and stalks to make dinner stretch further.

But she'd never lost her temper with me, the way I took my unhappiness out on other people. I cringed when I thought about my recent reaction to Louise's end of term report. I'd been glowing at all the wonderful comments: 'She writes stories with ideas beyond her years', 'Her understanding of geography is exceptional for her age', 'Her contribution is always thoughtful and intelligent.' But Louise was only interested in what the music teacher had said, twirling around with excitement when she read the words, 'A musician and singer of outstanding talent'.

She'd looked at me shyly. 'Do you think I'm good enough to become a pop star?'

I'd turned on her. 'Absolutely no chance. You'll get a proper job like everyone else. I haven't brought you up to hang around with a bunch of hippies who think they're the next Rolling Stones.' I'd pushed away the memory of myself singing on stage, in the silver hot pants I'd bought from the market and worn *that* night.

She'd stood there, hands on her hips, and said, 'Just because *you* weren't good enough, it doesn't mean I won't be.'

I'd shouted back, 'You have no idea how tough it is to make it in the music industry, you silly little girl.'

She'd burst into tears, screaming back at me until Danny had come running in.

'For god's sake, why on earth are you arguing over what Louise might or might not do in ten years' time?' He ordered me into the kitchen while he calmed Louise down, his face a mixture of fury and puzzlement. And yet again, everyone I loved was pushed a fraction further away from me.

As my sobs subsided, Mum leant forward and put her hand on my stomach. 'This little one is going to have a lovely life.'

I hoped she was right.

CHAPTER NINE

October 1977

I shouldn't have been surprised that with baby number three, my stomach muscles were shot, but by the time I was seven months' pregnant, my walk was a lumbering shuffle and Danny affectionately described me as 'the battleship coming through'. At least, I hoped it was affectionately. As the due date grew nearer, I'd spend large chunks of the night with raging indigestion, propped up on pillows just to stop the flames firing up my oesophagus. And those night-time hours, when I'd pad over to the window and stare up at the North Star, were fertile compost for my fears. Would a stranger snatch this baby from the park, would he/she drink bleach when my back was turned, would a huge dog run up and bite this child? I'd try to force out my worries by thinking about how excited Danny was about the baby's arrival, the nursery he'd painted in his spare time, little ships decorating the walls. 'We might get one with wanderlust like me, wanting to see the world,' he'd said. I knew he hoped we'd have a boy. I didn't dare think about what I preferred because any thoughts about the new baby led me back to you.

Despite my best intentions, when Louise was at school and Danny was at work, I'd stand in the nursery, running my fingers over the cot Danny had sanded and varnished and feel the absence of you burrowing out of me, until the precious few images I had of you twirled around my brain, making me dizzy. Sometimes the need to know how you were was so intense, it was like an acute hunger gnawing away at me. The only solution was to walk, miles and miles, way further than my achy-breaky body wanted to waddle, until I was too exhausted to think any more. And today was one of those days.

I'd already walked along the front towards the dockyard, thinking about how I used to wait for Danny when he was coming off the ship, physically yearning for that first moment when I'd fold myself into him, all the holding together while he'd been away sagging into the solid reality of him, always a little different from how I'd remembered, a bit more tanned, his hair shorter, his hands rougher. But one thing that never changed: the way he made me feel. As though there was someone on this planet who was in my corner. And look how I'd repaid him.

Despite my aching back and swollen ankles, I forced myself to carry on walking, up past the Guildhall, the physical exertion stopping unwanted memories creeping in.

I didn't see her in time to escape. She was there right in front of me, pushing the baby in a pram, with a bigger boy, about four, holding the edge and whining along beside her.

But still she broke into a big smile. 'Paula!'

I shook my head. 'Sorry, you've made a mistake.' I tried to push past her, but the pavement was too narrow and the traffic was roaring by. I had no choice but to flatten myself against the wall.

Her face drooped in resignation. 'It is you. I knew it was you the minute I saw you at the Jubilee. It's your eyes. No disguising them beauties.' Her eyes dropped to my stomach. I put my hands over the bump in a pathetic attempt to disguise it, as though I'd somehow been disloyal to you.

I wanted to dash out into the traffic, dodge between the cars and disappear. She saw me looking and hauled her little boy onto her hip, wiping the green slime from his nose with her thumb. 'Don't blame you for not wanting any reminders of that time. Bloody awful, weren't it?'

Denial sprang to my lips. How could she prove it? But panic bulldozed my ability to pretend out of the way. I could hear the begging tone in my voice. 'You can't tell anyone. My husband and daughter don't know.' My mind thrashed about wildly, unable to compute that my entire life could crash down in minutes one random day. I started to turn away from her.

She grabbed my arm. 'You've never told your husband?'

She obviously hadn't bothered with the maths of the eleven-year-old daughter announced loudly for all to hear at the beauty contest, when she knew that my baby had been adopted nine years ago.

I pulled my arm away. 'I've never told anyone. Only my mum knows.'

She nodded. Her face was soft, compassionate. The face of someone who knew what it was to be judged. 'Bless you.' She nodded at my stomach. 'When's this one due then?'

'First week of December.'

'Is that the only one you've had since the home?'

I nodded, knowing I should leave but somehow drawn to this woman, the only other person who understood.

'So what's the age gap going to be between this one and your daughter?'

I wanted to lie. Wanted to take an India rubber to the truth, wear a hole in the page of my past, as Louise sometimes did in her maths book. But I couldn't. I couldn't deny the daughter I had. I tried to fudge it. 'She's going up to senior school this year.'

But Lizzy wasn't stupid. I watched as the bits all moved into place, like the penny-pusher machine in the damn amusement arcade Louise always wanted to go to. One thought shoving against another, dropping down a level until it cascaded into understanding. She narrowed her eyes. 'How did that work then, if your daughter is older than the baby you gave away? Is *she* your husband's?'

I was torn, wanting to race back to my house where I could slam the door, hide from the shame that she had witnessed my disgrace. Her words should have sounded nosy, insensitive, accusatory even. But there was something about her, something unshockable as though she'd fallen so far herself, anyone else's dingy and dirty secrets would never merit more than a half-raised eyebrow. I found myself answering her questions, tentatively to begin with, then elaborating on Danny being away in the navy as she responded with 'You poor bugger. Keeping all that to yourself. No wonder you darted off like an injured cat when I saw you at the Jubilee. I shouldn't have said anything in front of Louise. It just came out, it was such a surprise.'

My mind flicked back to that day, when I'd seen her surrounded by her ginger brood. That tall son of hers had haunted me. He looked about nine, the same age as you would be by now.

I forced my voice to sound light, as though I was making polite conversation. 'You didn't keep your baby then?' I felt myself tense backwards, away from the answer, an answer I dreaded in case it confirmed that someone else, in the same circumstances, had turned out to be a better, braver mother than me. But I needed to know she'd lost her baby too, that she hadn't found a way to hang onto him. That she understood what it was like to live life with half of your heart missing.

Before she could answer, her little lad shifted on her hip, his fingers twirling her ringlets until she winced. 'Oi, Carl, off, that hurts.' She turned to me. 'They all pull my hair. Even he did, little tinker.'

Bittersweet memories flashed across her face, but I still felt a sag of relief at the back of my knees when she said, 'I didn't keep him, no. How could I? No way my dad was going to have a daughter with an illegitimate bastard shaming him in front of his friends. He nearly beat me half to death when he found out as it was. It was only after I'd signed the adoption papers my mother told me I couldn't come home anyway.'

'You must have had another one quite quickly though. How old is your oldest son?'

'Only seven. Rick's big for his age. Often wonder whether Bobby turned out tall. I've never told any of the kids I had another baby. Breaks my heart that Rick's got a big brother out there that he don't know about.'

A lorry rattled past, making conversation impossible, giving us a moment to knit our wounds back together.

'Did you meet your husband after you gave your baby away? Did you tell him?' My desire to understand someone else's experience made me intrusive.

'I made out it happened a long while before I met him. My old man doesn't like me to talk about it. It makes him edgy, touchy.' She rolled her eyes. 'You know what they're like. Starts revving up if he even hears an American accent, because I told him the father was a Yank who left me high and dry.' She laughed, a sound without much basis in humour. 'Thought that was safer than having him prowling the dance hall wondering if every chap in the room had slept with his wife.'

The baby girl in the pram starting to cry and Lizzy shoved a dummy in her mouth.

'I more or less married the first bloke that came along, mainly to prove my mother wrong.' She did an impression of her mother. 'No man will want to look at you now. If you've got any sense, you'll never breathe a word about that little bastard you gave away.'

She looked over my shoulder, her face pinched with pain.

'All in the name of bloody religion. She was more worried about what the church congregation would be tittle-tattling about than packing her eighteen-year-old daughter off to London to get rid of her grandchild.'

She jiggled the pram with one hand, gesticulating with the other. 'Them bloody nuns. If that was religion, they can shove it where the Pope won't see it. I went to live with my sister afterwards but there wasn't really room for me. She was already cramped as it was. Got chatting with Simon when he came selling insurance door-to-door – he had the gift of the gab all right. I just married him to have somewhere to call my own.'

That explained the toughness about her, her lack of self-pity. At least I'd had a life to slot back into, a mum to give me a hug. I hadn't been cast out to sink or swim on my own.

She stroked her son's head as his eyelids drooped and he relaxed into her shoulder. 'I wasn't going to tell Simon about the adoption but I'd had enough of being ashamed. My mother was hiding the fact she was seeing me from my own father. I decided I'd be a better mother than that, even if I hadn't been able to keep my baby. At least I'd acknowledge he'd existed.'

I wanted to cheer her courage. I no longer wanted to run away from Lizzy, I wanted to cling to her, another fraud mother, another impostor parent, the only person I'd ever met who knew what it was like to exist with a dull aching void without remedy. I had to understand how she'd survived, if she felt she might go mad if she contemplated never seeing that little boy again, never knowing if he'd been looked after, loved, *cherished*.

She looked down, scuffing at the kerb with her sandals.

'He was a gorgeous boy, you know. Had a headful of hair. Ginger, of course. I didn't want to give him up, but what life could I have given a little 'un? A mum on welfare and nowhere to live? And we didn't stand a chance anyway with those nuns lurking in every corridor waiting to snatch the babies from us.' She turned to me, her eyes begging for my agreement. 'Did we?'

'We really didn't. Do you remember Sister Patricia?'

She screwed up her eyes against the memory. 'Bitch.'

She was, but I still couldn't speak about the nuns like that. Though I admired Lizzy for her lack of hypocrisy.

I nodded at her baby. 'Has having another one helped?'

Her eyes flicked over my face as if assessing how much truth I could withstand. She sighed. 'I was that desperate to have another baby. I was pregnant less than two months after marrying Simon. I haven't been able to stop having them since. Got four now.' She looked down. 'But I still think of myself as a mum to five, feels like one's missing the whole time.'

She tried to smile but I recognised the pain that flashed across her face, the same ragged yearning in her voice. I was obviously a poor excuse for a human being but I felt my spirits lift. Someone else in the world was carrying the same burden as me, her sadness bound to her tightly, tucked away from view, a poisonous kernel festering and fermenting from within.

She lowered her voice. 'I'm a dab hand at getting pregnant, but I'm not much cop at choosing men.'

I had to laugh at the irony of it. 'I've been hopeless at getting pregnant but my husband's turned out all right.' Then I worried about sounding smug. 'I mean, he still leaves his socks on the floor and doesn't empty his ashtrays, but he's a good dad.'

The baby started crying then and the moment for confidences was broken. She swung the boy over to me, protesting at being moved from his perch on her hip. He was heavy and I struggled to hold him comfortably. He sensed my unease immediately and pushed away from me, crying for his mother and straining to reach back to her.

Lizzy leant over the baby girl in the pram, slipping her little finger into her mouth. 'I'd better go, she's hungry.' She grabbed the boy from me, blowing raspberries against his cheek until he was throwing his head back, laughing. I envied her, those unselfconscious gestures, that sense of fun. I couldn't remember the last time Louise and I had laughed together. I hadn't spent nearly enough time blowing bubbles, making mud pies or castles out of Plasticine when she was their age. I'd been far too fixated on making sure she could read and write by the time she started school. Maybe I'd be able to redress the balance with this one.

'I'll push the pram to the corner for you,' I said, wanting to absorb Lizzy's joyful company for a moment longer.

She hugged me with her free arm.

'Nice seeing you. I'm always in St Edward's Park of an afternoon. Till about three when the other kids finish school. Come and find me anytime you want. Bye, Paula.'

I nodded, weighing up whether I could trust her. 'It's Susie.'

'Jeanie.'

CHAPTER TEN

December 1977

My second daughter was born on 1 December 1977. The midwife laughed when my first question was whether the baby was okay, not what sex it was. I couldn't tell her that I'd been waiting to be punished. And now she'd arrived in the world bellowing lustily, I had nightmares about all the ways I might accidentally harm her: slipping on the parquet floor and smashing her skull open, her pram rolling off into traffic because I'd forgotten the brake, fainting while she was in the bath.

Danny dismissed my worries, waving them away. 'You've never let anything happen to Louise, touch wood. You're a great mum. Your biggest concern is making sure we choose the right name for her.'

Danny wanted to call her Leia because he'd loved the *Star Wars* film so much. And of course, it was 'the perfect name for a princess'. But I was desperate to call her Grace, because every time I heard the hymn 'Amazing Grace', I thought of the day you were born. I wanted you to be involved in her life, to be part of your sister somehow, a link, however tenuous, even though you'd never meet.

Danny tried out the name a few times. 'Grace. Gracie. My gorgeous Gracie.' Then he nodded. 'I can live with that. You've done all the hard work, you get to choose.' So the new girl in our lives became Grace Leia.

I didn't sleep for three days after I got home from hospital with her. Away from the nurses pattering in and out, nodding at how well she was feeding, exclaiming over how bonny she looked, I was afraid to drop off in case something happened to her. Every time I closed my eyes, I could see the grand old stairs at the Mother and Baby home, the long bannister some poor girl had to polish. My left hand clutching at it for support, a suitcase in the other hand, my feet stumbling down the steps. And no you.

In the end, Danny prised Grace from me. 'You need to sleep, Susie. You'll get ill otherwise. Come on, you weren't like this with Louise and she turned out fine. I'll sit with her.'

'Promise? Promise me you won't fall asleep?'

I saw the weariness in Danny, the slump of his shoulders as he realised that having another baby hadn't 'fixed' me, just catapulted me into another set of concerns. He'd probably spent the last decade wondering where the girl who leapt out of her chair at the opening bars of 'Let's Twist Again' had disappeared to and hoped that having the baby I'd longed for would bring me back to him. But instead of filling in the channel between us, the before and after I lost you, Grace's arrival had excavated everything I'd tried to bury.

And far from me finally achieving the two-up, two-down family I'd dreamt of, Louise showed very little interest in Grace. 'There's no point in talking to you when *she's* here.' I tried not to get distracted when Louise was telling me something, but one murmur from Grace and I was rushing to adjust her cardigan, tuck in her blanket, wind her, cuddle her, rock her.

My obsession with Louise and her grades gave way to a fixation about fresh air for the baby. I walked miles every day, pounding the pavements to keep my fears at bay. When she was in her pram, I knew she was safe. When she was upstairs at home, I could barely do the washing up without going to check that she hadn't somehow got her head stuck between the bars of her cot. I'd sit, in the silence of Grace's afternoon nap, telling myself that I wouldn't go up and look until the grandfather clock struck the quarter hour. But more often than not, I dashed up to the nursery, my heart hammering, licking my forefinger and putting it under her nostrils, to feel the reassurance of the warm air cooling across it.

Danny was tolerant at first, almost taking pride in my dedication to our daughter, teasing me. 'How many carrots have you pureed today?' 'Don't worry, I've sterilised the princess's spoon.' 'How long did you let her cry for? A whole two seconds? Crikey!' But his joking gave way to whispered conversations in the kitchen with my mother, littered with phrases like, 'Do you think she needs to see a doctor?' 'The effect on Louise'. 'At my wit's end'.

By the time Grace was five months old, I knew something had to change. So after Easter, like a mouse skirting a trap to steal the cheese, knowing it could easily go wrong, I headed to the park where I hoped Jeanie would be with her children. I told myself two broken people were unlikely to fix each other. But my desire to talk to someone who might understand the tornado of emotions unleashed by having another baby was stronger than my common sense.

It didn't take many days for me to locate her. She waved as though she wasn't even surprised to see me.

She leant into the pram to have a look at Grace. 'You had another girl then?'

I knew she was asking if I wanted a boy to replace you. I never pried into other people's business, to justify never offering up much information about myself. But as though I'd known her all my life, I asked, 'Did you feel better when you had another son?'

And as though I had every right to delve into the feelings deep in her heart without even a preamble about the lovely sunshine, she answered: 'It hasn't made any difference. It's been worse as I've gone along. I kept hoping that one of them, the next one, would wave the magic wand and make giving him up, if not okay, at least not feel like my guts had a sword through them. But it hasn't. Each time I've nearly fell apart. Though the advantage of four is that I haven't got time to think about him.'

I loved her for her honesty. It was like someone turning the button to the left on the volume of my insanity. Mum's sympathy had given way to fear that Danny would leave me. 'Don't think he won't divorce you. It's much easier now than it used to be. Young ones don't just shut up and put up like we had to and there'll be no shortage of women waiting in the wings. You've got to stop bellyaching about what you haven't got and focus on what you have.'

Jeanie and I stood there for a minute, watching three of her kids in the playground. Her oldest son was pushing his sister and the little boy so high on the Witches' Hat that I had to remember not to hold my breath. In the end, I nodded towards them. 'Is the youngest one all right on there?' Desperate to sound as though I was just making conversation rather than poised to go screaming over, yelling, 'Stop, stop, you'll kill someone!'

Jeanie just shrugged. 'They're fine.' She laughed. 'That's nothing. When I went upstairs the other day, Rick and Sarah were climbing onto the top of the wardrobe and launching themselves onto the bed. The week before, Rick helped himself to my husband's saw and hacked our garden bench in half. Little bugger.'

I thought of how I patrolled the house, looking for sharp edges, anything Grace might pull down on herself once she started to crawl, refusing to let Danny order any coal for winter because I kept imagining her falling in the fire.

'Don't you worry about them hurting themselves?'

Jeanie looked at me. 'I suppose so, a bit. But my old dad wouldn't let me do anything, always had some bloody rule about having to be in early, going bonkers if you got a speck of mud on you, giving us a good belt if we left our toys on the floor in the living room. And in the end, I went off the rails. My kids are going to remember me as fun if it's the last thing I do.'

I envied her that attitude. I was pretty sure of all the adjectives Louise would use to describe me, 'fun' wouldn't be one of them.

'I wish I was more like you. I worry about everything.'

She turned to me. 'The worst thing has already happened to us. We can survive anything now.'

I stood in front of her, studying her freckly face, her chin up, her absolute refusal to apologise for who she was. She didn't care that half the mothers in the playground were tutting at her son standing up in the swing, twisting it round and round until it nearly reached the bar at the top. She didn't bat an eyelid when he charged through the sandpit, flicking grit into everyone's faces. In years gone by, I would have been chiselling my outrage with the best of them. I'd have gathered up Louise, murmuring into her ear, 'Stay away from that horrid little boy.'

But instead I admired her. She'd been judged by society and now she was sticking up two fingers to what anyone thought about anything. I could learn a lot from her.

It took me a couple of years of weekly meetings in the park before I trusted Jeanie enough to introduce her to Danny. When I'd told her for the fiftieth time that Danny didn't know anything about my time in the Mother and Baby home, she'd said, 'Oddly enough, I don't run around advertising the fact that I was pregnant at eighteen by a sailor on a last hurrah before he buggered off to Brunei. Don't really think that's a subject I'm going to be rushing to discuss. No, we'll tell them the truth. The truth we've decided on, that is. We bumped into each other at the Silver Jubilee then came across each other again in the park and got friendly because we've got kids of a similar age. All there is to it.'

And as always, Jeanie made everything sound so simple.

CHAPTER ELEVEN

July 1983

'You're a funny one, Susie. All those navy wives you wouldn't even invite round for coffee, yet you let her come here with her kids and wreck the whole bloody house!' Danny said, almost every time Jeanie came round.

I could see his point. Over the four or so years she'd been visiting, the house had taken a battering. Egged on by the youngest boy, Carl, who, now he was ten, should have known better – the kids went on the rampage, jumping off the settee, playing hide-and-seek in the wardrobes and foraging in the kitchen cupboards without asking. I'd find bits of Fig Roll stuck on door handles and chocolate teacakes squashed behind the curtains for days afterwards. Louise would barricade herself in her room with her music until they'd gone.

If Danny came in from work before I'd had a chance to clear up, he'd say, 'That lot are like a bloody zoo on the loose.'

I'd carry on picking up the wrappers stuffed behind the settee. 'But Grace gets on so well with little Stella. And I'm trying not to be as strict as I was with Louise and frighten off all her friends. They're all right really, just a bit wild.'

He'd shake his head in disbelief and step through the chaos to get changed upstairs. I didn't want him to stop me seeing Jeanie. When she popped round, I felt like I did before I gave you away. That nothing mattered as much as laughing, singing and living life to the full. And she'd been right about one thing: 'When Grace looks less like the baby you gave up and more like a proper kid, you won't worry so much. It's that baby stage that does your nut in, thinking history's going to repeat itself and you'll have been waddling round for nine months and end up with nothing at the end of it.'

Thankfully Danny tolerated the occasional chip out of a skirting board or scuff along the wall because he saw that Jeanie's optimistic attitude about everything: 'Could be worse, couldn't it?' had rubbed off on me. That, not before time, as Grace was nearly six, I'd stopped making a drama out of a slight cold, a fall in the park, a bike whizzing past too close to her. Danny was just happy to have a sunnier wife and less day-to-day aggro. And of course, he was a bloke, so he didn't do forensic investigations in the same way I would have done, always on the lookout for something that wasn't straightforward, sniffing out a half-truth, or digging out a secret. I'd been uptight for so long now, Danny no longer questioned why I'd changed from a carefree person into someone who couldn't sleep if the landing light wasn't on, if I hadn't triple-checked the lock on the front door.

Jeanie had managed it differently. She didn't have that lead-enness, that hesitation about being happy, quite the opposite. I spoilt everything, unable to take pleasure in watching Grace flying around the garden on her roller skates without ruining the moment wondering whether you would have turned out sporty, dynamic on the football pitch, even a bulldozer on the rugby field if you'd ended up at a posh school.

I usually invited Jeanie over when Danny wasn't around, but work was scarce and he was on a three-day week at the factory. On this particular occasion, she'd brought her thirteen-year-old son Rick along when Stella came to play with Grace at the start of the summer holiday. He'd whirled in, a boisterous bundle of hormones and spots. His voice alternated between sounding as

though he was in the backing chorus of The Three Degrees and
barking out commands in the Royal Marines. As soon as he started
banging on our fish bowl, sending the goldfish Danny had won
at the fair flailing under its plastic fern, Danny had tapped him
on the shoulder, 'Come on, mate. You come outside and help
me in my shed. I've got a couple of things you can do for me.'

Through the window, we could see Rick hammering in nails,
chiselling and planing.

Jeanie had clapped her hands. 'Jesus, that's the first time I've
seen him focus on anything for more than five minutes. My
husband's far too interested in the dog track to spend any time
with him.'

I smiled, proud of Danny for bringing out the best in everyone.

Eventually Rick came back in, waving a crudely fashioned
box. 'Look what I made, Mum!'

Jeanie cradled it in her hands as though it was an exquisitely
carved owl in the finest oak. It made me ashamed of how I'd leap
on the smallest spelling mistake in Louise's essays.

Danny said, 'Your lad has got a good eye for woodwork. You
should encourage that. Says he's never been fishing either? Maybe
you'd let me take him down the river one day?'

My stomach went all hollow as I watched Jeanie perk up,
leaning towards Danny as he told her how brilliant it was to have
a boy to teach things to, moaning about how he'd never managed
to get Louise interested in woodwork.

'If it doesn't have a tune to it, she won't give it the time of
day. Grace is too little at the moment, but she seems more into
her dollies than anything else. You send Rick over to me – I've
always wanted to have a go at making a treehouse. Perhaps he
could give me a hand with that.'

Rick was all wide-eyed enthusiasm.

Jeanie laughed. 'Be fab if you taught him something useful.
My husband used a mallet to hammer in a nail and now we've

got a great chunk of plaster missing in the front room. Does a
job and makes a job, does Simon.'

I muttered something about making more tea, just to get out
of the room. I couldn't stand it. Couldn't bear Danny talking
about what projects he'd like to do with a boy. It made me want
to rush out into the street, dash up and down, beg people to help
me find you. There was room for a son in our lives. Danny would
have been a brilliant father to a boy.

Just not you.

When I went back in, Danny and Rick were sitting doing
drawings of treehouses at the table. Rick was all hastily scribbled
ladders, gun holes and escape hatches. Danny was the complete
contrast, with his rubber, rulers and light pencil lines. I couldn't
watch. Couldn't look at those two heads bent over, the bright
ginger against Danny's dark curls, engaged in one common
goal. I couldn't settle, didn't bustle round telling Jeanie I was
just about to make some ham and eggs, that they'd all be very
welcome, as I usually would. She kept glancing at me, frowning.
In the end, she called her brood and started buttoning up coats
and shoving on shoes, brushing away the protests of 'Aren't we
staying for tea?'

Jeanie whispered to me as she left. 'It's the son thing, isn't it?
Sorry. I didn't think about that. I got all excited because no one
really likes Rick, he's got none of the charm of the other three.
Too much like his father. Just made such a change for someone
to be interested in him. And Danny was great with him.'

I hugged her, hating myself for my mean spirit. 'Sorry for
being such a misery guts. It's lovely for Danny to have a boy in
the house.'

Despite my best intentions, after Jeanie's visit, I was prickly
all evening, telling Louise off for singing too loudly, impatient
with Grace for spilling a beaker of orange squash, having a go at
Danny about his messy shed.

But for once he didn't back down. 'Give it a rest, Susie. You never even go into the shed. What does it matter to you whether my nails are all over the workbench and there are wood shavings on the floor?'

I then diverted the argument onto how he thought I felt, watching him spend all afternoon with someone else's child when he never read with Grace, never made Louise practise the piano, seemed to prefer going out to the working man's club with his mates than staying at home with his family.

That evening, Danny didn't do what he normally did: walk away and gather the children to watch television until 'Mummy feels a bit better'. He gave me both barrels, not in the hysterical, toys out of the pram way I did, but calmly, no-nonsense. His voice was so cold, so detached, it was like being catapulted off a sunlounger where I'd been baking nicely into a freezing pool.

'Susie, I'm sorry I'm not enough for you. I'm sorry I haven't been a good husband. I've tried. I really have. I came out of the navy, I do a job where I'm trapped inside all day so I can be at home more. I do all the overtime I can. I think we've got a good life. And I'm really *bloody* sorry that you're so miserable. If you think someone else could make you happier, then maybe it really is time to take stock before we sleepwalk into old age and realise we've wasted our entire lives.'

With that, he picked up his jacket, ran his fingers through his hair and walked out the door.

Louise poked her head out of the lounge. 'Are you and Dad going to get divorced?'

I put my arms out to her and, for once, her seventeen-year-old edges and corners folded into me. 'Don't be silly. I won't ever stop loving your dad. And he loves us all so much. We've just had a bit of a disagreement, that's all.'

I knew at least one of those statements was true. I'd have to shape up to make sure they both were.

CHAPTER TWELVE

August 1983

When Danny came home that night, I expected him to be calm and forgiving, brushing everything under the carpet as he always did. But he wasn't. He stumbled up to bed, a waft of beer trailing in his wake. Grace woke as he banged the bathroom door. I perched on her little bed, stroking her forehead until she dropped off again, wrestling with the stupidity of giving you away to save the rest of the family, and losing you causing so much pain that I was destroying everyone else anyway.

I crept into our bed. Danny was rumbling out the wheezy snores of a man who hadn't just had half a bitter, while I lay there, in the hot air of the summer night, thinking about what I'd been like before I'd started singing with The Shakers on a regular basis. Before I'd started filtering what I put in my letters to Danny. When I slipped in now and again that I'd been doing a few turns on stage at the dance hall rather than the truth: I was singing full sets on Saturday nights and rehearsing with the band every Wednesday evening. I left Louise overnight with my mum while I went to my 'pottery class'. 'You have a break, love, get a good night's sleep.'

She wouldn't have understood my compulsion to sing and would have certainly disapproved. The pull of the music, the desire to try out new arrangements, to work on dance routines, was so strong that my guilt about lying about where I was going only lasted as far as the corner. I convinced myself that Danny wouldn't mind. He often said, 'I can't expect you just to sit at home twiddling your thumbs until I get home.' But there was a vast difference between a night out at the pictures with a friend and staying up to the early hours drinking, the only woman in a group of men. And letting myself get dragged into thinking that a rock 'n' roll lifestyle could ever be mine? Utter madness.

But there'd been that tiny moment, that one evening, when I'd toyed with the idea. Thought I could make everyone see sense, could convince them to let me have a go. I'd allowed myself to fantasise about being famous, about making so much money that we'd never have to worry about anything ever again. If only we knew those tiny moments, the minutes in our lives we overlook, the happenings that slip in with no more disturbance than a breeze ruffling a net curtain, were sometimes the pivotal turning points. The moments that should be heralded with a fanfare, fireworks, a bright red BEWARE.

And now, fifteen years after I'd had you, I had pushed Danny right up to his limit, rubbing shoulders with beware. For more than a decade, Danny's easy-going nature had allowed me to fool myself that what I wanted was what he wanted. But with his mid-forties approaching, it looked as though I couldn't rely on that any more. It was all too easy to imagine him standing in our bedroom, saying, 'Suze, I've done everything I can, but I can't carry on like this, trying to make you happy when nothing ever does.'

And with a surge of fear, the words in my head sounded so plausible, so real, that I wanted to leap out of bed and check there wasn't a half-packed suitcase hidden in the wardrobe.

As dawn broke, I realised I'd have to bury thoughts of you forever. No more buying presents for your birthday. No more staring up at the North Star. No more whispering to Jeanie about my dreams of somehow being reunited with you one day, without anyone knowing. You needed to be dead to me if my remaining family was to survive.

By the time I'd dragged myself out of bed, I was resolute. A feeling akin to intoxication rushed through me, as though I'd understood a truth: I could never think about you again.

Instead I focused on Danny. Really looked at him. As a man, not as the person I could never relax with, in case you crept out in the crevices of our conversation. His face, soft in sleep. Those big hands that were capable of fixing the tiniest screws on Grace's bike, which tucked a strand of hair behind Louise's ear with a spontaneity I could never master, which could communicate love, safety and 'I've got this' with a simple squeeze.

And that gorgeous mouth that made me want to trace the outline of it with my finger, to recapture those heady days when he was on leave from the navy and we could lock ourselves away into a private world just by focusing on each other's faces.

I ran downstairs and made him tea and toast on a tray.

I smiled as he opened his eyes, squinting against the light. I couldn't wait to tell him my idea. 'Danny, I've been thinking. Do you fancy having a party for your birthday? I think the weather's supposed to stay fine for the rest of August.'

But instead of him jumping at the chance as I thought he would, he shook his head. 'Not really.'

'Why not? Louise can help, she's old enough.'

He struggled up onto his elbows.

'Do you want the truth?'

I nodded, even though I wasn't sure I did.

'I don't want to look forward to a party, get the girls all excited, just for you to cancel at the last minute because you're too worn out, you've got a migraine, because you can't face all those people, because the catering's too much for you, because it's getting too expensive and wouldn't I rather just have a family dinner anyway?'

He flopped back down onto the pillow, pulling the sheets around him.

I stared at the back of his head. It seemed a long time since he'd held me in his arms at the Portsmouth Palais and said, 'Every man here wants you.' Then he'd looked away shyly. 'But you chose me.'

I'd show him that I could be that girl again. His forty-second birthday would be one to remember. I had three weeks to plan my surprise.

By the time the day of the party rolled around on the third Saturday of August, Louise and I were working like a team of special agents. Initially, she had been reluctant to get involved. 'You always say we're going to do something and it never happens.' But when she saw me stockpiling beer in the coal shed and spending three afternoons in a row making sausage rolls and mushroom vol-au-vents, she agreed to take Grace round our cul-de-sac to invite the neighbours. No one could resist Grace. She was a mischief-magnet but had that innate ability to reel people in with a cheeky smile. It was the inviting I found awkward, as though I might have to justify a sudden desire to fill bowls with Twiglets and chop fruit for the punch. I put off phoning Danny's ex-navy mates until any later would have looked plain weird. Without exception, they all paused when I announced who was calling and why, as though 'Susie' and 'party' didn't fit in the same sentence. But they still said yes.

I'd told Danny we were going to have a nice family meal, but he should go down to the club with his mates for a few drinks before Mum joined us for dinner at eight. He'd looked blank, as though his expectations for any celebration I might be involved in would require a microscope. While he was out, Jeanie and I flew around decorating the garden, hanging lights in the trees, while Mum clucked about, fussing over her rice salad and coronation chicken. Louise was busy with the balloons. For the first time in a long time, I felt like the fun parent rather than the teacher, the disciplinarian, the manners monitor.

Just before seven-thirty, I put the Bay City Rollers on the cassette player. I chose 'Bye Bye Baby' as a deliberate challenge and forced myself to sing along to every word. We all danced, waving our hands in the air as though we were at a concert at Wembley rather than a backyard in Portsmouth. I refused to feel guilty about singing and dancing. It would get easier. It had to.

Guests started to arrive and I had no time to think about anything. Louise stationed herself as a lookout at our front gate, while I dashed about pouring drinks. Jeanie was chief cocktail maker, though she wasn't much of a stickler for measures, slopping Galliano, vodka and orange juice into glasses and telling everyone that it was 'the nearest thing to being in Magaluf'.

When Louise gave the word, we switched the lights off in the garden and everyone crouched down. I went to the front door and let Danny in. Instead of my usual peck on the cheek, I stopped in front of him, lifted my face to his and kissed him hard on the lips. He paused for a second in surprise and then melted into me, greedy for this moment of spontaneity.

'I love you.' I was never first to say those words any more; I only ever volunteered them as a response. They felt clunky and wooden to me, my hypocrisy radiating out of every pore.

The surliness that had been darkening Danny's face for weeks lifted, his eyes holding mine. He kissed my neck. 'Love you too. Where's your mum? The girls?'

A trickle of relief ran through me. I stepped away reluctantly. 'They're in the garden waiting for you.' His face fell in mock disappointment. I kissed him again. 'Later.'

As we stepped through the back door, a huge cheer went up, the lights snapped on and Louise sang 'Happy Birthday' standing on the stage we'd fashioned out of crates and an old pallet, her soulful sound turning a hackneyed refrain into something exquisite, throwing the other voices in the mix into sharp relief.

'You little minx!' Danny said, throwing his arms around me and covering me in kisses until a shout went up from his mates to 'get a room'.

It was a long time since I'd been mischievous enough to be considered a minx.

Jeanie weaved her way over with a couple of Harvey Wall-bangers.

'Simon coming along later?' Danny asked.

'Nah. He's a miserable sod anyway.' Jeanie hadn't read the good wife guide to being loyal to useless husbands. 'He'll probably be down the pub himself. His mam is watching the kids.'

'You should have brought them,' Danny said.

'My four? You got to be kidding, love. You know what little hooligans they are. And the little one, she's the worst, proper little tike.'

Jeanie winked at me when Danny had moved off to greet his guests.

'Told Simon I was babysitting for some extra cash. Knew he'd spoil my fun otherwise. He chats up other women all the time, but gets a right old cob on if I even talk to another man. Thinks the fact I had a baby with someone else is eternal proof that I'm a right old scrubber.'

And as though she needed to make up for his absence, Jeanie attacked the cocktails as though her sole purpose in life was to mainline vodka. There was no denying the woman could party though. She even got Mum swigging back the fruit punch and shaking her tail feathers to The Blues Brothers.

Grace finally conked out on a deckchair, not even stirring when the whole party started congaing around the yard and through the house. Louise was in her element, playing the guitar and singing a whole repertoire of songs that Danny and I had danced to when we were first dating, songs I didn't even know she knew. When Danny joined her in 'When I'm Sixty-Four', his off-key notes crashing across her gutsy, vibrant rendition, I wanted to stop the clock and let all the good things in my life fill my heart, like rain in a reservoir. I looked round at all the faces laughing and singing along, and if I ignored the twinge where you were missing, I could consider myself happy.

By midnight, the party was starting to thin out and Danny kept leaning on me, kissing my neck and running his hands over my backside. 'I've had a lovely time. Lovely. You're the best wife ever.'

Normally I'd have felt a burst of anxiety about how tired I'd be the next day if I got to bed after midnight. But tonight I didn't want the evening to end. Apart from a tiny moment when I wondered if you'd been there – a fifteen-year-old with the beginnings of a moustache – whether you'd have handed round crisps, chatting with the guests, or hidden in the kitchen pretending to look after Mum, I banished you from my mind. Which with Jeanie as a guest wasn't too difficult: she needed no encouragement to party on. 'Come on! The night is young!' She twirled around, pirouetting about with a wine glass. She kept requesting songs from Louise, who was in her element on the electric guitar Danny had insisted on buying her for her seventeenth birthday. 'Yeah, I know it's extravagant but she deserves it. She's a good girl.'

Jeanie dragged up a man to dance, but he refused to be parted from his beer. There was something comical about them stumbling about dancing entirely out of time with the music while endeavouring not to spill their drinks. And just as I got up to join in, my whole body alive with the joy of dancing, the rhythms and shapes settling on me with easy familiarity, the back gate onto the alley crashed open. Jeanie's husband, Simon, stormed in with all the purpose of a silverback gorilla intent on laying claim to a territory. He steamed over to where Jeanie was playing imaginary one-handed drums in a world of her own.

Jeanie took a moment or two to stop dancing, grinding to a halt like Gracie's toy dog when it ran out of battery. He grabbed hold of her. She winced and wrenched herself free. 'You're supposed to be babysitting, not here acting like a little scrubber. Again.'

She didn't hesitate. Just swung her hand back and cracked him one right around the face. 'Don't you dare call me a scrubber. Don't you dare. In fact, I'm far too bloody good for you.'

Danny had been lying in a deckchair with his head back, half-asleep, grinning soporifically under the August stars, reaching out for my hand every time I walked past and mumbling about, 'The best birthday ever. And you're not so bad either.' He sat bolt upright at the commotion, glancing about him in a daze before leaping up. He didn't manage to get in-between them before Simon shoved Jeanie backwards and she landed in a heap on the grass. I heard the breath leave her body as she jolted down but bravado made her laugh.

'Go on then, show everyone how tough you are, what a fantastic example you are to the kids. No wonder Rick's always in trouble.'

Louise stood folded around her guitar, looking over at me in a panic. I ran over to stand with her, ready to crack Simon one myself if he came anywhere near her. With way more confidence than I felt, I said, 'Dad'll sort him out, don't worry.'

Danny was wide awake now, arms out to keep them apart. 'Jeanie! Simon! Cut it out.'

But Simon wasn't done yet and raged towards her again. Thankfully, a couple of the navy lads grabbed hold of him and propelled him towards the back gate.

'Out you go. Go and cool down, mate. Go on, home.'

He was still shouting about not going anywhere without his wife as the two lads lifted him off the ground, his feet windmilling in the air, before they threw open the gate and dumped him outside, then dragged a garden bench in front of it. The gate shuddered as he kicked it, until one of the men told him they'd punch his lights out if he didn't get lost.

Danny helped Jeanie to her feet, his face a mixture of concern and anger. 'Are you okay?'

She stood up straight and smiled, the sort of smile that people like us had developed over the years as an alternative to crying. 'And now for my next trick.' She hiccupped and turned to me. 'Sorry about that. He can get a bit handy when he's had a drink, but I can look after meself.'

I put my arm round her, feeling the defiance in her shoulders, the toughness within that wouldn't let her wilt, even in front of me.

We sat on the bench. The remaining guests made their excuses and left, while Danny went inside to fetch some coffee.

Jeanie leaned forward and rested her chin in her hands. 'Simon's my punishment for giving my baby away.'

'Don't be stupid,' I whispered. 'You sound like one of the nuns. Our punishment is having to live without our babies. That's bad enough.'

Jeanie lolled over to one side. 'Are you glad you stayed with Danny? Or do you wish you'd gone off with the baby's father?'

'Sshhh! He'll hear you.'

She persisted. 'I never did understand why you were unfaithful to Danny. Isn't he everything a girl wants? Handsome, kind, a good father, hard-working, brings home the housekeeping? Did you really think you'd get someone better? Talk about having your cake and eating it. Christ, I'd have nailed a bloke like that to the floor.'

I felt my stomach sink. Jeanie had always smudged the edges of brutal truths to make them easier to bear. And now she was flinging them at me with arrow-sharp accuracy. I didn't need anyone to point out how lucky I was to have Danny. Or how stupid I was to have done what I did. I scuffed at the grass with my sandal, one eye on Danny moving about, oblivious, in the kitchen. I managed, 'I don't think it's the right time to discuss it now,' when really I wanted to stomp about the garden kicking over the tables and smashing those stupid mushroom vol-au-vents into a million pastry flakes, screaming, 'You have no bloody idea what it was like!' at the top of my voice.

But Jeanie was slurring on, rolling away from my control like a football down a hill. 'Why? What made your mistake so special? Was he was the love of your life? Not just a shag behind the pub like mine?'

Danny appeared at the back door with two cups of coffee just as I hissed, 'Shut up!' Thankfully, she slumped back into the corner of the bench.

As he handed Jeanie her coffee, he frowned at me. My heart skipped as I wondered if Jeanie's words had travelled in the quiet of the darkness. But Danny smiled and held out his hand to me. 'Let's make Jeanie a bed up on the settee.'

Not for the first time, I wished he wasn't so kind.

CHAPTER THIRTEEN
August 1983

When Gracie climbed into bed and woke us up the next day, Danny snuggled up to me. 'Wonder if Jeanie made it through the night without puking on the parquet.'

I elbowed him. 'You're full of sweet nothings this morning. How about "Morning, love of my life, that was a wonderful party you threw for me"?'

'That you're the love of my life goes without saying.'

Grace started to bounce up and down on Danny, eliciting a groan from him.

'What's the matter? Didn't you like your party, Daddy?' she asked.

He sat up, rubbing his hands over his face. 'I loved it. We should do it more often. Bet there are a few sore heads this morning. Not least Jeanie's. And Simon must have been pretty drunk to come barrelling in like that. I don't feel that clever myself.'

I wanted to stay there and luxuriate, share the delicious party aftermath of who said what, who put their foot in it, who'd crossed a line, who'd been surprisingly entertaining, all the fragments of human interaction we compared ourselves against, that made us feel better – or worse – about who we were. I longed to enjoy that moment of closeness with Danny, of feeling that he was still in our marriage, not planning how to leave. But the knowledge that Jeanie was downstairs, the unreliable holder of my secret, made me fidgety. She'd never once mentioned you when Danny had been in the vicinity, but then we'd only ever been drinking tea and Tizer before. Now the fuddle of alcohol had cleared, the sheer terror at how easily my life could be destroyed with a few Galliano-fuelled words had developed its own drumbeat.

And then Danny said, 'What were you talking to Jeanie about? You looked like you were arguing when I came out with the coffee.'

I rolled away from him, fright turning my stomach to liquid. 'I can't really remember. We'd both had a bit too much to drink.'

'You were telling her to shut up.'

'God knows. She was probably giving me advice on how to bring up the kids. Yes, I think that was it. She was telling me I was too strict. Which given how her brood are capable of wrecking our whole house in fifteen minutes, I thought was a bit rich.'

I held my breath, my mind racing. Danny stared at me for moment, as though he wanted to ask something else. Thankfully Grace wasn't going to be ignored and started jumping about. Danny laughed and said, 'You might have been strict with Louise, but this little monkey gets away with murder,' he said, tickling Grace until she squealed. He was right, but in that precise second my inability to tell off my youngest daughter wasn't my top priority. I needed to make sure Jeanie's blabbermouth moment was a one-off.

I swung my legs out of bed. 'Stay there. I'll go and make some tea. You can be the birthday boy for a bit longer.'

'I knew there was a reason I loved you,' he said, blowing me a kiss before fighting with Grace, who was trying to pull the bedclothes off him.

Before Danny got downstairs, I needed to set Jeanie straight on a few things.

I crept down, ready to leap on her if she showed any signs of uttering anything other than 'my head hurts'. The lounge had the stale smell of an old pool hall. I shut the door after me and perched on the edge of the settee. I shook Jeanie's shoulder, nowhere near as gently as I would have done if the embers of resentment and anger hadn't still been scorching through me.

She shot up cartoon-like, arms flailing. 'Jesus Christ. I thought it was a school day and I'd overslept.' Then she groaned. 'Tell me we didn't have that conversation.' She grimaced. 'Was I prattling on about how lucky you were?'

I didn't feel like letting her off the hook. I hissed back, 'At the top of your voice, so Danny could hear.'

Her eyes, what was left of them in their piggy pink state, flew open. 'No! Did I say anything too bad? Tell me I haven't dropped you in it.'

She didn't sound anywhere near horrified enough. 'Not for the want of bloody trying. What were you thinking? Blaring about whether I wished I'd stayed with the baby's father at a hundred million decibels. Do you even realise what you could have done?'

In other circumstances, I'd have had a bit of sympathy for her as she screwed up her eyes and massaged her forehead. But fear, combined with the shock that someone who knew my most shameful secret might just blurt it out, blasé, one August night, because she was on the wrong end of a couple of cocktails, made me savage.

'One, you have no idea what my circumstances were before you start judging me. And two, I thought I could trust you. You, of all people, know that the thing that was in "everyone's best interests" turned out to be an enormous great cross to lug through life. I don't need you to make me feel guilty, I can get there on my bloody own. And I definitely don't need you broadcasting it to the people who love me and know nothing about it! It's fine for you, you could tell Simon. I can't say a word to Danny because – as you well know – I got pregnant when I was *already* married.' Despite myself, my voice was rising, tears were stinging my eyes.

I'd never had a go at Jeanie before. She'd always been my soft landing. But the girl who'd been forced out of home at eighteen and been fighting to survive ever since was quick to surface. 'Christ, keep your hair on, Susie. I'm sorry. I was drunk. And don't take this the wrong way...'

I immediately geared up to take maximum offence.

'...but Danny is so good to you and you can be so difficult, never wanting to go out with him. Poor bloke always has to go to the social club on his own. Bet they think you're someone he's made up. You don't even make much effort to keep him, but he never gives you any aggro. You saw what an oik Simon is. If he weren't the father of my kids, I'd have buggered off long ago.'

In my family, I had a reputation for being the 'difficult one'. Louise rolling her eyes, 'Mum is bound to have some problem with it', Danny saying, 'Just listen to my suggestion before you say no' – but I still felt the burn of injustice fan the flames of my anger.

'For god's sake! I am so sick of being grateful. Grateful the nuns gave a sinner like me a roof over my head. Grateful another couple were prepared to take on my illegitimate son, grateful for a husband who everyone thinks is a bloody saint for putting up with bad-tempered, deceitful, unfaithful me!'

Jeanie put her hand up to stop me, but the words were crashing out of me with the force of winter waves.

'Get out. Just get out. I don't need you telling me how bloody lucky I am. Just go.'

Jeanie's face was a mixture of horror and fury. Her hands were up in surrender. It was her turn to tell me to keep my voice down.

I took a breath. 'Jeanie, you've got to leave. I can't have you here.'

She got to her feet. 'You're being really unfair. Yeah, I made a mistake, Susie, but no harm done and all that. I've learnt my lesson, I won't ever say anything like it again. I don't know what got into me.' She pulled a face. 'Don't get much opportunity to let my hair down. Took it a bit far but didn't realise you'd burn me at the stake for it. I'll hop off now. See you soon though, eh? Say thanks to Danny for looking after me.'

I didn't even respond. Just ushered her out of the front door and banged it behind her, leaning against the stained glass, feeling my heart slow, the surging of frantic energy slackening to a dull pulse.

Danny shouted from the bedroom. 'Oi! I thought you were making me tea.'

And like a wife with nothing more pressing on her mind than scuttling up the stairs with her best bone china, I shouted back, 'Just coming.'

CHAPTER FOURTEEN
September 1983

After Danny's initial curiosity about why Jeanie had been in such a rush to get off, a haste I dismissed as needing to get back for the kids, no one noticed her absence for a few weeks. Eventually Danny said, 'I'm thinking of going fishing at the weekend. Do you want to ask Jeanie if Rick wants to join me? I promised her ages ago I'd take him. God knows, that husband of hers doesn't sound like he shows much interest.'

'I think they're really busy at the moment. Simon's got Rick working with him on the vans at weekends.'

Danny shrugged. 'Never mind. I just feel bad for not doing what I said I'd do.' He paused and looked at me. 'You two haven't fallen out, have you? Haven't seen her lately.'

I bent down to get a cloth out from under the sink so that he wouldn't see my face. 'No. She's just tied up with all those kids and I'm having such a struggle trying to get Louise to see sense about taking up that place at bloody music school, we haven't had as much time to catch up with each other.'

I started scrubbing at the limescale around the kitchen tap, willing my face to lose its heat.

Danny shuffled about behind me, the air weighty with 'something needing to be said'.

Eventually I turned round. 'What?'

He came towards me. 'Put that cloth down and stop being such a grump.' He threaded his arms around me and I leaned into him, feeling myself soften. 'I know you feel strongly about Louise going into teaching, but don't you think we should let her try out the music thing? She's so passionate about it. As long as she works hard and gets the grades for university so that there's a plan B to fall back on if it doesn't work out, I can't see what harm it could do. She's got a full grant.'

I leaned away from him. 'She's not going, Danny. We'd just be building her up for disappointment. Who makes it in the music industry? A handful of people out of the ones who try. She thinks a few years at music school and she'll be entertaining the crowds at Wembley, but that's never going to happen. We don't know anyone in those circles. We're not a family that produces pop stars.'

'I don't suppose Paul McCartney's mum thought they were a family of pop stars either. Someone has to be successful. Why not her?'

Because she was my daughter. Because she was precious and I was bloody well going to protect her. I wished I could find the words. I wanted to start smashing crockery at the thought of her believing that some man was going to deliver her dream. However unpopular it made me, I couldn't let my seventeen-year-old daughter out into a world where she'd be agreeing to dinners, drinks, laughing off a touch of the hand, letting someone stroke her glossy hair, all the while pushing away an uneasy feeling in her stomach because the power to 'make her a star' lay within his grasp.

No sharp-suited record producer was going to sit in front of her with his head on one side, ostensibly assessing her vocals but secretly wondering whether he'd be able to persuade her to come back to his hotel to discuss contracts. She'd never find herself urged on by her bandmates, already making jokes about filling stadiums and travelling in private jets.

I could see Rob now, that Saturday night in September 1967, steaming into the manky backstage room at the Portsmouth Palais, little more than an understairs cupboard, where we were taking a break, midway through the set. His face was a blaze of excitement.

He punched the air. 'Guess who is in the audience?' We all waited for him to tell us he'd seen 'the woman I'm going to marry', which he did every other week. But he burst out with, 'A scout from Top Note Records! He's just come over and told me he wants to "explore the band's potential, sort out a demo"! The Shakers are going to be famous!'

I threw my arms around him. 'Oh my god! Promise me you'll still let me do the backing to "I'll Never Fall In Love Again" for old time's sake when you're rich and famous.'

He grasped my wrists, his eyes wide with delight. 'What do you mean? He wants everyone, you as well, Susie. In fact, he's taken a real shine to you, thinks you round off the group perfectly, likes the "chemistry" between us all apparently.'

I remembered my heart leaping with the pleasure of being included, then the sick feeling of disappointment as I knew I couldn't ever be more than a singer on a Saturday night at the dance hall. I wasn't free like them.

I tried to smile, not wanting to dull Rob's excitement. 'I can't be part of that, Rob. How am I going to be a "recording artist" with a two-year-old daughter and a husband on the other side of the world? I'm already lucky that Danny hasn't put his foot down about me singing at the Palais. There's no way I can be part of a band. I'm a wife and a mother. I can't spend my life rehearsing and recording. We'd have to tour and all sorts.'

Rob's face clouded over. 'But this is our big chance. We can't do it without you. He wants a woman in the group, said he likes the way it fits together, broadens the appeal.'

I couldn't do it. Of course I wanted to stand on stage and sing to an audience of thousands. In that moment, I was ashamed of how much I wanted it. So much so that part of me wished that I hadn't rushed to get married at nineteen as though settling down with a handsome navy petty officer and having a baby was the pinnacle of everything a girl like me could hope for. I loved Danny but it was hard to feel that presence, that sense of building a family together through letters. I needed someone to say, 'Here, give Louise to me, let me take her for a bit,' when she'd been teething and grouchy. Someone to light the candles in a power cut. Someone to tell me, 'You sit down. You haven't stopped all day. Cup of tea?'

Danny and I could never live in the moment, existing either to look forward to being reunited or dreading being separated. I'd tick off the weeks when he was away at sea or feel the sick pit in my stomach as the days became measured in 'the last time that'. The last film we'd see together. The last Sunday we'd stay in bed all morning. The last trip to feed the ducks with Louise. Until the last day, when we'd make love, wordlessly, tenderly, trying to transmit enough love to sustain us through to the next leave.

And sometimes, after months of knitting yet another jumper for Danny for when he came home, flicking through *Good House-keeping* when Louise had gone to bed, watching *The Avengers* when Mum popped round to keep me company, I wished I could just throw it all in, go off with Rob and Jim on an adventure. How I longed to be the one pointing my compass into the unknown, not silently marking another birthday, another Christmas, another ordinary Tuesday on my own.

Danny had never really understood that loneliness. How could he? When he was away, with fifteen of them to a mess deck, he'd complain about never having a moment on his own. He'd never understand how the little greenhouse of unremarkable circumstances produced such a crop of disaster.

I closed my eyes against the memory, diverting my energy back to the argument over that bloody music school. Louise's rage rumbling through the house like a rockfall down a cliff face. All her whispered entreaties to Danny. 'Tell her, Dad! Tell her it's the only thing I want to do.' Her immediate silence if I ever joined in when she was singing. The way she wavered between begging me to let her go and outright hostility, especially after the headmistress had written a personal note, detailing what a fantastic opportunity this represented for someone 'with such a remarkable gift'.

Today, I sensed that Danny was going to deal with the subject once and for all, try and dig behind why I was so rigid, so uncompromising. He tried to pull me close, but my whole body was taut with the frustration that I'd never be able to explain. Because if he knew what I knew, he'd snip the strings on Louise's guitar himself. He tried again. 'Is it the fact that she'd have to live up in London that's putting you off? If we made sure she was living somewhere safe, with other girls, would it be so bad? You'd have given your right arm for an opportunity like that. She's desperate to go, Susie.'

I knew all about desperation. I could smell it on Rob that night, the raw need in his voice, the longing for a chance to release a record, to be more than the cute guy in the fluorescent suit, doing a turn at the Portsmouth Palais. Those eyes that stared down, teasing and flirtatious, into the faces of all the groupies by the stage, making every woman feel she could be the one, were pleading with me. 'Come on, Susie. Just go and have a drink with him.' He'd tried to joke, 'Turn all that little-girl-lost charm on him. He'll be eating out of your hand. Please.'

And Jim, slumped against the wall, tapping a drumstick on his knee, seeing his chance of realising his dreams ebbing away with my refusal. He wasn't begging like Rob. He was angry, resentful their opportunity of fame and fortune depended on me; the person who'd started off singing the occasional chorus now held their fate in her hands. I paced up and down, tears threatening, my throat tightening around the apologies I'd ever got involved.

Jim was cold, lethargic. Nothing like the soulful presence on the drums and guitar every Saturday night, the one who mesmerised the crowd with his rhythm, exuding sheer joy and energy, whether it was the slowest love song or the liveliest jive. He threw a drumstick into the cracked old mirror, causing a shower of plaster to rain down. 'Don't screw this up for us, Susie. Just fucking go along with it, tell him you'll be the lead bloody singer. Let's just give it our best shot for six months, try and get a record out there. It might not happen anyway, but it definitely won't if you jump ship.' He kicked the heels of his Doc Martens into the stained carpet with a dull thud.

So I never said an outright 'No', the sort of no that meant 'This can't and won't happen'. I'd tried, mumbled a few objections. But in the end, I'd put on my lipstick, run an extra line of kohl under my eyes and strutted out on stage in my silver hot pants and purple turtleneck. Sung our best song, putting every last ounce of emotion into each trembling lyric. And despite the knowledge that a pop career was out of the question for me, I still felt a little rush of adrenaline when I picked out the scout Rob had described: 'Pin-striped jacket, mid-thirties, dark hair, quite long. Looks very "London".'

He was leaning on a pillar at the front, blowing smoke rings. Striking, quite dark-skinned, as though he had some exotic ancestry. His face had the expression of someone who expected people to please him. He didn't take his eyes off me. Even when I focused on other faces in the crowd, there was a hotspot in my peripheral vision, where I sensed his gaze. As the song drew to a close, he looked up at me and winked, nodding slightly, bottom lip jutting in a 'not too bad at all' expression. The challenge in his stance, the 'Hey, pretty girl, you're welcome to come over but I won't be moving a muscle' ignited that responding, hands-on-hip

'Come and have a try if you think you're good enough' in me. The confidence I'd had when I met Danny, the vanity of youth that made everything a catch-me-if-you-can game, fluttered out a faded heartbeat. I'd just see if I could reel him in, get him onside for Rob and Jim before I bowed out. Back to the bloody doilies that Mum liked to come round and crochet with me. 'That'll look lovely on your coffee table.' Back to rolling snakes out of Plasticine, pretending to pour tea out of Louise's plastic teapot, watching that Slinky roll down our stairs for the five hundredth time, feeling ashamed that I'd rather have been at work gossiping to my friends like I did before I was married.

But here, up on stage, I felt alive. More than just a twenty-one-year-old who'd married too young, for whom the most exciting event in the foreseeable future might be finding a pound note in the park. More than just a dutiful wife who found Hilda Ogden's disappearance in *Coronation Street* more thrilling than her own life.

As we came off stage, I walked slowly, my hips swinging as though I knew the world would wait for me. Danny always said I'd won him over with my 'Portsmouth pout'.

I let the boys go first, Rob bounding ahead, eager like a puppy at a picnic. Jim hiding his shyness with a slouch and a handshake that gave the impression he was doing the scout a favour by moving the muscles of his hand into a clasp.

'Jim.'

'Mal, A&R department at Top Note. Great sound you got going there.' He paused and looked over to me. 'And this is…?'

'Susie.' I put my hand out, making sure to grip firmly. I just stopped myself asking what the A&R department was; I'd get Rob to explain later.

'Susie.' That appraising look again. 'You, me and the boys here have got some talking to do. Let's see if we can make something out of you.'

We followed him out to his Morris Minor, a white convertible that made me feel like Audrey Hepburn. I was torn between wanting the girls I used to work with to see me and fear that news of me gallivanting around would reach Danny on the ship.

Mal ushered me into the front seat. 'Good looks are everything in this business. Let's start as we mean to go on.'

Later that evening, when we all stood in the bar at a hotel on the seafront, he didn't ask us what we wanted to drink, just nodded at the bartender. 'Jack Daniel's on the rocks, four.' I concentrated on sipping the whisky without my eyes watering. He led us outside onto the terrace. 'Bit of peace and quiet out here. Not too cold for September, is it? Anyway, we've got the whisky to keep us warm.'

Then he launched into what he had in mind for us, how we'd have to make a demo, how we'd need a bit of patience, but he was very excited by what he'd heard, thought we were 'very box office, especially with Susie fronting it. No promises, but if you play your cards properly, you could be very rich.'

I glanced at Rob. He was doing a great job of arranging his expression to accept his demotion from lead singer. He gave me a little wink. I forced my face into a smile, pushing away the disloyal thought that, with any luck, the demo tape would end up in the bin. Six months from now, I hoped we'd just see it as an exciting interlude before Rob resigned himself to working in his dad's fish and chip shop by the hospital and Jim went back to fixing cars. A treacherous corner of my brain allowed me a brief flirtation with the idea of cruising about the south of France, arm dangling out of the side of an open-top car, complete with Jackie Onassis sunglasses and headscarf.

Rob was rubbing his hands together. 'What will happen next? What's the next step if the big boss comes on board?' Even Jim dropped his broody artiste façade for the evening and started making jokes about private jets and yachts.

After the fourth round of drinks, Mal was leaning on the table, chin resting on his fist, laughing and saying to the boys, 'You'll get any girl you want. It'll be like being at the Pick 'n' Mix counter. One of those, then maybe one of those, or perhaps that one instead. Especially when you start making money.' Rob looked like that was the best news he'd heard all year and even Jim was making Les Dawson faces. But my laugh was getting strained. Danny hated men talking like that in front of women. I always teased him that they must nickname him 'the monk' on the ship.

He'd shrug. 'I join in the banter, but I don't like it when they take it too far. Especially the lads with wives and daughters. They should know better. They know not to say anything about you, not even as a joke if they don't want to end up in a fight.'

In that moment, I'd have done anything to be at home with Danny. To sit on the settee with Louise propped up between us watching *The Great Escape* again, cheering Steve McQueen on his motorbike, even though we knew how it ended. My head felt fuzzy, I was having to concentrate to smile at the right moments and look like the prospect of a record deal was a great glittering gift rather than a huge abyss of problems opening up in front of me. Would Danny be able to accept me having a recording career? Maybe it wouldn't actually take up that much time if we didn't tour. But there was no mistaking the dread in my heart. He wouldn't be happy.

And Mum would be horrified. She wouldn't listen to The Beatles ever since they had backed a call to legalise marijuana in July. 'I told you all those singers are on drugs. Can't be right living in hotel rooms and never being at home with your family.'

I was just wondering how to make my excuses to leave, when Mal turned to me, his voice gentle. 'And what about you, Susie? Will you have a man in every port?'

I hesitated. 'I'm already married.' I hated myself for the apology in my voice.

Mal wrinkled his nose. 'Where's your husband then?'

I explained about the navy, watching Mal's face fall as he realised I might not be so appealing to the punters after all. He narrowed his eyes. 'I don't think we need to burden anyone with that knowledge. We'd have to keep him out of the press. Shouldn't be too hard if he's away for fifteen months at a time. Not really like being married, is it?'

Even though I often used those very words to Danny when I was upset about him leaving, I felt the stab of hurt that Mal should consider my marriage somehow inferior to one where a husband and wife sat ignoring each other over a pork chop and peas seven days a week. 'I've got used to it.' I closed one eye slightly to keep his face in focus. 'Anyway, on that note, I need to get going. I've got to collect my daughter from my mum's at 8.30 tomorrow morning.' I gathered all the pride and conviction I could into those words, though I stopped myself adding, 'So Mum can go to church'. Even though I drew the line at admitting Mum still thought attending a Sunday service was as essential as a vest in winter, I wasn't going to apologise for Louise, whether she fitted his plan for The Shakers or not.

Mal's shoulders slumped. 'Didn't realise you had a kid. Jesus, did you give birth when you were still at school?'

There was something in his tone that made me feel stupid, as though I hadn't understood how getting pregnant happened. 'No. I was twenty. A proper grown-up, quite capable of looking after another little human being.'

Rob darted me a look of alarm as he caught the defiance in my words. But Mal laughed. 'Great, we need all the grown-ups we can get. At least someone will know how to iron the boys' shirts when we're on the road.'

'Actually my husband irons his own. All that navy training – he's much better than me.' I loved that something I was ashamed of – that I was a bit of a rubbish wife – had become something I could use to defend myself.

Mal looked round at Rob and Jim. 'God, this girl's a feisty one. She's going to need a bit of managing. Do you think we're up to the job, lads?'

Jim laughed but Rob took a sip of his drink and said, 'Susie's brilliant to work with. Fitted in since the first time she hopped up on stage with us. Hard-working, fun and a bloody fantastic singer.'

Mal grinned. 'That's a glowing reference if ever I heard one. And ups the good looks of the band by about fifty per cent.' He paused, his face turning serious, his dark eyes intense, staring into mine. 'And in all the years I've been doing this, well over a decade now, I've never heard someone so young with such a powerful range. How you reach those top notes, god only knows.'

I felt myself glow, noticing how dark his eyelashes were. He must have some Spanish or Italian blood in him. Similar colouring to Danny actually. Pride was smoothing over my earlier irritation. I'd always been a plodder, with no real flair for anything. My school reports had always said, 'She does her best', 'She works at a steady pace', 'She must be commended for her continuing efforts'. And now, this man, this *talent scout* who had no reason to tell anything but the truth, thought I was extraordinary.

I glanced down, self-conscious. 'Thank you.'

Mal patted my arm. 'I mean it. You've no idea how good you are. Eh, boys?'

They both nodded but I felt awkward that he'd singled me out. This was their dream. As soon as I could, I'd have to leave them to it. Though even as I told myself that, my brain was scratching away, wondering how I could negotiate a compromise between wife and mother and lead singer. Maybe Danny and Louise would be able to join me on tour. Perhaps we'd be able to see some places together instead of me just hearing about where he'd been. Paris. Rome. Maybe even New York. A girl like me from a tiny terraced house in New York! Louise wouldn't ever have to clip 2p-off coupons out of the newspaper. For a moment I allowed myself to dream. A house in the country. A pony for Louise. A swimming pool. Me, glamorous in long sparkly dresses slit to the thigh. Danny in a sharp suit.

And then I looked round at Rob in the tank top his mother had knitted, Jim with the Afghan coat he thought made him look like John Lennon but just made him smell like a wet Labrador, and got to my feet.

'I'm going to love you and leave you. Think of me when you're all still asleep at midday.' I stuck my hand out. 'Nice to meet you, Mal. Thank you for the drinks.'

Rob put his hand on my arm. 'How are you getting home, Suze? The buses have stopped running now.'

I peered at my watch. 'Half one already. Shanks's pony then, I guess. Never mind. The fresh air will do me good.'

Rob said, 'I'll walk you home. I don't like the thought of you wandering about late at night, especially not when a ship's just come in.' He paused. 'Sorry, no offence to Danny, but you know what the sailors can get like.'

I wanted to hug him for that kindness when I knew he wanted to stay and hang off Mal's every word. 'You're all right, Rob, thanks, it's the wrong direction for you. I'll be fine. I'll stay on the main streets.'

But Mal was on his feet, reaching for his keys. 'I'll drive you all home. Can't risk anything happening to my new superstars.'

Jim shook his head. 'I only live round the corner, mate. Not worth wasting your petrol on me.'

Mal clapped him on the back. 'Go steady then. I'll be in touch soon.'

Rob and I followed Mal out. Rob made a big show about wanting to sit in the front, so he could have a look at the car. 'Always been a bit of a grease monkey. Jim's the mechanic but I'm far more interested in motors than he is.'

Mal lifted the seat forward and helped me into the back. He asked for our addresses, then told Rob he'd drop him off first.

Rob argued back. 'You'd be better off taking the coast road to Susie's and then doubling back round. You can drop me by the petrol station and then you've got a straight run to the A3.'

Mal ignored him and carried on to Rob's. As Rob got out, he leant over to me in the back seat. I was half-asleep, drowsy with whisky and their conversation about the idiosyncrasies of the leather roof and the temperamental choke.

He shook me gently. 'You could sleep on the couch for the night if you want, save Mal the trouble of going all the way back into town. My mother won't mind.'

Mal turned round. 'No problem at all. I'm a night owl. Won't go to bed for hours yet anyway. But I don't want to be a taxi driver, so you come and get in the front with me, Little Susie.'

I wasn't really at my best to start doing the meet and greet with Rob's family. And if I didn't go home now, I'd have to leave at the crack of dawn to fetch Louise. And there was no way I could go straight there in my silver hot pants, otherwise Mum would start lecturing me about what I'd been up to 'while that husband of yours is working so hard to provide'. I just wanted my own bed.

Rob helped me out of the car. He hugged me as I moved to sit in the front seat. 'Be careful,' he whispered into my ear. I pecked him on the cheek. Rob always looked out for me but tonight he was clucking about like my mother. I'd be home in ten minutes.

Rob was still reluctant to move away, but Mal leaned towards us. 'Come on, chop, chop. Night, Rob!'

I slid in beside him. 'See you Wednesday,' I shouted.

Rob stumbled up his path, waving before bending down to fish out a key from under the flowerpot by the door.

'So, which way now?' Mal asked.

I only ever got the bus or walked so I wasn't much good on directions but I told him to head towards the sea. He pushed in a cassette and sang along to 'Wake Up Little Susie'. Initially I thought he was laying a trap for me to see if I'd dare comment on his tunelessness, but he was tapping his hand on the wheel, doing all the moves as though he was an international rock star. It struck me as hilarious that someone who was involved in talent-spotting singers was so tone-deaf himself. I stared out of the window, desperate to think of something to talk about before I got the giggles. I sifted through topics: Where did he have to drive back to? Discarded for sounding as though I'd like to go with him. How many bands had he discovered? Dismissed in case he started naming ones I'd never heard of and laughed at me for being Portsmouth parochial rather than London sophisticated. I was still mulling over a suitable conversational start-up when he pulled into a car park by the beach and switched off the engine.

He sat back against his door and turned to me. 'Do you mind if we just walk down to the sea before I head off to the Big Smoke? Can't remember the last time I felt the sand between my toes. Especially not on a lovely starry night like this.'

He sounded like a little boy excited about a day trip to the seaside. But there was no way Danny would want me strolling about on the seashore at two in the morning with a bloke I'd just met. I tried to make my words come out straight. 'I really ought to be getting back. I don't have the luxury of staying in bed tomorrow morning.' I tried to make a joke, 'It's all right for you, all footloose and fancy-free. I've got responsibilities, you know.'

'Oh live a little. Five minutes and then I'll run you home. Go on. When was the last time you did anything a bit wild?'

I wanted to come up with something to shock him, to show him how rock 'n' roll I was, but I didn't think he'd be impressed with Rob and me smoking the stub end of a joint we found in the dressing room. Next to Mal, I felt so ignorant of the world, as though my horizons had all the depth and breadth of a rabbit hutch.

Mal got out and came round to my side of the car. 'Five minutes. Please.'

I rolled my eyes. 'Five minutes. Then I really have to go.'

We walked down the beach. My wedges were sinking into the shingle, so I pulled them off. I had to concentrate on not staggering while Mal chattered on about the starry sky, how there were so many lights in London that stopped you seeing them and how one day he'd like to settle down somewhere in the country, with a wife and kids. 'In fact, I want what you've got. A family to go home to.'

I glanced at him to see if he was teasing me, hovering between being flattered he thought I wasn't so stupid after all for having a baby at twenty and fear that he was going to laugh in my face if I took him seriously.

I dared to tease him a little. 'I don't see you like that at all. What about the bands, the cocktail bars, all the hundreds of women you were promising Rob and Jim?'

He sat down near the water's edge, craning his head back to look up at me. 'That's just a front. This sort of job doesn't really allow for much home life, you're out all hours, not many women are going to put up with that. Sure, there's lots of glamour, plenty of champagne and all that jazz, but it can be a bit lonely.'

I stood, scrunching my toes in the shingle. 'It's about finding the right sort of woman. I put up with my husband being away for fifteen months at a time. It would be a luxury to have him at home even three nights a week.'

Mal patted the ground beside him. 'Sit down for a second, then we'll go. Believe it or not, I don't often get to have real conversations with bright women.'

I knelt down, the cold of the night making me shiver.

Mal moved over and put his arm round me. 'Sorry. I'm letting you freeze to death while I ramble on. It's just so nice sitting here in the fresh air.'

I sat stock-still, wondering how to move away without looking rude. I didn't want to give him another opportunity to think I was a silly little girl, one who ran for the hills if a man so much as sat next to her. But after a while, when he'd talked about how his mother had worried about him moving to London – 'There's all sorts there' – I started to relax, even allowing myself to enjoy the warmth of an arm around me after three lonely months of re-reading Danny's letters and saying good night to his photo. Especially someone who seemed interested in what I had to say, as though my opinions were really thought-provoking and intelligent. So nice to be appreciated for something other than my ability to point to the right hole for Louise to post a pink triangle through. Particularly a man like Mal, who talked about 'Engelbert', 'Jimi' and 'Aretha' as though he was out drinking with them in the streets of Soho on a regular basis.

'So Little Susie, what do you think about being in a band? I didn't really get a chance to hear your take on it? How are you going to manage with a husband and baby?'

I nearly blurted out the truth. I felt guilty for stringing him along, making him think that I was as committed as Rob and Jim. I kept imagining him enthusiastically presenting our demo tape to his bosses, championing us through god knows how many hoops, just for me to say, 'The Royal Albert Hall sounds lovely, but can we do Southampton so I can put Louise to bed first?' But I remembered Rob's eagerness, Jim's anguish. I battled to put my thoughts into order. With far more confidence than I felt, I tried to shut down that avenue of conversation, hearing the slur in my words as I said, 'Don't know yet. I'll think of something. About time I lived a little, as you were so keen to point out.'

And with that, the whole temperature of the evening changed. Mal put his hand on my chin and turned my face towards him. 'Is that so?' There was a beat, the noise of car brakes squealing in the distance, the rustle of the waves lapping at the shore, and then he kissed me so gently, so sweetly, it took me a moment to pull away from him.

'We should go.'

'Come on, Suze, it's just a kiss. Just two people keeping each other company under the stars. No big deal. Just a little bit of London loving a little bit of Portsmouth.'

And before I could say anything else, he put his lips on mine and kissed me so sensually, I couldn't help but respond. My body was treacherous, lost in the sheer rush of giddiness, of abandonment that accompanies kissing someone who knows just how hard, how soft, how insistent to be. It was as though everything in me was reaching up to him, the culmination of standing on the sidelines for months, existing in a world that was paired off everywhere I looked: the teenagers lying entwined on the beach, couples kissing on the dance floor, even Mr and Mrs Jones next door holding hands as they admired their lupins in the front garden. My brain was fighting to call a halt to it, struggling to instruct my limbs to push him away, not to sprawl back onto the pebbles, not to be anywhere near as intimate with someone who wasn't Danny.

As Mal pushed me backwards, his fingers snagged on the chain around my neck, the gold heart that Danny had given me before he went away last time. 'This is my heart to keep with you until I come back again.'

With a jolt, I turned my head away, trying to sit up. 'I shouldn't be doing this. I need to go home.'

But Mal lay me down on the sand again. 'Don't be a spoilsport,' he said, kissing the tip of my nose and pushing himself up so his eyes were directly above mine. 'I could really fall for someone like you.' His fingers were brushing against my chest, circling my nipples through my top.

I tried to find the words to make him stop. I wanted to run to the sea and dip my head in the cold water to jumpstart my brain. I'd obviously sent out the wrong signals, made him think he was in with a chance. I tried again. 'Mal, you're very lovely but I'm married. And I love my husband.'

And even as he undid my bra and lowered his head, I felt embarrassed at how childish saying I loved Danny sounded, as though I was still at school, drawing hearts with arrows on the back of my exercise books.

Mal paused, lifting his head up to say, 'You really are something special, Little Susie. What is your husband thinking of, leaving you on your own for months at a time? If you were mine, I wouldn't leave you for a night, a lovely woman like you.'

I tried to pull my top down. Singing was one thing, but there was nothing I could say to Danny about this that would get anywhere close to excusing it. His last letter had been full of how hard it was to get through the time apart, how he pretended to be snuggled up to me when he was stuck in a hammock 'where I'm either kept awake by mosquitoes or snoring'. I tried to wriggle out from under Mal but he was too heavy. 'I've got to go. I really have.' My voice sounded high, panicky.

'Sus-ieee. The old man is miles away, probably out in a port having a good time with the girls as we speak. All those Wrens making eyes at him. You don't think he's going without, do you?'

I shook my head. I wanted to rush the words out, decisive and firm, but instead they were stumbling out, staggering out of my mouth as though they weren't quite sure which direction to head in. 'Danny's not like that. He doesn't get involved with that sort of thing.'

Mal ran his fingers through my hair. 'That's what he tells you, anyway. Do you really think he goes for a whole year or more without touching another woman?' He leaned down to kiss me again but I pulled away.

'I don't know. I mean, it doesn't matter what he does. I know what I should be doing and it's not cavorting with you on the beach.'

Mal shrugged. 'Come on, Susie. Who's going to know we're "cavorting"?' He made my words sound as though they'd been uttered by a Sunday School teacher. He put his hand up to my cheek. 'You must have got married young. How many men have you slept with?'

I tried to push against his chest. 'I'm not discussing that with you. It's none of your business.'

'Just the one, then, is it? Time we sorted that out.'

I heard him unbuckle his trousers.

'No. No. I can't do this, Mal.'

'Little Susie. I think you're quite keen to do this. A moment ago, I thought I was going to have trouble keeping up. Didn't realise quite what a little firebrand I had on my hands when I saw you on stage tonight. I shall take my duty as only the second man you might sleep with very seriously. You won't regret it, Susie. Think of it as a little gift to keep you going until hubby returns.' He kissed me, dragging my hot pants off me.

I attempted to tug my clothes back into place but Mal lay on top of me, one hand unzipping his fly. I looked along the beach. Just the occasional flash of headlights lighting the road. 'I'm sorry, I've given you the wrong impression. I don't know what got into me, I must have been missing Danny, or maybe it was the whisky.' The feeble justifications tumbled out into the darkness, dissolving into the sounds of the sea. My voice sounded strange, hesitant and pleading as though I was asking for a favour from someone I didn't know very well.

But there was no point. Mal was going to show me what I'd been missing and all I could do was turn my head to the side, my eyes screwed up, tears squeezing out between my eyelids and running down into my ear.

When he'd finished, he collapsed on top of me. 'He's a lucky man, your husband. You're a sweetheart. And a sexy one at that.'

I adjusted my clothes, let him drape his jacket round my shoulders as we walked back to the car – 'Don't want you catching a chill' – and sat clutching my wedge shoes on my knees as he drove me home, answering his questions about where to turn, whether it was a quiet neighbourhood, how far my mother lived from my house, as though we'd done nothing more than share a port and lemon at the bar. He drew up outside my house, patted my arm and said, 'Thanks, Susie, for a lovely evening. I'll let Rob know when we can do the demo. Sleep well.'

My last words were, 'Thanks for driving me home,' whispered into the darkness so as not to disturb the neighbours.

CHAPTER FIFTEEN

September 1983

Louise walked in while Danny was trying to persuade me we should give her a chance, a year at the College of Modern Music, to see if she liked it. She stood fiddling with the fly screen beads across the back door, no longer hostile, just defeated by weeks of discussion. However, the memory of Mal stopped me getting distracted. I was coming out with every argument I could think of. 'She needs to build a career that's going to give her a stable income for the rest of her life. Women shouldn't expect a handsome prince to rescue them. The world's moved on, they need to take responsibility for their own jobs, their own finances.'

Although both Danny and Louise thought everything I came up with was just a ploy to get Louise into teaching, I did really believe that. It seemed alien to me now that, at Louise's age, none of us had thought beyond who we'd marry. Me and all the girls in my office had seen work as a toe-tapping exercise until we found 'the one'.

On another occasion, Danny would have teased me about becoming a 'bra burner' but we were beyond joking. 'I'm just thinking about Louise. Being a pop star's a nice fantasy but she'll be much better off doing a teacher training course at Portsmouth Poly. She'll still be able to keep up with her singing as a hobby, but that music college has only been going for two years and they've got no track record of people finding work afterwards. With a teaching degree, the world's her oyster.'

Louise rolled her eyes as I pointed out that she'd be able to live at home without bankrupting herself paying for digs and that she'd have a qualification to fall back on even if she had time off to have children.

And quietly, in the middle of that, I sprinkled in the fact that the pop world was full of weirdoes and predatory men. I turned to Danny. 'Would you want Louise being taken out to dinner by a forty-year-old record producer who promised her the earth? You know when I sometimes sang with The Shakers, we used to get all sorts of dodgy blokes hanging around, telling us we'd be the next big thing if I just went for a drive or back to the hotel with them?'

Danny frowned. 'Really? You never told me that.'

I still felt sick whenever I thought about Mal. 'I didn't think that was the sort of news you'd want to read while you were in Singapore.' I paused. 'I never went anyway, obviously.'

The words contained in a lie have a heaviness all of their own, rolling out into the world, followed by a wait to see if they meet with any resistance.

I saw I'd hit home with that. Just the day before, Danny had gone steaming out of the front door when he'd heard a couple of lads shouting 'Sexy bitch' at Louise as she walked up our path.

I pressed on. 'Is that the sort of world we want her in? Sex, drugs and rock 'n' roll? Partying away with god knows who? She's not worldly-wise. She's been at a girls' grammar for all these years, hasn't even had a boyfriend yet and we're going to pack her off to London where any bloke who even sweeps up at a recording studio will be wondering how he can work that to his advantage.'

I recognised the fight go out of Danny. His brow furrowed. He was chewing on the corner of his lip, wavering between letting Louise fly and tethering her to home to keep her safe. The little seed of doubt that I wasn't just being a killjoy, devoid of faith in Louise's ability, had been sown.

Louise was shaking her head. 'I'm not that stupid, Mum. I just want to go there for the vocals and the guitar lessons. I won't even go out in the evening. I'll come home every weekend. I just don't get why you won't let me do the only thing I love. When I'm sitting at some stupid desk job instead of listening to my records on the radio ten years from now, it will be your fault.'

She stormed out of the kitchen, slamming the door so hard, all her music awards and cups rattled on the dresser.

I nearly gave in. The sheer rawness of her desire to make music, to perform, to get somewhere in the business reminded me of Rob. I'd tried so hard not to think about him. His kindness. How he wanted to protect me. How I pushed Louise all the way to his house that Sunday afternoon, her crying piercing my hangover, feeling sick with the exertion of propelling the heavy pram along the pavement. How his mother stood rigid at the front door as she looked into the pram, her whole demeanour brightening with relief as I explained who I was. Rob blundering out of his room, still half-asleep, dragging a mohair sweater over his head. Ignoring his mother's invitation to 'bring your friend and the baby into the front room'. The look on his face as we walked towards the dockyard, the devastation when I told him I'd been up all night thinking about it, that I'd had second thoughts, that I couldn't be part of the band, not even for a few months. My apologies, my platitudes that Mal would probably still want them anyway, without me. His absolute disbelief. Anger, frustration and then finally, sitting on a garden wall, head in his hands, trying to hide his tears from me.

Then that last moment on the street corner, when I swivelled the pram round to head for home. Rob was plucking at the fluff on his jumper. 'What happened last night, Suze? After you left me? Did Mal try it on with you? You were beginning to believe in it, to work out how to make it happen. I know you were. This just doesn't make sense. Danny might struggle to begin with but he'd soon change his tune if you earned enough money to make a better life for you all. You could move to a bigger house, give Louise a good start.'

I shouted, a big bellow rooted in fear and strengthened by shame. 'Nothing happened, Rob. He took me straight home from yours! What do you think I am?'

He paused. 'Sorry, I didn't mean… I just wondered if he'd upset you somehow.'

I glared at him. 'It's nothing to do with Mal. I just sobered up and saw it for what it was. A bloody pipe dream we could waste our lives on! You can go and throw yours away sucking up to men like Mal, hoping they'll chuck you a couple of crumbs from their table, but I've got better things to do.'

He tried to grab my arm, but I shook him off, banging the pram down the kerb and making Louise cry out in alarm as I rushed away.

I sobbed all the way along the coast road, tears bouncing off the hood of the pram. I was convinced I could could feel bits of grit chafing between my buttocks, a slight wetness between my legs, despite bathing and rubbing my skin with a kitchen scourer before I'd gone to Rob's.

The memory of the humiliation, the self-loathing weighing down every step as I trudged home, the knowledge that I'd broken my vows and could never again be the person everyone thought I was, stopped me chasing after Louise now to tell her she'd ground me down, that she could go to London with my blessing.

I couldn't let her dreams become a nightmare.

CHAPTER SIXTEEN

December 1986

I decided to make the Christmas before Louise graduated from Poly an occasion to remember, just in case she got a job teaching somewhere else the following year and decided not to come home.

I wanted to sob every time I thought about her as a toddler, when her eyes followed me about the room, her whole face creasing into a smile the second she saw me, the girl who'd sit for hours squeaking the nose on the pig in her book as long as I was within touching distance. And now, because I'd stopped her doing what she was passionate about, she'd frozen me out, hugging Danny every morning when she left for Poly without even shouting goodbye to me.

Unlike Grace who could stage a sit-in in her bedroom for hours, knowing that the key to coming downstairs was an apology but refusing to surrender, Louise had been a compliant child. I'd thought that, given time, she'd thaw, but just last night I'd asked her, 'Are you coming with us to see the fireworks on New Year's Eve?'

She'd looked vague. 'I'll probably go out with my friends.'

'The girls on your course? Emma and Judy?'

She barely lifted her eyes from her book. 'Does it matter who?'

And yet again I was left wanting a little bit more, yearning to clarify the bigger picture, feeling as though I was glimpsing her world through a keyhole.

Occasionally, she'd mention there were opportunities for placements in Manchester, Edinburgh and, memorably, the Isle of Skye. I had no idea whether she said it to test my reaction. Whether she hoped I'd wish her well and send her on her way, or if she wanted proof I'd miss her. I tried to ask questions that didn't sound judgemental. 'Where would you like to work?'

She'd purse her lips and say something like, 'I'll see what comes up when I've finished college.'

This evening I'd snapped. 'You'll stand more chance of making the most of life if you actually decide what you want and go for it. At your age, I already had a baby. I didn't have that luxury of drifting about seeing what came my way. Dad and I got our heads down and did everything we could to make sure we could give you the best possible start.' Before she'd stomped off into the lounge, Louise looked at me with something akin to pity, as though it was incredible I had the audacity to try to give her any advice when my own life experience was so limited. It was the same look Mal had given me that night when I told him I'd been a proper grown-up with a baby at twenty. Thank god he'd never had the satisfaction of seeing what a frightened child I'd become with another baby at twenty-two.

Grace appeared in the kitchen. She hated anyone falling out, unless it was her picking the fight. She plugged in her cassette player. 'Mum, dance with me.' I tried to refuse. 'I've got all the washing up to do' but she wouldn't take no for an answer, grabbing my hand and pulling me about to 'Papa Don't Preach' until we were laughing and twirling round the kitchen until gone ten o'clock. In the end, Danny had come in.

'You should be in bed, young lady. School tomorrow.'

Grace hugged him. 'Just one more song. Pleee-ase.'

Danny frowned at me. 'She'll be worn out in the morning. Louise never stayed up this late at her age.'

'Two minutes, and then I'll send her up,' I said, waving him away as we sang Kool and the Gang's 'Get Down on It' at the top of our voices. I almost managed to ignore the sulkiness I could feel radiating from Louise on the other side of the wall.

So that Christmas, I made a concerted effort to plant a happy memory of us as a family in Louise's mind in the hope that she might fly away but would eventually migrate back when she realised no one had the perfect home life.

I sent Danny off with the girls to choose the real tree Louise had always hankered after. I resigned myself to a cleaning nightmare in January and allowed Grace and Louise to spray stencils of snowmen and reindeer on the windows. Louise sprayed sparingly, her outlines crisp and clean, while Grace's looked as though she'd used a fire extinguisher. We made a Christmas pudding, stirring in a sixpence from the collection Mum had gathered since they'd been discontinued in 1980, convinced that they'd become valuable. Grace was fascinated. 'So if I find it, I get to make a wish?'

I nodded.

'I'm going to wish to be a pop star on *Top of the Pops*.'

I didn't dare look at Louise as I said, 'You can't wish that now because you've told us. It has to be a secret. You'll have to think of something else.'

But Grace wouldn't be derailed. 'You'll have forgotten that I told you by then.'

With the extra cash I was earning from working a few days a week, I was determined to splash out on things Louise wanted rather than my usual repertoire of things she needed like slippers, socks and shampoo. I bought her some hair crimpers, which I deliberated over for ages, balancing out her joy at opening them with my sadness at seeing her gorgeous hair standing out like she'd been the victim of dodgy electrics. But the big gun in my Christmas present armoury was a CD Walkman – or 'Oh… you mean a *Discman*', according to the boy in the shop, who screwed

up his face as though I'd spoken to him in Japanese. I was sure
any CDs I chose would never make it out of their cases, so I
asked him to suggest some, though whether a boy with a mane
of blonde highlights and a feather hanging out of his ear would
have tastes any closer to Louise's, I had no idea. But at least I'd
tried and I wrapped them up weeks before Christmas, enjoying
the 'You'll never guess what I've bought you' teasing and watching
Louise unfurl. I caught her more than once shaking the boxes
under the tree, more like Grace who circled piles of presents like
a cat round a bowl at feeding time.

I even agreed to a lunchtime drinks party on the Sunday before
Christmas. Normally I refused point blank to invite any friends
or neighbours round over the festive season in case I had to hear
about how 'our Christopher/Stuart/Andrew moved heaven and
earth so we could all be together for Christmas Day', followed by
a general nodding and murmuring that 'Christmas was a time for
family'. Even with my family around me, I always felt as though
one crucial piece was missing.

Danny raised his eyebrows. 'You're all mistletoe and mince pies
this year. Where's my little Susie Scrooge disappeared to?' He'd
hugged me tight and I felt the certainty grow that I'd brought
him back from the brink of giving up on me.

Grace threw herself wholeheartedly into party mode, handing
round cheesy footballs and Twiglets, saying, 'I don't believe in
Father Christmas any more, *obviously*.' Then making everyone
laugh by adding, 'But I'm going to leave out some sherry, and a
carrot for Rudolph, just in case.'

I'd invited Jeanie, one of the rare times since Danny's birthday
party three years ago that she'd come to the house. Since then, I'd
confined our meetings to the coffee shop in the city centre, the
park or the cinema. Jeanie had apologised again and again for
getting drunk and being a 'great big rent-a-gob', turning up at my
door a few weeks after the party with a huge bunch of flowers I

knew she couldn't afford. But I couldn't let her mistake go. Every time she was in the same room as Danny, I was monitoring her, watching what she drank, earwigging on what she was saying, ready to leap in. She'd never put a foot wrong again, often dropping into conversation how lucky we'd been to meet at the Silver Jubilee and then bump into each other in the park. Although I'd just about forgiven her, I refused to discuss you with her any more. You'd turned eighteen in June this year and become an adult without me. I'd broken my rule about not thinking about you by writing a letter on your birthday. It was a special one, after all. But apart from exceptional red-letter days, I'd almost managed to forget about you. Not forget. But to release you. And me. To the lives we were meant to have.

Today, Jeanie was on her best behaviour, even taking her turn with Mr Arnold from across the road who had a 'deaf aid' but never switched it on to save the battery, so any conversation had to be carried out at top volume and usually went along the lines of 'Are you still going to the allotment?' followed by a completely random answer such as, 'Yes, I think I saw something about that in the newspaper. I don't know what gets into these young ones.' A pause would follow while the questioner tried to guess what he'd been referring to and switch to the right topic. Gracie would squeal with laughter when he gave an odd response and Louise would tell her off for being rude. Mr Arnold didn't seem to mind and she still ended up with his entire stash of Devon toffees.

Louise hovered on the edges of the party, not barging up to noisy groups but gravitating to the people who were standing looking at the photos on the mantelpiece or loitering shyly by the Christmas tree. I'd hoped going to college would give her some spirit; that confidence Grace had always had. I wasn't sure it ever occurred to her younger sister that she *wasn't* the most fascinating person in the room. I tried not to notice Louise only ever looked totally at ease when she was singing, as though a couple of bars of music loosened something in her, transported her to a place where she wasn't even judging herself because she knew how good she was.

As I watched Eddie from number twenty-one stop her to ask for another drink, talking directly to her chest without bothering to disguise the direction of his gaze, I reminded myself why I hadn't let her go.

Jeanie appeared at my side. She nodded towards Grace, who was showing off her latest 'magic' tricks, which seemed to consist of her mainly fluffing the shuffling of a pack of cards, dropping them all over the floor, then laughing her head off and saying, 'That's not it! Wait!'

'That girl's not backwards at coming forwards. Good on her.'

I nodded, still thinking about Louise.

Jeanie turned to look at me. 'You all right? Christmas can be a funny time of year, can't it? Makes you take stock,' she said. I could see her sieving her words, doing that thing we often did, making our conversation sound normal for the casual listener, while weaving in an extra meaning for us.

'Nothing to do with the time of year,' I said, wanting to believe it. 'I was just wondering whether I'd done the right thing not letting Lou go to the music school.'

Jeanie shrugged. 'No use crying over spilt milk now. She tells me she'll be starting work in September. A teacher in the family! Fancy that. She's done ever so well. And at least she's not as likely to end up with some bloke snorting stuff up his nose. Has she got a boyfriend?'

I shook my head. 'She doesn't seem very interested in men.'

'Good girl. Got her head screwed on right. She's going to go far. You've done a great job.' Jeanie's admiration for Louise warmed me, especially as she launched into her latest dramas with Rick, and his brushes with the law, shoplifting and nicking bikes. I wished I'd been a better friend to her.

Despite feeling that I managed to alienate everyone I cared about in my life, when Danny and I congratulated ourselves on a successful party later that evening, I was struck by an unfamiliar sensation: I was actually looking forward to Christmas.

CHAPTER SEVENTEEN
December 1986

On the Tuesday before Christmas, Grace had gone to the park with her friends. I zipped her into her coat. She darted off down the road, singing my instructions back to me, 'No, Mum, I won't go off with any strangers, won't run in front of a swing, won't jump off the roundabout till it stops...' I envied the other mothers in the street who chucked their kids out of the house with a bottle of squash and a few sandwiches and moaned if they came back before teatime even when it was freezing cold like today. Louise was carol-singing in town with a group of college friends to raise money for Amnesty International and Danny was at work. I was pottering about, hanging up cards on gold ribbon suspended from the ceiling, re-reading the round robins from some of the navy wives. I had to hand it to them. They'd stuck with that odd life of enforced separation interspersed with chunks of precious time together pouring away, relentlessly, through the egg timer. I knew Danny missed those days but whenever I probed, he just said, 'Gracie might not have happened if I'd have stayed in.'

I heard the postman coming up the path with the second post and nipped out to give him a tip. He handed me another pile of cards with a 'You're a popular family, aren't you?' Given that we barely socialised, I thought it said more about people's unwillingness to edit their address books. I flicked through them to see if there were any stamps Grace hadn't yet had for her collection. I smiled as I saw one she didn't have – three men in a boat. I stared at the writing, trying to work out who it was from, a habit that drove Danny mad: 'Just open it! All will be revealed without you wearing out your brain.'

I slit it open.

It wasn't a Christmas card.

22 December 1986

Dear Suzanne

    I hope you won't mind me writing to you. I realise you might not want to hear from me, though I really hope you will. If you haven't guessed already, my name is Adam, the son you gave up for adoption in 1968. I was eighteen on 13 June this year (in case you don't remember my birthday) and my parents gave me a memory box, which contained my adoption file for me to do what I wanted with it. They told me they'd have to arrange counselling with a social worker if I wanted to look for you. I didn't fancy that, so I tried to find you on my own. My real name, Edward Duarte, was on the court adoption order, and you'd signed a vaccination form, so I knew your name was Suzanne.

    I learnt to swim very quickly and my Mum told me I was a special 'sea baby' because you were from the south coast somewhere. It was surprising how easy it was to find you, but there aren't many Duartes in England – I found your number and address in the phone directories at the library. I rang a few days ago but a young girl answered – your daughter? My sister?!! – and said you were at work. I lost my nerve then and pretended I was calling from the bank. I haven't dared ring back since, so I thought I'd write instead.

    So here I am. Adam Edward Bramley. You can call me Edward if you like. I'm living in Bristol at the moment where I've just started at university. But I grew up in Bath with my parents and my little sister, Kate, who's also adopted.

My mum, Shona, couldn't have children so she always says she was so lucky to have had the chance to bring us up. My dad, Clive, jokes a lot about all the lovely holidays they could have gone on if they hadn't adopted us, but I don't think he means it. People who don't know I'm adopted say I'm like Dad because we both love sport – we watch everything – darts, rugby, golf, football. We're really competitive too, even if we're playing cards. Dad came to every football match I was in at school. I was always the goalie because I'm tall. It was a bit embarrassing if Mum came with him because she went crazy if I saved a goal, even if it was an easy one. They still watch all of my sister's netball matches and she hasn't scored a goal for years.

I haven't told them that I'm looking for you. Mum would be really sad. I don't know why you gave me away – Mum just said you wanted to give me the chance of a better life than the one you could offer, but I don't know if she told me that to make me feel better. You might not want to know me so I don't want to upset her for nothing.

I've always felt a bit different because I was adopted – I've known since I was little – but since I turned eighteen I keep thinking about it much more, wondering why you gave me away. Did my dad know about me? Was it a hard decision? Did you regret it ever? Sorry if these questions make you feel bad but I feel I should know the answers now I'm an adult. I wonder if I look like you or my other dad – I'm skinny with dark hair and big brown eyes. My friends call me 'Toothpick'. I'm good at art and I'm quite musical. My dad bought me an electric keyboard for my eighteenth birthday and I'm driving everyone mad practising. I'm really good at 'Hotel California' by the Eagles.

If you are happy to be in touch, could you write to me at the address above, but mark the envelope 'private and confidential'? I will tell my parents eventually.

Yours sincerely,
Adam (Edward)

My chest was so full of conflicting emotions, it was as though I didn't have enough space within me to contain them. I sank to the floor, right where I was. I didn't know which feeling to isolate first. Fear was flooding through me. You'd called and spoken to Grace. You'd made contact with someone in my family who didn't know anything about you. A phone call so irrelevant to her that she'd forgotten to mention it. But behind the fear was joy that you didn't hate me. Relief. Yes, relief was solidly in the mix; you'd had a good life. Your parents sounded nice. I knew I'd pick and squeeze at the 'I don't want to upset her for nothing' later on. How much worse if you didn't care about your parents, were desperate to find me because you'd hated them every day of your life. How small of me to feel a sliver of jealousy, even a pinprick. But my eyes were drawn to the 'Yours sincerely'. The same thing a librarian might write in a letter notifying me of overdue books.

Of course, for you, I was that cold person, who'd handed a six-week-old over to strangers. Not a woman who'd wrapped you in a blanket and watched numbly as a nun whisked you out of the room. It still astounded me that I'd lived through that moment without screaming so loudly that my throat blistered, without collapsing from the searing pain of separation that left me unable to breathe. 'Was it a hard decision?' was a fair question to ask, though the notion you might think it had been anything else winded me.

I combed the letter for information, throwing myself on the scraps of knowledge you'd handed me like a starling on a suet ball. Skinny, dark and musical like me, tall, sporty and competitive like Mal. We'd shared out the gene pool. And you'd gone to university. I told you you'd be clever. I imagined the photos of you in your parents' front room. You playing the guitar. You clutching your A level certificates. You standing alongside your dad, towering over your mum and sister. You belonging so resoundingly to someone else's family. Fitting in. Thriving. Thank goodness. Your mum sounded so proud of you. I had an image of a blonde-haired woman, well-turned out, with leather gloves and fancy scarves, shocking the spectators with ferocious cheering for her son. My son.

You gave the impression of being close to her. Did you sit chatting over dinner, in no hurry to rush away? Or were you like Louise? 'Is it all right if I get down? I need to carry on with my essay.' 'I'd better get on, I've got my revision notes to do.' 'Can I be excused? I haven't finished my preparation for tomorrow's class.'

You sounded open, aware of your family's emotions. How well they'd done to make you like that. I bet you weren't distilling information into bland morsels like Louise, sanitising her world to prevent me having an opinion.

I must have sat on the floor for an hour or more, studying your writing, your uneven letters as though you had stopped on every word, interrupting the flow. I pictured you sweeping your dark fringe away in concentration.

What could I say in return? That ever since I kissed your head, feeling your feathery hair tickle my chin one last time, my heart had struggled on like a faulty boiler, firing up properly on the odd occasion but generally lukewarm with the odd waft of noxious fumes? That I'd pushed away people until they cut off from me. Or smothered them with love, until they'd wriggled away, mistaking my protection for control.

But pushing through all of these feelings, electric and exciting, was the thought that I had the chance to explain, possibly even face-to-face, that I loved you from the minute you arrived with your shock of dark hair, shouting your energy to the world. And losing you meant every day since had been threaded with sadness, a sepia tint washing over the brightness of blowing out birthday candles, opening Christmas presents, any ordinary family day missing a figure at the edges.

As I contemplated turning the meeting I'd fantasised about so often into reality, I glanced around my front room. Louise's teaching notes stacked neatly on top of the piano. Grace's attempt at knitting a tie for Danny unravelling and abandoned on the armchair. Danny's slippers tossed aside in front of the fire. I put my head in my hands, my palm resting against my forehead, taut with tension, my thoughts whirling around a labyrinth of possibilities and impossibilities.

Even though I knew no one was in the house, I still checked every room before calling Jeanie and arranging to meet her in the park.

CHAPTER EIGHTEEN

December 1986

The prospect of telling Jeanie that you'd got in touch immediately quietened the jittery sense that I could no longer keep the truth from Danny. I felt as though it might burst out, unfiltered and unchecked, as I flew out of the door, ready to leap onto a train to Bath. A calm descended on me as I saw Jeanie hurrying towards me, that nervous energy giving her the gait of a teacher late for an unruly class.

We sat ourselves down on a bench away from the main thoroughfare. She turned to face me. 'So, my lovely, where's the fire? Your Danny been up to no good?'

I shook my head. I knew she didn't mean anything by it – her view of men was so warped it was a question of when, not if, they'd let you down.

'No. Nothing to do with Danny. Not really anyway.'

Her pale eyebrows shot up. 'Come on, stop being all bloody secret agent. Spill the beans. I had to abandon the shepherd's pie I was making to rush here. If I don't get back soon, it will be Pot Noodle for dinner.'

Still I hesitated, knowing that my news would cause her pain.

She frowned at me, then gasped. 'Oh my god. Is it him? You've heard from Edward?'

I nodded. Jeanie winced as though she had to still her own hurt before she could open herself up to my story. I knew I couldn't tell her your words without crying. I handed her your letter, imagining your fingers folding it into the envelope as I did so. Her face as she read it tightened and slackened, her emotions parading across her freckled skin as clearly as if she'd spoken them out loud. When her features finally relaxed, she didn't look up. Her voice, when it came, was small, nothing like the full-bodied boom I associated with her. 'You're so lucky. You know now. He's had a good life.'

I was lucky; it was what we'd always said to each other: 'I just need to know he's been happy.'

Her gaze strayed back to the letter.

'A sister, too. That's good he didn't end up on his own. Someone else who's adopted, who'll understand what that means.' She cleared her throat. 'Sounds like he looks like you, don't it?' Her voice caught, snagged on her own longing for the news she'd been waiting eighteen years to hear. She gathered herself; I saw her dig deep to be pleased for me. Her generous heart didn't let her down. 'What are you going to write back?' She shifted on the bench, grabbing my knee with excitement. 'You could have met your son by the end of January! I'll come with you if you like. I mean, not to meet him. But I can hold your hand on the bus. Might feel a bit bloody terrifying. What do you think the first thing is that you'll say?'

I looked at the ground. 'I'm not sure I'm going to meet him.'

'What? Why not? Dan doesn't have to know. Don't be silly. You must want to see him.' She looked outraged, as though my mind had popped out of my head and was running round in circles on the pavement.

'Of course I *want* to see him. But I don't want to lie to Danny. Well, not more than I have done already.'

'But that's precisely it. You've told him this great big lie for years and years. How can a silly little fib about where you're going for a day be worse than that?'

'But what if it doesn't stop there? What if I'm not satisfied with just meeting him once? What if he wants to see me again? How am I going to tell him I've loved and missed him all these years, then say he's not good enough to introduce to my "real" family?'

Jeanie leapt to her feet and started pacing up and down in front of me. 'I don't get it. We've talked about finding our boys for years and now you've got the chance to meet him, you're coming up with a million bloody reasons why you can't.'

I was starting to shiver in the December wind. 'Say I do go and see him. That we get on well. That he still feels like my son rather than just any old guy and he wants me in his life as, I don't know, some sort of second mother, or aunt figure, or something. At some point, I'm going to have to tell Danny and the kids and then where will that leave us all? Danny's not just going to nod, clap his hands and say, "Let's get him round for fish and chips." And you can imagine how Louise would react. Gracie might be okay with it, but she's younger.'

Jeanie shoved her hands in her pockets. 'You're trying to run before you can walk. He might not even like you. You might hate him. Maybe you'll talk about whatever you need to talk about and then decide that's enough, curiosity satisfied, have a nice life. I don't understand why you wouldn't just have one meeting and worry about the rest later.'

'But what about his mother? It seems so awful to repay her by encouraging him to go behind her back.'

'You're his mother! She wouldn't even have a son if you hadn't given birth to him.'

She waved the letter at me, jabbing her finger into the paper. 'Even he says his mum thinks she was lucky.'

I held out my hand for the letter, as protective as if she was poking Edward in the chest. 'I know, but in the end she looked after him, she did what I couldn't. I have to be grateful to her.'

'Grateful! Grateful? We were just a money-making machine for those nuns. I bet there were some girls in there who could have kept their babies, me included, if they'd explained all our options to us. But there was never any question of that, not when there were all those perfect married couples queuing up to make a nice donation in return for our kids. Just a bloody "sign here, it's for the best."'

Jeanie was rubbing her hands, which were red from the cold. Her voice was forceful, almost shrill. 'You've got a chance to set things right with him, to let him know how much you've thought about him all these years. How much you love him. I'd *kill* for that opportunity.'

My stomach knotted with recognition that the conversation had taken an entirely different turn from the soft landing filled with compassion that I'd been expecting. Jeanie had always been very vocal in her admiration that I'd managed to keep Edward a secret from Danny for so long – 'Don't know how you do it, Suze. My head would have blown off. Though sometimes I wish I hadn't ever told Simon. He's so nasty about him, always going on about my "bastard Yankee son". Which is a joke because I'm pretty sure his dad was either Scottish or from Yorkshire.'

But today, she wasn't joking. 'Promise me you won't decide yet. Give it some thought. You can't rush this one. I'll help you write a letter. I'm good with words, though you'd better do the spelling. Get through Christmas and then we'll come up with a plan in the New Year.'

I sat on the bus home re-reading your letter, tracing your writing with my finger. All the reasons I'd given Jeanie to stay well away were running around my head.

But nowhere near as strong as the reasons to see you growing and multiplying in my heart.

CHAPTER NINETEEN

December 1986

I'd envisaged a joyful Christmas, the first one when I'd be completely immersed in the family I had, rather than torturing myself with the image of you delving into a stocking, another year gone by without me. Instead, this year was the worst one of all. Every time I sat down to watch TV with the family, a heaviness weighed on me as I see-sawed between what I wanted to do and what I needed to do. I burnt the gravy and let the carrots boil dry. I snapped at Grace. 'I'm not the only person in the world who can read the instructions to a board game. Ask Dad.' I spoiled Louise's delight when she opened her new Discman with a sour-faced, 'You'd better not go losing it on the bus.'

I forced myself to play Monopoly, my poor decisions bankrupting me within a short space of time, with Grace trying to save me, to keep me in the game, then getting cross when I made an excuse about having to get dinner ready. 'We don't care about dinner, we want you to join in.'

Sleep became my shelter. Three minutes into the Queen's speech my eyes clanged shut and my thoughts took refuge in oblivion. Danny kept asking me if I was ill as, yet again, I drifted off in the armchair, unable to fight against the lure of blankness. When I was awake, I couldn't stop myself peering out of the front window in case you were waiting out there. Grace noticed and I pretended I was looking at the sky, hoping for a white Christmas.

She slipped her hand in mine and said, 'I hope it snows because it might make you happy.'

With a supreme effort I managed to laugh and say, 'Who could possibly be unhappy with you around?'

But I just couldn't keep it up. Every demand from Grace to cast off on her new knitting needles, to help Louise rescue the cassette that had snagged in her old machine and was now covering the front room in brown spaghetti, even listening to Mum's rundown of the ailments of her fellow churchgoers – 'Poor Marge, you should see the state of her feet, can barely walk for her bunions' – felt like a drain on my inadequate resources. The thin veneer papering over the crevices of my life had become like a book dropped into the bath, peeling away from the central support in clumps.

I studied my daughters' faces, wishing I had a photo of you to hold up against them, to rejoice in the similarities, to deny the differences. Would you furrow your brow like Louise? Wave your hands about with excitement like Grace? Have your own unique set of mannerisms?

I nearly convinced myself I'd done my best to be a good mother to them both, that I deserved a moment of transgression, a day, just six or seven hours out of my whole life, when it was only fair, only right, that you had my attention. I wanted to rush to the address on the letter, bang on your door, throw my arms around you and fill in the eighteen years I'd missed. The answers to everything I'd wondered about: when you walked and talked, the names of your friends, your favourite food. I longed to study your hands, your nails, your ears, see where bits of me had come out in you.

But then I'd feel a wave of sickness, the fear of more deceit, and the flicker of hope would fade. I'd watch Danny patiently helping Grace set up her Dymo sticker machine, discussing job possibilities with Louise and I'd recognise the folly of putting the family I had in jeopardy for a child who already had another mother. However much I wanted you to forgive me, someone else had got up to you in the night, shivered on the edge of a football pitch, explained why your first mum couldn't keep you. It was too late for me to be a mother to you but I still had two daughters I couldn't let down.

I clapped my hands. 'Come on, let's have a game of consequences, the more outrageous, the better.'

Just for a moment, I got a glimpse of the family life I hoped for.

Mum laughing and saying, 'I don't know what to put. I've got no imagination.'

Grace's head bent over the paper, writing, 'What she said to him: "Bugger!"' Then scribbling it out and changing it to 'Bother!' before she got told off.

Danny, the smooth-talker that he was, wrote, 'What he said to her: "He wished he'd found a wife as wonderful as Susie."'

Even though it was a joke, Louise looked disgusted. I tried not to be hurt by her reading out: 'And the consequence was… they got divorced.'

Grace slipped her hand into mine. 'You and Daddy won't ever get divorced, will you?'

The trust in her face decided me. There was no halfway house to be had. I didn't want to taint you with my shame. I had no right to whirlwind in and destroy your settled life – or ours – just because you were welcoming me in, full of youthful optimism we could make up for lost time.

I tried to imagine us all sitting round at dinner, Grace doing her usual, 'You know I hate cauliflower!' Louise discussing a difficult student with Danny – 'He's bright, but just can't see the point of school.' The doorbell ringing, me answering and you standing there. I couldn't pretend that a tiny part of me didn't hope that would happen, that the decision would be taken out of my hands. But I couldn't ever explain away a grown-up son, younger than Louise but older than Grace, appearing now. And there were no more excuses. I wasn't a naïve twenty-two-year-old any more. I was forty-one. If ever there was a moment to make a good strong decision and stick to it, it was now.

By the time the thirtieth of December came round, I'd stopped allowing myself to think there was an alternative. I told everyone I had a headache and was going for a nap, then fetched my notelets and my ink pen. I never used real ink any more but I wanted to show you that I hadn't just dashed off my letter in a hurry, just another chore to get through before I could sit down with my *Family Circle* magazine. It was optimistic to think blue ink would make a difference to the words.

As I checked the cartridge, I wondered about discussing it with Jeanie again. But I could hear her words already. 'No, Suze, no! I won't let you do that. You'll regret it for ever.'

I had to deal with this one myself, before I made another mistake that would send my life careering off in the wrong direction like a car accelerating too fast into a corner.

I considered writing a heartfelt letter, telling you how devastating I found it that you even considered for one minute I could possibly not know when your birthday was; I had a chest full of presents to prove that Thursday 13 June was etched on my heart. But I couldn't put the responsibility on you of how my life turned out. I'd caused you enough harm. I'd forfeited my right to share any part of that eighteen years ago, on 25 July, when I'd disentangled your tiny hand from my little finger and sent you on your way, my throat so tight that afterwards I worried you wouldn't have heard my last 'I love you, be happy little one'.

I steeled myself. I had to be clear, cold. I couldn't write anything that could be construed as a maybe, a 'not now but later', a 'sometime in the future'. Definitely not a 'You'd be very welcome if you showed up unexpectedly.'

Dear Adam,

It was a very difficult decision to give you up and I am delighted to hear you've had a good life. Please know that I've thought about you often and wondered how you are, but I'm afraid to say I don't think it is fair on your mother for us to be in touch now and I would hate her to be upset when she's obviously looked after you so well. I know this might be disappointing to you but I think we should let the past stay in the past. Please don't contact me again. It's for the best.

Suzanne

Then I told everyone I was just popping out for a breath of fresh air to clear my head. I walked to the postbox, kissed the back of the envelope and pushed it into the slot before I could change my mind.

I had no idea how I would get through New Year.

CHAPTER TWENTY

New Year's Eve 1986

On New Year's Eve, when we all walked down to the seafront to watch the fireworks, I stood with a scarf wrapped across my face, quiet tears seeping into the wool as Grace entertained everyone around us with her dramatic reaction to the noisy rockets.

On the stroke of midnight, Danny pulled me into his arms. 'Here's to a very Happy New Year for all of us.' I kissed him hard on the mouth, the sort of kiss that I hoped would transport me, just for a minute, to a place where I couldn't think. He laughed and whispered, 'How soon can we get home?' He didn't notice that I was miming to 'Auld Lang Syne', my throat constricted with the effort of keeping the secret of you on the right side of the dam – now cracked and crumbling – that I'd tucked you behind.

I got up before everyone else on New Year's Day. If the post was working properly, you'd have received my letter the day before. I kept picturing you snatching the envelope off the mat, studying the postmark, my handwriting, a smile spreading across your face as you imagined what 1987 might hold for you. A smile that faded as you read my note. The pain that image caused me made me want to tear my heart out of my chest, just to relieve the unrelenting agony. I grabbed my handbag, slipped out of the house and ran to the phone box on the corner.

I had to talk to the one person who might understand. Jeanie wheezed down the phone as though she'd just stubbed out her last Benson and Hedges moments before. 'Jesus. You're up with the lark. I didn't get to bed till two.' But bless her, she rallied quickly when I pleaded with her to see me. 'Give us three-quarters of an hour and I'll meet you down at the Esplanade, by the kiosk.'

Before she put the phone down, I heard Simon shouting, 'You come here, you little sod!' followed by a scream. The sound of a man who thought the loudest voice equalled the person in the right. He didn't deserve Jeanie. And I didn't deserve Danny.

I stumbled through the throng of early morning strollers along the seafront, wishing I had nothing more taxing to do than make a New Year's resolution that I'd have forgotten by the fifth of January.

Jeanie was already at the kiosk, sipping a black coffee. She took one look at me and said, 'Christ. What time did you get to bed? You look like you've been sleeping under a hedge. Here, have this coffee. I'll get another one.'

I shook my head. 'I'm all right. You drink it.'

Her eyes lit up. 'Don't tell me you've been having sleepless nights planning "the visit"?'

'I'm not going to see him.'

'What? Don't be silly.' She looked almost amused as though what I was saying was so far-fetched as to be laughable.

'I just can't, Jeanie. It's too complicated. I gave him away to keep the daughter and husband I already had.'

She blew on her coffee, her eyes flicking out over the horizon. 'They don't need to know about him. I'll cover for you. Between us we can make up some story so you can escape, say you're helping me visit my aunt in hospital or some old rubbish. It's just one day, Susie. One day in eighteen bloody years.'

Jeanie looked excited at the prospect.

I couldn't lie to the one real friend I had.

'It's too late.'

'Course it's not too late. Some people find their real parents when they're in their fifties. Edward's only eighteen.'

'No, I mean, I've already written back.'

'Saying what?'

'That I can't ever have any contact with him.'

The silence while Jeanie paused, her coffee suspended in mid-air, was like waiting for the flash of lightning after a thunder crack.

'Please tell me you haven't posted it.' Her mouth was open in disbelief. 'You absolute idiot. Christ. Think how many mothers there with us would give anything to have had that letter. Do you remember Sandra, running out of the home, nearly getting hit by a bus after she gave her baby away? Ginny, screaming and being pinned down by three nuns? That little Irish girl who tried to hide in the laundry with her baby? And you've just acted like it's nothing. When it's *everything*. How could you reject him like that? He's not some pen pal popping up from the past. He's your *son*.'

I didn't know I could feel any worse, but her fury drilled into the dull lethargy that had engulfed me over Christmas, igniting a rage that could have started a forest fire. I couldn't believe that she was taking such a 'first against the wall' approach and blowing me to smithereens.

'Do you think I haven't thought of that? Do you think I don't wonder how distraught he'll feel when he gets my letter? What hard-hearted creature could deliver a "thanks but no thanks" after all this time? Well, I bloody wish your son had written to you instead, put a bomb under your family, so you could see what it felt like. How was I going to sell that one to Danny? "Ah, yes, I did just forget to mention when you got back from Singapore, that October in 1968, that I'd had a son and given him away…" What did you expect me to do?'

Jeanie's face had taken on a hard expression, the sort of face I imagined her presenting to one of the supermarket customers daring to complain she'd packed the baked beans on top of the grapes and squashed them.

'I expected you to do the decent thing and let your poor boy know where he came from.'

I felt as though I'd swilled down a toxic combination of lethal chemicals.

'There is no "decent thing". Let's say I go and meet him once, lie to Danny, have Edward tell his parents and get them all upset in case I somehow try to take over their role and then say, "Sorry, I can't see you any more because I've got two daughters I love more who don't know anything about you".'

Jeanie was shaking her head, as though I was deliberately causing problems where none existed.

I jumped up. 'Here, I'll pretend I never heard from him and then perhaps you'll feel a bit better that your son has never bothered to find you.'

And with that, I pulled Edward's letter from my bag, tore it into little pieces and scattered it into the January wind as I stormed away.

CHAPTER TWENTY-ONE

1987

Initially I thought Jeanie might pop round when Danny was at work. Every time the doorbell went, I looked along the hallway expecting to see her crazy curls silhouetted against the glass. My heart would leap, 'sorry' forming on my lips, knowing that giving our sons away had exposed nerves that aggravated and obliterated all rational behaviour. I lay in bed at night trying every which way to make the words, 'Your son has never bothered to find you' sound less cruel, to make them less important in my mind. I knew I'd overstepped a line. We'd always told each other our sons must love us a little bit, just because we'd given birth to them. We'd remained stuck in 1968 when it came to dealing with our loss. Jeanie's reactions were those of an eighteen-year-old, and mine a proper playground retaliation.

But she didn't come.

Sometimes I'd set out to walk over to her side of town in the hope I might bump into her in the park. My courage always deserted me before I got there. I was paralysed by how sorry I was, endlessly sifting through different ways to craft the perfect apology, the one that could undo my vicious words. But nothing seemed adequate. I hadn't got the reaction I wanted from her, the 'Bless you, Susie, I don't know what else you could have done', so I'd taken the delicate feelings she'd trusted me with and inflicted maximum damage. And as time went on, I convinced myself she didn't want to see me, that she would never forgive me for my unkindness and for refusing to see Edward when she dreamed of finding her son.

And now there was a Jeanie-shaped hole in my life too.

Every day there were several instances when I thought, 'That would make Jeanie laugh'. Without her company, I became a paler version of myself, quieter, more reserved again. I missed how she threw her head back in laughter, never caring if people looked round in the coffee shop to see what the joke was, never feeling the need to moderate her admiration for Tom Cruise at the cinema, treating the surrounding audience to a loud, 'Cor, wouldn't say no if he crept into my bed. Love a chance to wipe the sweat off his brow.'

I loved her irreverence about everything, her belligerent ability to shrug off the judgements of others, unafraid to take people on if they were talking down to her. How she managed to keep her job at the Co-op after she told one customer 'to pop his plums up his posh little arse', I didn't know. Without her, I felt as though the funfair had passed through and packed up, leaving tattered reminders of bustle and bright lights.

But all her strong opinions, her ideas about how the world should unfold came at a price. I'd slowly re-engaged in family life after New Year by blanking you from my mind, but the equilibrium I'd carved out for myself was so fragile, I couldn't allow Jeanie to take me to task about you ever again. The mere mention of the names Adam or Edward on the radio sent a stab of pain through me. Any reference to the city of Bath made me want to tuck up into a tight ball and shut out the world. And by February when Danny asked me why I hadn't seen Jeanie lately, I told him something approaching the truth. 'She's so angry all the time. Last time I saw her she went on about how I deal with the children.'

'Because you won't let Louise study music?'

I grunted in a way that Danny took to be a yes.

Danny was frowning as though he couldn't imagine Jeanie behaving like that. 'Maybe she's envious because our kids aren't as naughty as hers. But that's Simon's fault. That Rick needs a firm hand, but with the right guidance, he could be a great lad.'

I wanted to weep when I thought about what a brilliant dad Danny could have been to a boy.

'She's been sniping about a lot of things lately. We haven't fallen out, but I think a bit of a break from each other will do us good.'

Danny defended her. 'Really? She's always struck me as having a kind heart. I mean, she doesn't suffer fools gladly but I never thought of her as someone who couldn't be happy for someone else. She'll come round soon enough, perhaps she's just having another rough patch with Simon that she can't face admitting to.'

In normal circumstances, he'd have been spot on. But as the days turned into weeks, what had seemed like a serious row revealed itself to be not so much a fracture as a clean break, with neither one of us capable of bridging the gap. I didn't blame Jeanie if she never wanted to see me again. What sort of friend would ever, even in a fury, release that level of spite into the world? I'd looked for the chink in her armour and used it. But even knowing that, I couldn't put it right. What if I tried and failed, fanning the flames of her upset further until she decided Danny had a right to know, and bugger the consequences? I couldn't risk it.

What a coward I was.

CHAPTER TWENTY-TWO

March 1990

Over the years I'd grown to hate 'big' days – birthdays, Christmas, Easter, anniversaries of anything. But contrarily, everyone else in the family loved a good celebration: no occasion was too small for a 'suuur-priiise', no birthday falling on an ordinary weekday too insignificant to avoid the whole cake with exactly the right number of candles routine: 'Wish! Wish!'

Saturday 10 March was our silver wedding anniversary. A whole twenty-five years since I'd walked down the aisle with my dad, who squeezed my hand as he positioned me next to Danny, a simple gesture so full of complex emotions. In the interests of my mascara, I'd nodded to acknowledge his whispered, 'Love you, darling. Be happy.' Now I knew he'd be dead two years later, I wish I'd stopped and given him a great big hug, told him how much I appreciated his quiet gentle ways and that Danny wasn't replacing him as the man I looked up to, he was complementing him. But I was nineteen and hadn't yet taken on board that parents weren't immortal. That those mums and dads parked in the cosy lounges of our lives, an odd combination of vital and unimportant because they'd always been there, would leave an earthquake-sized hole in their absence.

On my wedding day though, I wasn't thinking about my dad. I was fretting about whether the hem of my dress had dragged in the wet when we got out of the car. Smiling about how handsome

Danny was, how lucky I was that he'd chosen me. How funny it would be to move out of my little bedroom at home, into a proper house where I wouldn't have to ask Mum's permission to invite people round.

Nothing anywhere near as important as making sure Dad knew I loved him.

And everything about our silver wedding anniversary made me miss him, all over again. But Danny was determined the event wouldn't pass unnoticed. 'We can't do nothing, Suze. I want to celebrate, to make you feel special,' Danny said. He suggested posh restaurants in London, hotels in Brighton, trips to the theatre.

I waved his ideas away. 'I'm quite happy staying in with fish and chips. I'm not a wife who needs a lot of wining and dining.'

Mum kept nudging me. 'Let your husband spoil his wife if he wants to.'

Grace and Louise joined in, sensing an opportunity to get Danny spending his money on them – a new dress for the occasion – soft touch that he was.

In the end, we settled for a day out at the seaside, which didn't fit with Louise's idea of celebration. 'But it's March. It'll be freezing.'

I tried to jolly her along with how lovely it would be to have the beach to ourselves. Ice creams. Hot chocolate. Bracing walks in the sea air.

'I am nearly twenty-four, Mum, not ten.' But instead of withdrawing like she normally did, she laughed. 'If that's how you and Dad want to celebrate your anniversary, who am I to argue?'

I couldn't face sitting in a restaurant, a cake coming out, waiters clapping, everyone gawking over to see who had made it through twenty-five years of the subtle and intricate steps that constituted a marriage. Knowing none of them would look at me and suspect I'd done anything worse than told a few fibs about the price of a pair of new shoes.

I didn't even bother trying to win Grace round. Since she turned twelve, the sunshine she'd brought into our lives had disappeared behind a permanent cloud of belligerent hormones. She'd taken to tucking her thin frame into Danny's cotton shirts, worn billowing over jeans she'd hacked to bits with scissors. But even that was preferable to the low-cut tops and short skirts she bought from the market, modelling herself on Julia Roberts' hooker look in *Pretty Woman*. I did my best to ignore the hennaed hair, the extra earring that appeared after her friend Stacey had stayed the night. My mother, on the other hand, couldn't help passing comment. 'She'll be getting herself a reputation going out like that. You should have a word.'

On the day, one of those nearly spring days with just enough warmth and brightness to feel summer was no longer down a dark and distant tunnel, we managed to get Grace, Louise and Mum into Danny's car with minimal dashing back into the house for coats, gloves and foldaway chairs. I'd nipped into the attic to fetch the windbreak before he'd even suggested it, carefully rearranging the suitcases in front of the chest where I kept everything to do with Edward. He'd always accepted it contained my dad's private letters and mementoes but I never liked to remind him of its existence in case he got curious.

Before we set off, Danny gave me a little rectangle present. He was fidgeting just like Grace when she thought she'd found something I'd really like, which immediately made me nervous of opening it. Inside was a cassette with all of the songs that had meant something to us over the years. Mum gave me the 'What a wonderful husband' eyebrow raise while Grace pulled a face as though she'd chewed rather than swallowed the cod liver oil tablets I made her take in the winter.

Danny noticed and said, 'No need to look like that, Gracie, there's a special song in there for you.'

He pushed the cassette in. And there it was filling the car. 'Amazing Grace', conjuring up, as always, a slideshow of images in my mind. The nuns' faces without a wisp of hair poking beyond their coifs. Your own dark hair, so much of it, plastered to your head. Sister Domenica hesitating before handing you to me. And that rush of love, knowing that I couldn't, shouldn't feel it. That split second when I stood on the edge of the precipice telling myself not to open my heart, not to let you in, then realising that it was too late and abandoning myself to the smell, the touch of you, far enough away from my six-week deadline to rejoice at your safe entry into the world.

I concentrated on Mum and Louise singing along, keeping my breathing steady, watching them in the wing mirror, reminding myself how lucky I was to have the family I had. Today would be a good day.

By the time we'd driven the half an hour to East Wittering, I'd been through a roller coaster of emotions – 'Some Kind of Wonderful' that Danny and I danced to at our wedding; 'Isn't She Lovely?' that Danny played every day for months after I came home from hospital with Gracie; 'Delilah' that he used to dance round the room to with Louise in his arms. The one that really made me sob and didn't do Mum much good either was 'They Long to Be (Close to You)'. My old dad used to sing it to me, flapping imaginary wings when he came to the bit about the angels getting together. I found it so embarrassing. Yet how I would have loved the opportunity to be mortified again now.

When we got out of the car on Shore Road, I hugged Danny. 'Thank you. That was really thoughtful, even if two out of the five of us have cried so far.'

For a second he looked a bit crestfallen. 'Sorry. It's supposed to be a happy occasion.'

I kissed him gently on the lips. 'We're going to have a great day.'

Louise winked at Danny. 'Come on, Grace, let's go and see if there's anyone on the beach.' Grace shot off at a trot, clumping along in her Doc Martens, a nightdress she'd taken to wearing as a dress and one of my dad's old pinstriped jackets. She looked a fright but I loved seeing his clothes on her.

I knew something was up because Grace never ran anywhere any more, usually scuffing along reluctantly whatever anyone suggested. Danny, on the other hand, was walking so slowly he made Mum look sprightly at sixty-seven.

When we got onto the beach, I couldn't see the girls. Even though I knew they wouldn't be in the water in March, I immediately started scanning the sea, imagining a freak wave sweeping them both in – my mind always defaulting to the catastrophe setting.

'Where did they go?' I asked, trying not to spoil the moment by alerting Danny to the disaster unfolding in my head.

Danny turned to me. 'Wait there till I shout you,' he said, all twinkly and excited.

I got it now. There was going to be some kind of 'suuur-priiise!'

While he disappeared off into one of the beach huts further along, Mum and I crunched along the pebbles. She put her hand in mine, rare enough for me to register surprise at how bony her hands had become, the skin so thin, as though her fingerprints had worn away over the years. 'He's been a good husband, hasn't he?'

I wanted to head her off. I wasn't in the mood for the 'We were right to do what we did' discussion today.

I squeezed her hand, then withdrew mine. 'He's been lovely. Still is lovely. I wonder what they are up to. Do you know what they've got planned?'

And with that, Grace came running out with Danny, throwing a kite high into the air. It caught on the wind and soared up, the letters of the tail whirling and twirling until they settled enough for me to decipher, 'Happy anniversary, I love you'.

The diamond of the kite silhouetted against a bright sky, ducking and diving, Grace tearing along the beach, Louise grinning, standing with her hands on her hips, Danny cheering on

Grace. My mind clicked the shutter on that perfect moment. Then Danny put his hands over my eyes and led me, shuffling and stumbling over the pebbles into the beach hut. In it was champagne, cakes and sandwiches, with anniversary bunting.

'Where did all this come from?'

Danny laughed. 'The bakery up the road knew someone who owned a beach hut and they did the rest.'

We toasted each other, the children, Mum, our good fortune at having such a lovely family. I decided to take everything at face value for once, to live in the moment. We paddled, squealing at the cold. We played French cricket. We huddled in the hut playing rummy during a sudden downpour. Danny's face was alive with the pleasure of planning a successful surprise. And just as I turned to Mum and said, 'I'd like to do this all again next week', Grace slipped off the wooden sea defence she'd been using as a makeshift stage and flopped into a heap in the shallow water. I heard her shout and went flying out, calling her name, dashing into the water. She pushed herself to her feet but I could see blood, lots of it, spreading like an ink stain over the bottom of her nightdress.

I didn't seem to have much buffer between 'It's only a graze' and 'You're going to need a blood transfusion', but thankfully Danny wasn't far behind.

'All right, calm down, let's just have a little look and see what you've done.'

Grace had gone pale and was doing that one-eyed squinty thing when you're frightened to inspect the damage in case a vital piece of the body is hanging by a thread. I let Danny take charge, pinning my arms firmly by my side – I didn't think an actual flapping motion would be a helpful addition to the circumstances.

Grace was whimpering but managing not to cry. I held her hand while Danny peeled away the nightdress that was wrapping itself around her legs. Grace snapped, 'Shut up!' when I grunted out an involuntary 'Oh my god'. She'd managed to catch her leg on a piece of metal, which had sliced a huge cut across her knee and down her shin.

Danny helped her up the beach. 'I'm going to wash it with some seawater. It's going to sting but then we'll be able to see how deep it is.'

My knees went weak as Danny cleaned the wound. I held my breath, but really I wanted to make all sorts of shocked noises.

'It's not too bad, but I think we should get it looked at,' he said.

I risked peering at it myself. I thought it looked terrible. 'We're going to need to wrap something around it to stop it bleeding.'

Grace leaned on me and hopped up the beach. Mum was wringing her hands and I willed her not to stoke up my own panic.

Danny ran back with a clean tea towel. 'Here, you tie that around her leg. I'll just shut up the beach hut and fetch the car. I'll come back tomorrow for all the stuff.'

Louise took one side of Grace and I took the other and crab-like we managed to stagger to the car.

I sat in the back with her, snuggling her up in the picnic blanket. She closed her eyes and put her head on my shoulder. I cuddled her close, trying to warm her up. It was so long since I'd had anyone to mother. My life now consisted of backing out of rooms I wasn't welcome in, trying to make my point through a door shut firmly in my face and puzzling over the stream of invective set off by asking what sort of day she'd had at school.

'How's it looking? Do you think we need to drive straight to the hospital?' Danny asked.

'The bleeding has slowed a bit. I don't know.' I was afraid to disturb the wound by peeling back the tea towel to see. And the bit of me hacked straight from my mum was worried about what a sight we were with Grace in her bloodied nightdress, plus me and Danny with wet shoes and trousers.

Mum chose that moment to crane round from the front seat with a story about her friend who'd got lockjaw from a rusty rake, which tipped me into the camp of straight to Portsmouth Hospital and sod the sight of us.

Thankfully, two o'clock on a Saturday in March seemed to be a fairly unusual time for drama, so Grace was seen quickly. She emerged with a spectacular dressing and a dramatic limp that was already subsiding by the time we made it back to the car.

Grace declared herself starving. Mum was fussing about the waste of the sandwiches we'd left behind in the beach hut in our haste, but I was so damn grateful Grace was all right I didn't give a hoot about a few egg mayonnaise sandwiches the seagulls could enjoy.

'What do you fancy?' Danny asked.

Grace said, 'Chips.'

With a great effort, I managed not to say, 'Have some fish as well.' Instead I said, 'I'm not sure there'll be anywhere open at half past three in the afternoon,' but minutes later, we turned up a street with a fish and chip shop with the lights on.

Danny parked right in front. 'Funky Fish Café. God knows what that will be like, but anyway it will fill a hole.'

Everyone apart from Mum piled out, even Grace, who just 'wanted to see what else they've got other than chips', despite me instructing her to stay put. She didn't take any notice and I didn't want a big fight in the middle of the road. I was so busy watching how she was walking, I didn't pay much attention to the man serving behind the counter initially. But when I did, halfway through apologising for our appearance, I gasped, then tried to turn my face away, pretending to be engrossed in the price list. Too late.

'Susie?' He was bald now and looked as though he'd been eating saveloys and battered onion rings on a daily basis for a good few years.

I managed to say, 'Hello, how are you?' but before I let him answer, I rushed out with, 'Rob, do you remember my husband,

Danny? And these are my daughters, Louise and Grace.' I hoped he heard the warning.

Rob leaned over the counter, all expansive, still that easy way about him, the charm that had made him the heart-throb of the group. 'I used to be in a band with your mum,' he said to the girls.

I corrected him. 'Well, you had the band, and I used to join you on stage sometimes.' I could hear the note of panic, the desire to escape in my voice.

Grace was a mixture of disbelieving and impressed. 'Mum used to sing with a band?'

Rob pointed behind him to some poster-sized black and white photos on the walls, dulled with grease. 'If you look really carefully in that picture on the far right, do you recognise anyone?'

Suddenly the smell of fat frying was turning my stomach. It was me, on *that* night, in my silver hot pants and purple turtleneck. The clothes I'd burned in a metal bin in the back yard the day after.

Grace was agog. 'Oh my god, is that you, Mum? You look so different.'

I nodded. 'A long time ago. We'd better get going, Rob, we've just come from the hospital. Right, tell him what you want.'

But Rob was asking the girls whether they could sing and Danny was explaining how I'd got out of the habit and how he wished I'd kept it up as a hobby. I butted in with Mum's order for a bit of haddock, but Rob was off on one, lost in memory lane with stories of the Portsmouth Palais. I was staring at him so hard I could feel my eyeballs drying out in the heat of the shop, willing him not to mention the night with the talent scout. Then just as he was finally, slowly, wrapping the last battered sausage, Louise said, 'Did you ever make a record?'

He glanced at me. I opened my mouth to close the conversation down but I couldn't make any words come out. His eyes narrowed with a question, then he bit his bottom lip and ran his hand over his bald head. 'No. Would have loved to, but we never quite made it that far. It's a very tough business, the music industry.'

'Yes, that's what I've been saying all along, isn't it, Louise? Right, come on, let's get you home. Nice to see you, Rob.'

I sat with the food on my lap, not caring that the grease was seeping through onto my trousers, monosyllabic in the face of Grace's questions, the most interest she'd shown in anything I had to say for months.

Twenty-five years and a single night still dominated my marriage.

CHAPTER TWENTY-THREE
1992

It was the fourth time that term I'd had the call from the school. 'Mrs Duarte, I'm just calling to let you know Grace wasn't in class this morning. Is she ill again?' The school secretary managed to put all the emphasis on 'again', tapping right into my bad mother paranoia. I couldn't bring myself to tell her that I had no idea where she was. Or better still, I did have an idea: she was down at the park hanging out with the boys from the tech college instead of reciting Shakespeare's 'All the World's a Stage' that I'd been trying to force her to learn for the last week.

'Yes, sorry, I meant to phone earlier. She's really suffering today with a bad period pain, but she'll be in tomorrow.' I didn't add, 'If I have to drag her in by her ear!'

I slammed down the phone and yanked on my boots. The last six months had been like living with a feral cat, a world away from the little girl who used to sneak in and sleep across the end of our bed. I'd only know she was there when my feet connected with something soft. 'I had a nightmare, but I didn't want to wake you.'

And I'd make room for her between Danny and me. 'You climb in with us. There's no reason to be frightened.'

But for the last couple of years, Grace hadn't worried about how much love I could give. Our relationship seemed more about how much hate I could withstand. And as I rounded the corner to the

park, I gathered my weary soul for another showdown. I headed
to the playground, scanning for a group of teenagers shoving each
other about. I felt a pang of envy at the mothers pushing their
children on swings. I wanted to rush up to them and say, 'Make
the most of it. Enjoy them thinking you are wonderful and never
wanting to spend a single moment away from you.'

No sign of Grace. I headed over to the pitch and putt. And
there she was, the little madam, wrapped around a boy in a black
and yellow stripy jumper. I stood back for a moment, fighting
my desire to go steaming over and wrench her away. She never
told me anything any more, so I had to amass my information carefully, sieving through the lies that poured out of her to
ascertain a single truth. The boy was much older, maybe eighteen,
with a stubbly face. And running his hands over Grace, squeezing
her buttocks with a sense of ownership that made me want to
grab the golf club and do some damage.

They were taking it in turns to puff on a cigarette and blow
smoke into each other's mouths, before plunging in for kisses,
which even from my distant vantage point reminded me of my
old twin tub in motion.

When his hands started making their way under Grace's shirt,
I stormed over. She jumped away, a flash of fear quickly replaced
by defiance.

The boy didn't hang around. He flicked the cigarette they'd
been sharing into the bushes with the action of someone who's
smoked not one, but thousands. He snatched up his bike and
pedalled off with a 'See you around, Grace'.

I didn't dare touch her because I felt as though I might start
shaking her and never stop.

She put her hands up. 'Save it. I'm not interested in a lecture.'

'Don't you dare talk to me like that. Don't you dare. You are
coming home right now. And when we get there, you are going
to get it into your head once and for all that if you ever, *ever*,

play truant again, I will march you to school every day and hand you over to your teacher like I used to do when you were five.'

She scuffed along beside me, hostility radiating from every pore.

I didn't know why I thought about you in that moment. Probably because I'd failed so spectacularly with both of my children that it was easier to think about the one who might be out there worrying about his mother's feelings, rather than the daughter next to me, acting as though it would be a blessing if a car mounted the pavement and squashed me flat.

I wasn't sure what was worse. Going home and having to follow through with my earlier threat that I'd confiscate Grace's CD player if she skipped school, smoked or stole from me again. Or suffering another lecture from Louise about how I'd been 'far too soft with Grace', followed by advice from her teacher friends who, like Louise, were in their mid-twenties, didn't have kids and thought being a parent was a breeze. A breeze whistling through a blossom tree, if you just 'set some boundaries and some consequences'.

Ironically, I'd been delighted when Louise had found a job at a lovely little primary school in Portsmouth, so she could still live at home. But with Danny encouraging me 'to be a bit firmer with Grace – she doesn't speak to me like that' and Louise shaking her head every time Grace was downright rude, I was beginning to wish that Louise would start a whirlwind romance. Preferably with a man who had his own flat, so I could escape the little jury resident in my front room, shouting out 'nul points' for mothering ability.

When we got home, I went straight up to Grace's bedroom and unplugged her CD player.

She flew up the stairs and tried to wrench it out of my hands. 'I need that.'

I held tight. 'I told you what would happen if you didn't go to school.'

'I need it to practise for an assembly we're doing. I'm singing "Hey Jude". I'll be in even more trouble if I don't do it. Mum, please!'

'You should have thought about that before you decided to bunk off with that moron from the park.'

I tugged the player towards me, but she twisted away from me and the plastic handle snapped.

'Now look what you've done.' She started to cry.

I'd never been able to stand her crying. Even though I knew that if Louise had been there, she'd have been rolling her eyes. 'You're not going to fall for that, are you? Grace always turns the waterworks on to get her own way.'

Grace sniffed. 'I do really need it. I'll be letting everyone down if I haven't got it perfect by Tuesday.'

Christ the girl was bright. Turning my own words back on me, about not letting people down. But Grace didn't find school easy, unlike Louise who'd had a breakdown if she got less than eighty per cent in anything. And maybe the teachers would go easy on her if she did a great performance next week. I could hear Danny's words in my head. 'I'm sorry, Suze, but you do have to be the one who's unpopular. I'll take over when I get home from work, but there's nothing I can do during the day. She won't stop loving you if you tell her off.'

I tried not to look at her blotchy face. I wanted to pull her to me as I had done when she was a baby and make everything right.

'I'll give it back to you after the weekend. You can't keep behaving badly and expecting never to be punished. It's not fair on Dad and me. We're worried out of our heads half the time, not knowing where you are.'

'But if I ask you, you always say no. Everyone else is going to parties, half my class goes clubbing at the weekend. But you, you've always got a problem with whatever I want to do.' She did an impression of me, her voice high and simpering. 'I don't think so, Grace. Nothing good ever happens after midnight. You'd have to let Daddy pick you up at ten-thirty. No, you're not just wandering the streets with your friends. No, I don't like the sound of you going up to London just the two of you.

'And now, because I missed *one day* of school, you're going to take away my music. I knew you'd find a way to spoil that too.' She slumped down onto the floor. 'Why couldn't I have been born into a family that had a bit of fun? In this house everything is a bloody problem. You're all so serious. Louise still living at home at twenty-six, going to bed with a hot-water bottle every night. Jesus, as soon as I'm old enough, I'm out of here. There's Dad thinking he's a right old rebel if he has half a lager and lime with dinner, and you, god, you'd still hold my hand crossing the road if I let you. Cluck bloody cluck. I can't breathe without you fussing round me.' She pushed her hair back from her face, her cheeks red and angry. 'I wish I'd been adopted.'

I tried not to let her see how much she hurt me, desperate to do what Danny suggested and let it wash over me. 'She's a teenager with a perfectly nice home life. She gets everything she needs, but not everything she wants, which are two different things. She's looking for things to be angry about, to rebel against. Don't get drawn in.'

But her last comment pierced my resolve. 'Do you really mean that?'

I felt the rawness of recognition in my chest, as though she'd suddenly articulated something I'd long been denying. Maybe you would have felt like that too, one day.

Her eyes dropped to the floor and she shrugged. 'I don't want to talk to you. And you're not taking my CD player.'

I felt the fight drain out of me. Everything in me drooped, weary. 'All right. You can have it, but that's the last time. I mean it. I'm not covering for you any more. You'll end up getting expelled if you carry on like this. You won't get any O levels and then you'll never get a good job.'

But Grace had already plugged in the CD player, singing Whitney Houston's 'I'll Always Love You' into an imaginary microphone. 'I don't need any O levels. I'm going to be a pop star.'

I slunk out of her room defeated. I had no appetite left for that battle today.

CHAPTER TWENTY-FOUR

December 1995

The platitude, 'It's just a phase' had never rung so hollow as when I watched Grace bump her holdall down the stairs the day after her eighteenth birthday on the first of December. She pushed past me, shouting over her shoulder, 'Don't even think about coming to look for me. Just leave me alone to get on with my life. I mean it. You'll never see me again if you try and bring me back here.' She stormed out towards a rusty old Vauxhall Corsa that looked as though its axle might clank off at any moment. Danny stood on the front path, blocking the gate and trying to reason with her.

I got a little flashback to my mother, always waving me inside so the neighbours didn't 'know our business'. Too late for that. They'd witnessed enough of Grace screaming at us as she stomped out, coming home drunk – throwing up in next door's grape hyacinths on one humiliating occasion – not to be under any illusions about our perfect family unit. Frankly, I didn't care any more how much tut-tutting Reg did as he hosed down his hyacinths, or how high Ivy's eyebrows disappeared into her hair-line. I cared that the gorgeous, funny little girl who'd swept into my life eighteen years ago hated me so much, she was leaving of her own accord. Not wrenched from my grip by some stranger's hand but by her own volition.

Danny argued with her, but not like I argued with her. 'Grace, just listen to me. Hear me out, so you've got all the facts in front of you, then if you still want to go, I won't stand in your way.'

I wished I could be like him. Keep chugging along, quietly insistent in second gear, nimbly negotiating the twists in the conversation. Far better than my tried and failed techniques of either collapsing immediately and letting her do what she wanted or going from 0–60 in seconds, bringing in every misdemeanour from the last ten years at an increasingly hysterical volume.

I looked to see who was driving the rust heap while Danny said, 'You've only got a couple of terms left at school. Surely it makes sense to get your art and music A levels? You can always go and work in the hotel next summer, if that's what you want to do.'

Grace argued back. 'I'm sick of school. At least I'll be earning money. They'll give me a room in the hotel and pay me for waitressing in the restaurant. And singing at weekends.'

I stood there, my arms folded, watching her slip away from me. In her drainpipe jeans, long black sweater where she'd poked her thumbs through the sleeves and clumpy monkey boots, she didn't look like someone capable of setting an alarm to get up in the morning. Let alone someone who could cook for herself, clean a bathroom and, god, fend off bloody men, drunken sailors straight off the ship, who thought she was available for the taking. She was still my baby.

But Grace was in broadcast, not listening mode. Eventually, the bloke driving the car slithered out, leaning on the roof, looking as though the emotional devastation unfolding before him was just an inconvenience standing between him and an appointment examining his belly button fluff. 'You coming or not, Grace?'

She wavered. I wanted to rush out to her, tell her that we'd work it out, that she didn't need to prove anything to us, that maybe I had tried to control her too much but only because I loved her. But her need to be free was greater than her need for security, for us. She glanced at the house then back to Danny, her eyes skipping over me as though I was just another face in a crowd.

She gave Danny a brief hug. 'Love you, Dad. Don't worry. I'll be fine.'

She wrenched open the door, chucked her holdall in the back and with a screech of tyres, she shot out of sight.

Danny took my arm and led me inside. 'She'll soon be back, you'll see.'

He disappeared into his shed where the sound of ferocious hammering ensued. He emerged several hours later rubbing his face and muttering about the sawdust irritating his eyes. I wasn't fooled. I pulled him to me and we stood for ages draped around each other in the kitchen, propping up rather than comforting one another.

'Do you think Louise might be able to talk some sense into her?' he asked.

I shook my head. It would be like trying to put out a fire with a blowtorch. Louise's methodical reasoning: 'Just stop to think that through for a moment and listen to what people have to say' acted like petrol on the flames of Grace's knee-jerk reactions of 'There's no point in talking to me about it because I've made up my mind.'

I wondered about Craig, Louise's boyfriend. 'Maybe Grace might listen to him?'

It was Danny's turn to look doubtful. 'He's quite staid though. I'm not sure Grace would relate to him any better than us.'

I loved that he included me in that sentence, but the truth was, Grace had shut me out for years, cutting her conversation short on the telephone if I walked into the room, refusing to tell me who she was going out with, even when it was just a girlfriend I knew and liked. Secrets were Grace's power and she cuddled them to her like a comfort blanket. Mum always said Grace was so like me, but I couldn't see how. And didn't even know if I wished it was the case.

But I couldn't really see myself in Louise either, who was certainly Grace's opposite.

Before she'd moved out to live with Craig two years earlier, she'd told us what she was planning. Danny had a small huff about them not getting married first, but frankly, I was just relieved that she was showing signs of wanting to be independent from us. Living at home circling the programmes she wanted to watch in the *Radio Times* didn't constitute making the most of being young. But she still managed her breaking out into the big wide world in a very Louise-like way. 'Dad, will you come and look at the flat we want to rent? I'm not sure about the security. Would you help me fit some window locks?'

Now, however, I was grateful for Louise's steadfastness; I could fill my worry basket entirely with Grace-related thoughts without having to cover two bases at once.

Danny instructed me to stay away from the hotel, to wait for Grace to get in touch 'even if you have to chop your fingers off and your tongue out of your head'. If I hadn't heard him pretending to sleep at four in the morning, I'd have felt ridiculous sloping into her room whenever I could, tracing my fingers in the dust on all her jewellery boxes, picking absent-mindedly at the Blu-Tack staining her walls, breathing in the scent of Charlie I imagined still lingered there.

Two weeks in, we hadn't heard a word. Every time I asked Danny whether we should 'just go and have lunch at the hotel/ just phone and check she is still working there/go and watch her sing', he shook his head.

'Just let her be. The best way to cut short her rebellion is to stop giving it oxygen by arguing with her.'

But I couldn't stay away. The house seemed cavernous without Grace's emotions careering off every wall, without her singing spilling down the stairs. It was so quiet, my own footsteps sounded loud; I noticed the noise of the tap dripping, of the radiators creaking, the electric oven humming. And when I wasn't in the café distracted by customers fussing about butter versus margarine or white versus brown, I let my worries fill the silence, swelling up until they pinned me to my seat, unable to read, watch TV or even talk to Danny. I kept picking up the phone to see that it was working, and when it did ring, I had to stop myself shouting, 'Why would I want to speak to you? Get off the line in case my daughter rings!'

With a week to go until Christmas and a whole fortnight and three days since Grace stormed off, I took a bus towards the dockyard. This time I didn't close my eyes as we drove past the part of the beach that set this all in motion twenty-eight years ago. Meeting Mal had been like a ball in the Mousetrap game Grace once loved to play, dominoing through the various obstacles before snapping a trap down on me forever.

I hoped Grace was smarter than me. Though judging by the bloke driving her 'getaway' car, I couldn't take that for granted. I hopped off the bus near the hotel, standing on the pavement like a dog who wasn't sure which direction his owner had taken. I hadn't really planned what I'd say if I saw her. But I had to know she was actually there. At two in the morning, I'd lie awake, imagining the police knocking on the door to tell me she'd been found dead in a hotel room in Edinburgh. I couldn't bear to be that mother, the one who'd thought her daughter was down the road in Portsmouth, serving whisky chasers and singing 'Sailing' to a rowdy audience, but was so utterly hopeless she hadn't even known that her daughter was four hundred and fifty miles away in Scotland.

I walked up to the hotel and stood outside. It was bigger and more modern than I'd expected. I'd imagined a sign with faded lettering, peeling paint around the windows, a scruffy bloke with big gut and a fag hanging out of his mouth leaning on a wall by the entrance. Every time I thought about what sort of room Grace might be living in, dingy stairs leading to a stained bathroom and a mattress on the floor sprang to mind. Instead, the glass doors were spotless with spider plants tumbling from every corner in the reception area. The woman behind the desk bore no relation to the brothel madam of my imagination. Instead of red lipstick bleeding into her wrinkles, she was young enough to have that smooth skin I wished I'd appreciated more. The doors flung open automatically, leaving me exposed in the doorway, and although I hadn't intended to go in, I didn't quite get it together to dash away.

She smiled. 'Can I help?'

I said the first thing that came into my mind. 'Actually, I was wondering if you had a toilet I could use? I hadn't realised how far it was to the dockyard.'

She waved me through some double doors without batting an eyelid. I tried to work out how I could discover whether Grace was employed there, now I'd lied about needing the loo. But as I left the ladies' I saw a sign to the restaurant. I couldn't resist. She might be there, just thirty yards away. If she was on duty. If she even worked there at all. I looked at my watch. Half-past twelve. I tiptoed along the corridor, wishing I was one of those people who could march into anywhere with such confidence everyone would wonder whether I owned the place, rather than whether I was burgling it. I stood to the side peering through the doors at an angle, her words, 'Don't come and look for me, leave me to get on with my life' ringing in my ears. I couldn't see her. I dropped my head in despair. Now I was here, I couldn't leave without knowing she was safe.

I gathered myself to go and ask at reception, to come clean with the woman at the desk. I hoped she had children, understood that need to know. But as I turned to leave, music started up. I glanced behind me, then scooted along to the double doors at the end of the corridor. I pressed my nose against a little diamond window, where I was rewarded with the view of Grace on a stage, singing her heart out. I cursed my lack of height, clutching the edge of the window with my fingertips and balancing on the toes of my boots. She was mesmerising, her eyes half-closed, her fingers moving over the guitar strings, the relaxed demeanour of someone who has found their place in the world. The piano stopped. Grace stood up, waving her hands about the way she did when she was trying to explain something she believed in passionately. She sang a few bars, then pointed to whoever was sitting at the piano, nodding as strong deep notes resounded. And then she was back to singing. All the tension that dogged her, those sharp angles defining her body for years, her shoulders and elbows jutting in permanent defence had softened. Whether it was the chance to sing freely or the distance from me, I didn't know.

I stood for a fraction longer. Grace didn't just look happy, she looked *liberated*. Nothing about her suggested she'd spent a single evening sitting on a bed with a moth-eaten eiderdown, wishing she had the courage to ring for her dad. I walked out, ignoring the receptionist as I left.

Two out of three of my children were better off without me.

CHAPTER TWENTY-FIVE

December 1995

A few days after my visit to the hotel, Grace waited outside the printing works for Danny to let him know she wouldn't be home for Christmas.

'She said she got paid time and a half over the Christmas period and it was a good opportunity to make some money. She sent her love.'

I didn't believe him but didn't want to force him to admit to a lie. He was trying to be upbeat.

'She sounded like the management were pleased with her. She was quite chatty really, much less grumpy than she's been lately, anyway.'

The fresh, sharp pain of Grace disappearing from my life imprinted itself onto the dull ache of your absence. It was Christmas nine years ago that you'd tried to contact me. My contrary heart still hoped you'd try again. My rational mind prayed you'd forgotten me.

We'd held off telling Louise that Grace had walked out until we knew it was a long-term thing, but when she popped in to drop off our presents so we'd have them to open first thing on Christmas morning, we couldn't keep it a secret any longer.

She shook her head, appalled.

'Mum! She hasn't even finished school. How's she going to support herself? She's just a child.'

Danny stepped in. 'Not technically. Anyway, she knows her own mind.'

Louise looked dumbfounded. 'Where's she living? How much does she earn? Does she eat in the restaurant? She can't cook anything.'

I couldn't decide whether Louise's questions stemmed from concern for her sister or astonishment at my lack of control.

I couldn't look her in the eye when I said Grace was earning her keep by waitressing. But when Danny chipped in, 'And singing.' I could have happily taken a chainsaw to him and cheered while it ground through chunks of his flesh.

Louise's big bubble of resentment that I hadn't let her go to music school had shrunk but not burst in the intervening eleven years. 'So she gets to sing for a living? And live wherever she wants?'

Danny realised his faux pas. 'Just until she comes to her senses. I expect she'll go to technical college next year and retake her A levels, perhaps go into, er, nursing.'

I tried not to raise my eyebrows at Danny's random clutching at straws. Grace was the worst nurse I'd ever come across, telling people off if they coughed anywhere near her or shouting at them to sneeze elsewhere.

Louise scooted off soon afterwards, saying she still had presents to wrap for Craig's parents.

Christmas Day rolled around without a card or a word from Grace. Louise, on the other hand, did exactly what she said she would: spent the morning opening presents with Craig's family then came to us with Craig for lunch. I was pathetically grateful that she hadn't given into the pressure from Craig's parents to stay with them for lunch and just come to us for the Queen's speech. Christmas Day already had enough ghosts wafting their complicated histories around the cranberry sauce without Danny and I trying to think up conversation that didn't revolve around the fact that neither of our children wanted to spend the day with us.

The day was oddly relaxing without Louise dispensing wisdom to Grace: 'You'll damage your feet if you keep wearing shoes that high' or Grace goading Louise about her narrow horizons – 'I mean, living all your life in Portsmouth? It's hardly round the world in eighty days, is it?'

And even more surprisingly, Louise stepped into the entertaining role we associated with her younger sister. As soon as we sat down, she made us pull the crackers, wear our hats and read out the jokes. I went along with it, hoping my laughter wouldn't turn into a sob. God knows, I wanted to rip my purple crown off and shred it into tiny pieces. She'd obviously schooled Craig on 'staying off the topic of Grace so as not to upset Mum' because every time he mentioned his own brother, he blushed at his lack of tact. I had often joked that you could fit Louise's sense of humour in a tobacco tin, thinking of Grace as 'the funny one'. But as I sat there listening to her telling stories about the teachers at work, I realised, with a big rush of love, that she could be really witty. Maybe now she was with Craig, she had the confidence to be who she was rather than just 'the reliable one', the person we'd poured into a mould and not allowed to break out nearly three decades later.

Although Craig would never have suited me with his precise way of dabbing the corners of his mouth with his serviette and his eager leaning forward whenever there was a debate to be had: 'Your point is well made, however…' I could see he respected her opinions, often turning to me with an earnest furrowing of the brow, 'Louise is brilliant at organising/staff issues/motivating the students. She's so bright.'

Louise kept flicking his arm and saying, 'I'm not that bright. I just work really hard.' She repeatedly changed the subject to showcase all his good qualities. A proper mutual admiration team. As soon as we'd had our Christmas pudding, Louise put on the radio for Christmas carols, singing along so sweetly, I kept forgetting to scrape the plates while I listened.

And when I looked at her with Craig, I wanted to march her back to the Mother and Baby Home and parade her in front of the weasly Sister Patricia and prove that although I'd done hundreds, probably thousands, of things wrong, I'd also done lots of things right.

With that one daughter at least.

My poor eldest child who'd borne the brunt of my mistake, the distracted years of yo-yoing between frantic activity and numbing melancholy while I tried to come to terms with losing you. As I watched her drying up, holding the glasses up to the light to check for smears, making sure the knives all faced the same direction in the drawer, I wondered if I had given her enough love. Had my energy for her been diverted into my mourning for you? Had I told her often enough how special she was? How important? I hoped she hadn't seen our jubilation at Grace's birth and absorbed the message she wasn't enough. The trouble with wanting to manipulate the past into a sanitised version – highlighting all our triumphs and kicking sand over our failures – was that memories were so random.

When Jeanie and I had talked about that bloody home in London, we argued over so many details, each convinced that we had the monopoly on our history.

'That laundry was the cushy place to work. You were all right if you got a job in there,' she'd say.

'You are joking? It was a hothouse. Every time I stepped through the door, I'd have sweat pouring down my bump. And that nun who ran it wouldn't even let me hold my wrists under cold water.'

And so it went on, with me convinced we all went to church every day, lined up like sinners on one side, while Jeanie recalled it as a Sunday-only experience.

I had no doubt that Louise's view of our life would be entirely at odds with my own. I could only hope the underlying 'feel' of her life at home – whether or not I'd read the right quota of bedtime stories, baked enough butterfly cakes, kissed enough grazed knees – was one of love. But who knew or could guarantee what she would have snatched and immortalised in her mind from the unreliable patchwork of family life.

I watched her line up the glasses in my cupboard, the ones the rest of us stuffed in willy-nilly, wherever they fitted, then I went over to hug her. Unlike Grace who, on the rare occasion that the stars aligned, just drooped into me, relaxing every muscle to hang from me like a baby koala, Louise submitted, a receptacle of physical affection rather than an active participant. 'Thank you for coming home today. I know it's really hard when you've got Craig's family to think of as well. We've loved having you here.'

'Don't worry about Grace, Mum. She's always been a law unto herself. She's probably sitting in her room right now wishing she was eating Twiglets and watching *The Wizard of Oz* with Dad.'

I tried not to hear the judgement in her voice.

CHAPTER TWENTY-SIX

February 1996

I didn't dare risk going back to the hotel to spy on Grace, though it nearly killed me to stay away. But as January rolled into February, there were signs she'd started to miss us. Or Danny at least. A couple of times she'd waited for him outside work and they'd gone for a drink. I pushed aside the hurt she wanted to see him but not me. Instead, like a greedy Labrador coming across an unexpected bowlful of food, I barely paused for breath between questions, hungry for answers. 'What did she say about work? Is she doing more singing or more waitressing? Are they paying her properly? Did she say anything about me?' But however hard Danny tried to remember their conversations, I always felt he hadn't 'got to the bottom of it' in the way I would have done. Which was probably why she chose to see him. He ran his hand through his hair, trying to find a response that would satisfy 'How did she look?' Obviously the blokey 'Just the same' didn't tell me what I needed to know. 'Was she fatter, thinner, did she look tired, do you think she's eating all right?'

In the end, he'd get exasperated. 'I don't know, love. She seemed fine.'

Which mother in the entire world had ever been satisfied with their offspring being described as 'fine'? It made me want to jump on the bus with vats of home-made soup, a new pack of M&S

pants and a fresh toothbrush. I wondered if she ever changed her bed or hoovered her room. 'Did she mention a boyfriend?'

Danny frowned. 'She mentioned various men who worked at the hotel, but I didn't get the impression she was seeing anyone. She seems far more interested in her music, to be honest. Said she was writing some songs and that she'd teamed up with a guy who puts them to music.'

'What guy? Someone her age?'

'I'm not sure. I think it's someone who does some of the music spots at the hotel at weekends.'

'Didn't you ask?'

Finally, Danny got cross. 'For god's sake, Suze! I don't bloody ask anything. I sit and let her talk and hope to God that one day we'll have a normal relationship with her and she'll come round for Sunday lunch like any other daughter, instead of sitting waiting for me on a wall outside the factory in the rain.'

I knew he was right. I wanted to turn the clock back and do it all again. But do it right this time.

Initially, I'd agreed with Danny and thought that Grace would come home within weeks if not days. But when it became clear that she had left permanently with no intention of coming back, it dawned on me I had no idea when I would see her again.

Some nights I'd sit in front of the telly with Danny, the figures moving on the screen, the dialogue washing over me. Eventually I'd blurt out, 'Have I really been such a terrible mother?'

The first few times he'd talked about how it wasn't only my influence that had shaped Grace. 'She's my daughter too and I didn't manage to control her either.' But I knew deep down that Danny hadn't tried to control her; he'd tried to be steady. I'd treated her like a princess to be waited on, dressed up, appeased and celebrated. And by the time she'd reached her teens, she was so used to getting her own way, my remonstrations had as much impact as a feather duster.

After several weeks of asking the same questions – 'Could you go pop down to the hotel and see if you could persuade her to nip back for a visit?' 'Could you at least phone and see if she needs anything?' – he snapped.

'No. No. She is a grown-up and she's going to have to make her own mistakes. I'm not going begging her, to be honest, she should be a bit more grateful for what she had. We haven't been perfect, but then again, neither were your parents, neither were mine and we've turned out okay.'

I sat in silence. Danny barely criticised either of our daughters. His checklist was so much shorter than mine. If you paid your own way and stayed out of trouble, you were halfway to Danny's seal of approval. Consequently he had much less to blame himself for than I did when the kids didn't live up to my many and varied expectations.

More gently he said, 'We can't affect what Grace does now, so I want to get on and live our lives, Susie. Enjoy ourselves. We've brought the kids up the best we can and now I'd like to have a nice time with you without every moment being devoted to Grace and what she might need. You were so wrapped up in her, I didn't even have a conversation with you for ten years after she was born. Now she doesn't even live here, I'd like to talk about something else.'

Not for the first time I wondered if heaving the blame for my shortcomings onto losing you was in fact a huge exercise in smoke and mirrors. Perhaps I just wasn't cut out for motherhood.

More than ever, I missed Jeanie. Nine years since we fell out. I wondered whether she took the opportunity to slag me off to anyone who'd listened. Or whether, like me, she wished we'd sorted it out earlier, nipping our quarrel in the bud there and then, rather than letting it spill over and spread, an upturned paint pot of regrets and recriminations, spooling down the years. She wouldn't have judged me, wouldn't have made the face the neighbours did when I bumped into them at the shops. 'We've not seen Grace around lately?', their features imprinted with gleeful anticipation of no good having come of her. With Jeanie, I could have let my brave face slip, admitted my despair at losing contact with not one child, but two. And she'd have found a way to make it seem just a little bit better.

Danny convinced himself that focusing on my upcoming fiftieth birthday would cheer me up and became increasingly frustrated at my refusal to do anything. Just to shut him up, I said, 'Let's invite Louise round with Craig. I'll cook.'

Danny pulled a face. 'Really? That's your "special" birthday treat? No restaurant?'

I couldn't face the idea of 'Table for four?' when it should have been 'Table for six?'

It was already a miracle I hadn't decided to ignore it all together.

CHAPTER TWENTY-SEVEN
February 1996

Louise was rigorous about sharing herself out between Craig's parents and us. Tonight, Thursday 8 February, wasn't actually our night, but as it was my fiftieth birthday, there'd been a departure from their rigid schedule. I was so unsure of my place in the family these days, I was slightly surprised she didn't tell me we'd have to celebrate the following week. Out of sheer gratitude that one of my three children would be there for my birthday, I said, 'Invite Craig's parents too, if you want to.' I regretted it as soon as the words were out of my mouth. However, given that I'd made the same offer several times to no avail since Craig and Louise had moved in together three years earlier, I didn't think I needed to worry.

But this time she hesitated, her eyes narrowing for a moment, as though she was considering something. 'I won't invite them for your birthday, but I do think we should have dinner with them in the not too distant future.'

I tried not to look excited. Louise was coming up to thirty. Although Danny told me off every time I even mentioned the fact women were leaving it so late to have children, I hoped that Louise's low-key suggestion meant a marriage proposal might be in the offing. Instead of thinking about where to book for a simple supper with Audrey and Ron, I kept drifting off into planning what hat I might wear for the big day.

I thought I'd do a little more fishing over my birthday dinner. But I didn't need to. As soon as we sat down, Craig asked whether we were free the following week to meet his parents, 'to grab a bite to eat with them, finally do the introductions, as they're back in the country for a bit'. Louise caught his eye, a little smile, quite coquettish for her, brightening her face. It was all I could do to stop myself humming my entire repertoire of wedding songs.

But before I knew whether the dinner next week was to make small talk over a piece of battered cod or discuss the carnations for the button holes, the doorbell went. Danny was obviously on the same page as me because he said, 'Shall we ignore it? We're not expecting anyone.'

'It's probably a Jehovah's Witness,' I said, failing to keep the 'We're expecting big news from you, Louise' excitement out of my voice.

So we all sat there, me willing myself to keep quiet, to let Louise tell us what we were desperate to know at her own pace. But whoever it was started banging on the door as urgently as if someone was bleeding to death on the street outside.

Danny got up, patting Louise on the shoulder. 'Sorry, excuse me a sec, I'd better just check who that is.'

He opened the door, but I only heard one little exclamation, then no other conversation.

Louise sat back, doing that one-shouldered shrug that used to drive me mad when she was a teenager. Again, that funny little look at Craig. But as I sat there, irritated by the interruption, a big bouquet of flowers appeared in the doorway. Grace's face appeared round the side of it, looking a bit hesitant.

'Heard it was a big birthday today.'

I wanted to be calm, wanted to welcome her in as though we'd been quietly getting on with our lives, not staggering around in the void of her absence. I'd intended to keep it all low-key and manageable if she ever came back. But I couldn't. I leapt out of my chair, knocking my knife onto the floor. 'Gracie!'

I took the roses, thanking her and pressing my face into them, to give me a moment to react. Then I handed them to Danny and tentatively reached out to hug her, every cell on the surface of my skin straining, that primeval instinct to make a connection with my child overwhelming me.

And just for one brief moment, Grace hugged me back and said, 'Happy birthday'. I felt the complex emotions contained in those two words. The admission: 'I'm here because I wasn't ready to break so far from the family that I'd ignore a major birthday.' The warning: 'I'm only here because it's your birthday.' The face-saving: 'I'm glad to have your birthday as an excuse to be here.' Whatever was going on with her, whatever had become so unbearable she couldn't live under my roof a moment longer, it was quite clear it hadn't gone away. But I sensed a softening, a shift of perspective that only occurs when the heat of injustice has cooled and the door slammed in the face of a hundred grievances had creaked back open.

I pressed my fingers to my eyes but the tears squeezed out anyway. 'Sorry. I've missed you so much.' I tried to act natural, not to stare, but Grace didn't look like Grace. Short white blonde hair with just a trace of a dark fringe at the front. Oversized denim dungarees. Doc Martens. And enough black kohl around her eyes to help out in the panda enclosure should the need arise. I wanted to run my hand over her face, the neat little nose like Danny's, the high cheekbones like mine, that profile I'd sat and stared at for hours in the months after she was born.

Danny was semaphoring 'tread gently' with his eyes. I wiped my face. 'Are you hungry? You're in luck, we were just having a bit of celebration with Louise and Craig, so we've got plenty.'

Craig stood up and pulled a chair out for her, filling the shift in atmosphere with questions. 'How are you getting on? Are your digs okay? Does your boss give you a hard time?' I tried not to look like I was listening too hard to her answers.

I served Grace some lasagne, nervous of giving her too little or too much in case she saw it as a judgement on her weight, too thin, too fat. I was terrified of making a mistake, of breaking the tiny thread that still tied Grace to me, with a careless word, an ill-chosen question. It seemed years since we could all be in the same room and just act naturally. Instead, here we all were, tiptoeing around, making out it was normal for people to leave home in a storm then blow back in when the wind changed direction.

Louise fetched extra cutlery, then put the flowers in a vase, snipping the ends off, fiddling about getting the stem lengths just right. As she settled back into her chair, the family dynamics twisted into their old pattern. Grace, encouraged by what seemed like a genuine interest in the hotel business from Craig, was soon regaling us with stories of nightmare customers. With her talent for pinpointing other people's idiosyncrasies for comic effect, she described another member of staff who lived in the room next to her. 'Honestly, I don't think he's washed his clothes once since he got there, not even his pants. He just hangs them outside to air on the fire escape.'

I tried not to pull a disapproving face when she described the communal bathroom, complete with sights and smells. I knew it wouldn't take much to make her bolt again, to remind her of all our faults, rather than the qualities that she'd now had time to miss. So I encouraged her to carry on speaking, managing not to flinch at her swearing, her new-found coarseness. I was desperate to keep her there as long as possible. 'More tea? More lasagne? You'll stay for some pudding?'

I told myself to be more like Jeanie and less like me. After all these years, I could still imagine what she'd say to me: 'Don't you start bleating on about whether she wants to stay the night, when she's moving back, if she's eating enough carrots or when she last brushed her teeth.'

As soon as we'd all finished eating, Louise looked at her watch, put her hand on Craig's arm and said, 'Come on, we'd better go. I've got to be at work really early tomorrow.'

Danny tried to protest. 'Come on, it's not even nine o'clock. You haven't had a piece of birthday cake yet.'

But Louise was on her feet, widening her eyes at Craig when he didn't move to get up. He caught the message and pushed his chair back.

Louise turned to Grace. 'Take care. And keep in touch with Mum and Dad. They've been really worried about you.'

I waved my fingers airily as though I'd barely given Grace a thought. 'She looks like she's been absolutely fine to me. It's a mother's job to worry when you first leave home. I knew you had Craig looking out for you, Lou, so it wasn't as bad with you.' Then panicked in case Grace thought I was having a go at her for not having a boyfriend.

But she wasn't listening to me, more interested in patting Danny's stomach and teasing him, 'You been eating my rations while I've been gone?'

I went to the door with Louise and Craig. 'Hope you're not rushing off because Grace has turned up. It was lovely to see you both.' With a jolt, I remembered that we'd been on tenterhooks waiting for the big announcement. I didn't dare ask them outright in case they both looked at me blankly and said, 'Get married?' as though they'd never thought about it. I tried to make amends. 'You'll let us know when your parents are free, Craig? We'd love to meet them. And thank you for making such an effort with Grace. As you know, things have been a bit tricky.'

And I watched him shake his head as they walked towards their car, whisper something to Louise and flick his hands up in a gesture of 'What can we do?'

God knows how I would have managed to give three children the attention they needed.

CHAPTER TWENTY-EIGHT
July 1997

A year and a half later, Louise chose the week I gave you away to get married, which meant my emotions were already leaking out like a sponge unable to absorb any more liquid.

On the morning of the wedding, Danny zipped up my dress and kissed the back of my neck. 'I'm so lucky to have you.' I couldn't reply. A complex tangle of emotions sat at the bottom of my throat, dense as a fat ball left out for the winter birds. I turned and put my head on his chest, swallowing, trying – and failing – to find the words to convey everything he meant to me. And everything I should have done and never have done.

But Louise appearing at our bedroom door, her face softer than normal, framed by dark ringlets rather than the severe bob she usually favoured, interrupted the negative spiral of my thoughts. She looked so happy, as though making the decision to marry had released her to love fully, to commit to a future rather than existing reticently in the present. I understood that holding back, that foot out of the door, the sense that letting go could only lead to disappointment. My heart sang; she'd got there in the end. I wished Mum was still alive to see her.

Danny, as always, found the right words to express everything I would like to have said but couldn't begin to articulate for fear of what might rush out alongside it.

His simple sentences always sounded so special. 'Just so you know,' he said, clearing his throat, 'your mum and I are so proud of you. We couldn't have wished for a daughter we love more.'

Louise's eyes filled. I'd only seen her cry once in recent memory: at Mum's funeral six months ago. I wasn't sure that I'd ever stop sobbing myself if she started.

As always, I could only manage the practical. 'Don't cry! You'll spoil your mascara!' And another chance to tell my daughter how much she meant to me passed me by. Thank god for Danny. At fifty-five, he was still handsome. A little grey, a little thin on top, but still that same energy, that same twinkle about him, the quiet confidence that never tipped over into anything overbearing or arrogant.

But when I saw him walking down the aisle with Louise, when I should have been focusing on my daughter on a day that – if ever there was one – was all about her, I couldn't stop thinking about you. What you'd look like in a suit. How handsome you'd be. Whether you'd have my shiny straight hair or your dad's unruly mop. I hoped Jeanie had been right all those years ago, that you'd have my eyes. Which meant you'd look like Grace.

Who, right now, was standing next to me in a bright pink tie-dye dress that would have everyone wondering if she thought she was going to Glastonbury rather than a wedding, not even bothering to watch her sister's entrance. I was glad I was standing on her left side and couldn't see the yin and yang shaved into the side of her hair. I wished I'd been the sort of mother who'd been able to go shopping with her, giggling as we tried on the outrageous, the frilly, the bold. A mother who could cast her eyes along any rail and pull out the perfect garment with a 'Here, try this. It'll be great with your colouring.' A co-conspirator who could peer round a changing room curtain and not experience a moment's awkwardness at her daughter's state of undress. But when I'd dared to suggest 'popping into town to find an outfit for the wedding', she'd shrugged and said, 'I'm not spending money on something I'll never wear again.'

I didn't have the courage to say I'd like to treat her, to buy her something new. I knew she'd take it as a criticism, assume I meant I didn't like the way she dressed, that I wanted her to conform. I'd be setting myself up for 'I don't want to be like *you*!' And I couldn't find the words so that she'd understand I just wanted to share an experience with her, reach across all the misunderstandings, build a bridge into a world we could enjoy rather than tap straight into everything that separated us.

When did I become this woman who couldn't stand next to her own daughter without feeling a pressure to fill the silence? Throughout Gracie's tantrums, the drinking, the pot smoking, Danny was worried, but he wasn't asking himself where *he* went wrong. 'We've done our best, love. Sometimes, it's just the way they are. I expect she'll grow out of it.'

I was still bloody waiting.

I tried to ignore Grace yawning and fidgeting beside me. I forced myself to be grateful that she'd turned up on time and, so far, hadn't scandalised the congregation with one of her shocking swear words. I concentrated on Louise, who looked touchingly vulnerable, not at all the no-nonsense Head of English, on my back about my failure to keep Grace in check. 'You'd have gone mad when I was growing up if I'd dared to swear, let alone smoke. Yet she was hanging out of her window like Fag Ash Lil, telling you to F–off when it suited her and you didn't do anything about it. No wonder she can't stay in a job for more than five minutes. Did she tell you she's left the hotel because they wouldn't let her have time off to sing at a festival? Now she's living in a scummy flat with a load of dropouts.'

Some days her scathing remarks hit the bullseye and I just fell silent. Some days I didn't feel like taking her self-righteous shit. I'd start off all calm, 'Parenting isn't as straightforward as it looks.' And end up yelling, 'I hope I bloody live long enough to see you screw up being a mother!'

But today I was going to celebrate the fact Danny and I had managed to raise one daughter at least, who had a steady job and who was marrying a decent bloke. Though a disloyal bit of me couldn't help veering towards Grace's opinion of Craig that 'if he could bottle himself as a cure for insomnia, they'd be millionaires!' But god knows, everyone probably wondered why someone as charming as Danny had chosen someone as unsociable as me.

Danny's mouth contorted with emotion as he let go of Louise's arm and left her next to Craig. Grace – and probably Louise too – would be sniffy about the notion of 'giving a daughter away', but there was no doubt that the ritual of walking a child down the aisle and watching her commit to another man, even one she'd been living with for years, felt like a milestone for the family.

Danny joined me in the pew and squeezed my hand so tightly I could almost feel his heart constricting. I patted his arm and whispered, 'Well done.' He stood straight, unblinking, as though he couldn't allow his eyes to relax into tears. I wondered if, as Louise took her vows, he was seeing a parade of images from years ago. Louise earnestly licking the hinges to stick in the stamps she steamed off postcards into her album. Tongue out in concentration, colouring in her geography maps. And singing, always singing. In front of the mirror. To *Top of the Pops*. In the shower. On stage with me at the Silver Jubilee. Selfishly, I was glad she hadn't become a singer, suffering all the highs and lows that Grace had to withstand. And Louise didn't have Grace's easy charm. She liked certainty, reliability, a good rule to follow and the singing world didn't have many of those.

It really didn't.

And then it was over. Louise and Craig were kissing, self-consciously. When I'd kissed Danny at my wedding, my mother had told me off afterwards for 'making a spectacle' of myself. If I'd known how buttoned up I'd become, I'd have made a West End stage show of it with a sixty-piece orchestra.

Grace turned to me. 'She does look really happy, doesn't she?'

I couldn't quite pin down the emotion in her voice. Surprise? Envy? I felt a burst of sorrow. Despite my hundreds of faults, I'd always had Danny pouring warmth and love into the gaps where fear and worry resided. I hoped someone would do the same for Grace one day, though seeing past her prickles – 'I don't need a man around, too much like hard work' – would be a challenge and a half. I had no idea whether she'd ever been in love, ever had a proper relationship. Apart from the occasions in her late teens when we'd gone looking for her in the early hours and found hands and clothing where they shouldn't be, I knew nothing about her boyfriends. If she even had one.

We filed out behind Craig and Louise, trying to ignore the astonished whispers from Louise's teacher friends: 'Is that her *sister*?' I hated them for judging Grace on what she looked like, for failing to see her for the feisty, funny woman she was. A trap I'd tumbled into a million times. Danny linked arms with both of us, beaming away as though he had the good fortune to be in the company of the most magnificent women in the world.

We walked up the road to the reception. Grace had been so difficult in the lead-up to the wedding – 'She needn't think I'm going to be a bridesmaid in some satin lilac frock' – to being irrationally outraged when Louise decided not to have any bridesmaids at all: 'What's the point of even having a church wedding if you're not going to go the whole hog?' But today she seemed less opinionated, subdued even.

When she first heard Louise was having the wedding breakfast in a gastro pub, she'd said, 'Christ, no doubt we'll be having some microscopic meal with bloody chickpeas marinated in a jus de bollocks.' When we walked in and she saw the room, all the tables decorated with jam jars of miniature white roses, she raved about how pretty it all was. She passed absolutely no comment about having to sit with Craig's brother, Michael, on the top table, even though he looked as though he'd had a bowl on his head for his 'wedding haircut' and had white crusts of dried saliva gathering at the corner of his mouth. She even exchanged pleasantries with Craig's parents about how hard it had been to 'juggle their diaries', given their impending cruise to the Bahamas. Frankly, the 'all about themness' of the conversation made me want to poke them with a fork, so I had to applaud Grace's genuine-sounding, 'You've done well to get here then.'

I was relieved to see she took a glass of sparkling water as well as Prosecco when the waiters came round. I'd seen her drunk more times than I cared to remember. I'd asked Danny to have a word with her, remind her not to let Louise down. He refused, saying, 'If we go on at her too much, she won't come. I'll keep my eye on her and if she gets too lairy, I'll call a cab for her.'

I tried to relax into the day, to stop second-guessing all the things that could go wrong, stop assuming the responsibility for making everything right was only down to me. I glanced over at Craig's mother, Audrey, with her immaculate suit and manicured nails, the sort of fingers you could imagine politely but insistently summoning a waiter to complain about an underdone steak. I bet she wasn't looking at Michael and envisaging all sorts of humiliating worst-case scenarios that would flag her up as a failed mother.

I allowed myself one tiny moment while everyone was finding their seats to think about you. Would you be married? You were twenty-nine. I hoped your parents had loved you so much that you were stable and sure of yourself, despite living with the knowledge that I'd given you away. Maybe you'd been desperate to create a new family, one that was properly your own, not borrowed or chosen for you. I imagined you with a petite blonde wife, someone you felt protective of. I told myself you'd never bully a

woman, never force her into anything. That your father was the
product of a generation of men who thought it was their right
to take what they wanted from women. I had to believe you'd be
different. More like Danny.

Craig's best man dinging a spoon on a glass drew me back from
the familiar pain of imagining what you'd become without me.

Despite me.

Everyone sat down. Danny was smoothing the path for me as
always, charming Craig's parents with his easy manner. I knew
how his mind was working. What we lacked in money, we – or
rather he – would make up for in manners. We'd only met them
a few times because – according to Louise – they were jet-setting
around the world now Ron had retired, leading to huge negotia-
tions about the date of the wedding day.

Danny was facilitating the conversation, dropping in little
nuggets to include me, to make sure I charmed them too, whether
I wanted to or not. He was doing that thing with his eyes, long-
married speak for 'Come on, help me out on this.' I'd seen the
way Craig's mother had pursed her coral lips when she'd been
introduced to Grace, so I wasn't sure Craig's family would ever be
thanking their lucky stars their son fell in love with our daughter
but I admired Danny's ability to give it a go. I wished Jeanie was
there. She'd have been so naughty, daring me to tap Audrey on
the shoulder and say, 'Just so you know, I couldn't give a hoot
about your opinion of us, which, for all I care, you can stick up
your bony little arse.'

But Danny was so much more civilised. He was finding topics
for me to join in with, opening conversational doors and gently
ushering me through – 'Like you, Susie's lived in Portsmouth all
her life – third generation.' 'Susie loves cooking... does a mean
chicken curry.' But the one that actually made Craig's father, Ron,
stop pontificating about how hot it would be in the Bahamas at

this time of year was Danny's announcement that I used to sing on stage at the Portsmouth Palais.

'I met Audrey at the Portsmouth Palais! We used to love the dance bands. The Rocksters, The Banjos and The Shakers. Used to go every Saturday.'

I smiled vaguely and pretended to be looking for a waiter.

Danny frowned. 'Susie used to sing with The Shakers sometimes.'

I took a slug of water to give me time to formulate an answer. 'Not very often.' I tried to laugh. 'It wasn't really the done thing to be singing on stage every week when your husband was away on the other side of the world. Different times.'

Danny smiled. 'Susie's a great one for hiding her light under a bushel. She thinks people find it boring when she talks about her singing days. I can never get her to tell me about it. Good job I didn't know much about it at the time, I'd have driven myself mad with jealousy. But she's got an amazing voice.'

But Ron was a man who liked a bit of reminiscing and, surprisingly, the in-laws that he'd probably been dismissing as 'not really our sort of people, not much in common with them, nice enough though', had turned out to be a fraction more interesting than he'd anticipated. 'I used to love that band. Audrey was such a dancer, weren't you, Aud? I knew I'd have to get with it to keep her. We used to jive all night, I'd be dead beat by the end of the evening. Barely had enough energy to walk her home.'

He peered down the table at me. 'You weren't the one who used to sing the duets with that Rob chap, the one who had all the bright-coloured suits?'

I could feel a big flush spreading up my neck. 'Very occasionally. I just used to help out if someone had a bad throat. Or a bit too much to drink. But Grace is the singer in the family now – she's done some great shows.'

But Ron had obviously written off Grace as Louise's odd sister, devoid of talent and unworthy of a minute's attention. He was like a dog who'd discovered a long-buried bone and was determined to hang onto it at all costs. 'Did you used to have a sort of Cilla Black hairstyle?' His hand indicated how short my hair had been. 'We all thought you were better than her.' He started to hum 'The Last Waltz' that we used to sing as our closing number.

And despite not wanting to remember, I couldn't help myself joining in for a bar or two, the feel of the notes so familiar in my throat, turning back the clock thirty years with a simple lyric about love. The sheer energy that came from performing, the freedom to sing myself to surfing in California, to a Saturday night at the movies, to sitting on the dock of the bay. To be anyone other than me. I stopped abruptly, aware that a couple of heads were craning to see where the noise was coming from. This was Louise and Craig's day.

Nothing good ever came from talking about the past.

'What happened to The Shakers? Weren't they on the cusp of getting a record deal?'

I stared down at my hand-dived scallops, as though looking for the answer in the pea puree.

Danny nudged me. 'Susie, The Shakers? Do you know what happened about their record deal?'

I swallowed, my throat constricted as though I had a walnut stuck in the top of my windpipe. 'God knows.' I knew I sounded rude, that Danny was disappointed – again – at my inability to rise to the occasion.

Luckily, Grace chose that moment to decide she needed a helping hand with Michael. 'Mum, Michael was just telling me that he wants to audition for a West End musical next year and was wondering what sort of song might give him the best chance?'

The fact that she called me Mum, instead of Susie, was a measure of her desperation.

He turned to me to explain his strategy for success. 'You need three things: talent, stage presence and charisma.'

Behind him, Grace was doing a barely perceptible mime of what he might look like on stage, front teeth clamped to his bottom lip with eyes half closed in earnest sincerity. I had to suppress a smile, the stress of Ron poking his nose into my own singing days starting to recede. I wondered how Michael's parents had instilled such confidence into him, when the only thing I could imagine happening in his audition would be a unanimous 'Next!' from the panel before he'd even sung a note. Thankfully, we were saved from a debate about whether a song from *Les Misérables* or *Evita* would be more of a guarantee of success because the best man called for silence.

Craig made a speech peppered with intellectual in-jokes about how he knew Louise was the one for him when he'd seen her talking to herself and tutting over an article about education in the *Guardian*. Craig looked up, as though he was judging whether the audience could cope with his wit. 'When I saw how passionate she was about education, I couldn't help thinking that all that passion might bode well for elsewhere in our lives. And I was not wrong.' He did a 'nudge-nudge wink-wink' face in case we were too dense to understand his meaning.

There was a collective grimace around the room, the astonishment that this man who said, 'That'll do, that'll do,' if anyone ever dared mention anything as risqué as passing wind, chose his wedding day speech to allude to their wonderful sex life.

From the back, one of their teacher friends who'd obviously been swigging back plenty of the organic wine from a specific area of mountain in Alsace, yelled, 'Shall we all go and leave you to it?'

Louise looked mortified, as though separate bedrooms might be more likely than a night of marital passion. I daren't look at Grace, who had only weaned herself off calling him 'Cretinous Craig' since they'd got engaged. As I kept pointing out to her, it didn't matter what we thought of him as long as he made her happy. And it seemed he'd mastered turning up at the specified slots on Louise's rigid timetables, remembering to put the Sellotape back in its place the second he'd finished with it – something that Danny had never grasped and whose life regularly hung in the balance because of it – and knew not only what a washing machine was for but made Danny mutter about 'putting women out of work'.

I wondered if your mother liked your wife if you had one. Whether she felt like she was losing a son, not gaining a daughter. But I had no time to ponder imaginary family dynamics because Danny was standing up, unfurling a piece of paper he'd never let me read, to say a few words. Next to Ron, I knew he was conscious of his West Country accent, the rose with 'Susie' on the stem tattooed on the inside of his wrist, a twenty-seventh birthday present from his navy mates one drunken Singapore shore leave. I saw his chest fill with pride as he paid tribute to Louise, her hard work, her determination, her sense of right and wrong. 'I hope she'll bring all these qualities to her marriage.'

After we'd toasted Louise, he put his hand up for silence. 'One last thing before I do you all a favour and sit down. If Louise has made a success of her life, been determined to get to university, educate herself and do brilliantly in her career, I have to acknowledge the role my lovely wife, Susie, played in that.' And then he choked on his words. 'If Louise and Craig share the same love and happiness, the same respect and honesty we've managed for more than thirty years, they won't be doing badly at all.'

As the words left his mouth, the corkscrew of deceit hollowed out another layer in our relationship. Sometimes the betrayal felt so untenable, so unwieldy, I almost wanted to shout it out and face the consequences. If anyone would understand human capacity for poor judgement, Danny with his kind heart and 'It's easy to kick a man when he's down – much better to give him a hand up' mantra would. But he loved me, all of us, so much, the only way I could possibly atone for it was to keep it to myself.

And just as I was arranging my face to be the adored wife, the receiver of compliments, the mother of a charming bride, Grace scraped her chair back, clapped her hand over her mouth and threw up over Michael.

CHAPTER TWENTY-NINE

July 1997

Grace yelled an apology and ran out. Danny was first to his feet, grabbing Michael by the arm, cupping a napkin under the second-hand scallops and whisking him out of the room. I stood up, risking a glance down the top table to see whether there was any tiny hint of kindness or forgiveness. Louise, Craig and his fridge-freezer parents had the same look Olympic team coaches have when someone they've trained for ten years fluffs a forward roll in the battle for gold. Michael's mum fished out a lacy handkerchief from her bag. I almost laughed at the absurdity of it. Even Audrey apparently clocked that her little monogrammed offering would be like trying to put out a bonfire by spitting on it. Eventually I couldn't stand the accusatory lip-pursing any more and mumbled something about 'Going to see how they were getting on.'

As I shot out of the room, the embarrassed silence was giving way to the buzzy chatter that follows a spectacle, where people are trying to look concerned but are dying to kill themselves laughing at the hideousness of it all.

Bloody Grace. She would have to pick Louise's wedding day to drink herself senseless, though I'd actually thought she was being very restrained. Louise would be celebrating her silver wedding anniversary before she saw the funny side.

I heard Danny in the gents' helping Michael strip off his suit. 'Just hold that arm horizontal so it doesn't all splatter on the floor.

I've got a T-shirt in the boot of the car. Not quite wedding gear but at least you won't be wearing chocolate truffles.' God bless that man. Nothing about Michael's voice suggested he'd put on a brave face to not ruin the day. Mum would have called him a wuss. Though the stink of vomit wasn't going to add to his paper-thin charisma for sure.

I found Grace in the loo hanging over the sink. 'I'm sorry for spoiling Louise's day.'

As always, I couldn't quite bring myself to do the catastrophe combover that Danny would manage with a 'Never mind, it's not the end of the world'. Instead I said, 'Didn't you realise you'd had too much to drink?'

'I'm not drunk! I've barely had a sip of Prosecco.' Grace glanced into the mirror. 'Where's Dad?'

'Next door mopping down Michael. Why?'

And as always, I had the sensation of sitting on the outside, no one trusting or liking me enough to be the first port of call.

Grace tried to look me in the eye, but faltered and chose a spot on the loo door to stare at. She was jutting her chin out in an attempt at defiance, but if her words had been written in a cartoon, the lettering would have been all shaky. 'I'd been feeling a bit queasy, not too bad, but I got a little bit of skin from the coffee stuck on my lip and it just tipped me over the edge.'

I almost saw Grace count to three, eyes to the ceiling, teeth biting her bottom lip, then release: 'I'm pregnant.' The sentence thudded out, lumpen and wrong, with none of the lightness of possibility that those words should bring.

I blurted out the first thought that came into my head. 'I didn't even know you had a boyfriend.'

Then she did look at me. As though I'd asked her who she was 'courting'.

'Have you never heard me talk about Ollie? I don't think you ever listen to me. I've been with him for nearly a year.'

I racked my brains. 'Perhaps you told Dad? What does this Ollie think about it?'

Her face crumpled. 'It's such a cliché, isn't it? "Children aren't really my thing."' She wiped her eyes. 'He doesn't want to know.'

The gents' door banged and I heard Danny shout to Michael that he was just popping out to the car. I wanted to fly out there, hook him in and say, 'Never mind about Sicky Stan in there, just come and hear what Grace has got to say.'

But before I could marshal any thoughts at all, Grace said, 'I'll have to have an abortion.'

And then I had the right reaction. One lost baby in our family was enough. I hugged her. And she let me, her hot tears soaking my shoulder. I couldn't remember the last time I'd had any physical contact with her beyond a peck on the cheek. Her curvy warmth reminded me of how she'd clamber onto me when she was little, 'Cuddlies, Mummy', swiping the knitting off my knee and demanding affection, taking my chin between her little forefinger and thumb and swivelling me round to look at her. She'd always required a hundred per cent attention. And when she'd realised that I couldn't give enough – because a whole chunk of my heart was elsewhere – she'd backed off, protecting herself instead against my push-pull parenting. I couldn't seem to help it, despite hearing my words and *knowing* they were guaranteed to cause confusion. One minute I'd sit there stroking her hair, saying, 'I'm so proud of you. You're going to do so well in life, you clever thing.' The next I'd be shouting, 'What do you mean you forgot to say thank you to Ellen's mother? Now she'll be telling all her friends how rude my daughter is!'

But today, I simply said, 'You won't have to do anything you don't want to, Gracie. Getting rid of a baby is such a big decision. Let's talk it over with Dad.'

Emotions scudded across Grace's face – distrust and disbelief finally settling into relief, a chink of hope lifting her eyes off the ground and dropping her shoulders from around her ears.

But whether that was because she thought I'd help her sort out an abortion or encourage her to have the baby, I didn't know.

PART TWO

GRACE

CHAPTER THIRTY
January 1998

Out of the ward of six women, I was the only one who'd given birth without a partner there. Mum had said, 'I'm happy to stay with you' but in the sort of way people say, 'I'm happy to get the bus' when it's obvious they'd much rather you drove to pick them up. Plus she kept making noises about 'letting Ollie know' and that absolutely wasn't going to happen. Mum had been so weird about the whole pregnancy thing anyway. I kept waiting for her to rage about what an idiot I'd been, carry out a forensic investigation into exactly *how* in this day and age I'd managed to get pregnant. But apart from some rants about men not shouldering their responsibilities, happy to have 'intercourse' but unable to deal with the 'outcome', she'd been surprisingly uncritical. That was the thing with Mum, she was so bloody unpredictable. She'd had more of a shit-fit about me rolling a couple of Rizlas in the back garden than the up-the-duffness of me having a baby. I kept expecting her to give me a lecture on being reliable, along the lines of 'a baby's not just for Christmas'. But to give her her due, she'd never told me to get rid of it, even when it was clear I wouldn't be tripping down the aisle with the father.

When I'd been overwhelmed, trying to work out how I could carry on with my singing jobs and bring up a child and told her I didn't think I could go through with the pregnancy, she'd got really upset. 'Don't get rid of your baby. There'll be a way through it. It'll be the making of you, Gracie, you'll be a great mum. Dad and I will help out.' And then she'd nudged me and said, 'Anyway, you can't deprive me of being a grandmother. Grandma Susie. I like the sound of that.'

It was the most faith she'd ever shown in me. I wasn't sure what she was basing the 'great mum' on, since not so long ago she was telling me I needed to grow up, get a proper job and start thinking about saving up for my own place – 'You don't want to have a kitty for milk and bread when you're thirty-five.' But there must have been something in her words that tapped into my own self-belief, because I stopped wavering and started planning, not a word that had ever entered my vocabulary before.

And Dad, once he'd been forced to face up to my pregnancy not resulting from an immaculate conception, seemed quite excited. He'd bought a Scalextric after I had my twenty-week scan and assembled it in my old bedroom. And Mum, who was a great one for sucking every last bit of joy out of anything he enjoyed – 'Wasting all that time feeding the stupid tomato plants and we end up with about four tiddling things' – never batted an eyelid, just laughed. 'The cars will be worn out by the time the baby's old enough to play with it.'

But I didn't trust Mum not to have a big fat opinion on how I should give birth. She'd started to get a bit 'Gracie, I'm not sure that's a good idea' when I said I wanted a water birth. She trotted out her line of how she'd given birth to both of us with barely a suck of gas and air. She was never ill – or at least never had a day in bed – even when she looked half-dead. Dad, for all his tough old seadog talk, had made more fuss over an ingrowing toenail than Mum ever had when she had proper flu.

I didn't want to be thinking about Mum when I had my baby. Whether I was being brave enough. Whether I was making too much noise. I could just imagine her patting my arm and saying, 'Now that's enough, Gracie. We don't want you waking all the babies that have just got to sleep,' and turning to the midwife for approval that she was thoughtful and had brought up her daughter to be as well.

No. I wanted to focus on my baby, not on whether I was doing childbirth right. So I chose to be entirely alone, with music on my CD player to sing me through. In the event, Jude had sailed out, seven hours from start to finish, finally arriving to Simon & Garfunkel's 'Bridge Over Troubled Water'. When the midwife handed him to me and put him to my breast to suckle, I thought of Mum's words. 'A baby is so precious. You'll never know love like it.' It was rare for me to think a single word my mother uttered was worth the effort of expelling breath but, god, she was right about that. Aged twenty now, I knew that even if I lived to a hundred, I'd never wake up again without my first thought being whether Jude was safe.

Visiting time couldn't come soon enough. I couldn't wait to see how proud Mum and Dad would be. That their ne'er-do-well daughter had done something good, the daughter that everyone only dared ask after once they'd heard how well Louise was doing, in the frame to be the next headmistress, clutching her clipboards and stapling spreadsheets. I was the daughter who gave everyone a little catch in their voice when they asked after me, the question they weren't sure they should even articulate, 'And how's Grace?'

But apart from the obvious lack of a ring on my finger, I'd done something that Louise hadn't – yet, at least. I'd produced the next generation of the Duarte family – and owing to the absence of a father in the picture, I'd be keeping our unusual surname alive into the next generation.

I couldn't take my eyes off him. His little chest rising in the red and green stripy sleepsuit, his arms flung out to the side as though he had no need to protect himself because he knew I was watching every breath. Before, when anyone I'd worked with had brought a baby in for us to admire and coo over, I'd always wondered why they couldn't see that people were saying, 'Isn't he gorgeous?'

to be polite. Most of the time everyone gave far more of a hoot about who was doing the coffee run than they did about whether a five-week-old could sleep for four hours straight or empty an 8oz bottle in minutes. And, to my shame, I'd always dismissed women who popped a boob out for a feed at any opportunity as a bit weird: 'Most women do a right old rope trick to stop anyone seeing a flash of nipple in a communal changing room but once they have a baby, it's bap central for all to see.' But finally I got it. I only had one person in my viewfinder now, blocking out the panorama of everything else, and frankly, if he needed feeding, I could imagine flinging off my top wherever I was.

When the ward doors opened, there was a flurry of husbands, flowers and chocolates. And Dad. Dad, who never pushed in front of anyone, practically treading on their heels in an effort to get to me. Mum trailed in behind, letting everyone rush past her. Dad threw his arms around me. 'Love, love, love you! Congratulations! Let's have a look at the little man.'

While Dad bent over Jude in the cot, oohing and aahing, Mum stood back, not even glancing over to him. She managed a 'Hello, love. How are you feeling? Are you sore?'

I felt all the adrenaline, all the excitement drain out of me. 'I'm fine. Tired but fine.'

Mum looked as though she'd have found an evening at bingo more thrilling than meeting her first grandchild. Dad, on the other hand, was bouncing about, turning to Mum and saying, 'Look, Susie, he's the spitting image of our Gracie when she was born. She had that perfect little bow of a mouth. Do you remember?'

Still Mum stayed at the bottom of my bed.

Jude opened his eyes and started to cry. I picked him up, making a big show of supporting his head so I'd be spared a big intake of breath from Mum. I pressed him to me for a moment, almost unwilling to hand him over, to acknowledge that there would be other people in his life who might not be as besotted as I was.

Dad reached for him, then drew back. 'Do you want the first hold, Susie?'

Mum shook her head so hard, I felt insulted on Jude's behalf. I wanted to snatch him away.

But Dad smiled at me. 'Your mum was telling me in the car she hasn't picked up a baby since you were tiny and she thinks she's lost the knack. I told her it's like riding a bike. She never put you down when you were little, cuddled you half to death.' He put his hands out. 'Come here, my little one.' Dad kissed Jude's head so gently, I felt my eyes fill.

He held him in the crook of his arm, stroking the dark strands of hair on his head, whispering about all the things they'd do together. 'You're going to love coming to football. Hopefully Portsmouth will be doing a bit better by the time you're old enough. And I've got a lovely Ferrari for you, Scalextric that is.' I hoped my son would grow into a man like Dad. I didn't want a genius who could do algebra as a toddler or get a grade eight on the violin before he went to school. I wanted my son to be kind without being a walkover, to be reliable without being a fusspot and to have joy in his heart that he wasn't afraid to share. I smiled as I heard Dad saying, 'There are far more good people in the world than bad ones, but you won't have to worry about the horrible ones because we'll protect you.'

Mum was stealing little glances. What was her bloody problem? She was the one who was absolutely adamant I shouldn't have an abortion and had practically gnawed through Dad's neck when he mentioned adoption.

'Adoption? Nobody gives their baby away these days. It's barbaric. I'll adopt it myself before I'd let that happen in our family.'

And now here she was looking like Jude would bring her out in boils if she so much as stood next to him. Dad turned to her. 'He's gorgeous. Here, Susie, give your grandson a cuddle.'

She made a big fuss about sitting down: 'I don't want to drop him', with Dad laughing and telling her she wasn't so old and doddery yet. She put her arms out for him and held him in front of her for a moment as though inspecting him for signs of disease.

Dad was like one of the bands I'd often sung in, charged with the unhappy task of animating the crowd for the main event. He kept up a running commentary. 'Just like our Gracie, though his eyebrows are darker. He's got your face shape, Susie. I wonder if his eyes will stay blue.'

Mum cradled him awkwardly for a few seconds, her head looming over him. I wasn't a bit surprised when he started crying. Mum thrust him back towards me.

'I think he's hungry. We'd best go and leave you in peace. You'll need to rest anyway, you must be exhausted.'

I'd felt exhilarated until Mum had arrived. Now I was looking at the other women with envy. They all had someone to share their joy with, someone who would find every freckle, every tiny little fingernail, a source of fascination. Dad had done a pretty good job, but the idea that I might flip a breast out for a feed there and then had him jingling the car keys and muttering about making a move before the traffic got too bad. At three-thirty in the afternoon.

I hoped Jude would never have this thought: I wish I had a different mother.

CHAPTER THIRTY-ONE
June 1998

Much to Louise's disgust, Dad insisted on giving me money towards the rent for a one-bedroomed flat of my own. He winked at me. 'You'd be welcome to move back home, love, but I thought you might be happier in your own place.' I didn't want to take his money but my options were limited. Mum didn't seem as enthusiastic about the reality of being a grandma as I'd hoped. The house I'd moved to after I'd left my last job at the hotel didn't really lend itself to sterilising bottles, when it was already a triumph to get in a shower that wasn't blocked with someone else's hair.

I overheard Louise telling Mum that she and Craig had done a spreadsheet of their earnings and worked out how much they'd need to have in the bank to enable her to take a year's maternity leave. 'But Grace is so irresponsible; you and Dad are having to bankroll her, just when you should be looking forward to retirement. So she gets to have a baby without any of the sacrifices, while we're being sensible and having to wait.'

Surprisingly, Mum gave her both barrels for me. 'Just so you know, what Dad and I choose to do with our money is up to us. And if one of my daughters needs a helping hand, so be it. I'm not having my grandson crawling around on a floor where he might come across god knows what. I'd never forgive myself if anything happened to him.'

Louise was right though. Even though I hated her for pointing it out, I had been completely cavalier and had to run to Mum and Dad to rescue me. When I hugged Jude's little body to me, I found it hard to believe I'd ever been that woman who'd partied in clubs knocking back tequila shots, before – more often than not – having sex with someone just as directionless and lost as me. I didn't even want to think about the debacle with Jude's dad. Those days were over. For a start, I couldn't ever imagine being able to keep my eyes open after nine o'clock in the evening. And as for rolling in at 2 a.m., fishing a greasy plate out of cold washing-up water and eating toast swilled down with cheap vodka, definitely not. I'd show them all that Louise wasn't the only one whose loo you could visit without feeling the need to bleach the seat first.

Of course, within weeks, Mum's spirited defence of me morphed into 'helpful suggestions' that I should give up singing and start looking for a more child-friendly job. But the reality was I couldn't afford childcare during the day, and given that I barely had an O level to my name, I could earn more singing for four hours, than in any menial job for eight hours.

Dad backed me up. 'Susie, it's far easier for Grace to leave Jude here to sleep for the evening and pick him up later.' Dad was so straightforward. I never had to second-guess what his agenda was because there wasn't one beyond keeping his family safe and happy. With Mum, she'd been against my singing career right from the word go, so I couldn't work out whether she genuinely believed it would be better for Jude if I did something else, or whether this was her classic back-door strategy to impose her will.

Every time I turned up, Dad would whisk Jude off. 'Look, I carved this little train for you.' 'Here, have this spoon and give that tray a good bash. That's the way.'

Mum did all the back-end stuff of nappy changing and burping, but there was something restrained about her, as though she was going through the motions rather than relishing the time to bond with her grandson. If I ever had five minutes without my thought pattern being derailed by Jude's every whim, I'd have to give some serious consideration to why, when Mum was doing me such a huge favour, I felt on a knife-edge of resentment, so close to telling her, 'I'll bloody sort myself out if it's such a massive effort'. Louise would whip out her favourite theory: that siblings who are significantly younger than the other children in the family are treated as babies and never fully separate from the parents even in later life. I subscribed more to the idea that Mum's generosity of spirit was about the same size as a raisin, unlike Dad's, which would fill a field. Or maybe Louise was right: I was just an entitled brat who hadn't grasped what being a grown-up entailed. But until I got more than three consecutive hours of sleep and could stitch together a couple of rational thoughts in a row, I'd just have to bugger on and attempt not to blow up.

But on this particular Friday night, Dad had gone out to his monthly meeting with his old navy mates at the snooker hall. An exploding nappy had delayed me and I was behind schedule, so I practically thrust Jude at Mum before racing upstairs to finish my stage make-up. My stress at having to rush had obviously transmitted itself to Jude and I heard him wailing in the lounge. I couldn't afford to turn up even five minutes late, so with every bit of me yearning to sit and soothe him, I carried on with my liquid eyeliner, steeling myself to block out the noise. But suddenly it all went quiet. I resisted the urge to race downstairs and check Jude was okay. I finished backcombing my hair and crept back down in case Jude had dropped off to sleep. I peered through the crack in the lounge door to see Mum sitting on the settee with Jude lying in her arms. She was smoothing his eyebrows and smiling down at him. He was waving his little fists, his eyes following hers. Her face had taken on a softness I didn't often see, except occasionally when Dad would wolf-whistle her when she came downstairs when they were going out. She'd tell him off for his 'old flannel', but all her hard edges would melt away. Even though the minutes were ticking past, I stayed where I was.

'You're just like him, you know. The spitting image.'

She must be talking about Dad. I hadn't really noticed much of a resemblance. We didn't have any other men in our family. Unless she meant grandma's brother, Fred, who'd died in the war. But Mum wouldn't ever have met him. It was amazing how a baby could never be a unique addition to the world but had to be a little collage of everyone else, a photofit of eyebrows, nose and mouth. If he turned out to be clever, I'd never hear the end of how he was 'just like his Aunt Louise'.

Then the grandfather clock chimed quarter to seven. I had to go.

I popped my head round the door and she started, as though I'd caught her up to no good. She snatched up Jude. 'I'll put him to bed now.'

'He can stay up for a bit if you want some company. He loves being here.'

'I can't drop everything just because you've got to go out to work, Grace. I've still got plenty of my own chores to do. And anyway, someone needs to get this baby into some sort of a routine, otherwise when he's a toddler, he'll be up till all hours and then where will we be?'

I think it was fair to say she'd finally given up on all that 'It will be great to have a grandchild to spoil, Dad and I will love helping you out' bollocks she was peddling when she was afraid I might have an abortion.

I forced out a 'See you later, thank you,' instead of the 'Could you just explain why you tried to get pregnant with me for all those years?' that sprung to my lips.

I was never going to be like my mother. Ever.

CHAPTER THIRTY-TWO

February 2008

For a ten-year-old boy, Jude was as easy-going as they came. And for a kid who had a funny old family, he took them all at face value, never seeming to notice Mum's glass half-empty approach to life, or Louise's need to impart the corrective information that one 'dice' was actually a 'die'. Any time I mentioned we had a family occasion, his face would brighten, making me feel guilty for not providing anyone other than me at home. And today was Baby Matilda's first birthday which had been delivered with a set of instructions for strict arrival and departure times – 'Two-thirty, please, so she can still have a nap, and ending at five-thirty, so we have time to settle her before bedtime'. It wasn't an event I imagined would bring great joy to someone whose main passion was guns and guts, in whatever technological form they came. But Jude was thrilled. 'Will Granddad be there?'

I nodded. Dad had converted my old bedroom into a room for Jude now so he had all his things there to stay overnight if I was out singing. Jude was always coming back with stories about how Dad had taught him chess, showed him how to fix his bike and – a source of great pride – to build a fire 'without using firelighters'.

When we arrived at the birthday party, Louise didn't quite embrace me, more hovered her arms around me at a two-centimetre distance as though there was only so much actual touching she could tolerate. But she was the complete opposite with Jude. She gave him a big hug, saying, 'Go and look in the kitchen. I've made some lovely brownies.' I hoped that she hadn't made some unsweetened adzuki bean horror. She claimed all these weirdy ingredients were 'better for our teeth' – but in my view, that was only because we wouldn't be eating them. Craig stood at the door. Matilda was in his arms, a bundle of pink satin, a little band of rosebuds around her head, smiling with her one tooth. She wriggled towards me – it was a bit odd to be flattered by the favouritism of a one-year-old but she always made a beeline for me.

'Come here, my little one, come to your Auntie Gracie.' And I was rewarded by a little squeal of delight as I swooped her up into the air.

The lounge was festooned with balloons and streamers, a pile of presents stacked on the side. Normally, I would have had a little rant to myself. 'For god's sake, what a waste of money on a one-year-old who doesn't even know it's her birthday.'

But I knew how long it had taken Louise to conceive. Every time I saw her with Jude before she got pregnant, her face would flicker between genuine enjoyment at teaching him things and fear that motherhood might never happen for her. But she'd still been generous enough to remember Jude's birthday, send fabulous Lego sets, treat him to tickets to Chessington, Thorpe Park and the London Eye. And her suspicion – quite an accurate one – that I'd never bother to take him to a single museum, meant she'd also relieved me of the job of trailing round dinosaur exhibits, or admiring Formula One cars and astronaut paraphernalia. Her interest in Jude had brought me closer to her than all those years living under the same roof. And now, for the first time ever, I knew more about something than she did.

I knew about motherhood.

The one thing I'd come to terms with very early on was that babies were irrational creatures and I was less likely to go mad myself if I accepted Jude's desire to play might sometimes coincide with my desire to sleep. I had the advantage of years of unsociable hours and being awake when the whole world was asleep. But Louise, with her ten-thirty bedtime, her 'up and at 'em' attitude to early mornings, sobbed in despair. 'I just don't know what I'm doing wrong. She wakes up at 4 a.m. and drops off again when it's time to get up.' After two months of snatching sleep, with conflicting advice from Audrey, Mum and every other expert on babies, Louise sat defeated on the settee, tears pouring out of her, about how much she'd wanted this baby and how every day was an ordeal because she was so tired. Everything about her was ragged. 'And I'm beginning to hate Craig because he has to travel for work and he gets away from it, sleeps in a hotel, has time to finish a cup of coffee while it's hot. People make *toast* for him. Sometimes he can sleep till eight o'clock.' The desolation and envy in her voice nearly made me giggle.

For the first time, I was able to see Louise for who she was. Yes, she was a bit prissy, fell apart if a shoe got left in the hallway rather than lined up in a pair with a bloody shoe tree wedged in it, but in the end, she just wanted to do the right thing, to make everyone happy, sort things out, rather than bumble along haphazardly as I did, waiting for the most urgent or disastrous thing to come to the top. She didn't know how to shoehorn Tilly into the tidy structure of her life. And, of course, her brain, starved of sleep for weeks on end, could no longer see this period as a temporary phase that would pass soon enough, but as a life sentence with no hope of reprieve. I had shooed her off to bed and stayed for two nights, feeding Tilly Louise's expressed milk – 'Yes, don't worry, I'll follow the date order, now go' – while Louise slept. And slept. And finally emerged with a face that wasn't weighed down with despair and responsibility.

Allowing me sole charge of her baby was the greatest accolade Louise could have paid me, an indication that her view of me as a feckless twit who couldn't be trusted to switch the iron off properly had changed. I wasn't naïve enough to imagine we'd suddenly start planning holidays together – 'I was rather thinking we might go to Volterra to see those fourteenth-century frescoes' – when I could just about run to a week in a caravan in Bournemouth. But after so many years of feeling as though I'd burst into the cosy triangle that existed between her, Mum and Dad and never quite found a corner for myself, I started to feel I had a place in the family.

I loved Tilly nearly enough not to notice how Mum couldn't wait to pick her up, even when she was a tiny baby. 'Where's my precious little girlie?' How she'd always rushed in to scoop her out of the cot. How she was so much more at ease with her than she'd ever been around Jude. I tried not to mind.

But it was impossible not to.

CHAPTER THIRTY-THREE

March 2014

All I could think about as I carried the three drinks towards the intensive care unit was that Mum would have taken one look at the tea and pronounced it 'too weak to crawl out of the cup'. It was almost as though my mind was snagging on trivia, to avoid confronting the bigger picture that Mum had severe sepsis and the doctors we'd seen so far were distinctly cautious in their predictions.

Louise was sitting with Dad outside the unit. She jumped up as I approached them, bustling towards me as though she was the only one who could safely be in charge of a tray of hot drinks. 'I'll take that.' I was thirty-six, for god's sake, not twelve, and I had managed to carry a cup of tea without slopping it everywhere several times in my life. I reminded myself not being in control, not having the magic answer, was much harder for Louise, accustomed as she was to 'getting things sorted'. And even though she was irritating, I was glad I didn't have to go into the ward by myself. It wasn't so much Mum – though it was difficult to marry up the force of nature, good and bad, with the woman wired up to tubes and machines – it was Dad who unnerved me. He looked shrunken, suddenly small and old. Frightened. He kept shaking his head and saying, 'I just don't understand how a cut on her leg could have made her so ill.'

If I knew Mum, she wouldn't even have bothered to clean the wound where she'd tripped and caught her leg on some barbed wire. According to Dad, she'd insisted on finishing the walk, dabbing at the cut with some old tissue she'd found in her anorak pocket, wafting him away with 'It's just a scratch'. But Mum was so stubborn, she wouldn't show us the wound until she was keeling over in pain.

A couple of days earlier, Louise had popped in after Dad had mentioned in passing that 'your mother doesn't seem quite right.' She'd forced Mum to show her the swelling spreading up her leg, then realised she could barely lift herself out of the armchair without making a huge effort. Louise had gone straight into headmistress mode. She'd taken her temperature, which was sky-high, and called an ambulance, despite Mum saying she just needed some paracetamol.

And now we were here. In a place where people whispered about blood poisoning and intravenous antibiotics. I even heard one nurse muttering to another about a medically induced coma, 'though we're not there yet', which had made my stomach flip with fear. A coma was serious. Something that she might not come back from. That just couldn't happen, not because of a stupid bit of rusty barbed wire hanging over a path and Mum's misplaced stoicism.

We were only allowed in two at a time, so once we'd finished the drinks, I waved in Dad and Louise, delaying the moment when I'd have to test my own strength. I peered through the mesh of the window at them. Dad was stroking her hand, no doubt talking to her in a gentle voice, infused with love and tenderness. It made me want to rush in and hug the fear out of him. He was the one who always made everything right, who mediated, mollified and managed to make everyone feel that their view was understood, if not upheld.

I stood in the doorway, watching Louise trying to find the right words to help Dad. He suddenly crumpled, clamping a handkerchief over his face and blundering towards the door.

I grabbed hold of him. 'Dad, she's going to be okay.' I helped him to a seat, trying to sound certain and upbeat while choking down my own tears. 'Shall I pop in for a minute while you gather yourself?' He nodded.

I hesitated on the threshold, wanting to bury my head in the sand, to go home and let the 'grown-ups' deal. It was ironic that I'd always railed about being the youngest, that none of them trusted me to take responsibility for anything. If I wasn't careful, I'd prove them all right. I could be better than that. I steeled myself and stepped up to the bed.

'Mum. Can you hear me? It's Grace.' I paused, feeling self-conscious, as though Louise would be judging my pathetic attempts to engage. I felt wooden, unable to speak naturally, to say the things I really wanted to say, while the nurses were scurrying about, wiping, adjusting, monitoring.

I glanced round at Louise for support. She was nodding, 'I'm sure she can hear. I think we should keep talking to her, at least she'll know we're all here.'

'Mum, I just wanted you to know that Jude sends his love. If you don't go home soon, he'll come and see you, but he's working hard for his exams, you know, his GCSEs.' I tried to make a joke – 'Not like me, don't know where he came from, he really wants to do well at school' – but my voice came out all mangled and choked. My mind went blank. I'd never before considered how hard it was to have a one-way conversation with someone who might or might not be able to hear.

I turned to Louise. 'Do you think the nurses would mind if we sang to her? She might like it. She always used to sing when she was in a good mood.'

Louise ran off to ask whether it would disturb the other patients, the headteacher confident and on a level with the medical staff, rather than overawed and reverential like me.

She came back, nodding. 'As long as we keep it really quiet, they're okay with it. What shall we sing?'

I named a few of the songs Jude and I heard on the radio every morning.

Louise frowned. 'I don't know anything in the charts. Matilda isn't really interested in pop music yet.'

I squashed my uncharitable thought that poor old Tilly was probably too busy rushing from one sporting fixture to the next to have time for such frivolities. The child never had five seconds without some activity. Unlike Jude, who'd had to entertain himself growing up, sitting in the wings while I rehearsed various musicals. That was probably why he was such a bookworm, he'd bored himself into reading, then found he loved it. My clever boy. Despite not having Matilda's trips abroad, her enforced listening to Radio bloody Four, her tennis and piano lessons, Jude had an interest in the world beyond Portsmouth that lifted my heart. Plus he was funny and charming and, god knows, those two qualities alone could catapult you a fair distance in life.

I scanned my repertoire of songs Louise was likely to know, thinking through the requests I'd had at a seventy-fifth birthday party recently. But before I could suggest 'It's a Long Way to Tipperary', Louise said, 'How about "Amazing Grace"? Mum loves that.'

That song had become a blessing and curse. It was a relief that Dad wasn't there to chime in with, 'She named you after it, because we'd waited so long for you,' for the nine hundredth and ninety-ninth time.

'Do you know all the words?' I asked.

'Yes, we all learnt it for assembly at school the other week as part of our anti-slavery topic.'

It had to be said, my sister was so worthy, I had visions of her being reincarnated as a wind farm. Or maybe a wormery. A solar panel. She'd fall on the floor in fright if she heard some of the spectacularly un-PC backstage banter at the shows I performed in. Not sure it would meet her guidelines for 'appropriate' interaction.

We stepped closer to the bed. I took my cue from Louise, murmuring the words, conscious of not disturbing the ward.

Amazing grace, how sweet the sound
That saved a wretch like me.

It was almost impossible not to belt it out. Even though I'd sung it a hundred times, the words moved me and made me want to sing in a rousing and robust way. I resisted the temptation to sing over Louise. I had more power, more foghorn ability, but she had more finesse. Her voice was extraordinary with a much bigger range than mine. I remembered a huge hoo-ha when I was little about her not wanting to go to university, because she wanted to take up a place at music school. Mum wasn't having any of it. 'You're far too bright to waste your life messing about in clubs and pubs. It's a lovely hobby, but you need a proper job. Like a teacher.' And that was that. I wondered if she regretted giving in to Mum, if any part of her was envious I'd pursued the career she'd wanted. A few months worrying about bills and whether the car would pass its MOT would soon cure her of that.

We'd only got as far as '*The hour I first believed*' when Mum opened her eyes, funny guttural noises coming from her throat as though she couldn't get enough air in her lungs. The nurse glanced over and we stopped singing. Louise didn't hesitate to take Mum's hand. I was ashamed to admit I found touching her difficult. Her cold, dry skin with those age-thickened nails. Once I outgrew bedtime stories, she stopped kissing me good night. I didn't know whether it was deliberate, but we got out of the habit of hugging each other as I got older, as though cuddles had a cut-off point after the age of ten. As adults, we tended towards a bit of a pat on the back or arm, or a wave at a safe distance.

Nothing like how I was with Jude. Even now he was sixteen, we'd still give each other big, generous hugs good night, a proper gesture of 'I have great love for you' transmitted from one heart to the other. Though not if his friends were there, of course.

Mum tugged at Louise's hand. 'Paula.'

Louise stroked the hair back from Mum's face. 'Shush. It's Louise here. You need to rest.'

Mum's eyes flew open, all scary glassy. If I ever gave up singing, I was never going to make a nurse. I'd be seeing those eyes rolling around all wild every time I tried to sleep.

I leaned in. 'What's she saying?'

Mum was repeating, 'Paula.'

Louise was frowning.

'Who's Paula?'

Mum's lips were twitching as though she was still formulating a thought, dragging a thread of lucidity from somewhere, one that required incubating before it could be born into the world. She made a groaning noise, as though she wanted to shout but didn't have the strength.

While I stood, rooted to the spot, unable to move forward to comfort Mum, Louise jumped up and grabbed hold of her arms. 'Mum! Susie! It's okay, you're all right. I'm here. It's me, Louise. You're in hospital, you're quite safe.'

I sensed the effort it cost her, but Mum lifted her head slightly and opened her eyes. 'Danny?'

I found my voice. 'He's just outside. Do you want me to get him for you?'

'Danny mustn't know.'

'Know what, Mum?' I asked, putting my ear right by her mouth, straining to catch her rasp of words.

Then we both heard her, clear as anything. 'I'm Paula.'

My sister's face clouded. She looked at Mum, studying her intently for a moment. Then Louise's expression cleared as though she was privy to something the rest of us were not.

But before I could ask her any more, one of the machines she was hooked up to started to beep, and a nurse flew over in a whirl of efficiency. 'You need to let her rest now.'

I was embarrassed at how welcome the suggestion that we came back in the morning sounded.

CHAPTER THIRTY-FOUR
March 2014

I hated the fact there was no contest as to who Dad would go home with. In the hasty conversation Louise and I had while Dad popped to the loo, we both agreed he couldn't go home on his own. But a bedroom with fat quilted eiderdowns and an en-suite beckoned at Louise's, rather than a sofa bed squashed in next to Jude's drum kit at mine. Despite looking down on Louise and her husband as 'wage slaves', claiming moral superiority as a 'creative', I was pretty envious of the ease that having money created. Not because I'd rush out and buy fifty Rolexes but because it meant we'd have a bit of space and I could keep the heating on permanently so Dad didn't have to sit there all stoic, saying, 'I'm fine, love. I've got another jumper if I get cold.' I'd be able to take some time off, instead of worrying that there'd be a queue of young hopefuls happy to sing at a wedding or take the lead in a show for half the money if I dropped out.

I scrutinised Louise. 'Any idea what Mum was on about, all that Paula stuff?'

There it was, that funny little flicker of comprehension, of recognition.

For a moment, I thought she was going to be the holder of the knowledge, eke out any information as and when she thought I could handle it. But she frowned, shaking her head. 'I'm not sure. I've got this weird memory of winning the beauty contest at the Silver Jubilee party and Mum's old friend, Jeanie, coming up to her and saying, "It's Paula, isn't it?" Mum got really angry and dragged me away. I spilt orange squash down my dress and started crying. I don't know why, but I had the impression she didn't want Dad to know.'

Nothing new in Mum getting really angry. That didn't move us forward in the proving or disproving stakes. 'Are you sure she called her Paula? Did Mum even know Jeanie then? I thought they met at the park when she'd just had me? Why would Jeanie think Mum was called that? She hasn't got a second name I don't know about, has she?'

Louise shrugged. 'I don't think Mum and Jeanie were friends then. She was just the mother of the other girl who won a prize, you know, the oldest daughter, Sarah. And I'm pretty sure Mum hasn't got a middle name. Just Suzanne. Susie. At least, I can't remember anyone ever mentioning one or seeing it written anywhere.'

It was a bit basic trying to establish at this late stage what our mum's real name was.

I glanced back towards the ward. I did what I always did in times of stress, tried to make a joke of it. 'Maybe she's led a double life. Perhaps she's married to someone else and she's forgotten she's supposed to be Susie when she's with us. Maybe we'll walk straight into her other family when we leave here.'

Louise frowned impatiently. 'She's probably just confused with all the drugs and stuff she's taking. And I'm not certain about the Paula thing.'

Then the conversation ended as Dad came back from the loo. Slow and a little unsteady as though he was feeling the ground for obstacles before planting his foot. How much I'd taken my parents for granted. There were so many things I thought I'd have time to resolve with Mum. Such as why she'd made such a meal out of helping when Jude was little and I was fighting to get myself known on the singing circuit, but Louise only had to say, 'Running late at school' to have Mum waltzing down with a blueberry muffin and carton of orange juice to fetch Matilda. Though, weirdly, whenever I overheard her talking about Jude, she was always, 'You should see Grace's boy, such a handsome lad, all A*s in his mocks, the sciences and English as well. He's a clever one.' Even now, with her lying there so poorly, the old hurts, diamond-sharp, diamond-hard, were still banging into each other like out of control bumper cars.

We walked out to the car park. I took Dad's arm, suddenly conscious of how he no longer felt so solid. I wondered when that had happened, that slow erosion of the man who was the steadfast backdrop to the family, the person who'd sit at the table when Mum was picking fault with something or other and say, 'Come on, Susie, it won't matter in five years' time.' And behind her back, we'd all mouth, 'Or even one week.'

I hugged him goodbye, breathing in the very essence of him. The scent of a hundred bedtime stories, late-night cups of tea when I got back from a gig, the solidity of a man who kickstarted my boiler, fixed my ancient fuse box, filled up my windscreen washers with water. The smell of love.

He waited until my rust box of a car started, then hopped in with Louise. 'See you tomorrow, love. Drive safely.'

I started towards home, Mum's nonsensical words rattling round my mind.

Over the next few days, we moved up and down the greasy pole of serious illness – a slight improvement in response to antibiotics counterbalanced by a worsening in the wound on her leg; her temperature stabilising, cancelled out by a concern about her blood pressure… every day there was something new and frightening.

Today, a week after Mum had first been admitted, I was at the hospital before Dad, and Louise, who'd texted to say she had to go into school for a quick staff meeting. I was nervous about going in on my own in case she became agitated again.

As I pressed the buttons in the lift to the ward, I realised I envied my parents. Envied their love story. That sense of fitting, belonging, of absolutes. In a strange, 'you bloody weirdo' sort of way, I even envied Dad's sense of devastation that he might have to live without her. That someone in the world was essential for his survival. I didn't want to be one of these women who couldn't take out the bins or light the boiler without a man in the wings, but at this rate, I'd be lucky if I wasn't found fossilised in my living room with the neighbourhood cats enjoying an unexpected banquet when I died. Especially if Jude married someone who didn't like me. And judging by the relationship I'd forged with my mother, my family hit-rate wasn't that hot.

I didn't know how Dad had stood Mum's moods, yet to hear him speak of her when she was young, she sounded like a carefree livewire. 'I used to get letters on the ship, saying she'd been out dancing, even singing on stage sometimes. I knew if I tried to clip her wings, we'd end up unhappy, that free-spiritedness was the essence of her. That's why we got married so young. Wanted to make sure she was mine before someone else snapped her up. She was, still is, so beautiful.' He'd turned to wink at me. 'I thought of it as an insurance and ended up feeling as though I'd won the pools.'

I wished Dad was with me now. I hesitated when the lift doors opened. Mum's ramblings unnerved me. I didn't really believe in spirits, but it was a bit like sitting round a Ouija board, with a ghostly voice in residence 'I'm Pauuu-laaa'. I could almost hear the reluctance in my steps as I headed along the corridor, a friction on the lino with my feet slowing as I reached the reception area. I waited until a nurse looked up from her notes. 'My mum's in the ICU. Susie Duarte?'

She nodded. 'Just a minute. I'll just get the nurse who was looking after her last night before she finishes her shift. She wanted a word with you.'

'Is there a problem?'

'She's very unsettled. Just hold on there for a minute and I'll see if I can find out a bit more.'

I couldn't believe how cowardly I was. I looked down the corridor, hoping for the sight of Louise tapping along in her opaque tights and court shoes, with her lists of questions. But the only person who appeared was a dainty Chinese nurse, with lovely smooth skin. I wish I looked like that when I'd been up all night.

She smiled and spoke to me in such a gentle voice, I had a sudden urge to cry. 'Morning. I'll take you to your mother in a minute. All last night she kept calling out for Edward. She was getting so distressed. I wondered if you knew who she's talking about? We've done her bloods and we're giving her a more specific antibiotic now. She should be responding better than this. The doctor was wondering whether the upset about this "Edward" was preventing her recovery.'

I felt ridiculously protective towards Dad. I couldn't let him find out that she'd been in love with someone else all her life. I snapped at her. 'I've no idea who Edward is. Could be any random name. She's only really close to one man, my Dad – Danny. And I suppose she spends a bit of time with my sister's husband, Craig.'

I regretted my sharp tone immediately as her neat little eyebrows shot up in surprise. God. The poor woman was only trying to help. Mum always accused me of being snappy, but I thought that was just because my opinion was different from hers. I tried to soften my voice. 'I'll ask my sister when she comes in. Thank you. Thank you very much.'

She nodded and pitter-pattered through to the ward, looking as though she would barely have the strength to lift a bedpan.

Mum seemed to be asleep. I hung back a bit, hoping that the nurse would just check she hadn't died. She pulled the curtain round her bed. 'The doctor gave her a light sedative but it should start to wear off soon.'

I perched on the chair by the bed, watching her chest rise up and down, her face pale. Was this woman really full of secrets, secrets that now, at this late stage, were trying to break loose? I leaned back, sieving, searching through my memories for anything that stood out. The trouble with your own family was that however barking bonkers they were, they eventually seemed normal. Normal for you, that is. It just seemed so unlikely that this woman who'd gone into meltdown if I went to school with dirty shoes, if I sneaked out of school and into town at lunchtime, if I did anything that would 'make her look like a mother who didn't know or care what her daughter was up to' would have been up to no good herself. The biggest accolade in our house was always 'good girl', not 'courageous girl' or 'beautiful girl' or 'clever girl'. Which is probably why she seemed to get on better with Louise.

Mum coughing pulled me back into the present. She opened her eyes. Then she smiled. 'Gracie.'

I held my breath to stop me crying. I wasn't a daughter who cried. Seeing her youngest child dissolve into sobs of 'Please get better' would definitely make Mum think she was on her deathbed. And no one seemed to know whether she was or not.

Her eyes flickered round as though she was checking who else was there.

'Dad and Louise are coming later, Mum. Louise had to go to work for a bit, you know, at the school?' I wasn't sure how much Mum remembered about our world, as opposed to the one populated by Edward and Paula.

Her face relaxed in recognition.

'I'll stay until they get here, then I need to go and rehearse for the weekend show. I'm in *West Side Story* at the local theatre.'

Her fingers twitched. Then she started doing an intense blinking thing with her eyes. A fluttering of panic began to stir in my stomach, but I realised she was trying to get me to come closer.

I leant towards her.

'Sit me up.'

'I don't know whether that's a good idea, Mum.' I looked at the tube up her nose and the drip in her hand. 'Shall I get the nurse?'

'No!'

'Okay. Can you stay lying down? Are you comfortable?' I had visions of all the tubes falling out, bleepers going off and, I don't know, a crash team arriving with trollies and shit.

Mum fluttered her fingers as if to say, 'Forget it.'

And then she whispered, 'Find Edward.'

'Who's Edward, Mum?'

Her eyes closed. 'Don't tell Dad.'

I decided to play along. 'Where do I need to look for Edward?'

'In the attic.'

This felt like something out of Roald Dahl's *Tales of the Unexpected* and just as freaky. 'The attic at your house?'

Mum grunted, her lips moving, but I couldn't make out what she was saying.

'Edward is in the attic at your house?'

'Corner.'

I tried not to think about *Silence of the Lambs* and the scene with the granny rotting in the bath in the basement.

Then her fingers started worrying at the edge of the sheet. 'Danny mustn't know.'

And with that, Dad walked into the ward. I took one look at his old face, braced for bad news and decided to keep 'Edward' to myself. I'd get Louise to come with me. I bloody hoped Edward was a teddy bear or other forgotten toy from our childhood that Mum had a sudden desire to see.

'How is she?' Dad asked, as he looked at Mum sleeping.

'She had a rough night but she's had a sedative so she's okay at the moment.'

My heart ached as he bent over and stroked her hair. 'Happy wedding anniversary, darling.'

'Oh my god, I'd forgotten. Is it the tenth of March today?'

Dad turned to me. 'I can't live without her, Gracie. I just can't.'

I hugged him, trying not to feel how bony his shoulder blades were. 'Don't talk like that, Dad. There's a long way to go but they're not out of ideas yet.'

At least, I hoped they weren't. My parents were the original Noah's Ark pair. I couldn't imagine either of them surviving without the other.

I sneaked a look at my watch. 'Dad, I'm really sorry. I don't want to leave but I've got to go and rehearse now. Will you be all right?'

'Your sister's outside. She just had an urgent call to deal with from school. Said she'd be up in a minute.' Dad sighed. 'I do worry about how much pressure she's under, trying to visit Mum, do her job properly, keep her household ticking over, look after Matilda and everything.'

Now was not the right time to feel irritated by the unspoken assumption that my job was just a question of trotting out a chorus and couple of can-cans that could bend and stretch to any timetable, plug any gap in the family emergency schedule. And of course, Craig could pick up some of the slack for Louise, whereas, in my house, the slack-gatherer was me.

As though Dad read my thoughts, he said, 'I know how hard you work, too, love.' He tried to smile. 'But you've always been a survivor.'

And like the dutiful daughter I was learning to be, I accepted my place in the family pigeonhole.

CHAPTER THIRTY-FIVE
Monday 10 March 2014

I was so bad in rehearsals for my new show that the whole cast was getting fed up with me. Every time I hit my stride, the thought that Mum might not make it crept in, her plaintive repetition of Edward and the whole attic business, knocking me off balance.

Six o'clock couldn't come quickly enough.

I needed to look in the bloody attic and satisfy myself there wasn't some flipping body rotting away up there. We'd have to make up some bullshit so Dad didn't realise what we were up to. I'd tell him a half-truth; that we were looking for Mum's old photo albums to give us something to talk about. At any rate, it would be better than staring out of the hospital windows, making inane comments about how we could 'smell spring in the air today' and how 'the daffodils will soon be poking their noses through'. Hospitals were the suckers of scintillating conversation.

I phoned Louise as soon as I got home. 'Is Dad still with you?'

'No, I dropped him off so Mum could have a rest.'

I filled her in on my exchange with Mum.

'She's just delirious, I think. The nurse said the illness could make her confused.'

I tried my most conciliatory voice, though there was something familiar about Louise's tone, some suggestion that Mum wouldn't have let Very Important Communications loose on her youngest, frivolous daughter.

With a great effort, I managed, 'I feel we should check the attic. She was quite vehement about it, so something is obviously playing on her mind. I thought I might pop round there this evening, so at least I can tell her tomorrow that Edward is no longer hiding up there.'

Judging by the noise in the background, Louise was deciding whether my hunch was worth tearing herself away from Matilda's piano practice for. She sighed. 'I suppose it's a good chance to make sure Dad's had some dinner. He didn't want to come back to stay here tonight, said he'd better get used to sleeping in the house on his own.' I heard her voice catch and my resentment drained away.

We agreed on seven-thirty. I left Jude with a pizza and guilt that he'd be home alone for the evening. Though I had no doubt he relished control of the telly and the opportunity to watch unsuitable things on the iPad.

I arrived at Mum and Dad's at the same time as Louise. She whipped her keys out of her handbag and let herself in, 'Coo-ee, Dad?' I didn't realise she had her own keys. I always used the one under the stone planter by the side gate. Mum probably thought I'd lose it. And to be fair, I did have a bit of a history of leaving my bag in pubs, clubs and cabs. Louise had probably never even dropped a pound coin.

The Chase was booming out in the front room, with Dad shouting out the answers. When I was little, the room seemed huge, but now the space seemed tiny, with its ancient velour settee and the piano still taking up most of one wall. I left it to Louise to peddle the stuff about the photo albums, feeling shoddy and deceitful when Dad nodded gratefully and said, 'Will you be all right on that ladder? I can't come up myself, haven't been able to for years, all that trouble with my ears has done my balance in.'

Realising I'd probably been a little too enthusiastic in my 'No worries at all, Dad, you stay right here in the warm,' I tried to look like I wasn't in a big rush to get up there and stopped to study the mementoes in the glass cabinet on the way out. Shells we'd found on days out at the beach. A Silver Jubilee mug next to a photo of Louise winning the beauty pageant. You'd never know we were sisters. I had Mum's small features and shiny, straight hair, whereas Louise had Dad's curly dark hair and olive, almost Mediterranean skin, a throwback to Danny's great-grandfather, who'd given us the Duarte name. I glanced at the postcards Louise and I had sent from school trips propped up at the back. The Isle of Wight. The Isle of Man. Edinburgh. My gaze fell on a photo of us at the funfair down by the docks. We were all smiling. But that wasn't how I remembered that day. Or at least not the end of it. Dad had just won a stuffed rabbit on the shooting range, when a fortune teller grabbed hold of Mum's hand as she walked past. Mum laughed and said, 'Can you see a future of washing-up, ironing and cleaning?'

The fortune teller frowned at her palm. 'You should share your secret.'

Mum had grabbed me then and marched off, practically pushing the woman out of the way. 'Load of old nonsense. They just guess at anything and hope that you'll give them a clue. Charlatans, all of them.' But, after that, the energy seeped out of the day and Mum stopped coming on the rides with us, watching instead of joining in.

As Louise pulled down the ladder to the loft, she was all brisk. I had no doubt that even fourteen-year-old boys became a lot less lippy when they saw her striding down the corridor. 'Can't be too long because I've barely seen Craig this week.'

I did wonder if they had a little timetable, a quota of hours they had to be in the same room. I wasn't sure I'd ever be able to stand the pressure of having to be somewhere because it was expected of me, because that's what people in relationships did. I'd probably never find out.

As we stepped into the roof space, I said, 'Mum said "he" was in the corner.'

Louise rolled her eyes, her whole face set in 'the sooner I get this nonsense out of the way, the quicker I can get home' stance. She peered into a couple of boxes. 'This one's got some photo albums in it,' she said, pushing it towards the hatch. 'That'll give us something to talk to Mum about anyway.'

Now I was here, my heart was thumping. I was glad of Louise's certainty there was nothing to find but, at the same time, a little bit of me craved a discovery. Something that would explain why, when Mum loved us so much, she never allowed us to get to know her, almost as though we were pressing our palms together on either side of a window, a thin pane of glass between us, mouthing words but having to make a rough guess at the answer.

Louise marched over to the far corner and started riffling through old suitcases, boxes of crockery. 'Do you remember this?' She held up a tall silver figurine, one of the things we hadn't been able to bring ourselves to part with when Nan died.

I nodded. 'Yes. I used to love looking at the necklaces she hung round its neck.' Nan had been so different from Mum. So cuddly and warm. The way I was with Jude. The hugging gene had obviously skipped a generation. I wished Nan had had a chance to meet him.

Louise directed me to the windbreak and deckchairs. I lifted the corner rather gingerly in case a big spider came scuttling out. It was only the not-quite-suppressed sigh from Louise that got me shifting things with a bit of oomph, before she could get all competitive over who'd really put their back into the matter in hand – her – and who'd stood around spectating as usual – me.

I dragged the windbreak out of the way. Christ knows why they kept it. They'd probably last used it in about 1980. Did they even sell windbreaks any more? Underneath that was a cool box. I remembered Dad lugging it down to the beach full of cans of

Coke and Long Life beer. Mum would have been carrying a big wicker basket with creams for every eventuality – sun cream, sand rash, wasp stings, antiseptic – plus sun hats, which I'd refuse to wear and she'd go into a big mardy sulk.

Then I saw it. A big wooden chest. The sort you see in films, when the music goes all der-der-deeerrr and you just know the heroine is going to find something she can't ignore.

'Lou. Look here.'

She came over. 'Never seen this before. Have you?'

I shook my head. There was a bit of me that was backing away from looking inside. I tried to lift the lid. I was embarrassed that my voice came out in a feeble whine. 'It's locked. Do we really want to know Mum's secrets? What if it's something that will hurt Dad?'

Louise shrugged as though I was making a drama out of nothing. 'I'm sure it's nothing very exciting. At the most, I bet we'll find the odd love letter to some bloke she knew before she married Dad.'

I couldn't help wondering whether Louise lacked imagination about what a can of worms could be coiled within because she'd never had an ill-judged moment in her life. Whereas I could offer up a whole range of men I thought I'd loved or I'd fooled myself had loved me. And some of these 'acquaintances' had translated into letters, cards and photos. Not to mention quite a spectrum of behaviours that would merit not only a locked chest but a hefty padlock. Jude's father for one.

I didn't know what I hoped for. Maybe an answer to all the little fragments of odd behaviour, of things that didn't quite add up, of feeling that Mum was going through the motions of loving me, without experiencing that powerful all-encompassing surge of ferociousness I felt whenever anyone so much as teased Jude about a spot. Perhaps a sense of the woman Dad talked about, the vivacious girl five years his junior rather than the discontented person who often gave the impression she didn't really like any of us.

I looked up at Louise. 'Where would she keep the key?'

Louise could never answer, 'I don't know'. If you asked her what the inner core of Saturn was made from or how long a woodpecker's intestines were, she'd make a stab at it. So instead of pulling a face and echoing my thoughts of 'needle in a haystack', she suggested having a look in Mum's jewellery box on her dressing table. Which, to be fair, wasn't a bad plan.

'Won't Dad hear us creeping about in their bedroom?' I asked.

'I doubt it. He's got the telly on so loud.'

'Why don't you go and look for the key and I'll carry on having a poke about up here, see if there's anything else of interest?' The reality was I didn't want to go through Mum's things. I didn't want to touch her necklaces, lift up her bracelets, sift through her rings and wonder whether she'd ever wear them again. Ever sleep in her bedroom again. Ever open her wardrobe on the rare occasion Dad insisted she joined him for a 'do' and dither between eight different blouses. I blinked against the surge of emotion, the wanting, the desire for things to be different. The realisation I might not ever have the chance to *make* things different.

Louise disappeared off down the ladder without comment. She always made me feel as though I had the stability of a dandelion clock. Which I probably did compared to her bulldozer 'nothing to see here' approach.

I inspected the lock on the chest. Quite a chunky key. It could be anywhere. I tried to imagine where someone would hide a key. I lifted the chest up just in case. It obviously hadn't been moved for a while as there was an exact oblong dust mark on the floorboards. No key. I looked around, shaking a pair of wellies to see if anything rattled inside them, searching for a little box tucked away somewhere.

Louise came climbing back up, 'No luck'. She turned the chest round. 'I thought we might be able to unscrew the hinges but they're on the inside.' Louise was so practical. Dad always joked she didn't need a husband, at which point Mum would purse her lips as though one daughter no one wanted to marry was already quite enough to bear.

We both stood for a moment with our hands on our hips. 'Could we pick the lock with something?'

I knelt down to look.

Louise sighed. 'Dad would know how to get it open.'

'I honestly think we should see what's in there before we involve him. He loves her so much, I'd hate to ruin that for him. Especially if she doesn't make it.' I looked at Louise. 'Do you think Mum will die?'

Impatience flashed across her face. 'I don't think there's any point in speculating. I'd say it's fifty-fifty at the moment.' Louise always managed to sound so rational. I bet she'd never gone into Matilda's bedroom when she was little and woken her up checking she was still alive, like I used to with Jude. Or unlocked the windows whenever she'd had an open fire in case a spark or ember suddenly burrowed out of the chimney breast and they all needed to get out in a hurry. Nope. Louise only dealt with certainties. I don't know how she'd escaped Mum's neuroses, which had replicated themselves a hundred-fold in me.

Louise moved towards the hatch. 'Look, I'll come back for the chest when Dad's at the hospital. We can't start trying to sneak it out without him seeing. I'd hate him to think we were making off with Mum's stuff,' she hesitated, 'prematurely.'

All the adrenaline, all the psyching up to unravel – or not – the mystery that was my mother drained away. I felt weighed down as though I'd eaten a pile of greasy meat pies. I sat down on the floor, defeated, resting the back of my head on the chest. And as I looked up, there it was, hanging on a nail, tucked behind a rafter. A chunky key.

CHAPTER THIRTY-SIX

Monday 10 March 2014

As I lifted the lid of the chest, it was as though the past was fluttering out. Louise was impatient. 'I need to get going soon. Craig and I like to be in bed by 10.15 otherwise we're fit for nothing the next day.' I didn't want to get into a 'who'd had the least sleep' contest, but when I did a show, I often didn't get to sleep until 1.30 in the morning but still had to get up to take Jude to school. I kept the thought to myself.

But all of those thoughts disappeared when we saw what was in the chest. A vintage treasure trove of toys. I picked out a Scalextric Lamborghini, a wooden pull-along train, a Dinky tipper truck. 'I don't get it. A chest full of toys?' I couldn't remember Mum ever being interested in cars, and these had never belonged to me or Louise. Mum had never even learnt to drive.

'I told you there wasn't anything to know. God knows why Mum has been hoarding these. Mind you, they're probably worth something now.'

Frustration was surging through me. I couldn't believe that the big mystery was just a giant bloody toy box. I dug deeper, dislodging a Guinness Book of Records 1975 and a 1974 Dr Who Annual with Jon Pertwee on the cover. And then my heart leapt as I saw a pile of cards. 'Edward'. I pulled them out, waving them at Louise. 'Oh my god. Look!'

She snatched them from me as though she couldn't believe I'd been right about something.

I hesitated. 'Shall we open them?' Even though Mum had sort of given us permission to go snooping, it still seemed wrong to start opening cards and letters that weren't addressed to us. But again, Louise was far more pragmatic.

'Well, there's not much point in going to all this trouble without understanding why we're here.' She fanned them out. 'They've got the date written in the corner. The first one's 13 June 1969.' She slid her finger under the flap and the ancient glue offered no resistance, flipping open.

She drew the card out. It had a 'One today!' badge on it. I peered over her shoulder to read my mother's careful italics: *My darling Edward. That's perhaps not even your name now, but you'll always be Edward to me, or perhaps you'll be known as Teddy. I don't know where you are or who you are with but I hope that you can see the North Star at night and somehow feel that I can see what you can. I didn't manage to look after you but that doesn't mean I didn't love you. Happy birthday, my darling. I hope you are happy. Love Mum xx*

I felt like I did when Jude was little and used to come flying out of school and barrel into me, knocking the wind out of me. I'd been geared up for some intimate love letters, distantly braced for some hideous stomach-churning revelation about how much my mother had enjoyed sex with some other man. But not this.

Louise's face was screwed up as though her lightning-fast teacher brain needed an emergency jumpstart. Her voice, when it came, was taut and strained. 'What on earth is she on about?'

'Did *you* know Mum had had another baby before me?' I asked

Louise was almost shouting. 'Don't be so bloody silly! Do you not think I might have mentioned that we had a brother at some point in the last forty years?'

'He must have died. Why didn't they ever say anything about him? I mean, fair enough, Mum's always been a bit secret squirrel, but Dad's quite open.' I kept staring down at the card, as though if I looked for long enough, the words would mean something else.

Louise sat back on her heels. 'Perhaps it was just so traumatic. It sounds as though he died in an accident. Mum obviously felt responsible for it.'

'But why would she say "That's perhaps not even your name now"?'

Louise was pulling out the next card, reading it aloud. '*I hope your new Mum and Dad are looking after you. I often think about you.*' Her eyes flew open. 'Oh my god. He's not dead. They gave him away.'

I shook my head. 'They'd never do that. I overheard Dad telling Jude how much he loved "his girls" – us – but how he was so delighted to have a boy in the family at last. Then he made some joke about how he couldn't bear the thought of the Duarte passion for Portsmouth FC dying out with him. Why would they give a child away and then keep me?'

Louise was scrabbling at the envelopes. 'How could they do that? All that stuff about "Amazing Grace" and how they thought they couldn't have any more kids? If anyone in the street had a baby when I was growing up, Mum would get all tearful and sob to Dad about how she didn't feel complete.' There was real anger in her voice. 'It's just so hypocritical! All those years feeling like I wasn't enough for them, Mum muttering to Dad about how she'd hated being an only child herself and she really wanted me to have a sibling.' Her voice was rising, so much so I thought Dad might hear.

I put my finger to my lips. 'Shhh. They might have had a good reason for it.'

Louise's jaw was set. 'Such as? Why would anyone give a baby away?'

Louise's rage was frightening me. She never lost her temper. She was the mistress of 'We all just need to calm down here.'

'Maybe they couldn't afford another baby at that time?' I said.

In the dim light of the attic, Louise's cheeks were glowing red. 'They had a house they'd inherited from Dad's parents! Dad was in the navy with a regular income. Your boyfriend did a moonlight flit when you got pregnant with Jude. You were living in that dump of a flat, but you didn't go giving him away.'

I concentrated on not taking offence at her damning verdict on my living conditions, as though only people with four-bedroomed houses, an airing cupboard and a husband who'd jammed a ring on your finger should be allowed to have kids.

Then I had a thought that was so off the wall, I had to steel myself to articulate it in front of Louise. 'What if the baby wasn't Dad's? Mum keeps saying he mustn't know.'

'Don't be *ridiculous*! How could Mum have had a baby without Dad knowing?'

'He was away for ages at a time. It might just have been possible.' I pushed my fringe away from my face. 'But if the baby was Dad's as well, why wouldn't Mum want him to know she's looking for him?'

'Because Dad isn't stupid enough to start raking up the past after forty bloody years, disrupting two families. And now she's trying to get us to do her dirty work without telling him.' Louise's head was shaking, tiny little movements of acute disapproval.

I dug deep for my calmest, most rational voice. 'Before we jump to any conclusions, why don't we read the rest of the cards? We might find out one way or the other whose baby it was. Shall I pop down and check Dad is okay first?'

'We could get him up here to save us the trouble of opening the envelopes. Why don't we hear the explanation from the horse's mouth?' I didn't recognise this woman. She'd always been the one protecting Mum and Dad, telling me off for having a go at them.

'Shall we just see what we're in for first? Prepare ourselves a bit? On the off-chance that Dad doesn't know anything about it?'

Louise huffed but held out her hand for the pile of cards I passed her. I gave her 1970–8 and took the later ones, deciding to work backwards. I spread them out, puzzling over the fact that June 1984 and 1985 were missing. I'd start with June 1986. I looked at the 'Eighteen today!' badge, remembering how the whole lead-up to my eighteenth birthday had been a series of rows. Mum shouting. 'If you don't want to follow my rules, you'd better find yourself somewhere else to live!' Mum begging. 'Don't leave, Gracie. Just talk to me. I'm not an ogre. I promise I'll listen.' My bravado battling with my fear as I stomped down the stairs and out to Zed's waiting car. I'd refused to see her for weeks. I'd be so devastated if Jude did that to me, but at the time, I didn't even give it much thought, was just happy to be doing my thing without Mum's opinions. I cringed at my cruelty.

Fortunately, Louise put a stop to the guilt flowing through me by stabbing at a fourth birthday card with her finger. 'Look, here she calls herself "your other mother". Presumably Dad is "your other father". How can they live with themselves? Craig and I would have been on the streets before we'd have given Matilda away.'

Louise wasn't going to unhand the sweeping broom of judgement any time soon. I was burrowing into everything I thought I knew about Mum and Dad. I couldn't imagine my soft old dad lifting a baby off his shoulder, handing it to a stranger and hopping back into his Cortina. I struggled to see Mum doing it to be fair, but there was a hardness in her, a steel that, given the right circumstances, she'd be capable of anything. I turned my attention back to the eighteenth birthday card, feeling as though I was peering through one of those shop windows that had been sprayed white to see what was beyond.

And then the mist started to lift.

Dear Edward, I've never really explained why I couldn't keep you, but now you're an adult, a man, I feel it's time. You must wonder how I could possibly hand you over to someone else. I know I would if I was in your position. I loved you so much but the circumstances were so complicated. This is hard for me to write, but my husband isn't your father. When you were born, he was away at sea for fifteen months. To this day, I've never been able to tell my husband even though he's a good man – and ironically, I know he would have loved you if I hadn't done what I did.

Written down, it all seems so weak, so pathetic. But everything I did once you were born was because of my love for you. I already had a little girl, Louise, (your half-sister) and I knew that if my husband threw me out, I couldn't offer you even a fraction of what your new parents would be able to. I'd be the bad mother the nuns predicted, so I let you go, even though it absolutely broke my heart. Please forgive me. It doesn't help you now but there hasn't been a single day when I haven't thought about you and wished our lives had turned out differently. I hope, I hope so, so much you are happy and that you go on to have a lovely family of your own. Love your other Mum.

PS Make sure you look at the North Star tonight. I look at it before I go to bed on your birthday every year and wish I could see you again. I know that's selfish, but that hasn't changed in eighteen years and I don't think it ever will.

PPS I'm sorry for not writing on your sixteenth and seventeenth birthdays. I thought it was better to let you go and allow everyone to get on with their own lives, without endlessly raking up the past. I don't think I've been very successful.

My throat was tight, constricted against the longing, the sadness radiating from the words in my mother's careful script.

I could see her in my mind's eye, filling her fountain pen with Quink, gently pressing blotting paper onto everything she wrote, endlessly despairing of my scrawled messages, scratched out with a biro.

I swallowed, hesitating before showing it to Louise, pausing before I rolled the dynamite stick into our family history. One word from me and everything we knew would be rearranged into an altogether different picture, as though we'd entertained ourselves by cutting out the heads in family photos and sticking them onto the wrong bodies.

Wow. Mum had had an affair. Mum with her Pledge and her Marigolds, her insistence on watching documentaries on Winston Churchill, wildlife programmes about meerkats, anything that would 'expand your brain, your horizons', had shagged someone who wasn't my dad. A one-night stand? An ongoing affair? A few days long, or years, bolting out of the door and into his arms as soon as Dad set sail to sea? My eyes scooted down the words, all the various strands of wrong congealing into a homogenous clump that, for a moment, stopped me processing the biggest truth: Dad didn't know Mum had had another baby.

I put my head in my hands, doing a quick calculation. If her son was one in June 1969, he was born in 1968. Forty-five now. Forty-five years keeping a secret. I thought back to the months when I was expecting Jude, before I told Mum and Dad. How I'd had to leave my job at the hotel and find work in a club, knowing I was already pregnant. How I'd tried to hold my stomach in, disguise my baby bump to cling onto my job. The dart of fear every time someone's eyes dropped down, as though they knew something was amiss. The days I'd wanted to ring Dad and tell him, but couldn't face being that daughter, who, yet again, had let them all down. The weeks of inaction, unable to make a decision to have a termination, yet powerless to plan for a different outcome. The surge of shame, then relief on Louise's wedding day when it all came out. The image of Mum's face, concerned rather than harsh and angry. Her voice had been gentle: 'How long, Grace?' Her complete refusal to let me contemplate an abortion.

Dad wanted to find Ollie, to make him take responsibility, but I wouldn't let him. I'd waved him away. 'Dad, there's no point. I'd rather bring Jude up on my own than have his dad paying lip service to him, squeezing in a visit every other Sunday. Jude's not going to be missing out on a lot by not having him in his life. Besides, he's got you as a role model.'

And Dad would launch into a list of everything he was going to teach Jude, and over time, no one even mentioned his father any more. Thankfully.

But Mum, poor Mum, had been hanging onto her shame for nearly half a century. No wonder she'd gone a bit cuckoo. Imagine keeping a lid on a secret of that magnitude. How far down would you have to bury that knowledge, how tightly would you have to seal up your emotions just to survive? I wanted to rush over to the hospital, hug her skinny frame to me and tell her it was okay.

But of course, it wasn't okay. Dad didn't know. He was looking forward to their golden wedding anniversary next year, already making plans. I had no doubt he'd have us all oohing and ahhing at his soppy speech, which would basically be something like, 'You, Susie, have quite simply been my life.' Were we really going to strip away the foundation of his whole world now? Aged seventy-two?

I didn't want to be the one making a decision about protecting my dad from Mum's mistakes. I glanced at Louise, her expression set and angry as she skimmed the cards. Her ability to put herself into someone else's shoes wasn't as noticeable as, say, her talent for pointing the finger and apportioning blame. But I couldn't keep this from her.

'Lou, there's something you should see.'

With a big huff, she held out her hand, all the muscles in her face quivering with tension.

I sat back on my heels, biting my lip, feeling like I used to as a little girl, when Dad lit a rocket in a milk bottle on Fireworks Night and we didn't know whether it would go straight up or take on a will of its own and smash into the neighbour's greenhouse.

'For god's sake!' She threw down the pile of cards resting on her lap as she finished reading the letter. 'Why now, after all these years? Does she somehow think we're all going to find our long-lost brother and sit around drinking Ovaltine and playing Snap, catching him up on the forty-plus years that he's missed out on? Not to mention Dad… ah, yes, that son you always wanted, well, here's one Mum made earlier with someone else. I don't want to find him! We're happy as we are.'

And then she burst into noisy tears, leaving me patting her arm awkwardly. I was desperate to stick my head back in the trunk and check what else was in there, but Dad's voice floated up through the hatch. 'Are you all right up there?'

I darted over and called down, 'Yes, sorry, we just came across of few mementoes of Nan. Got a bit lost reminiscing.'

He shouted something about having a cup of tea waiting for us when we got down.

Louise shot me a furious look, but this particular discovery wasn't something we should trot out without a sizeable chunk of forward planning. Which, for me, was groundbreaking as a concept.

Having resented being treated as the silly youngest all these years, I wasn't so keen that the sensible oldest seemed to have abdicated her position without consultation.

CHAPTER THIRTY-SEVEN
Tuesday 11 March 2014

My sister was a baffling human being. She and Craig were always posting messages of outrage on Facebook, government cuts, dog-eating in China, appeals for boycotting this, that and the other. I'd always considered myself a bit heartless with my inability to gather up sufficient fury about anything that didn't directly affect me. But I felt so sorry for Mum. She was bloody nineteen when she got married. It was a big ask to sit in night after night when Dad's letters were full of cocktail parties in the ship's wardroom on the other side of the world. Sometimes after a couple of glasses of wine sitting in on yet another Saturday night when Jude was little, I'd almost convinced myself that Gareth in the downstairs flat was a viable option. And he was a man who paddled around barefoot with visible sock cack stuck in his big toenails and couldn't have a conversation without his fingers excavating some part of his body and eating the findings.

Louise didn't get married until she was thirty-one, so she'd had plenty of freedom to experiment and ensure that she didn't balls it up like Mum – and me. Though knowing old Sandra Dee, she'd probably only held hands with a couple of other men before she got together with Craig. Of course Mum had 'betrayed' Dad, 'let all of us down' (though I didn't include myself in that as I wasn't even born), but Christ, a little bit of human kindness and forgiveness. I got goose pimples just imagining handing over a tiny human being to strangers, a child you knew better than anyone else, whose needs you'd begun to anticipate. I wasn't rich or clever, but I'd never doubted that I was the best person to love Jude. No one else knew that stroking his eyebrows would send him to sleep, that he liked to be walked around rather than rocked, that he hated anything with a hood, and don't even think about socks. Without Jude, I'd only be a fraction of myself, a whisper of the person I was, with barely enough substance to anchor myself down.

But Louise seemed to overlook the whole 'giving away a baby' trauma and was resolutely focused on 'Dad has a right to know what she's done.' We stood hissing at each other in the hallway.

'At least sleep on it. Let's speak to Mum when she's well enough before we go blundering in upsetting everyone.'

Louise put her hands on her hips. 'She might never be well enough. I'm not even going to see her tomorrow. I think she's despicable for dragging us into it. You go. I'm not. And she can forget me giving up one second of my life to look for "Edward" or whatever he's called now.'

'Lou… she's probably not even aware of what she's saying. It must just be something so deep-rooted eating away at her, that she can't keep it in any more.' I couldn't believe my sister, the person who had always taken Mum's side, was so hard-hearted.

'Even so. We shouldn't be the ones to deal with it all. I'm not visiting while she's coming out with all this nonsense. I'll tell Dad I can't get away from work. Which is true.'

So, the following day, Dad and I trotted in alone mid-morning. Just so we weren't walking along the corridors in a mournful silence, I made a comment about Dad's shiny shoes. His eyes filled with tears. 'If she goes, I want her to know that I was making an effort for her right till the end.'

I'd have to beg Louise not to say anything to Dad yet. Louise was so flipping black and white, so bound up by injustice and rights and wrongs. It was fair to say that my personality palette encompassed a far greater array of greys. If Mum died, Dad would be broken anyway. If we added in what we'd just found out, he'd be smashed to smithereens.

As soon as we arrived at the ward, we checked with the nurse to see how Mum had been during the night. 'Not great, I'm afraid. She was shouting about "him not being here, finding him before it's too late".'

I went flying in with, 'She hates being away from Dad. They've been married nearly fifty years, I expect she wonders why he's not with her.'

Dad looked like he might keel over himself. And then he uttered the words that none of us had allowed into the air in front of medical staff, though my internal worrywart definitely had them on the megaphone rota: 'She's going to die, isn't she?'

The nurse shot a glance at me, a cross between pity and disbelief that the idea might only just have occurred to us. She put her face into neutral. 'We're doing all we can. The doctor should be able to give you a clearer picture later.'

I let Dad go in, then nipped out to grab the nurse to find out what time the doctor was coming round. Through the window, I saw him kiss her gently on the cheek, then stand there, head on one side. I couldn't imagine what was going through his mind. But I was pretty sure it wasn't a question about who the hell she'd had an affair with and where the resulting baby might be now.

I joined him, shuffling through the albums we'd found in the loft, talking Mum through the photos and memories, with Dad chipping in, 'Oh lordy, remember our twenty-fifth wedding anniversary? Louise rented that beach hut in East Wittering. Gracie here toppled off the sea defences and cut her leg open and we had to rush to hospital.'

I know Dad didn't mean to make me sound a troublemaker but everything we talked about took on a hue of 'And then

Gracie disappeared...' 'And then we had to go home because Gracie...' and 'Gracie gave us such a fright when...' There were never any stories about Louise ruining the day, or being naughty. Of course, I had been pretty difficult in the teenage years, but I couldn't help feeling that all my misdemeanours as a kid were logged and highlighted so that no one would forget, whereas everything Louise did wrong was dismissed as an exception, out of character, buried like a cat turd on a litter tray. I wondered if, after trying for me for so many years, either of them had ever wished I hadn't come along.

There wasn't much reaction from Mum. A bit of grunting and throat clearing. Dad kept saying, 'See, she's smiling at that.' I didn't argue, though I thought he was being optimistic, the way people deceived themselves that a baby was smiling, when really it had wind.

I looked at my watch. 'Dad, I'm going to have to go and rehearse soon.'

He nodded. 'But you haven't had anything to eat. Let me get you a sandwich from the canteen.'

'I'm fine, I'll grab something later.'

He got to his feet. 'No. Your mother would never let you go to work without something proper inside you.'

There was no stopping him. And as he walked out, still with his shoulders back, still straight, but somehow diminished and vulnerable, Mum's eyes flickered.

I might never be with her on my own again. 'Mum, I know about Edward.' I took her hand. 'It must have been awful for you. I'm so sorry.'

I knew she could hear me. Her breathing became quicker, as though she was trying to gather enough air to tell me something.

'I understand. I really do.'

I wanted to pause life like I did films with a complex plot, to rewind and watch again the bits I hadn't quite grasped, to process it all in small manageable chunks. But before I could begin to make sense of it all, Mum screwed her eyes up, forcing the word, 'Find', from between her lips.

I found myself nodding, the fury on Louise's face from yesterday blazing through my mind as the words, the foolish, foolhardy words, left my mouth. 'I'll try, Mum.' As I said it, I knew Louise would kill me. 'Do you know where he is?'

She tried to speak, the effort making the drip coming out of her hand rattle. 'Bath.'

'What, the city, Bath? Do you know his surname?'

But she didn't try to answer.

The enormity of a promise I couldn't possibly keep sank in. I tried to backpedal. 'I don't know where to start.'

She was making a grand effort to say something, her dry lips twisting with exertion. I felt like a vulture waiting to swoop as the prey flipped this way and that in agony.

'Shhh. You need to rest.'

And there it came, spat out like a cough. 'Ask Jeanie.'

'Jeanie?'

Mum's eyes blinked out a nod.

'Your friend, Jeanie? With the ginger hair?'

A small nod, then Mum sank back into the pillow.

I'd loved Jeanie. She was one of the few people who didn't compare me to Louise. If Mum ever criticised me, Jeanie would just pat my arm and say, 'You're lovely the way you are, aren't you, ducky?' We'd seen loads of her when I was little and then she'd disappeared. I tried to think when I'd last seen her. When I was a teenager? No, before.

I had a vague memory of Dad quizzing Mum about why Jeanie hadn't been round and Mum flaring up. 'Why haven't you seen Dave? Why haven't you seen Lenny lately? You used to be best friends with them, but I don't go on about why you haven't seen them.'

And poor old Dad looking sad and saying, 'They still have the navy in common and I'm not part of that life any more.'

I didn't remember anyone ever talking about her after that. I was probably about ten and didn't think about anyone other than myself for long enough to notice her absence. I didn't even know where Jeanie lived. We'd never gone to her house. She always came to ours. Mum would go into a frenzy of tidying up before she came, then go on and on about what a mess everywhere was when Jeanie arrived.

'You lot live in a palace. Don't know you're born.' But she'd say it with affection, as though she was pleased for us.

I wracked my brains for what I'd learnt about her over the years. I came up with precious little. I remembered Mum clearing out Louise's chest of drawers one afternoon. 'She's got four kids and they're a bit tight for money, so I said I'd pass on some of the things Louise has grown out of. You won't wear them anyway, so they'll do for Sarah.' I'd seen it as a right result: an excuse to sidestep all Louise's hand-me-downs and campaign for some Dunlop Green Flash and a ra-ra skirt.

When Dad grumbled Mum never wanted to go to the pub with him but she was always off to the pictures with Jeanie, Mum would say, 'She's having a bit of a tough time with that husband of hers, just needs a bit of a listening ear.' I hadn't understood then that 'a tough time' wasn't Mum telling off Dad for trailing mud onto the hall carpet or Dad rattling his paper irritably when Mum moaned about him spilling beer down his new suede jacket.

What I needed my memory to come up with was where she worked, where she'd lived. There were no guarantees she'd still be in the same house anyway. I remembered Dad driving past her when I was about fourteen or fifteen. It was pouring with rain and Dad offered her a lift home but she wouldn't get in. Dad had tutted with frustration as she trudged off in the rain. 'God knows what those two fell out about.'

She'd been in her supermarket uniform. Brown? Blue? I could only remember the hideous Rainmate with her bright ginger hair hanging like wet ropes out of the bottom.

Perhaps Louise might remember more about Jeanie. But then she'd want to know why I was interested. I couldn't tell her I was planning to look for Edward.

Dad might know where Jeanie lived. But what if he got all suspicious if I started asking random questions about her? Jesus. Nothing was straightforward. Perhaps I was worrying unnecessarily. Twenty-seven years had passed since Mum wrote that eighteenth birthday card. Maybe she'd told Dad the truth at some point?

I had to know. I leaned right in. 'Does Dad know?'

She made a few noises that could have been mainly yes or mainly no. I kept glancing at the door. 'Does Danny know about Edward, Mum?' I tried not to sound impatient, but my voice was coming out in a frantic hiss.

'No. Can't… know.'

It was like hoping to stumble across the eighth wonder of the world without even a faded atlas and a couple of crosses marking possible locations. Find Edward with absolutely nothing to go on. Keep it from Dad. Stop Louise blabbing and blowing Dad's world apart. Avoid falling out with her because I wanted to find Edward and she didn't. Concentrate enough to avoid losing my job. And, if possible, manage all that before Mum died.

Out loud, I said, 'Enough. One thing at a time. Make a list.' I was sounding more and more like my sister. The irony of Mum entrusting all of this to me, hopeless, haphazard, silly little sister Grace, was not lost on me. Would Edward want to be found anyway? Maybe he didn't even know he was adopted. And Jeanie? Where did she fit in? I turned back to Mum to try and piece another tiny fragment of the puzzle together before the egg timer ran out.

'Mum, what's Jeanie's surname?' I asked. But Mum's eyes had closed. I touched her shoulder. 'Jeanie's surname?'

But I didn't get any further as Dad appeared with an egg and cress sandwich. He looked so pleased with his hunter-gathering, I didn't have the heart to tell him that against the heat of the hospital, it smelt like the bathroom when Jude's friends had stayed and had a few too many ciders.

I stuffed it in my handbag, hugged him and left him to Mum, wondering where the hell I could find Jeanie without a surname, let alone Edward.

CHAPTER THIRTY-EIGHT
Tuesday 11 March 2014

By the time I got home at three, after singing and dancing as though my whole world was a rose garden and I just had to decide which variety to pick – even the director offered up a grudging 'Much better' – I lay on the settee completely drained. When Jude wandered in after school, he managed to tear his eyes away from Snapchat long enough to look concerned. 'You all right?'

Usually I'd have just said, 'I'm fine'. But this afternoon, my coping skills eluded me and big fat tears plopped onto the cushions. After a lifetime of saying to Jude, 'Look on the bright side, plenty of people would love to have our problems', it seemed that I'd found a whole new set that no one would want.

Jude gave me a hug. 'Don't worry, Mum. We'll be okay.' It was pathetic that I was relying on a sixteen-year-old to prop me up. I pushed my luck by giving him a kiss on the cheek. He endured it for a split second, then wriggled free and scooted off to his bedroom. How would I ever have been able to kiss Jude *knowing* it was the last time? I had to find Edward, which meant having another look at the chest in the attic. I'd have to sneak in when I knew Dad was at the hospital.

I hauled myself off the settee and picked up the phone.

'Portsmouth 9281 9312'

Dad must be the only man in the UK who still recited his number when the phone rang. Those numbers represented so

much to me. Ringing Dad in the middle of the night when I'd
fallen out of a nightclub drunk. Sobbing down the phone when
yet another man who'd promised me the world turned out to be
a shit. And that call at three in the morning: 'Dad, my waters
have just broken.'

Every time there'd been a calm response. His voice, down the
line, soothing and safe. 'Stay where you are. I'm on my way.' With
the selfishness of youth, I never considered that he might have
something better to do – like sleep. I just knew he'd be there,
arms out. 'I've got you, pet.' The four most comforting words I
could ever hear.

And now I was going to have to trick him.

We had a quick discussion about how Mum wasn't improving,
then I asked, 'Have any of Mum's friends been in touch to see
how she is?'

'There were a couple of messages. But you know what your
mum was like. A bit shy with people. Family was the thing that
mattered to her.'

I took a deep breath. 'What about Jeanie? Have you let her
know Mum is ill?'

'Jeanie?'

I wanted to hurry Dad along. His inability to recall names was
legendary in our house. Mum used to laugh at him. He'd flutter
his hand and say, 'You know, Alan thingummy, no, not Alan,
Chris.' And Mum would sigh in mock-exasperation and say, 'Paul.'

'Yes, Jeanie, you know, bright ginger hair, loads of kids, not
very nice husband? Used to come to the house a lot when we
were little.'

I could sense Dad frowning at the other end of the phone.
'Mum hasn't seen her for years. I don't know why. They used to
be great friends.'

'Could it help if she visited? A different voice. Perhaps a face
from the past might help.'

He said, 'I don't know. Not sure what could help at this point.' He sounded a bit impatient I was even having a conversation about introducing other, long-forgotten people into the mix when Mum might not make the weekend.

I gave it one last shot. 'Have you got her number anywhere?'

I could hear the reluctance in his voice, the lack of energy to do anything other than worry about Mum. 'Might be in the address book, but I'm not sure where it is. Your mum takes care of all that stuff.'

I tried not to huff down the phone. 'Try the hall table. It's brown with a rose on the front.'

I heard Dad shuffling down the hallway, the noise of the drawer creaking open. 'Hang on a minute. Just trying to think of her surname. Lock. Something Lock.'

My frustration was growing. But finally Dad blurted out, 'Whitelock. Jeanie Whitelock. Great sense of humour, that woman. Made us all laugh.'

Flick, flick of the pages, with Dad murmuring, 'T, U, V, W...' Silence. 'Nothing here, love, sorry. Only the Whitsteads.'

'Just try under J, in case Mum put it under Jeanie.'

'Nope, love, nothing under J either. But I don't think Jeanie can help. I'm not sure anyone can.'

Poor Dad. Mum dying and me haranguing him over phone numbers. And now I was having to lie. I hoped it would be worth it. That I would find Jeanie and somehow she'd help me find Edward. I paused for a minute, thinking about the choice I'd have to make if I did find him. The outside chance that Mum might improve if he would even agree to come to the bedside of the dying woman who gave him away. Versus breaking Dad's heart.

I clung to one of Mum's favourite sayings. 'We'll cross that bridge when we come to it.'

I dedicated the next hour to googling Whitelock. But none of the ones in Portsmouth looked likely. I was sure she lived near

St Edward's Park somewhere, but the Whitelocks I'd found on 192.com didn't have the right names living at any of the addresses. Maybe she'd moved out of the area.

Facebook didn't offer up any likely suspects either. I'd have to ask Jude. He'd probably do some flicky-fingered thing on my ancient computer that would not only bring up her address but her last shopping list and favourite film.

My mind was replaying over and over again any fragments of memories I had of Jeanie. I could try to find the supermarket she used to work in but there must be well over twenty in Portsmouth now. I had visions of a whole frustrating string of conversations along the lines of 'Jeanie, you say? I've been here twenty-eight years. Nope. Doesn't ring a bell at all,' all conducted with customers revving up their trollies in the queue behind, champing at the bit to get their fishcakes and fruit juice packed away in a bag for life.

I couldn't sit still any more. I drove round to Dad's. Mum's hyacinths were out. I'd cut some and take them into hospital for her; maybe the scent of them would tap into some survival instinct.

I rang the doorbell, just in case Dad hadn't left for the hospital at five-thirty as we'd discussed. No answer, so I dug out the key, let myself in and ran upstairs. I hovered for a minute in the doorway of my old bedroom. The times I'd sat with my back against the door, pockmarked with Blu-Tack from the posters of George Michael long gone. I could still recall the sensation of the wood against my shoulder blades, the self-righteous rebellion straightening my spine, my determination to stay up there forever, to starve myself to death, to teach Mum a lesson.

I felt sick with guilt. The pain of giving one child away and the one who followed rarely missing the opportunity to say, 'I wish you weren't my mother.' How I must have hurt her. But I had a miniscule chance to make it up to her now. I pulled down the attic ladder and headed straight for the chest, grabbing the key from the rafter.

I had to steel myself to open it. None of the anticipation or excitement I felt last time, just an internal bracing against more shocks to absorb. I threw the lid back and lifted the cards out first, piling them to one side. A fresh wave of sadness washed over me at the sight of the birthday presents, macabre in their perfect condition, the giggling and mischief silenced, trapped inside the boxes. In the corner of the chest, underneath a Slinky, was a folded nappy, a terry towelling one, the sort I remember putting on my dolls with giant safety pins. I shook it out. The name Paula embroidered in the corner. The name Mum had shouted out. I didn't get any of this. I wished Nan was still alive. Would she have known? Or would Mum have tried to keep the pregnancy a secret from her as well? But how, when she already had Louise? My eyes smarted in the dust. Or maybe I was about to cry again. I peered right inside the chest, squinting in the dim light of the bulb.

Right there, tucked in the seam of the wood was a piece of tissue paper. I opened it up to reveal a black and white photo of a little boy propped up on a pillow, bare-chested, in a huge nappy that reached up to his armpits. Jude. It was Jude as a tiny baby. The same dark eyebrows arched in surprise, the same cheekbones. I put my hands to my face, pressing my fingertips into my eyes. My god. No wonder Mum never wanted to go near him as a baby. It must have been like seeing a ghost.

I flipped the photo over. Edward Duarte, born 13 June 1968. Westmill Mother and Baby Home, London. My poor mother, sent away in disgrace. I studied the background of the photo, only able to make out a bare white wall with a cross. I wondered if that explained my mum's lifelong aversion to religion, her absolute refusal to step foot in church, even when we were singing in the choir, harrumphing away whenever anyone spoke about 'God's will'.

But at least I had an address to work with. And then came the dispiriting thought that the mother and baby homes probably didn't exist any more. I'd never heard of anyone going into one.

I did a quick once-over to double-check there was nothing else left in the chest, then put everything back in as I'd found it, as reverential as a curator of a priceless work of art. I paused before shutting the lid, thanking god – sorry, Mum – that I'd been born in the seventies. Getting pregnant with Jude without a husband in sight hadn't exactly led to a round of applause but I didn't remember anyone treating it as a disaster.

Perhaps Google would be my friend this time. As I hurried down the hallway, I caught sight of the address book on the table, open at the Js. Just seeing Mum's writing brought me to a halt, a surge of sadness rushing through me. If she didn't get better, how would I ever be able to look at her writing again? Accept that I'd never see her scribbling little notes in the margins of her recipe books, her careful capitals in her crossword puzzles, her name signed with a kiss at the bottom of little notes she left for Dad as though someone else might have written 'Just popped to the bank'? No wonder Mum had sometimes burst into tears when she smelt someone wearing Nan's perfume. And I'd just found her silly and embarrassing.

I paused. I'd just check Dad hadn't made a mistake about Jeanie's address. Mum was zealous about sending Christmas cards even though she never wanted to see people in the flesh. I scanned the Js to no avail, then turned to W. He was right. No sign of Jeanie. I went back to the beginning, unable to stop myself looking to see how many people we'd have to contact if Mum died, how many people's emotions we'd have to deal with alongside our own. Not many in the As. A few more in the Bs. And then my eyes fell on Jean Blacklock. Of course, Blacklock. Dad and his bloody Whitelock. And there were all her details, her phone number, her address not far from the Guildhall. I scribbled it down on the pad.

I shut everything up and dashed down the path. I dithered. Which would produce the quickest results? Jeanie or getting in contact with the Mother and Baby Home? I couldn't see how Jeanie would know where Edward was if Mum didn't. And the idea of my mother sharing the story of the illegitimate baby with anyone, even someone she considered a good friend, seemed unlikely. Westmill Mother and Baby Home would be a better starting point. I might not have to speak to Jeanie at all. Maybe I'd be able to contact someone there and find out what happened to him. Even as I had the thought, with my limited knowledge of adoption processes, I knew there'd be some stinking great obstacle that meant I'd probably be too late to help Mum. But I'd try and follow the advice I gave Jude, 'Don't give up before you've tried.'

When I arrived home, I ran straight in and switched on my computer.

Jude emerged from his room, went to the fridge and started chugging milk straight out of the carton. I knew I should tell him off, but so many things no longer mattered to me any more.

He stood over me, staring at the screen. 'What are you looking for?'

I explained what I'd found in the attic, about Mum's insistence that I should speak to Jeanie. About how his granddad was completely in the dark about it all. Jude's teenage brain seemed less bothered about the possible family catastrophe if we actually found Edward and more irritated with my computing ineptitude. He fluttered me out the way, impatient with my one-fingered typing, talent for clicking on the wrong icon and laborious menu selection instead of flicking through the screens using a selection of baffling shortcuts.

Within seconds he'd brought up some information relating to the Westmill Mother and Baby Home. Closed in 1973. Replaced with a multi-storey car park. I felt everything slump in me. 'I'll have to go and see Jeanie.'

'Shall I go and see Nan?' Jude sounded as though he'd rather eat a plate of mushrooms – his pet hate – but I loved him for offering. She'd been odd and awkward with him forever but he still plugged away.

'Let's see what happens. Maybe you could come with me one day.' I smiled at him. 'Edward looked just like you as a baby, you know.'

'Really? Wow. He'd be my uncle, wouldn't he?'

I allowed myself a little flight of fantasy that 'Edward' or whatever he was called now might be the sort of uncle who wanted to play Xbox, watch rugby games and discuss cars ad bloody nauseam. Someone who was actually interested in how fast a Volvo with a Lamborghini engine could go. But why would he even want to be part of our family when he'd spent over forty years slotting into someone else's?

I shook my head to dislodge those thoughts. Running before I could walk and all that. Judging by the car park concreting over Mum's secrets, what Edward wanted wasn't an issue that would be troubling us any time soon. And perhaps Louise was right. I should just let sleeping dogs lie.

But before I could go any further down that route, Dad's number came up on my mobile. His voice was all taut as he said, 'Love, I just wanted to let you know your mum's taken a turn for the worse. There's a problem with her kidneys. She's getting very muddled. Kept shouting about someone taking a baby.'

CHAPTER THIRTY-NINE
Tuesday 11 March 2014

I ploughed my way to the hospital through the slow-moving traffic, which hadn't eased even at seven-thirty. In between some aggressive lane-changing, I thought back to the times I'd argued with Mum over wanting to be a singer, dismissing her as 'just a housewife and a mother', lacking in ambition. How ungrateful I'd been when – on the rare occasions she'd spent time with Jude – she'd encouraged him to read instead of going with him to the park. I'd taken it all the wrong way, feeling slighted that she thought I wasn't doing a good enough job, assuming she was disappointed with what I'd achieved academically and determined to spare Jude the same fate. I'd been prickly: 'Mum, boys aren't like girls, they don't want to sit down with books, they want to get out and run off some energy.' All that time growing up, with Mum just out of reach, veering between over-the-top interest in what I was doing followed by periods of withdrawal when I felt the neighbour's goldfish held more fascination for her than I did.

I wanted a mother who walked around nodding amiably at the success stories of other people's offspring but who carried the absolute certainty within her that her own daughter was the most magnificent of all. Just like I did with Jude. When anybody said of a son, nephew, grandson, 'He's a lovely boy', my brain automatically whispered, 'Not as lovely as Jude though.'

Of course, I still got enraged by tomato ketchup on the carpet, hoodies draped over every bit of furniture, empty toilet rolls left for the loo roll fairy to change. But I was pretty sure Jude had never doubted the fact I was one hundred per cent overjoyed to have him in my life. Whereas Mum often seemed a bit 60:40. I'd hoped at some nebulous point in the future we'd bump that ratio up to at least an 80:20. But maybe we'd never get the opportunity now.

My mind was groping its way around these thoughts as I walked onto the ward. The fact that the nurse let three of us into intensive care instead of the strict two we were normally allowed wobbled me. Dad made a huge effort to smile a welcome at me, his face bearing a grey sheen as though he had the beginnings of a beard pushing through, yet I knew he wouldn't have come without shaving. Louise had obviously abandoned her boycott on visiting Mum and raised puffy eyes to me. Mum looked serene enough if you discounted the elaborate hamster house of tubes surrounding her. It seemed superfluous to utter the words, 'How is she?'

Louise said, 'She's got acute kidney injury.'

'What does that mean?' Anything acute sounded terrifying.

'That her kidneys aren't working properly, so all the toxins are building up in her body. That's why she's so confused,' Louise said.

Dad fought to get his face under control. 'It's something to do with her heart pumping out less blood because of the sepsis. I'm not sure she'll make it, Grace.'

Louise burst in with, 'They didn't say that, Dad! They've given her more fluids to stop her getting dehydrated, but they need to find out whether the antibiotics they were giving her have caused this problem.' She sounded furious Dad was even prepared to accept that Mum might die. In every other circumstance, she always favoured the most pessimistic outcome – Matilda only had to bang her head on a kitchen cupboard for Louise to start announcing concussion. But now she sounded like a child, stamping her foot in the face of incontrovertible evidence that the tooth fairy was actually a parent bumbling about under the pillow with a pound coin. I didn't know how to respond. My sister had never been anything other than doggedly practical.

I was scared to get close to Mum, childishly frightened in case she died right there and then. We all sat, a trio of garden gnomes, while the sound of trolleys, coughing and the regular mechanical beeps filled the silence.

Eventually Dad steepled his fingers and said, 'I want her to know we're here. Could you sing for her?'

Louise shook her head, tears rolling down her face.

'I'll give it a go. What should I sing?' I asked.

'"If You Were the Only Girl in the World?" It's the first song we ever danced to.'

I hummed for a bit, mentally running through the words as I did so. Then I gritted my teeth and held Mum's hand, curling my palm around those familiar fingers, sometimes comforting, sometimes accusatory. When I let the words out into the air, peace settled on me as it always did when I sang, the rhythm of air filling and leaving the lungs, soothing and giving shape to the world. Nothing flickered in Mum to acknowledge I was singing. I turned away so I couldn't see the raw pain on Dad's face, the struggle within him, even now, to stay strong for his daughters battling against his devastation at losing her.

And as I sang, the conviction grew in me that a trauma, a secret as toxic and painful as giving a baby away, festering over decades, would work against her immune system.

I came to the end of the song and Dad started talking about the old days, when they used to go to the dance hall, when he met Mum. Stories we'd heard hundreds of times, that before had bored us but now we wanted to hear again, a thousand times more, clinging onto the familiarity of our history. Any tiny fragment of conversation we could bounce around was preferable to falling back into the silence where the only thing we could hear was the sound of time running out.

I was itching to leave. Desperate to drive over to Jeanie's to see if she could help me. It was the best chance I had. I looked at the new tube in Mum's arm, carrying god knows what potion around her body. If Jeanie knew anything about Edward, it couldn't wait.

'I'm really sorry but I've got to go, Dad. To fetch Jude.'

Louise looked up. 'What time will you be in tomorrow?'

I knew what she was thinking. That I was leaving it all to her. It couldn't be helped. 'I'll text you.'

Dad simply squeezed my hand. 'You do what you have to do, love. I'm not sure any of us are doing much good just sitting here.'

I dreaded having to tell him the one chance I had of saving her would destroy him.

CHAPTER FORTY

Tuesday 11 March 2014

I drove away from the hospital, trying to work out how I could approach Jeanie after all these years of absence – if she was at home, if she even lived there any more. It would be nine o'clock by the time I got there, hardly the perfect hour for dropping in on someone I hadn't seen for twenty-eight years. But she was more likely to talk to me if I turned up on her doorstep than if I phoned.

I found my way to the little bungalow with its rusty blue gates and nettles a foot high. I wished Louise was with me. She'd take charge and smooth the conversation, keep it civilised, even if Jeanie was confrontational. I walked up the path, feeling as though I was trespassing, trying not to make any noise on the gravel. I wondered if she'd recognise me. I hoped her husband wasn't in. Mum had often talked about 'Poor Jeanie, being married to a brute like him.'

I banged on the door. And then there she was. She frowned, letting out a suspicious 'Hello'. Her ginger ringlets had whole clumps of grey in them.

I remembered her as a twinkly, smiley person but the passage of time had weighed heavily on her features. I swallowed. 'Jeanie?'

Her face took on the look of someone for whom life was a series of unpleasant surprises. She nodded. I could see she recognised me but couldn't place me.

'I'm Grace. Grace Duarte. You used to be friends with my mother, Susie.'

Her whole expression changed. She flew forwards and hugged me. 'Oh my god. Little Gracie. Big Gracie now. You look just like your mum. I can see it now.' She paused, clapping her hand to her mouth. 'She's not dead, is she?'

'No. Very ill though. And I was hoping you could help me with something that might make her better. I'm not even sure you know anything about it.'

I watched her face carefully. Her mouth flew open, the words racing to find their audience, but then she pursed her lips and folded her arms. 'I haven't seen your mother for years. Nearly thirty, I'd say.' She looked at the ground.

'Does the name "Edward" mean anything to you?'

Shock didn't wash over her face, it invaded it. Colonised every corner, tightened every wrinkle. She glanced over her shoulder, back into her hallway. 'You'd better come in.' She led me through to her kitchen. 'Let's go in here. My husband's watching telly and he'll start shouting if we talk over it.'

Recently I'd begun to appreciate the advantages of being single.

On a little plastic chair, with a cup of coffee and a bourbon biscuit, I filled her in on what Mum had said, the stuff in the attic and Mum's insistence that I ask Jeanie for help.

'I gather Mum had Edward in the Westmill Mother and Baby Home?'

Jeanie had been listening as I told her what I knew, nodding as though it wasn't news to her but not really commenting. But now she gave a jolt of recognition and began to speak. I waited for the secrets of the past to stretch and uncurl.

'I was in there too, with my baby. I met Susie not long before she gave Edward away. Might even have been the day before. I can't remember. But she's striking to look at, like you, so I recognised her immediately on Jubilee day.'

'So who was Edward's dad? Was it a big love affair?' I had to concentrate on my breathing to get those words out without sounding accusatory. Whichever way this ended, Dad was going to get hurt.

Jeanie frowned. 'She never talked about him. She used to get really angry if I asked her about it. What I do know is she loved your dad. He was the light of her life. I never really understood how she'd ended up in the predicament she did. Unlike me, who… well, never mind.' She tailed off. I was relieved. I couldn't associate this person who looked like a cosy school dinner lady with a racy teenager.

But I didn't want her to think I was judging her, so I told her about Jude, that I was a single mum. She smiled. 'You kept your baby. You'll have given him enough love for two parents.'

I pulled a photo out of my wallet. 'That's him as a baby. That's him now.'

'He's the spitting image of Edward. That must have been hard for your mother.'

Jeanie was so easy to talk to, I ended up telling her about leaving home at eighteen, all of Mum's funny ways that I didn't understand back then. We drank more tea and then I plucked up courage to ask her. 'I need to find Edward. Mum keeps asking for him. I was hoping you might be able to tell me something that would help.'

She slopped her tea with the strength of her reaction. 'No. No. I don't think that would be a good idea. Your mum never wanted to see him. And your father can't possibly know. No point upsetting him at this age. Lovely man.'

I tried to stay calm, scrabbling about to find words that would get Jeanie on my side, rather than send her rearing up like a frightened horse.

'I think finding Edward might help Mum get better. The doctors don't understand why she's not responding to treatment.

One of the nurses said it was as though she'd given up. Seeing Edward after all these years would give her something to fight for.'

'But your mum was always adamant, absolutely adamant, that your dad could never know. I nearly let the cat out of the bag when I was a bit tipsy once and your mum was livid. Didn't speak to me for weeks.'

'But Dad would rather deal with the past than let Mum die. She's his life.'

Jeanie started pacing around the kitchen. 'I know she is. But the thing that was most important to her was that you girls, and particularly your dad, should never know about him. You know, to sort of make giving him up worth it.'

'She definitely asked me to find him. And specifically asked me to speak to you. She probably thinks that now she's dying, it's time to set the record straight.' My voice faltered. 'Please, Jeanie. If you know anything that could help... I don't have time to go through the official channels. It could take months. And we don't have months. She said he was in Bath, but I couldn't get anything else out of her. She keeps drifting off, as though she can't think straight. Do you know any of the details?'

'That's why we fell out,' Jeanie said.

I stayed silent. Jeanie's face was a canvas of emotions, her eyes blinking rapidly. She looked up and said, 'Edward wrote to your mother when he was eighteen and she told him she didn't want anything to do with him, that it wouldn't be fair on his family or hers.'

If I'd been more shocked about anything in my life, I really couldn't remember when.

'Oh my god. Poor boy.' I tried and failed to imagine giving Jude away and refusing any contact when he came looking for me. I did a quick calculation. Nearly thirty years ago. Poor man.

Jeanie's face quivered but she didn't cry. I was witnessing years of holding onto feelings with the tightest of reins. 'I couldn't believe it. The thing we all wanted when we gave our babies away, what kept us from going mad, was the thought that we might see them again. Your mother included. And when I found out what she'd done, we had an almighty row. I was so jealous that her son had come looking for her. I couldn't get past the fact she'd turned down the opportunity to meet him.'

But I'd seen the raw desperation on Mum's face in the hospital. She didn't do it to be cruel. She did it to protect us. I breathed out. 'I get how that would be hard to understand. Did you…?' I didn't finish my question.

'No. I've looked but I can't find him. Maybe he doesn't want to be found.'

In normal circumstances I would never have carried on torturing her with questions, but I couldn't allow Jeanie's grief to derail me now. 'Can you remember anything she said about Edward – surname, road, anything about where he'd gone to school?' As I said it, a wave of hopelessness washed over me.

Jeanie shook her head. 'It was such a long time ago.'

Frustration overwhelmed me. 'I can't believe I've got a brother out there, my own flesh and blood, and I've no idea how to find him.'

Suddenly Jeanie jumped to her feet. 'God help me.' She marched out of the room and ran upstairs. I sat at the kitchen table, the sounds of shooting on the TV echoing through the house. I waited. I got up and examined the photos crammed onto a cork board, all manner of ginger kids, some faded Polaroids with boys in 1970s tank tops and wellies, some recent, a grown-up woman – was that Stella I used to play with? – holding the cutest twins. Still Jeanie didn't come down. I didn't dare venture into the hallway in case big bad Simon appeared, but I was starting to wonder if Jeanie had climbed out the bathroom window to escape me. I told myself I'd give it another ten minutes and then I'd call up the stairs. Then Jeanie appeared, looking flustered. 'Sorry about that. I've found this for you.'

She handed me a patchwork of paper, held together with yellowing Sellotape.

'It's the letter he sent your mum. She ripped it up and threw it on the pavement when we argued.' She paused, frowning at the memory. 'I felt so guilty that we'd had such a horrible row when she needed someone to comfort her. I went back in the afternoon and gathered up as much as I could find. I always meant to give it back to her at the right time but we never spoke to each other again.'

The paper was crackling between my fingers, its words calling to me. 'She missed you so much, Jeanie.'

She leaned forward and hugged me. 'She was my best friend. The only one who understood. Don't make our mistakes, Gracie. Don't be too bloody proud, stubborn or stupid to apologise. I've thought about her so much over the years, so many times when I wanted to talk to her. Give her my love.'

CHAPTER FORTY-ONE
Wednesday 12 March 2014

Wednesday was my only day off from rehearsing. I dropped Jude at school before heading off to Bath. He'd begged to come with me but I wanted to manage my feelings without having to account for anyone else's. I rang Dad to tell him I was popping into the hospital first thing, wrote and deleted several texts to Louise, then just decided I'd let her think badly of me until I had something concrete to report. And with a mixture of excitement, fear and nerves, I headed west. I'd googled the address. If online directory enquiries were correct, his parents still lived in the family home. Rockshaw Road. I looked on Zoopla. The house next door was worth over half a million pounds. Half a million! He'd landed on his feet. I wished I'd been able to talk to Louise, to share what I was planning, what I'd found out. It made me realise how lonely Mum had been without Jeanie to confide in.

How many events of my childhood, of my adulthood, would now change shape, stretching into a different truth entirely, the razor-sharp edges of bitterness rounding out into something softer and more forgiving? If there was a word in English to sum up the concept of understanding a difficult family member now you knew their secrets and wishing you'd been a bit kinder, today was a day when it would have come in handy.

I turned on the radio, my mind flitting between the years, dragging up conversations, comments from my mother that had stuck in my memory as odd, to see if I could make sense of them now. By the time I got to Swindon, I'd moved on to thinking about Edward and what my mum's response of 'Thanks but no thanks' when he was eighteen would have done to him. Would he have shrugged it off and thanked his lucky stars that someone lovely adopted him? Would it have been a double rejection? Would he have gone off the rails, too young to think about why she might have acted like that? I made myself sing to the radio to blot out the macabre thoughts trying to muscle their way in, the extreme ways he could have reacted.

I found the terraced house easily, pulling up a few metres past it. The front garden was neat, the shrubs clipped, the front door newly painted. Which suggested that they were either well off enough to pay someone to do it or were still pretty active. I hoped I wouldn't be confronted by two elderly infirm people who would chase me out of the house with their walking sticks. I studied the big sash windows for signs of life. My heart seemed as loud as a baby's on an ultrasound. I couldn't see how this was going to be good news for them.

I counted to five and got out of the car, not allowing myself to pause before I rang the bell. It was his mother who opened the door, it had to be. Mid-seventies at a guess, but definitely in the category of active pensioner.

She didn't do what Mum did: open the door with a scowl in case the unexpected visitor was trying to sell something or peddle religion. She gave me a big smile, 'Hello dear.'

Which was just as well because I wasn't sure I'd have had the courage to speak otherwise. I'd only got as far as 'Sorry to disturb you but…' when she clapped her hands to her face.

'You're looking for Adam!'

I mumbled a yes, trying to decipher the tone of her words: shock, fear, anger, horror?

She looked as though she was going to sink to the floor.

I backed away slightly. 'Sorry, sorry, I don't want to upset you.'

She blinked a few times. 'You'd better come in.'

'Are you sure?' I wanted to slice my tongue off as soon as the words were out of my mouth. I'd driven all this way, put in all this effort and was handing the one person who could help me a get-out clause. But she turned on her heel, beckoning me through.

The house smelt of polish, lavender, the sort of place even Louise would sit on the loo seat. She led the way through into a kitchen with a glass panel in the roof, a lovely light space like you see in magazines, with granite surfaces and chrome appliances. She was clearly someone who moved with the times. I realised I'd imagined a house stuck in the sixties, complete with Formica kitchen and avocado bathrooms.

She sat down, dropping heavily onto a chair as though her legs had given up halfway through the action. 'I've been waiting for this day all of my life. I thought it would be his mother who came. Your mother?'

I nodded.

'How did you know who I was though?'

She pulled open one of the drawers and handed me a photo. 'That's Adam.'

No explanation needed. He had exactly the same heart-shaped face, the same heavy brows, the high cheekbones, the big dark eyes. I wanted to kiss the photo. Wanted to take a moment to stare at him, to process the fact that I had a brother. That I was one of three.

I searched for the right response. And searched. But no words came to me.

'I'm Shona, Adam's mother.' Her voice wavered on the word 'mother' as though she suddenly doubted her position after all these years.

'I'm Grace.' I cringed at the fact that I hadn't thought to say my name before. 'I'm sorry to turn up like this. I should have written, but the thing is my mother is ill, really ill, she might not make it...'

And as I launched into the whole story, I started to cry. Not a few emotional tears but a torrent, which ended with Shona pulling me to her, holding me tightly and telling me to 'have a good cry', as though I was her own daughter. I kept trying to remind myself in between sobs of the total weirdness of being comforted by someone else's mother, let alone my brother's adoptive mother, when I hadn't even met him. There was such a warmth about her, something generous and open, that in the end, I relaxed and waited to feel calmer.

Eventually I got my breathing back under control, though my voice still had that high-pitched whine that signalled I might have a relapse at any moment.

'We need tea. Tea makes everything better.' Shona trotted about, so precise with her tea strainer and fancy little biscuits.

And over tea, our stories came out. These stories that had been running along in parallel like railway tracks that run for miles, then intersect briefly before careering on and on across the countryside. I found out her husband, Clive, had died a couple of years earlier, that Adam's second name was Edward 'in deference to your mother', that they'd never actively encouraged Adam to look for Mum – 'an insecurity on my part, of course'. With a sigh, she said he'd always been restless. 'Bright, intelligent, articulate. Always trying to prove himself, had to be the best. Even at Cluedo.' I saw the memory flicker on her face. That little family moment of Adam getting competitive over the candlestick, Professor Plum and the library. I could imagine Shona gathering everyone round for a board game, maybe at Christmas. While a few hours' drive away, my mum was sneaking off for a lie-down, her determined Christmas cheer descending into inexplicable gloom by the time we settled down in the afternoon to watch *The Sound of Music.*

Shona explained how she'd given him what she had about Mum.
'The papers that came with him, really. The court adoption order.
The clothes he'd arrived in. I kept them. I guessed your mother had
knitted them. The nuns didn't tell us much and, in some ways, it
was easier not to know, so I didn't have to think about the poor
woman who'd given him up. All we knew was that she from the
south coast, one of the naval cities.' She smiled. 'He always loved
the water, right from small, so I assumed his Dad was a sailor.'

I didn't contradict her because I didn't know. And anyway, we
all rewrote family history when it suited us.

'He never spoke much about it, but I knew the day would
come when he'd want to find out about his birth parents. My
daughter Katie wasn't bothered, but Adam never felt he fitted in,
always asking when he was little why his mummy didn't want him.'

I wanted to cry but thought it would be insulting to start
blubbing again when Shona was managing to hold it together.

'I didn't even know he was looking for her until he heard
from her, saying she didn't want any contact. That was a terrible
time for him. For all of us. He only made it through university
by the skin of his teeth.' Her face hardened briefly. 'She had her
reasons, no doubt.'

I felt that tightening in my chest I got when anyone criticised
my family, that sense of indignation even though the comment
might be justified. But of course, Shona was only protecting her
son, the son she'd loved and cared for when my mother couldn't
and had stood by, witnessing him receive the most hurtful rejection in the world. Frankly, it was surprising she hadn't come
after my mother with a baseball bat. I'd had to talk myself down
from 'having my say' when one of Jude's 'girlfriends' dumped
him after three weeks.

I started to explain how Mum had got pregnant while Dad was
away and couldn't keep the baby. Shona's face softened. 'Bless your
mum. And your poor dad. Does he mind you looking for Adam?'

I grimaced. 'He doesn't know about Adam.'

She sighed with despair. 'She's never told him? How did you find out? How did you find us?'

I tried to be clear about what had happened without being disloyal, without making it sound like Mum was some kind of floozy and Dad some poor sap who had no idea who he was married to. I told her about Adam's letter. Jeanie's part in it. I wanted to tell her about the birthday cards, the presents in the attic. But it was so private, something so personal to Edward. Adam. I left that bit out. Though I did want her to know Mum had loved him, that she wasn't an evil person.

Even though Shona was so kind, managing by some miracle not to sound judgemental, I could see she was leaping ahead to the day that our family, Adam's other family, would have to deal with the existence of her son. And how her priority would be to look out for him, not us. Exactly as it should be.

After about an hour, when she hadn't mentioned where Adam was or even hinted at letting me talk to him, I had to ask. I could barely look at her in case she turned me down flat. 'Is there any chance I could speak to Adam?'

Her eyes dropped. She pressed her palms flat on the table and turned her face to me, her pale eyes rheumy with emotion. 'How can I say no? Adam was a gift to me. A privilege, not a possession.' She grabbed my hand. 'Don't hurt him. I don't love him any less because I didn't give birth to him. I'd do anything for him. Anything.'

How lucky my brother had been to have this lovely woman for a mother.

CHAPTER FORTY-TWO
Wednesday 12 March 2014

I left soon after that, pressing my contact details into her hand and asking, begging her to persuade Adam to get in touch. I wanted to say that there was no time to lose, that she had to do it today – 'Ring him tonight, as soon as he gets home from work!' That I needed to get Adam to Portsmouth before Mum died because it was the one thing that might bloody save her or at least let her die in peace. But I didn't say any of that. She knew. And I just had to hope that she was generous-spirited enough to give Mum a second chance, when it had been painful to give her any chance at all.

We hugged. The embrace of a mother who understood all the complexities of families, who was prepared to smother her own instinctive feelings, swallow down her jealousy, if it meant her son could find the answers he was looking for.

Not only did I want Adam to meet Mum for everything that would mean to her, but I felt such an emotional pull towards him myself. I had to meet him now, couldn't imagine how I'd put knowing I had a brother out there back in the box to be ignored forever more. I prayed he'd want to see me, if not Mum.

Back home I nearly wore holes in the carpet, pacing up and down. Maybe Shona would think about it for a week, for a fortnight, until it was too late. I tried to believe she'd be decent. And that Edward would risk another rejection.

In the end, I went to the supermarket, to stop myself looking at the phone, to stop second-guessing what might happen, whether I could have said something different to plead Mum's case. I cooked curry, Jude's favourite, as an apology for leaving him to fend for himself so often lately. Despite my best efforts: 'Don't forget the melon in the fridge', I was pretty sure KFC had seen a spike in profits the last couple of weeks.

Somewhere between measuring out the turmeric and adding the ginger, my phone rang and I nearly cut off the unknown caller with my fumbling fingers.

'Hello?'

And there he was. Despite knowing he was older than me, his deep voice surprised me as though I'd been expecting a boy's voice, the hesitant teenager who'd written to my mum all those years ago.

'Oh my god. It's you. Edward! I mean, Adam. I can't believe I've got a brother.'

He laughed, a lovely vivacious noise that reminded me of Mum when she was in a good mood. 'And I've gone from one sister to three overnight. How amazing is that? Is Louise okay with it?'

'She's a bit more serious than me – she likes to think things through and consider them from everyone's point of view, but she'll be thrilled once the news has sunk in,' I said, with about fifty times more confidence than I felt. 'Anyway, how does your Mum feel about me turning up? I gave her quite a shock, I think. She was lovely though.'

I heard the pride in his voice. 'She's been a fantastic mum.' He hesitated, 'Sorry, I don't mean Susie, your mother, wouldn't have been great, I just mean I've been very lucky. Obviously this is a bit hard for Shona. But I'd hate her, or anyone to think I wanted to find my birth mother because I hadn't been happy in my proper—' He corrected himself, 'Other family.'

I loved how open he was. His deep voice that somehow had the same rhythm as Mum's. He had so many questions: 'How did you even find out about me?' 'Does your dad know you're looking for me?' 'Do you think your mum is delirious or does she know what she's asking?' He didn't shy away from the tough stuff, didn't flick away my concerns or make a funny 'hmm' noise like Louise if I said something he didn't agree with. And I particularly loved him for his excitement over Jude. 'Oh my god. I've got a nephew! At last! Another man in the family. I can't wait to meet him.'

We finally got onto how ill Mum was. I spared Edward the gory details but I had to tell him the truth. 'We're not sure she'll pull through. I'm sorry. That's why I just turned up on your mum's doorstep, rather than writing to you. I thought I might be too late if I waited for you to get a letter and respond.' I paused, working up the courage to ask if he'd come and see her at the hospital. But I didn't need to.

'There's been so much wasted time,' he said. 'I don't want to sit here for the rest of my life thinking I had the chance to meet my mum and I blew it.' His voice dropped. 'You're absolutely sure she's asking to see me? I don't want to make it worse.'

'Yes, yes, she is. Would you do that? I know it's asking a lot.'

'Will you come with me?'

'Of course.'

We agreed he'd come in three days' time, on Saturday, which was the earliest he could get there. I offered to let him meet me at my flat, but he said he'd rather go straight to the hospital 'in case he lost his nerve'. I bloody hoped Saturday would be soon enough. I suggested the only place I could think of near there, the Funky Fish Café, which according to Louise had been 'gentrified': 'The food's not bad at all and there's a nice seating area at the back. Dad loves it.' At least we could have a quick cup of tea and introduce ourselves. And if they were still there, I'd be able to show him the pictures of Mum in the band.

Now I just had to work out how to tell Louise.

And Dad.

CHAPTER FORTY-THREE
Friday 14 March 2014

By Friday, Mum seemed to have stabilised, though whenever the doctor used that word, it always seemed like a pause before the next catastrophe dragged us down further in the wrong direction. I heard a lot of talk about creatinine levels that I didn't really understand but was too embarrassed to say so, though I did get the general gist that there were some positive signs. Apparently she was producing more urine. Dad's face lit up at that. 'That's a huge improvement, isn't it?' I wasn't sure that 'huge' was the right adjective, but I nodded enthusiastically, pathetically grateful when the consultant suggested I should get Dad home so he could rest.

I dropped him off and steeled myself for the least appealing Friday night ever: trotting over to Louise's to admit I'd disregarded her instructions to steer clear of finding Edward, and telling Louise that he would be coming to meet Mum.

Despite explaining that 'I just wanted to pop in and have a quick chat about something', she'd clearly decided that there was something dodgy about that as my role in the family wasn't discussing or sorting, so she'd primed herself for battle accordingly.

Craig threw the door open in an exaggerated welcome. He'd obviously chosen to be the counterbalance. 'Come in, come in. Let me make you some coffee.' I was grateful that the noise of the coffee grinder gave me a moment to rehearse my opening lines in my head.

Louise's face became more and more incredulous as I explained about my visit to Bath. My voice was little more than a whisper by the time I said, 'And I know you won't approve, Louise, but Adam is coming with me to see Mum tomorrow.'

Louise leaned forward in her chair, her glasses dropping down her nose in a scary headmistress fashion. 'Are you completely insane?'

I tried not to default to my sulky sixteen-year-old self, faced with yet another lecture of how unfair I was being on Mum and Dad from my older sister. I kept my voice neutral.

'I'm not insane, Louise. I think we should look at the facts. Mum is probably going to die. I think we are agreed on that. The thing she wants most is to see her son.'

Louise interrupted. 'He's someone else's son now. She hasn't even seen him for forty-five years.'

I swore that when my sister died, they'd open her up to find an empty husk in the place of her heart.

I put the photos that Shona had given me of Adam in front of her. 'Look at him. He looks just like her. Just like me. He's part of the family, whether you want to accept that or not. And she has a right to see him, to know that he's had a good life before she dies.'

Louise did raise her eyebrows at the photos. There was no mistaking whose son he was. But she pushed the pictures back towards me. 'I think you'll find signing the adoption papers was the end of her "rights".'

'There's no part of you that feels a bit sorry for Mum? That she's kept this huge secret all her life? No bit of you that thinks if she does die, she deserves to make peace with what happened? That Adam deserves to know the truth?'

The way Louise looked at me made me sorry for any fifteen-year-olds caught viewing 'inappropriate material' on a school computer. 'I'm not bothered about Adam, Edward, whatever his name is, I'm bothered about Dad.'

I thought I might gouge her eye out with the teaspoon, that smug assumption that I didn't give a shit about the bloke who'd been there for me, rescued me, loved me for my *whole* life.

'Do you think I'm not bothered about Dad? I'm dreading explaining this to him. But the one thing I'm certain of, is that if there is a way to get Mum better, by helping her deal with everything that's eating away at her, all the stuff she's had locked up inside for years and years, then he'd want us to do that. It's not a guarantee, but antibiotics and all the other shit they've pumped into her haven't worked that well so far. The alternative is, of course, that we just sit here, do fuck all and let her die.'

'Shh. Mind your language. Matilda's in the sitting room.'

I leaned my head on one hand. 'Sorry.' My inner sixteen-year-old was rattling at the door to get out.

Louise was shaking her head. 'No. I can't let you do this. What if you take Adam in, the shock of it makes Mum worse and she dies because of it? Or how about you take him in, it makes no difference and she dies, but Dad's life is turned upside down? He'll not only have lost his wife but everything he believed about their marriage. He loves her. I don't know how he'd come back from this.'

Craig cleared his throat. 'Can I put in my tuppence-worth?'

I resigned myself to being outnumbered. But I wasn't here to get permission. I was here to inform. I *would* be taking Adam into see Mum tomorrow. And I hoped I'd have some fragments of a family left afterwards.

Even Louise looked like she wasn't interest in hearing Craig's opinion, which contrarily made me want to give him the floor, if only to give myself a bit of breathing space to fine-tune my next failure to convince.

Craig put his hand on Louise's shoulder in a gesture of affection and solidarity that made me feel lonely. He looked at me. 'Lou, I know you're not going to want to hear this, but I do think

Grace has a point. Danny already knows that there's something up, something odd about her talking about a missing baby. And, god forbid, if she does die, he's going to go through all her stuff and there's bound to be something in there that gives it away.' He sat himself down in between us. 'Isn't it better that he deals with it now, while she's alive, while there's a slim possibility of some answers? I don't think you're going to keep a secret of this magnitude forever, not now Susie herself has broken the silence.'

Now that did surprise me. This fuddy-duddy man – with his collection of decanters, his obsession with checking tyre pressures before a long journey, his scientific approach to his compost heap 'not too much grass' – was the one bloody voice of reason.

Louise looked as though a fly had flown into her mouth. 'Thanks, Craig. Thank you for your very useful input.'

He wouldn't be getting any sex for a few weeks.

I put out my hand to touch Louise's arm but she shrank away. 'I'm sorry. I do see where you're coming from. I don't want to hurt Dad. But Mum is the one who brought all this out into the open and I don't think we can put the genie back into the bottle now.'

She shook her head. 'You're the one who went looking for him. We could have happily neglected to find him.'

I got up. 'I'm really sorry you're so against it. I am. Genuinely. But we've tried everything else and nothing's worked. I can't just stand by and watch her die. Just keep Dad away from the hospital until 6 p.m. tomorrow. Please. That's all I'm asking. Don't do it for me. Do it for him.'

She shrugged, so uncompromising. So Louise-like.

'On your head be it.'

CHAPTER FORTY-FOUR
Saturday 15 March 2014

I got to the Funky Fish Café early on Saturday to meet Adam. I hoped I hadn't invited him to the equivalent of a motorway caff for our first meeting, but Louise did come here occasionally and my sister wasn't someone for whom 'white coffee' was a drink. Her coffee order was always about three sentences of instructions with a smattering of disaster management if they were out of soya. So I was pretty confident that Adam and I would be able to bear a cup of tea there. I was out of luck with the photos: some turquoise drawings of seahorses and shoals of fish had replaced the pictures of The Shakers. The whole place was almost unrecognisable since I'd visited all those years ago when I cut my leg open at the beach. Just a nod to its history as a fish and chip shop with a catch of the day menu in the window. But really it was a posh café with shabby-chic furniture, lanterns and 'Gone fishing' driftwood signs.

A bloke in his early thirties served me, asking me if I wanted to order today's speciality, 'pollock and chips'.

I smiled, desperate to sit down in silence to compose myself before my nerves translated into actual throwing up. 'I'm just waiting for someone to go to the hospital. We might pop in for food on the way back.'

But he started chatting about how many people had discovered the café because they had relatives in hospital. 'We've had all sorts in here. People crying because relatives are ill, people laughing because they're getting better. Sometimes they're so upset they all start shouting at each other. It's a proper window on life here.'

I was so nervous I nearly blurted out I was meeting my brother for the first time. But I couldn't say that to anyone. I couldn't tell a complete stranger, when my dad didn't know.

Eventually I made my excuses and walked through to the tables at the back, where I could watch out of the window on one side and keep an eye on the entrance. My heart leapt every time the bell jingled on the door. Then finally, he was there. I couldn't get out of my chair fast enough. He caught sight of me and hurried towards me. And as if it was the most natural thing in the world to hug the life out of someone I'd never met before, we clung to each other, tears pouring out of us.

The guy behind the counter didn't even pretend not to stare, but I didn't notice until he said, 'Crikey. That's a welcome and a half.'

Adam wiped his face and with kindness rather than irritation, he said, 'We haven't seen each other for a long, long time.'

We took our seats. I kept looking at him, seeing myself in his face, me but heavier and squarer. 'Thank you. Thank you for coming. I can't tell you how much this means to me.'

The guy behind the counter nearly snapped his neck craning around the corner to see what had made us unravel in such a spectacular fashion, but I didn't care. I just couldn't stop smiling, then crumpling into tears, then laughing.

Adam sat opposite me. 'It's the first time I've ever seen anyone I'm related to. In my adult life, anyway. It's so weird. You should be a complete stranger, but you feel really familiar.' He clasped his hands together. 'There's so much I want to know, I'm not sure where to start. Tell me something about you. Anything. Are you close to your mum?'

'Not really. I wish we'd been closer.' And as I explained what she'd been like when we were growing up, I realised that there was a lot to be said for only getting to know your siblings in adulthood. Adam was so non-judgemental, with his 'That must have been hard for you.' So different from Louise who always made me feel I created my own bad luck.

We laughed over the fact that neither of us had been married. 'I've been a shocker with women. Always picked ones who were totally unavailable or over-the-top keen. I'm the original dead-end man when it comes to relationships,' he said. 'Sometimes I think it was deliberate, as though I was sabotaging myself.'

Suddenly, being single for so long in the family dynamic of Mum and Dad's decades of marriage and Louise and Craig's steady ship, didn't seem so odd. I said, 'From now on, you'll have to let me vet your girlfriends. I can spot a bunny-boiler from a mile off.' Then I blushed, thinking I'd sounded presumptuous, that he might not even want to see me again.

But he nodded enthusiastically. 'I need all the help I can get, believe me. My mum – other mum – despairs. Thank goodness my sister has provided her with some grandchildren.'

Over lunch, I discovered that, like me, he was restless, hopeless in nine-to-five jobs, better at working shifts, found it difficult to take orders. After many years, he'd set up his own business as a graphic designer and had started to win awards. We had more tea. And flapjacks. I could have sat there for hours, bouncing from topic to topic in a scattergun way. But eventually, he looked at me. 'Already two o'clock. I guess it's time for us to do what I came for.'

He was biting his lip, the way Jude did when he was worried about something. I couldn't believe that there was a tiny gene in charge of the lip-biting mannerism.

'It'll be fine. I'll stay with you.'

I popped to the loo and, to my delight, found the pictures of the band and Mum hanging in the corridor at the back of the café. It was like a black and white fashion shoot for the 1960s with photos labelled from 1962 to 1969. I called Adam out to see. I pointed to the one with 1966 underneath. 'There's Mum! Look, in the flowery top. She must have had Louise by then.'

He stood there for ages. I was sure he would have reached out to touch the photo if I hadn't been there. I couldn't help wondering what was in his head. I studied his profile as he stared, that face Mum must have stroked, knowing that in the morning she'd be giving him away. We stood back to let an older man carrying a crate come through. He laughed and said, 'That's me in those photos, in my glory days.'

Adam said, 'Which one are you?'

I loved it that he chatted to anyone just like me, rather than worrying about getting stuck with a weirdo like Louise did.

He balanced the crate on his knee and pointed. 'There I am, Rob. Lead singer of The Shakers. Didn't quite hit the big time but we had a lot of fun.'

I nodded at the photo. 'That's my mum with you there.'

'You're Susie's girl?'

I introduced myself.

'You look just like her. Jesus. Where did those years go?' Rob carried on. 'Your dad came in a few days ago with your sister, Lucy?'

'Louise.'

'They were going to visit your mum in hospital. Is she all right now?'

'About the same. We're about to go and see her.'

Rob made a sympathetic face. 'She's been in there a while now then. Poor Suze. None of us are getting any younger.'

There was an uncomfortable pause while he sucked in his lips and did that nodding people do when they want to investigate further but are afraid to hear the answer that the person in question is going to die.

He cleared his throat and turned to Adam. 'Is this your young man?' Then he shook his head. 'No, can't be. You've got to be related. You look just like each other.'

Adam was looking to me for guidance. Before we'd met up, I'd decided to introduce him as my cousin but I couldn't get the words out. I couldn't bring myself to deny his existence when he was standing there right in front of me. I stood rooted to the spot.

We stared at each other, waiting for the other one to speak.

In the end I just came out with it. 'Adam's my brother.'

Rob's eyebrows shot up. 'Never knew there were three of you. I didn't really hang out with Susie after the band split up, but I still used to bump into her from time to time. I knew she'd had you. I sometimes saw her out and about with you in the pram.'

I nodded, wanting to claw back the secret I'd just launched into the public domain. Adam stepped in, pointing to the photo labelled 1967. I could have kissed him for trying to divert Rob's attention. 'That's a great picture of you all. Love the velvet jacket.'

Rob laughed. 'Gawd, we all look so young. I thought I looked like Jimi Hendrix in that jacket. You're going to make me feel ancient now and tell me you weren't even born in 1967.'

'Sorry,' Adam said. 'A year out. I was born in '68.'

My turn to butt in. 'God, look at Mum in those hot pants. She used to go mad whenever I wore anything that revealing. I'd love to bring her in here and remind her what she used to look like.'

Adam shuffled along the corridor towards the photo of the band in 1968. Rob said, 'Susie had left the band by then.' He shrugged. 'She'd already worked out that we weren't ever going to be playing at Wembley. Took the rest of us a bit longer.' He pointed to the photo in 1969. 'That was our last gig at the Portsmouth Palais. We were never as good after your mum left. She was the real crowd-pleaser, even though she never officially joined the band. We just used to haul her on stage, but because she loved singing, she could never resist.'

Rob put his crate on the floor. He kept staring at Adam, blinking, as though he was trying to understand something.

I felt the atmosphere shift into one of puzzlement rather than general reminiscing. 'Anyway, we'd better get going,' I said, suddenly feeling claustrophobic under Rob's gaze. I thanked him and started back down the corridor.

Rob shook Adam's hand. Behind me, I heard Rob say, 'Give my love to your mum. And my regards to your dad. Is he coping all right while Susie's in hospital?'

I froze in the doorway, swinging round to answer for him, just as Adam said, 'Danny's not actually my dad, just Grace's.' It seemed the one family trait Adam and I definitely shared was an inability to fudge an answer to a direct question.

Of course, it had been entirely wrong of me to expect Adam to deny his father, Clive, the man who'd probably played football with him, taxied him about as a teenager, taught him how to be this thoughtful and kind man. I couldn't expect him to pretend Danny, a man he'd never met, was his dad.

But I really bloody wished he had.

Rob didn't look anywhere near as shocked as he should have been. I had a fleeting thought that perhaps Mum had been a right old girl about town, sleeping with all and sundry while Dad was away. But just as quickly as I had that idea, I dismissed it. Her love for Dad was genuine, it had to be. You couldn't fake those little strokes of affection, the casual touch of the hand, the little kisses on the head.

Understanding passed over Rob's face. He screwed up his eyes as though he was warding off a painful memory. I had no energy left to decipher what any of it meant.

I wanted to run away from them both, before I became stranded in a cul-de-sac of questions to which the answers would be disloyal to Dad. Even more disloyal than we had been already. Louise was going to be so unbelievably pissed off with me. But instead of giving in to my desire to run and keep running, I waved a cheery goodbye and marched towards the door, even putting my hand up to the chap behind the counter, as though we hadn't just flopped out the stonking family secret to a stranger. I might as well have stood on a chair and shouted, 'Meet my brother. We share the same mum but different dads,' over the frigging flapjacks. Followed by 'Oh… and if Dad pops in for some cake, forget you ever met Adam, will you? He doesn't know he exists yet.'

Louise would kill me.

CHAPTER FORTY-FIVE
Saturday 15 March 2014

The café door swung shut behind us. We both went to speak at once but Adam forged forwards with the most determination. 'Sorry. I panicked. It just felt so wrong to go along with the idea that Danny was my dad. I just couldn't. It seemed so insulting to you. And him.'

'My fault. I knew there was a chance we'd bump into Rob, but I wanted you to see the photos of Mum.' I stopped walking and turned to face him. 'I wanted you to have an image of her in your head of when she was young and in her prime. She's a fantastic singer and I was showing off.' My voice shrivelled up. 'I don't think I'd quite realised how important it was to me you should be proud of her too.'

Adam's expression was gentle. 'Thank you. It's a lot for us both to take in. We're going to make some mistakes. But thanks for not lying about who I am. You've no idea how brilliant I felt when you said, "Adam's my brother".'

I marvelled at the fact that Adam had found a way to make me feel as though I was doing my best. Louise always made it sound as though I was deliberately sabotaging everyone's happiness. I couldn't help wondering how different things would have been if Adam had grown up with us, diluting the intensity between me and Louise. I squeezed his arm. 'It's going to be okay. I'm not quite sure how, but we'll work it out.' I tried to tag an ironic 'bro' on the end, but it caught in my throat. I'd save the humour for another day.

We walked in silence to the hospital. If his head was as overloaded as mine, he needed all his energy to process thought rather than to create speech. As we entered the hospital, I could see beads of sweat on Adam's upper lip. He kept stopping in the corridor. 'Do you want to go in first and tell her I'm here?' 'What if your dad turns up?' 'Or Louise?'

By the time I'd managed to propel him to the intensive care unit, my nerves were shredded. The lovely Chinese nurse greeted us, quickly updating me on the fact that Mum had a comfortable night and seemed more settled.

I filled her in briefly, wincing as I said, 'If my dad comes this evening, would you mind not mentioning that I came with someone else?'

She nodded, with the sad smile of someone who'd seen way too many dysfunctional family scenarios to register surprise.

I turned to Adam. 'Sorry. That felt really rude but I just need to speak to Dad first. I don't know what he knows. If anything.'

Adam said, 'I get it. My conversation with Mum about wanting to look for my birth mother took a bit of planning. You've had this sprung upon you through circumstances. You've got to do what's right for you.' His eyes kept darting to the door. 'I feel really nervous.'

'I hope you won't be disappointed. She's hooked up to a lot of tubes. She might not even react to us. Sometimes she doesn't seem to know we're there.'

I pushed open the door and led Adam to Mum's bed. She was asleep, but her breathing seemed normal. 'I'll wake her up in a minute. Have a seat.'

Adam sat in the armchair. He looked completely poleaxed, swallowing and making little grunting noises as though he was trying and failing to contain a ferocious mix of emotions.

I felt oddly protective towards Mum. It seemed so unfair for her to be meeting the son she'd longed to see like this. I reached out for her hand. 'Mum, it's Gracie. I've brought someone to see you.' I turned to Adam. 'Can I call you Edward just for a bit? I'm not sure she'll cope with the name change at the moment.'

'Of course. I am Edward to her.'

Mum just about managed to open her eyes.

'I've found Edward. I've brought him to see you.'

I studied her face for a glimpse of understanding. For one horrible moment I thought she was just going to drift back to sleep.

'You know, your son Edward,' I said.

And as though someone had switched the light on in a dark cellar, her eyes flew open.

I took Edward's arm and brought him closer. 'Look, here he is.'

'Hello Mum,' he said, his lovely face creasing into a huge smile, at odds with the tears running down his face.

Mum's dark eyes filled. She stretched out her hand and Adam took it, squeezing it gently. Her face, that poor wan face, mottled and pale from the weeks in hospital, became animated in a way that I thought we'd never see again. Her words were muffled but clear enough: 'Forgive me. Never stopped loving you.'

There was a long pause as though Adam couldn't force his words out. 'There's nothing to forgive.' His voice cracked. 'Mum.'

Her hand flexed around his. Her knuckles were pale with exertion. How different Adam's hand must feel now, a man's hand with a lifetime of experience within its grip. Such a contrast to the tiny unformed grasp of a six-week-old baby. I looked down at their fingers entwined, struck by the sheer power of maternal love. Within that clasp was so much love and longing, such strength of feeling that time had done nothing to diminish. Mum looked serene, as though she was turning her face to the first of the spring sun after weeks of bruising winter rain. Adam was shaking his head slightly as though he couldn't believe this moment had ever arrived, that something he'd dreamed of, fantasised about, was now a tangible reality.

She managed to say, 'Tell me about your life.'

And I sat, listening to Adam who did a brilliant job of picking out anecdotes from his childhood. Such a tall order to condense your life down into a) something that sounded interesting and b) something that would reassure rather than wound the person who gave birth to you. But he struck just the right note: hitting a cricket ball through the dining room window, watching fireworks with his sister from the Royal Crescent, singing in the Abbey as a schoolboy, rainy days at Weston-super-Mare with his parents – 'Dad never went anywhere without a windbreak and a cool box.' It was ironic how much Adam's father would have had in common with Dad.

Now and again, I'd see Mum's lips twitch into a smile.

Eventually the nurse came round to check on us and said, 'I think she needs to rest.'

Adam lifted her hand to his lips. 'I'll come back another day.'

Whatever mistakes I'd made in my life, this time I'd done something right.

For these two at least.

CHAPTER FORTY-SIX
Saturday 15 March 2014

Adam had politely turned down my offer to stay with me for the weekend. Originally I'd been offended, leaping as I did into bulldozer mode, a hundred and ten per cent into every project, wanting to shoehorn a lifetime into two days. But Adam had let me down gently. 'Listen to your big brother. It's going to be an emotional day and we'll probably need a moment to catch our breath. I'll just come for the day – my own, my other Mum, will be desperate to hear how I got on, so I'll drive back in the evening.'

And now I couldn't be more grateful. The conversation I was going to have to have *tonight* with Dad wasn't going to be the sort of thing where I could say, 'Make yourself at home, beer in the fridge, here's the remote control, I'll be back in a minute.' Nope. This was definitely not going to be a discussion I could have in a minute. Rock, hard place had never, *never* seemed such an accurate phrase for what was coming next.

I buried my face in Jude's shoulder. 'Wish me luck.'

Jude hugged me, properly hugged me, as though the moment didn't allow for the self-conscious leaning away he often did these days. Poor Mum missing out on all those moments with Adam, the cuddles, the all-too-brief phase of childhood when your offspring think you are the font of all knowledge, when they want to be with you all the time before the inexorable move away, the fraying, the snipping, then the wholesale slashing of the ties of dependency. 'Granddad will understand, Mum. He loves Nanny.'

'It's going to really really hurt him, Jude.'

Jude frowned. 'But if it can make her better, won't he just get on with it?'

Bless my boy. After so many years of telling him that sometimes we had to just 'put up' with whatever irritations didn't suit us, 'getting on with it' had become part of his mantra too. 'I hope so, love. I really hope so.'

'Do you want me to come with you?'

I loved him for that, that goodness in him, a sense he could be relied on. I hadn't been the perfect mother but I hadn't completely failed.

It still remained to be seen whether I'd totally stuffed up as a daughter.

'You're lovely, but I think this is one of those horrible grown-up things I'm going to have to do on my own.'

I went before I crumbled completely. I knew Dad was planning to go to the hospital with Louise at six o'clock. Which gave me an hour and a half.

I dragged my way up the front path to his door, memory after memory superimposing itself. Dad standing on the pavement trying to talk me out of leaving home. Mum shouting down the street about coming back to have some breakfast before I went school. Me pretending not to hear, taking joy in her impotence. Dad standing in the kitchen between us, trying to prevent our arguments escalating. 'I hate you' reverberating around our hallway before I stormed upstairs.

I could have been so much nicer.

I rang the bell. The noise of fumbling with the top lock, followed by 'Just looking for the key.'

Finally Dad opened the door, his face lighting up with pleasure. 'Gracie! Louise told me you were away auditioning for the day. How did it go?'

'I'll tell you about it in a minute. Is there a cup of tea on offer?'

I followed him into the kitchen, noticing how his trousers were a little loose, his movements a little stiff. How was I going to tell him? How? That the Golden Wedding anniversary he was looking forward to celebrating next year wasn't quite so bloody glittering. But I had to. I had no choice. Not now. Not now Rob knew the truth. His café might be city gossip central for all I knew. I cursed my stupidity at taking Adam there. I could have bought myself more time. Thought it through. In the back of my mind, I'd been hoping I wouldn't be the one to have to tell Dad, that at some point, Mum would recover enough to do it herself.

I watched him warm the teapot. The comforting rituals that carried on, the tiny elements of family life, creating a whole framework within which to belong, to thrive or to rebel against. And now nearly fifty years of saying, 'Cup of tea?' to Mum, knowing the answer would be yes, would take on a different shape entirely. Almost half a century defined by the bearing of another man's child, five decades of a secret that had tarnished their lives and coated everything with a fine layer of toxicity. And I was going to be the one to open his eyes to what had always been there but so unthinkable that none of us could have dreamt it up.

'So, love, what's new?'

I looked at my dad, his face etched with worry, his hands a little more veiny, his movements lacking in energy, exhausted by the strain of willing Mum better, while trying to come to terms with the possibility that he might lose her. Selfishly I'd never had to worry about Dad before. The support had always been one way, Dad fixing me. And now I was going to break him.

'Dad, I've got some news about Mum. You're going to find it really hard to hear, but I just want to make it clear now that I only got involved for good reasons. And I'd never, ever do anything to hurt you on purpose.'

The enormity of what I had to say engulfed me and I couldn't speak.

Dad was all agitated, sugar flicking off the teaspoon as his hand shook. 'What? Is she going to die? Soon?'

'It's not really to do with her health. But – oh god – I don't know how to say this… you know she kept talking about finding a missing baby?'

Dad nodded uncertainly.

'The thing is,' I reached out to hold his hand, 'Mum had another baby after Louise.'

'A dead baby?'

I had no idea how the police broke bad news to relatives on a regular basis. I tried to focus. 'No, she had another baby, a son, Edward, while you were away in the navy.' I hesitated, knowing that Dad's world would never look the same again. 'She gave him up for adoption.'

Dad withdrew his hand. 'She gave our son away?'

Shit. I had missed out a vital piece of the story. I forced myself to grind out the words that had to come next. 'He wasn't your son, that's why she gave him away.'

Something collapsed in Dad, as though the scaffolding that had been keeping him upright had buckled in the middle. 'How do you know? What do you mean? Gave a baby away? Whose baby?' His voice was rising, I couldn't tell whether it was in panic or anger.

All the horrible imagined scenarios that had been running round my head since I'd known about Adam were pale impostors for the sheer devastation on Dad's face.

I tried to explain, attempting to be as clear as possible without adding unnecessary details to wound him further. He was shaking his head, repeating over and over again, 'How do you even know this?'

'I've met him, Dad.' I shrank back into the chair. Such cruel words. Such an ungrateful payback for everything this wonderful man had done for me.

I didn't want to tell him I'd had the bright idea of taking him into see Mum. How could I admit that I'd nosed about in the attic, gone behind his back, been to Bath, met Adam's mother? All those things I'd worried about but somehow convinced myself that they'd be okay, that Dad would accept them eventually if it made Mum better. I'd known at some level I was betraying him but I'd tossed the coin of loyalty and it had come down on the side of trying to give Mum a reason to live – or a peaceful death – rather than protecting Dad. But with Dad sitting opposite me on the rubble of his life, it didn't look quite as clear-cut. In fact, I had the distinct impression I'd just snatched away his own motivation to see his next birthday.

'I'm sorry. I should have told you before. I didn't want to upset you for nothing, if I couldn't find him, if he didn't want to see Mum, if – I don't know – if I could somehow make it all happen without you having to get hurt.' Tears were pouring out of me. 'I shouldn't even be telling you this, Mum should, but I was afraid she'd die and I thought bringing Adam to her might help. And I hoped you'd rather have her alive than dead. Even knowing about Adam.'

He sat back in his chair. I poured him some more tea. A silence hovered between us.

'Start from the beginning. Everything. I have a right to know what you know.' His voice was shaky but there was an underlying steel, a hardness, that I'd heard so rarely.

I gabbled rather than talked. The chest in the attic. Jeanie. The mother and baby home. Adam's mother. Adam. How he looked like me.

Dad didn't speak. Just sat with my explanation buffeting him, occasionally nodding in recognition of things slotting into place, sometimes grimacing as my words stuck into him like barbs. He stood up.

'Where are you going?' I had visions of him steaming down to the hospital, clattering into the intensive care unit and shaking Mum awake, demanding answers.

'Up to the attic.'

'I wouldn't do that, Dad. Not now. Let it sink in a bit. We can do it together when you've had time to think it through. I've told you everything I know, everything I've seen up there.' There was no way Dad could manage that rickety old ladder at the best of times. At this rate I'd have both my parents in hospital.

'So who was it then? Who was the father?'

At that my father's face crumpled and he leant forward onto his arms and sobbed. Proper broken-hearted sobs, as though everything in him was cracking and splitting like an old garden bench that had spent too many winters in the rain.

I stood up, not knowing what to do, how to make it right. 'I don't know, Dad.'

'Rob? Jim? One of The Shakers?'

Shit. Shit. Could it have been Rob? He'd been very interested in Adam. No wonder he'd had an odd look on his face. If it was him, I'd properly opened up a can of worms.

'I can't help you with that, Dad. Sorry.'

'I loved her so much. I would have done anything for your mum. Anything. I came out of the navy for her. She was so desperate to have another baby, to have you. Why would she have done that to me? I trusted her.' He bowed his head. 'She was everything to me.'

It was painful to watch, Dad flicking back through the Rolodex of his life with Mum, the things he'd dismissed, *we*'d dismissed, suddenly clicking into place – the way she'd suddenly look sad right in the middle of a birthday celebration, how she used to say her least favourite months were June and July, when we all loved them for the light nights and warm days.

I felt panicky, as though I'd rolled a great big bowling ball into his life and scored a strike, smashing our family into a million pieces. God knows what I'd been expecting. That Dad would say, 'It was a long time ago. What matters now is getting your mum better.' And then some manly observation about how he'd always wanted a son.

But even though I knew that sort of shit only happened in films, I had obviously been expecting some kind of Hollywood finale because I hadn't thought through my strategy for Dad's devastation.

The words I did manage to fluff out sounded hollow. 'Maybe it's not as bad as it sounds. I only agreed to look for him because I thought it would help her recover. Perhaps I was wrong, but I convinced myself you could cope with anything as long as she didn't die.'

'And she's seen him, has she?'

I looked at the floor. 'We went in this afternoon. I wasn't at an audition. Louise was dead against it, Dad. It's all my fault. She didn't want us to look for him. But I just thought it might give Mum a bit more fight.'

He took a deep breath, his chest shuddering with emotion. 'Did she know the boy? Did she speak?'

I nodded. 'Yes, she did, more than she has for a while.' I felt a surge of relief Dad hadn't had to witness the level of emotion in that room.

He closed his eyes, tears still squeezing out from under the lids. 'Thank god. Thank god for that.'

He loved her. I hoped that would carry us through.

CHAPTER FORTY-SEVEN

Sunday 16 March 2014

The next morning I felt hungover, my eyes aching in their sockets, despite having collapsed on the sofa with just a cup of tea the night before. It was as though my brain was bruised from the conflicting emotions charging around my head, the search for a solution that would suit everyone.

Louise had arrived to pick up Dad the previous evening, seen the state he was in and refused to take him to see Mum. 'She's going to have to manage on her own for one evening otherwise we're going to end up with both of you in hospital.' Right up until when she arrived, Dad had been insisting that he'd be fine, that he still wanted to go. But Louise wouldn't hear of it. She ran upstairs, packed him an overnight bag and bustled him into the car to stay at hers. I offered to go with her. She stopped short of saying, 'You've done enough damage for one day', opting instead for a clipped, 'We'll manage. You'll be needing a rest yourself after today.'

I was just gearing myself up to ring Louise to see how Dad was, trying desperately hard not to feel that I should have left the past well alone. But I kept coming back to Mum, her hand squeezing Adam's, her face serene, her burden released. And I was thinking about how much I'd liked Adam, how comfortable I'd felt with him, when 'Big bro' flashed up on my mobile.

'Just calling to see if you're okay? How did it go with your dad?'

'A bit emotional, to tell the truth.' I expected to see the word 'understatement' glittering around my sitting room.

'Poor you. Your dad's going to be in shock. It's only normal. That's a big old secret he's got to face up to. He's going to be a bit angry to start with. Phone me to let off steam if you need to, though, don't fall out with him.'

I was glad Adam couldn't see the tears starting to bubble up. He'd think I was a right crybaby. I tried to keep my voice strong. 'Thank you. I might have to take you up on that. How did you get on?'

'Not the easiest conversation I've ever had, though I know she understands really. Feeling a bit wrung out, to be honest.'

'It's so hard, isn't it? I don't want to hurt Dad, but at the same time I'm so thrilled that Mum has found you. And me too, actually.'

I could feel Adam smile down the phone. 'Ditto. I just keep worrying that Mum – Shona – will see me looking for Susie as a reflection on her.'

At that moment, Jude came blundering out of his bedroom, oblivious to the fact that I had a phone clamped to my ear. 'Is there any bread?'

I hissed at him to look in the freezer, not wanting Adam to think I was dismissive of his torn loyalties. 'Sorry about that. I am listening, it's just that teenagers think their rumbling stomachs are way more important than anything I could possibly be talking about.'

But unlike Louise, there was no audible huff that I'd failed on the instilling manners front. He laughed. 'I spent far too long thinking about myself at that age. I'm probably just about growing out of it now.'

I'd never achieved this level of familiarity with my sister in thirty-six years, this sense that who I was didn't require any corrective action. When I commented on it, he said, 'It's so weird. I feel like I've been sitting chatting to you every weekend for decades, rather than just three times in my whole life. How can that be? I thought I might meet you and think, "She's a nice person, I could be friends with her," but I didn't expect to feel such a powerful sense of family, a kind of "This is my sister, and if you upset her, I'll come after you".'

For the first time in years, I felt as though someone other than Dad had my back, that there was someone I could rely on. The way I'd always imagined other siblings supported each other. Siblings who weren't Louise, anyway. But Adam did have the bonus of negotiating the thirty-six-year-old me without witnessing the chaos of my teenage self.

Our conversation gave me the courage to phone Louise. Even though I couldn't see her, I knew she would be standing super-straight, her buttocks clenched at the mayhem I'd caused. 'Dad's refusing to go to the hospital now. Says he needs time to think things through before he sees Mum. Craig's been chatting with him, trying to help him put it into perspective.'

Good old Craig finding a perspective to put it into.

I felt simultaneously grateful to him and envious that Louise had someone to support her. And absolutely shit that I'd been the messenger to deliver the news to turn Dad's life upside down.

'What do you suggest we do about Dad?' I asked, braced for a tirade.

'I think we let him grieve a while for the life he thought he had, and then he'll just have to get on with it. Or get divorced.'

Even though my intellectual self knew what betrayals like these led to, my childish self couldn't begin to accept that my parents might divorce. 'That won't happen, will it?'

Louise did the sort of sigh I'm sure she reserved for parents who couldn't believe their child might not make it into the grammar. 'I think it's a possibility, yes.'

And over the next few days, I started to believe she was right. Dad closed in on himself, refusing to visit Mum. The smell of beer started to overtake the scent of polish. Louise's lasagnes, shepherd's pies and stews sat untouched in the fridge. Louise tried her school mistress technique of pointing out how he was letting everyone down. I tried to persuade him to visit Mum for us, if not for her. But like a politician expecting a landslide and ending up losing his seat, Dad sat in his chair, picking over old ground again and again. 'Why would she have done that to me? Then lied all these years? Why? Everything, *everything* I did was for her. For the family.' And I'd sit searching for the right words. But there weren't any. The whole situation was shit and unless Dad shifted in his thinking – a big ask given that he was undeniably the wounded party – we were quite buggered. Or 'challenged' as Louise would say.

The incredible thing about life was how a worry that had been all-consuming – Mum dying – suddenly morphed into something else entirely. After Adam's visit, Mum hadn't exactly leapt about in a 'take up your bed and walk' sort of way, but she definitely turned a corner. By Thursday morning, the nurse at the ICU had greeted me with a big smile. 'Your mother had a good night last night. Slept really well. She's even managed a bit of proper food. If she carries on like this, she'll be moved to a general ward tomorrow.' She put it down to the consultant working wonders with the right combination of antibiotics, but I knew it was because of Adam.

The good days started to outweigh the bad: she still had very little energy, but could manage ten-minute conversations before needing to rest. By the time Adam visited on Saturday, she was eating on her own and only had one drip in her hand. He'd walked in with a big grin. 'There you are. I can see you now all those tubes have gone. For a moment, I thought I was the son of an astronaut.'

I couldn't bring myself to regret what I'd done – not totally anyway – when I saw her sitting up, her face alight with joy as Adam talked her through his photo albums. 'Oh look at you there! Your sweet face. Is that your sister?' 'Bless you with that brace.

Grace had to have one too. You can blame me for that with my wonky old teeth.' 'Your dad's got a friendly face.' I had to turn away when I heard her voice wobble as she said, 'Your mother looks lovely. Thank god she loved you so much.'

There was no rancour, no agenda in Adam's reply, just warmth and love. 'No one could have taken better care of me. Really.' He squeezed Mum's hand. 'You don't need to feel guilty.'

Louise, grudgingly, was complicit in keeping Dad away 'only because I don't know what it will do to him if he accidentally bumps into Adam'. It was quickly becoming apparent that our problem wasn't any longer whether Mum was going to die, but where she'd end up now she was going to live. Dad refused to entertain the idea of her coming home. Every time I mentioned it, he shook his head. 'I can't face it. How many times did she lie? All those letters from Brighton where she was supposedly "helping" her aunt, when she was really in London. That chest of things "belonging to her dad". I feel such a fool.'

Mum kept asking where Dad was.

'It's such bad timing, but he's got shingles and he's not allowed to visit you. The last thing you need is another infection.'

She'd been far more worried about him than her own recovery. 'Are you making sure he's eating? Has he seen a doctor? I bet he hasn't been looking after himself properly.'

I felt like I'd planted a whole load of lies in a bucket of compost and they'd grown so fast, they needed staking.

When Adam had popped out to fetch some water, she'd turned to me. 'What does Dad know about Adam?'

Her eyes were boring into me and it took all my acting ability to reply, 'We haven't told him anything yet. I thought it would be better coming from you.' I felt like such a coward, but I didn't want to cause a relapse by breaking the happy news that he was probably flicking through the Yellow Pages for divorce solicitors as she was planning her homecoming.

'Thank you. Thank you for understanding. About everything.' And I did. The one area in which I could definitely trump Louise's knowledge was mistakes. Though I'd hoped that Mum would open up much more. I tried to ask her who Adam's father was but she got quite snappy and shrugged, 'What does it matter now? It's so long ago. I can't even remember his name. It's all in the past.'

Except it wasn't. Dad was in the depths of depression at home, I was adjusting to having a big brother and Louise was still adamant she didn't want to know him. But I didn't dare press her. I couldn't imagine Mum having a one-night stand. I concluded that Adam's dad had broken her heart and it was too painful for her to think about even at a distance of decades.

I couldn't dedicate too much time to worrying about Adam's biological heritage when a much more pressing problem was looming now that Mum was a few days from being discharged. Louise had compassion fatigue, haranguing Dad at every opportunity with 'Don't be stupid. Of course she'll have to come back here. What are you two going to do without each other at your time of life?'

But Dad didn't look like he was budging any time soon. 'I've probably been living in the same street as her bloody fancy man for half my life with the whole damn city whispering about it.'

But he still wouldn't let anyone use Mum's 'Best wife in the world' mug or sit in her chair.

Jude and I got brain ache trying to work out how we could persuade Dad to give her a second chance.

Whenever I visited Mum, I tried to gather a few more pieces of the puzzle to find one tiny thing that might change Dad's mind. Eventually Mum had burst into tears, saying, 'I'm not talking about this any more until I've spoken to your dad. I'm going to have to tell him. I've no idea how he'll take it.'

But the problem was I did know. I'd tried this morning to persuade him to come and visit. He'd lost his temper with me. 'Grace,

I know you're trying to help, but this is between me and your mum. And I'm not in the mood to speak to her at the moment.'

So, feeling like a traitor, I offered Mum all the platitudes of 'It was such a long time ago,' 'He's bound to be upset, but he loves you so much, I'm sure he'll come round in the end,' 'The thing that's most important to him is that you get better.'

The nurse told me as I left on Monday afternoon that her bloods were normal and she was well enough to come home tomorrow. 'As long as she's got proper support and someone to look after her.' I had to remind myself to look like it was the best news ever.

I got into the car, hating myself for rushing to fix one thing and making an even bigger problem somewhere else. For *someone* else.

The traffic was jammed coming out of the hospital and I became desperate for the loo. I pulled over by Rob's café and dashed in, praying that Rob wouldn't be there. But my luck was out that day. 'Grace! How are you doing? How's Mum?'

Mortifyingly, I burst into tears. After I'd been to the loo, he ushered me to a table and quickly rustled up a slab of consoling carrot cake. He was so gentle and kind, I ended up pouring out the whole story, with that odd rush of liberation that comes with talking to someone you barely know. Given he already knew about Adam, I didn't hold back.

He leaned back in his chair. 'Will you take me to see your dad?'

'He's not in very good shape at the moment.'

Rob ran his fingers through the little hair he had left. 'I might be able to help him.'

'How?'

He fiddled with a sugar sachet. 'I've got a good idea about how your mum came to be pregnant with someone else's baby.' I must have looked horrified because he laughed. 'I'm not Adam's father, if that's what you're thinking.'

Everything else had failed. And time was running out. 'Let's go.'

CHAPTER FORTY-EIGHT
Monday 24 March 2014

My heart ached when I saw the hinge on the front gate was broken. Dad was the master of cobbling together a bit of metal from this, a screw from that, to fix anything. He drove Mum mad with his squirrelling away of old saucepans, bits of pallet, ancient light fittings.

Rob stopped just before we got to the door. 'You might not want to hear what I've got to tell him.'

'Let's see what Dad wants.' If it was something really upsetting, there was no way I was going to leave Dad on his own.

I knocked on the door rather than letting Rob see where the key was kept. Soon I'd be one of those old women, carrying my handbag from room to room. No answer. I shouted through the letter box and eventually Dad appeared, unshaven. Mum would have waved him off to the bathroom immediately.

'Dad, do you remember Rob? He used to sing with Mum? He knows a bit about what's gone on and he wanted to talk to you.'

If I'd been expecting him to rush to put the kettle on, I couldn't have been more mistaken. Dad shook off the torpor he'd been existing in for the last few weeks and launched himself forward, shouting right in Rob's face.

'It's you, isn't it? You're the one who got her pregnant. You saw me with her every week at the dance hall. You knew we were happy. But all that time you were waiting to take her off me. You must have loved it every time my ship sailed out of the harbour. Then disappearing as soon as you got her up the duff.'

Rob had his hands up in surrender, trying to calm him down. 'Danny! Dan! It wasn't me.'

Dad's eyes were flitting about, searching Rob's face for the tiniest indication he might be lying. He looked as though only a fragile thread of civilisation was stopping him balling his fists and plunging them into Rob's face

'Wasn't you? Well, who was it then? That thin bloke on the drums, what was his name? Johnny?'

'Jim. It wasn't him either.'

Something about this conversation reminded me of the repetitive stories I used to read to Jude when he was about four.

I put my hand on Dad's arm, but he hadn't finished. He shook me off.

'Bit of a bloody coincidence though, isn't it? Susie's son appears and then you suddenly come crawling out of the woodwork. You've got some gall, asking after her when I came to the café the other week.'

'Dad. Dad! Shall we take this inside?' I knew what our green was like. They'd be chewing on this for months, making up what they didn't know. Louise would have nipped this in the bud straightaway.

My words seemed to break through whatever fog Dad was in, because he suddenly turned back into the seventy-two-year-old who would still offer his seat to a woman however young they were, rather than this gnarly bulldog gnashing its teeth.

Inside, I bustled about, gathering up dirty mugs and plates in the lounge while they sat down. Mum would have been mortified. I tried to redeem the situation by making tea in a teapot and putting the biscuits on a plate. I was my mother's daughter, after all.

'Danny,' Rob said. 'Listen, I know it looks odd me turning up here. But Grace said you were in a bad way and, well, there's something I've felt terrible about for years. I've never spoken about it because I hoped it wasn't true, but I think it's the right time to talk about it.'

Dad looked all belligerent again. 'What do you know about what happened?'

Rob glanced at me. Then he turned to Dad. 'Might be a conversation to have just us two?'

Dad sat back and folded his arms. 'She knows more about what's gone on than I do.'

'You sure?' Rob put his hands on the armrests, his fingers rubbing at the draylon. 'Do you know who Adam's father is?'

Dad shook his head.

I swallowed, nervous about what was coming. 'Not really, no. Mum won't tell me anything about him.'

Rob sighed. 'She's never breathed a word about him to anyone, as far as I know.'

And he launched into a story we'd never have believed if Mum had told us.

'She loved singing so much. She was bored being at home while you were at sea with just a baby for company.' He pulled a face. 'I didn't mean... She really loved Louise, adored her, but she was young with all this talent, and we were all so naïve, thinking we could hit the big time.'

I watched Dad's face. I couldn't read what he was thinking. It was as though all his softness had disappeared, replaced by a toughened varnish to withstand all weathers. Rob filled us in on the talent scout and how he'd really been taken by Mum. 'The thing that's haunted me all these years is that she didn't want to join in. She saw it for what it was, a pipe dream, that she couldn't ever be part of, because she was already married with a child. She never looked at men, never flirted with anyone, Danny. Yes, we sang together a lot, but she never once let any of us believe there

was anyone other than you for her. We used to tease her that she
was singing every love song across the ocean to you.'

Dad wasn't giving an inch, not even showing that he'd heard
him. He just stared ahead, blankly. Rob was starting to stumble
over his words, swiping at his lips with his fingers. I wanted to tell
him to take his time, that we weren't judging him, but I'd already
been disloyal enough to Dad, so I kept smiling encouragingly.
He talked us through how the talent scout had dangled a record
deal in front of them, how he and Jim had begged Mum to go
along with it, how they'd all gone out for drinks. 'Jim and I were
taking it all in, but Suze, she wanted to go home. She was worried
about getting up for Louise in the morning.'

I wanted to smile at that. My ferocious sister would be pleased
to know she'd been Mum's priority.

We didn't ask a single question, just sat mesmerised like kids
at story time.

Rob stopped and I sensed he was pausing to choose the right
words. 'I had a bad feeling about him driving us home. I tried
to make him drop Suze off first. I asked her to stay at mine.' He
looked at Dad. 'I was going to give her my room and sleep on
the couch. Told her my mam wouldn't mind, even though she'd
probably have gone apeshit. I didn't want her alone in the car
with him. He was too keen on her, too familiar. And maybe ten,
fifteen years older than us. Had all the patter. Smooth.'

He put down his teacup. 'The truth is I wanted the record
deal so much that I was afraid to insist, afraid to upset him by
making a scene. I shouldn't have let her go.' He swallowed. 'But I
did. The next morning she came to see me, all flustered, looking
awful, as though she hadn't slept at all. I asked her if something
had happened, why she'd gone back on her promise. She told me
she'd grown up. I didn't want to believe that he'd done anything
to her. I was a coward. I didn't want anything to get in the way of

us making records, so I let her down for the second time. I didn't run after her, didn't try to get her to tell me the truth.'

Dad spoke for the first time. 'What are you trying to say?'

Rob struggled to meet Dad's eye. 'I think he forced your wife to have sex with him.'

I gasped. 'Raped her?

Rob nodded.

Even though I'd guessed what might be coming, I still felt a jolt to my stomach. My poor mum, cutting me off whenever I asked about Adam's dad. Now I understood why.

Rob seemed to run out of words after that. Dad didn't speak but his face told me his imagination was alive and kicking. Horrible ugly words and images hovered in the silence that followed. No one articulated them. My blood boiled as I thought about how often this story was repeated the world over. Big man in power thinking he was entitled to take what he wanted. Yep. I could imagine what had happened to Mum.

Rob was barely controlling his emotions, turning his teaspoon over and over in his palm. Eventually he spoke again, his voice tight and distressed. 'Then, the other week when I saw Grace and the boy, and we started chatting about when Suze was in the band and when he was born, I couldn't lie to myself any more about that night. The dates add up. I might be wrong, but I don't think so.' A tear slid down his craggy old face. 'It's too late now, but I'm so sorry. I should have been more forceful, less selfish. Don't be too hard on her.'

'But why didn't she tell me if it wasn't her fault?' Dad's words sounded as though they were riding on a sob.

Rob all but rolled his eyes. 'Would you have believed her? Wife on her own at home for, what was it, fifteen months? Would you have accepted what she told you? How could she even have explained? She'd have had to put it in a letter. She couldn't just greet you at the dock with a baby in her arms. Would you have agreed to bring up another man's child, especially in those circumstances? In the end, she probably thought that if she lost her son, she'd keep her husband and her daughter.'

'It would have been difficult to accept, Dad, wouldn't it?' I was desperate for him to see Mum's side of the story. It rang so true to me. 'She tried to do the right thing, although it probably doesn't feel like it to you. She did it to protect you. Not to hurt you. You'd never have forgiven yourself for being on the other side of the world when she needed you.'

Dad scratched his forehead. 'But she's kept the secret from me for over forty years. I must have come home a few months after he was born. It makes me feel like our whole marriage was a lie. I made hundreds of excuses for her, thousands over the years, for all the odd things she did. I felt like I was never enough for her. That none of us were.'

Rob fidgeted in his chair. 'I wish I could turn the clock back, Danny. But we were young, ambitious. Stupid.'

Dad slumped into the chair. 'I'm the stupid one. The idiot husband who breezed back in and didn't even notice anything was wrong. Not even that my wife had been raped and had had a baby.' Tears were streaming down his cheeks. 'I thought she could tell me anything. I thought we were happy.'

I ran my finger around the rim of my coffee cup. 'You were, you *are* happily married. If she didn't love you so much, she would have kept the baby and risked losing you.'

Dad looked bewildered. 'But why would she even want the baby?'

I knew the answer to that. That when Jude had moved inside me, when I felt that little human being depending on me for life, when I allowed myself to consider everything my baby could be – despite knowing that it would be a hard road, with complications and consequences – the question became, 'Why would I *not* want this baby?'

Rob stood up and held out his hand. 'I'm going to get off now. Good to see you again, Danny. I know it's a shock, but don't be too hard on Suze. We led her into the lions' den, then deserted her.'

Dad just about managed to shake his hand.

Rob shoved his hands in his pockets. 'I'm sorry, sorry with all my heart. I'm not even sure I've done the right thing by telling you. But you had a right to know. She didn't betray you. We betrayed her.'

My heart went out to him. 'You're not to blame, Rob. The arsehole who did it to her is to blame.'

Dad remained silent.

'Dad, it's not Rob's fault. He was only young himself.'

Rob put his hand up. 'It's okay, Grace.'

But it wasn't and I couldn't see how it ever could be.

CHAPTER FORTY-NINE

Monday 24 March 2014

After Rob had gone, I tried to make Dad see that fear of not being believed had stopped Mum telling the truth. He sat there, clinging to the mantra that their whole marriage had been built on deceit.

I could feel my temper rising. 'Dad, if you react like this now, years bloody later, without thinking for a minute what it was like for her, you on the other side of the world, Mum totally isolated because she knew the whole group hated her for ruining their chances of making a record, terrified that she'd have Louise taken away from her, having to admit to Nan that she'd been going singing instead of to pottery classes, and now had a bun in the oven to boot because some wanker had forced himself on her, *why* would she have told you?'

'Because we never lied to each other. About anything. I just can't get past the fact that she's had another child without breathing a word about it to me. One that no doubt she'll want to continue to see. A *brother* you'll want to see. What are we going to do, invite him over for Christmas? A permanent reminder that another bloke took advantage of your mother. And I'll just sit there like the fall guy, the idiot in the corner, who had no bloody idea what was going on. You can all chuck me a few walnuts and satsumas and I'll just nod along.'

This version of my father frightened me. It was a measure of how much had changed that my mother's erratic behaviour in the past now seemed pretty sane, given what she had to deal with. Dad, on the other hand, was a blurred silhouette of the person I'd always run to, whose love for me always outweighed his disapproval.

I had one last trump card left. I'd promised myself I'd never tell him. And to date, my gamble on finding Adam and getting everyone to adjust to his existence, hadn't exactly ended in a royal flush. But I couldn't let Dad divorce Mum. Not at this age.

Not when he still loved her.

Louise would have called it reframing or some such management tosh. But I didn't care what we called it as long as Dad saw things differently. And if this didn't work, I was going to have a father who was devastated not only by his wife, but also by his daughter.

'Let me put it to you this way. You love Jude, right?'

For a second, Dad relaxed, then he frowned. 'What's Jude got to do with anything?'

'You've always thought his dad was my boyfriend Ollie, someone I was in love with, who disappeared when I got pregnant?'

Dad's face took on a wary expression.

I took a deep breath. If this didn't work, the disaster we were currently experiencing would be just the starting point of the calamity to come. I got going on the story before I chickened out. 'You know the last hotel I worked in, that really trendy place, the one I said I'd left because they wouldn't let me have time off to sing at a festival?'

Dad nodded.

'In fact, the hotel manager had promoted me to Entertainment Assistant, with the possibility of running the whole department if I proved myself. I was in charge of booking bands, scheduling the programme, discovering new talent. For the first time, I was starting to earn decent money and was beginning to think I might even make you proud, instead of you always thinking I was such a loser.'

Dad put his hand up. 'I didn't think you were a loser. You were just taking a bit longer to find your feet.'

'Mum did then.'

Dad didn't contradict me.

I ploughed on. 'To start with, I spent most of my time with the hotel manager – I was his protégé, the one who'd put the hotel on the map for the fantastic gig nights. I was working really hard, doing tons of singing slots myself and going to listen to loads of bands, a sort of scout for local talent. Sometimes he'd join me – even though he was about forty, he knew a lot about music and, of course, I was flattered he wanted my opinion. He was fun and charming and usually took me out for dinner afterwards.'

God knows how Dad would receive the next bit of information.

'Anyway, after a while he started to get a bit over-friendly.'

'What do you mean, over-friendly?'

I couldn't look Dad in the eye, directing my gaze onto one of the castors under the foot of the armchair. 'He wanted me to have sex with him.'

This was so flaming awkward. Who discusses their sex lives with their seventy-two-year-old dad? I bloody hoped my 'story' had the desired effect.

I switched my scrutiny to an ornament on the mantelpiece. 'I didn't want to sleep with him, but I just felt as though I'd led him on, that I should have known he wasn't dragging himself to bands in crappy pubs because he wanted to discover a new "artiste". But we kind of made a joke of it between us. He'd say, "If you want to keep your job, you know what to do to keep the management happy." And I'd laugh it off, but I felt as though he expected it for promoting me. And worse than that, I felt as though I owed him, for giving me the opportunity.'

Dad was scowling, his lips moving as though he was desperate to interrupt. But I had to finish before I lost my nerve.

'And then, one night, all the staff were drinking together after hours. It was a waiter's birthday and the manager was letting us have whatever we wanted, all sorts of things, tequila, vodka, rum. Anyway, I got really drunk and he insisted on helping me back to my room. The next thing I remember after that was him being on top of me.'

Dad had his hand over his mouth, a moan escaping through his fingers.

'I couldn't do anything; I was too drunk. I just went along with it. I wasn't even sure it had happened the next morning. But the worst bit was he then seemed to think he could have sex with me whenever he wanted now we were past that first hurdle. And even though I didn't want to do it, not in the first place, or ever again, I just didn't know how to say no. I was desperate not to lose my job and have to move again. I was so tired of looking for work, sleeping on people's settees, chasing off to job "interviews" which were more like auditions for strip clubs. I think I convinced myself we were in some kind of a relationship. Or at least, I just had to put up with it.'

Dad looked distraught. 'Why didn't you just come home?'

'Pride. I'd made such a stand over leaving, of telling you all I was going to make my living as a singer. I just couldn't face crawling back, with all that "I told you so" from Mum and Louise.'

'Your mum would be so upset to hear that. She worried about you so much.'

'I'm not telling you this to make you feel bad, Dad. I'm trying to help you understand why women don't speak up about what's happened to them.' I moved on quickly, 'So when I discovered I was pregnant with Jude, I felt utter shame. I didn't – couldn't – tell anyone what had happened. I just assumed everyone would think I'd got what was coming to me, that I deserved it for being so stupid and not having the guts to say, "No, sorry, the fact that you promoted me doesn't give you the right to have sex with me." I mean, obviously it wouldn't happen to me now, but I'm thirty-six. Not nineteen. Back then, I just told myself that was how the world worked and I was naïve to think otherwise. I just got on with it. Until I realised I was pregnant. And then of course it came out he was married. When I said I didn't know what I was going to do – keep it or have an abortion – he got really angry, frightened that his wife would find out, I suppose. He became quite threatening, so I just left and went to stay with a girl I'd met, another singer.'

Dad had his head in his hands. 'I'm so sorry, Grace. I wish you'd been able to talk to us. You were so young to cope with all that on your own. We really let you down. No wonder you've never seemed interested in finding a boyfriend since.'

I carried on before I crumpled completely. 'I'd probably have had an abortion if Mum hadn't found out and persuaded me to keep him. I was afraid I wouldn't be able to love the baby. And I've got Mum to thank for convincing me otherwise, because I don't care who his father was. He's a lovely boy and I wouldn't be without him.'

I cleared my throat to stop the tears getting in the way of the really important thing I had to say. 'In the end, I've stopped thinking about how he was conceived. You've always loved Jude and you've never thought once about his father, except to say that he was missing out on his son. It's the same with Adam. Mum's right to love him and to want to spend time with him. He's still her child. She couldn't tell you because she was ashamed. You'd never have believed she hadn't somehow brought it on herself or led that bloody record bloke on. I've never told anyone for the same reasons and I'm supposed to be a liberated woman living in a modern age. Think what it was like for Mum in the sixties.'

Dad bowed his head. 'I wish you'd told me. I wish she'd told me.' He was swallowing hard with the effort of not crying. His voice cracked. 'I could have got my shotgun out. Bastard.'

I smiled at the familiar joke from my teenage years.

'Will you tell Jude one day?'

'Jude is never going to know what happened to me. It's too big a burden. I'm not having my sixteen-year-old staring at himself in the mirror and wondering if he'll turn out like his father. I've let him think that I had a one-night stand. I'm not proud of that, but I'm going to put my energy into making him a decent man, respectful of women.'

'Come here and give me a hug.' He reached out for me, sighing heavily as though some of the toxic emotion circulating within him for weeks had found an outlet.

I leaned into him. I'd trusted him with my shameful secret and he hadn't let me down.

In that hug, brimming with the ferociousness of parental love, I felt a tiny tendril of hope.

CHAPTER FIFTY

Tuesday 25 March 2014

'What do you want to do? Bring Mum home or make sure Dad and the house are in a suitable state?' I asked Louise.

Even though she was quite right about who'd be best deployed where, it still irritated me that she'd put on her martyr voice and said, 'I think I'd better be the one to give the house a good clean, don't you?'

I waited, certain she'd have to make another little jibe of some sort. And I wasn't disappointed.

'And Dad knows I'm on his side.'

My voice trembled with fury as I said, 'It's not about sides! He knows I looked for Adam for all the right reasons.' And then I left the room. Very late in life, I was starting to learn that walking away instead of engaging in increasingly angry debates was the key to greater happiness and lower blood pressure.

Louise wouldn't accept that being reunited with Adam had helped Mum get better. 'I googled Acute Kidney Injury. It's quite common and, apparently, most people get better quickly once they get the right antibiotics and fluids. They obviously knew what they were doing at that hospital.' She stopped short of telling me that I was living in la-la land if I thought Adam had anything to do with Mum's recovery, but she never missed an opportunity to hint that I'd caused a great kerfuffle for no reason.

But whether or not Adam had helped Mum get back on her feet, he was certainly saving my sanity. I'd spoken to him the night before, the safety valve in the family pressure cooker, his words wise and reassuring. 'This is a really big thing. From what you've said, Louise doesn't do change well, so she's going to take a bit more time to come round. My own sister wasn't that keen on me upsetting the status quo either. Some people are just like that. We'll have to be patient. Best of luck in getting Susie home safely tomorrow. Give her my love.'

And now the moment was here. Mum clutching her handbag sitting in the armchair on the ward waiting for me. Just seeing her dressed and able to stand up on her own made me want to cry. I'd spent several nights lying in bed, wondering what I'd say about her at her funeral. Whether I'd even be able to speak at all. Whether any of us would. And now I'd had a reprieve; a chance to understand her rather than feel aggrieved that she didn't understand me.

'Did Dad come with you?' Her face lit up hopefully.

'No, but he's waiting for you at home. I think Louise is dashing about licking everything into shape as we speak.'

She smiled. 'Your father never was too good on his own.' She hurried on. 'He's lovely in lots of other ways though.'

I bloody hoped he was going to be lovely in the only way that counted right now. I had less than an hour to prepare Mum for how Dad might greet her. It had been all very well to spin the line about Dad having shingles and keeping away while she was ill but it made leading into the conversation I had to have in the next sixty minutes pretty tricky.

We signed all the formalities, said our thanks to the nursing staff and began the laborious journey to the car. Mum was always having a go at Dad for dawdling. 'For goodness sake, Danny. Get a march on, I've got things to do today.' Today though, she kept leaning on me, saying, 'Sorry for being so slow. It's like someone's pulled the plug on me.'

As I helped her into the car, I ran through my opening lines in my head. 'Dad knows a little bit about what's gone on.' 'I hope you won't mind, but we did have to tell Dad about Adam.' 'I know you said to keep Dad out of it but…'

In the end, I just blurted out what had happened with Rob when I'd first met Adam and then how he'd come over to talk to Dad, to explain about *that* night.

Mum went very still. 'Rob went round to see your dad? What did he say exactly?'

With a skill I had fine-tuned a lot lately, I gave her the bare bones.

She started to cry. 'I've never told anyone that. Ever. Does Adam know?'

I narrowly avoided going into the back of another car as the traffic lights turned red. 'No. I keep telling him I don't know anything about that side of things. That's up to you, Mum.'

I drove on, wanting to pull over and give Mum a hug, casting about for the right words to comfort her. Mum and I weren't used to talking about feelings. I'd managed to be a bit more open, a bit more honest while she'd been in hospital, even saying, 'I love you' several times without feeling stupid. I'd have to keep up the habit even without the fear I might not get another opportunity to say it driving me forwards. And right now, with my mother crying her eyes out in the passenger seat, was as good a time as any.

I took a deep breath. 'Mum. I know I'm the last person to tell you how to run your life. And I can't promise you, though I wish I could, that Dad will be okay with it all. But I want you to know that I understand exactly what happened. And I don't blame you at all. You don't have anything to be ashamed of. The arsehole who did it to you does, but you don't. And now, you've got to stop thinking about all of that and concentrate on getting better. I love you, Mum.'

Her hand slid onto my lap. 'Thank you, Gracie.' A few seconds ticked past. 'Amazing Grace.'

We drove the rest of the way in silence. As I turned the corner into their road, I didn't dare look at the windows of their house in case I glimpsed Dad storming out of the lounge. I busied myself with parking the car and helping Mum out, stunned that the door hadn't flung open the second we pulled up.

I supported Mum as we walked up the path. Finally, Louise opened the front door, still wearing her rubber gloves – just in case we were in danger of overlooking her contribution. 'Welcome home, Mum.' She leaned forward and grabbed Mum's bag. But Mum was craning to see where Dad was.

A mixture of fear and fury was fermenting inside me. He couldn't let Mum down now when she was so frail. Of course we understood where he was coming from, but he was a bigger man than that, decent and generous of spirit. The man who'd helped shape my son, who'd made sure he knew how to be a good man, who'd told him, 'You're a strong lad. That's a big responsibility. Make sure you use your strength to protect, not to hurt.'

Then suddenly Dad was in the hallway. His lips started to quiver, his eyes locking onto hers as though Louise and I weren't there. He held out his hand, the fingers of the other one wiping his face. 'You'll be wanting a cup of tea, I suppose?'

And just as she had, every time for forty-nine years, Mum said, 'Go on, then. That would be lovely.'

CHAPTER FIFTY-ONE
10 March 2015

If it had been another couple, I'd have been watching them, thinking they were putting on a show of harmony for everyone around them, then resisting the temptation to stab each other with nail scissors the second they were out of sight. But the last year had changed everything. That spiky, unpredictable core running through Mum had dissolved, giving way to a softer, approachable manner. So much so that Jude often told her things I'd hoped she'd never find out: 'We were talking about how boyfriends and girlfriends have changed since her day. She seemed quite surprised that lots of young people get with each other without being boyfriend and girlfriend.'

It was a measure of how much Mum had mellowed that she hadn't come trotting straight to me to discuss how I needed to have a word with Jude about the company he was keeping. But the biggest change was in how affectionate Mum was with Dad. If I didn't know the circumstances I'd probably have joined Jude in the face-pulling every time he stroked her face or she kissed him on the head. When I looked back now, she used to function as though she was braced for him to leave her, a hard shell encasing her, quick to anger and impossible to reason with, as though she didn't deserve Dad and was pushing him away before he turned on her.

Since she came out of hospital, it was Dad more than Mum on a short fuse: 'What sort of man doesn't notice that his wife has had a baby? Did you think so little of me that you couldn't tell me what had happened? Your experience shaped our whole family life and you didn't even think it was worth a conversation.'

We'd had months of outbursts from Dad, berating himself for not protecting Mum. 'If I'd known, I'd have made them give me leave. Me and a few of my mates would have liked to have paid him a visit.' And his eyes would dart about as though he could picture the whole revenge scenario in his mind. When he'd exhausted that, he'd threaten to hunt down Jude's dad and give him what for. Which was why I'd never mentioned any names. I definitely didn't need my seventy-three-year-old father on the warpath with a bunch of his friends in Zimmer frame convoy.

The mass of emotions that Dad was having to manage often caused me to question my meddling in the family history. But even when Mum first came out of hospital and he was grilling her, going over and over the past, she never shouted back or did the whole 'If you don't like it, you know where to shove your golden anniversary plans.' She just looked really sad and said, 'I'm sorry I made some bad decisions. I don't know what else to say. I wish I could change what happened but I can't. I never stopped loving you.'

And Dad would wince, pull her to him and say, 'I shouldn't take it out on you. I'd like to meet him on a dark night though.'

So tonight, I loved seeing them holding hands as they looked at the hellebores in the garden, everything about Mum relaxed, rather than coiled and critical as she would have been, overwhelmed by the need to make everything perfect. She hadn't even felt the need to readjust all the Happy Golden Anniversary balloons that Jude had tied round the garden in a haphazard way.

We'd pushed the boat out and squashed a tiny marquee into the back garden. It was nothing short of a miracle that we'd all made this fiftieth anniversary alive – and still together.

Matilda was twirling about in a frilly floaty dress I was sure had Louise choking on her feminist principles, but I'd noticed she'd abandoned lots of her opinions in favour of a couple of dominant themes: blaming Mum for her difficult childhood and not welcoming Adam into the family.

'I lost my chance of going to music college, because of what had happened to her,' she'd say.

I'd argue back. 'But she was just trying to protect you. If you feel that hard done by, why not apply for the *X Factor*? You're only forty-nine, not ninety-nine.'

Louise would huff and puff about not being able to throw everything in on a whim and how I needn't think she was going to start calling Adam her brother. 'I don't even know him.'

It was so unlike me to be the reasonable, measured one. 'But what happened wasn't his fault. Why should he be punished?'

'I'm not punishing him. I'm just not including him in my life at this late stage. He's the lucky one, growing up in a family where the world didn't fall apart if he didn't get an A in geography.'

'Was Mum really that bad?'

And on it went, both of us recalling our childhoods in a totally different way as though we'd grown up in two separate households. Eventually, just to avoid falling out completely, I'd agree that Mum had been more relaxed with me because she'd already proved that she could raise one intelligent, diligent daughter. And as a measure of my new-found maturity, I didn't even respond when Louise chipped in with, 'She let you run wild.'

Today I'd begged her to think of the bigger picture and put a face on for the celebrations. We had so much to be grateful for. Mum was so much better, though she still suffered with terrible joint pain.

Ten months in, Dad seemed to have made a fragile peace with the past, which made me less guilty about how much time I was spending with my new brother.

It was Dad's suggestion they should invite Adam and his mother to the golden anniversary celebration. He made the proposal one Sunday lunch, which ended up with both Mum and me blubbing into the Brussels. Dad went on about us going soft in the head, but I could see that the magnanimous gesture somehow lifted him above his own hurt and sense of betrayal. While we were snivelling, I'd done an 'in for a penny, in for a pound' and suggested inviting Jeanie as well. Dad had pulled a face and said, 'For Christ's sake, promise me Davina McCall won't turn up to film us. It'll be like a bloody episode of *Long Lost Family*.'

Mum smiled through her tears and whispered, 'Do you think Jeanie would come?'

I nodded. 'When I saw her last year, she'd really missed you. You know Jeanie, I bet she'd love to party on.'

Now it was nearly seven o'clock, my stomach was churning. I eyed the bottles of champagne, wondering if a quick swig might just dull the fear that instead of family unity I might have arranged a family bloodbath. Then Jude connected up his iPod, 'Uptown Funk' filled the marquee and Matilda, god bless her, took to the dance floor in the unselfconscious way that only an eight-year-old can pull off. Mum and Dad were hovering between the hallway and kitchen ready to welcome the guests and funnel them through into the party tent and I kept running to the loo, which wasn't quite the glamorous poise of party organiser that I'd envisaged.

First to arrive was Jeanie. Despite her sixty-four years, she'd embraced the anniversary theme with a gold sequinned dress and some heart tattoos up her forearm. 'Like them? My granddaughter did them for me, wash off ones. If I like them, I might have them done properly.'

She hadn't changed. Still made a beeline for the drinks, still bowling up to people with outrageous comments and laughing at their shock. 'This Judy, Judy, Judeeeee?' she sang at my bemused son. 'He's a stunner, isn't he?' Jude looked terrified and ran off to fetch some peanuts.

The reunion between her and Mum made me wonder about the stubborness of human beings. They folded into each other like people who'd been waiting for this moment to feel whole again. I watched them slip into their easy laughter and heartfelt empathy, bouncing from one subject to another. The death of Nan – 'My greatest regret is that she didn't live to meet Adam grown up.' Jeanie's unruly grandchildren – 'Little beggars they are.' Rick's surprising success at running his own furniture business – 'Your Dan is to thank for that'. Mum leaned in and asked a question. Jeanie's face clouded and she shook her head. Mum pulled her close, sorrow and regret on her face.

They weren't like two people who'd been estranged for nearly thirty years, more like two friends who'd seen each other the week before. How many people in the world missed great chunks of time with people they loved, time they could never get back, through a comment taken the wrong way or a misplaced reaction, which pride or fear of rejection exacerbated, spreading like ivy, covering all the paths back, all the avenues of apology, until the only way forward was alone?

I hugged Jude with the excitement of one part of my plan paying off. He allowed me three seconds before he disentangled himself.

Some of Dad's old colleagues came in then, with Craig doing a brilliant job as coat taker and wine waiter.

I kept looking at my watch. What if Adam bottled it at the last minute? What if the thought of meeting Dad for the first time was just too overwhelming? What if Shona persuaded him or herself out of it? I'd be sick with disappointment. I'd talked it through with Dad and he'd promised he'd be okay. 'Better at the party. Won't be so intense. We can just say hello and leave the proper getting to know each other for another time. But it gets us over the first hurdle.'

God bless my huge-hearted dad. He'd even gathered us all together to say he'd been thinking about Adam's 'dad' and how none of us were to make any reference to how he'd been conceived, that only Mum was to discuss his father, 'when and if she sees fit'.

If my Jude grew up to be half the man my dad was, I'd consider myself to have done a bloody good job.

Just as Mum looked at the clock in the kitchen before checking her lipstick again in the hallway mirror, the bell rang. I threw the door open, desperate to find Adam and his mother and not another of Dad's friends who couldn't believe I was thirty-seven and not seventeen with 'all those earrings'. There he stood, holding a bottle of port, with Shona half-hidden by a huge bouquet of yellow roses. I hugged him.

'We've been sitting round the corner for half an hour, psyching ourselves up.'

'You'll be fine, everyone's looking forward to seeing you.'

I shook Shona's hand. 'Thank you so much for coming.'

Mum came down the hallway, her limp more pronounced than ever.

If ever there was a moment for a scientific experiment on the ability of the human face to contain a hundred emotions, the BBC missed a trick. Mum's face softened.

Shona stepped forward and delivered the most generous words I've heard one human being say to another. 'Thank you so much for my son. Your son.'

Mum grasped both of her hands. 'Thank *you* for looking after him when I couldn't. He's been very lucky.'

And then all the carefully applied make-up, mine included, washed off in an avalanche of tears and laughter, that had us all dabbing at our faces with kitchen roll and checking our mascara.

Louise appeared at the kitchen door with two glasses of champagne, which she handed to Adam and Shona. 'You might need this. I'm Louise,' she said in a voice that sounded as though she was practising for her imminent ascension to the throne. But Adam grinned as though she'd clapped him on the back and told him she couldn't be happier.

'Thank you very much. I've heard such fantastic things about you from Grace.' He paused. 'I know how hard this has been on you, and it's very kind of you to let us join in tonight. I hope we're not intruding.'

Louise blinked rapidly. 'You're very welcome. I'll go and find Dad.' And she shot off.

Mum looked torn, as though she wanted to make sure Louise was okay but didn't want to leave Adam and Shona.

Adam turned to me. 'Is she all right with us coming?'

I nodded, understanding for the first time that Louise couldn't help the way she felt, that her feelings governing loyalty and love were instinctive, not logical. 'She takes a bit of getting used to. Give her time.'

But tonight, she'd extended the olive branch. Well, an olive twig, at least.

Mum put her arm through Shona's and I ushered Adam through.

Mum squeezed his shoulder. 'You've no idea how happy I am to have *all* of my family with me tonight.'

Before Adam could reply, Dad appeared. I felt Adam tense.

Mum moved over to Dad. 'Adam, Shona, this is Danny, my husband.'

Shona shook Dad's hand and didn't let go, her words bursting out of her, as though she'd been wanting to say them for so long. 'Thank you for welcoming Adam. I know it can't have been easy for you.' I loved that she tagged on, 'He's a really lovely man though,' as though even at forty-five she needed to fight his corner, make sure people appreciated what a jewel she was handing over. I'd be the same whatever age Jude was.

Adam put out his hand but Dad pulled him into a bear hug.

'Looking forward to not being the only bloke in a family of women. 'Bout time the balance was redressed.'

Dad was right. There were more good people in the world than bad and the best one of them all was standing right in front of me.

A LETTER FROM KERRY

Dear Reader,

I want to say a huge thank you for choosing to read *The Secret Child*. If you did enjoy it, and want to keep up to date with all my latest releases, just sign up at the following link. Your email address will never be shared and you can unsubscribe at any time.

www.bookouture.com/kerry-fisher

I never know where inspiration for a book is going to come from. I had a conversation with a friend of mine about the Mother and Baby homes that existed in the sixties and seventies, which set off a spark of an idea. That combined with watching *Long Lost Family* and seeing how desperately people want to find their birth families, set me thinking about how giving a baby up for adoption must colour everything else that comes afterwards. From reading about lots of women's experiences, the one thing that really touched and saddened me was that so many felt guilty and ashamed, unable to talk to anyone about their experience. And the idea for this book was born.

I love writing about the challenges of parenthood. Like Louise's friends in the story, I thought parenting was an absolute breeze until I had my own children. I found it quite cathartic writing about Grace going off the rails, putting (at least some of) my worst fears onto paper. I'm sitting here with my fingers crossed that my fictional character doesn't morph into reality in my own house.

I'm also intrigued by how siblings, brought up in the same household, with the same parents, can be so different (my own children included!). In Susie's case, giving up Edward affected what sort of mother she became to her other children, but I'd be interested to know whether readers think the fact that Grace and Louise were so different was the result of nature or nurture.

Somewhere, sprinkled into that mix, I became fascinated by how people who love each other fall out and never speak again because neither one can find the right moment to try to make amends. Eventually so much time elapses, it's hard to find a way back.

Finally, I wanted to end on a message of hope – that there are more good people in the world than bad, that decency, forgiveness and love will triumph. Even in these turbulent times, I still believe that.

I hope you enjoyed *The Secret Child* and would be very grateful if you could write a review if you did. I'd love to hear what you think, and it makes a real difference to helping new readers discover one of my books for the first time.

I love hearing from my readers – you can get in touch on my Facebook page, through Twitter, Goodreads or my website. Whenever I hear from readers, I am reminded of why I love my job – pure motivational gold!

Thank you so much for reading,

Kerry xx

kerryfisherauthor/

@KerryFSwayne

www.kerryfisherauthor.com/

ACKNOWLEDGEMENTS

As always, I write my acknowledgements with joy – that I'm lucky to have so many people help me write the best book I can – and trepidation – that I'm going to miss someone out.

I'm going to start with my lovely publishers, Bookouture. Writing, getting published, *staying* published is a tough business. I consider myself very fortunate to work with a company that is not only dynamic and professional but really looks after its authors. So a huge thank you to all the team at Bookouture, for working so hard to get our books out into the world in the best possible shape. Special thanks to Lydia Vassar-Smith for having faith in me, to Jenny Geras for her meticulous editing and endless cheerleading, and to Kim Nash for all the many hours she dedicates to publicising our books. It's been a huge privilege to be part of the supportive author community at Bookouture too.

Thank you to everyone at Darley Anderson – Mary Darby, Emma Winter and Kristina Egan have worked wonders in getting my books out into the wider world. My agent, Clare Wallace, has been her usual wonderful self – wise and calm – when I am not.

I've been lucky enough to make some great author friends along the way – thanks to Jane Lythell for keeping me company on a couple of writing retreats while this book got off the starting blocks. And to Julia White and Steve, for lending us their gorgeous cottage to get away from it all. A big shout-out to Jenny Ashcroft and to all the members of the DWLC – Claire, Kendra, Adrienne and Alison – your support means everything.

As always, the bloggers and FB book groups have been a force to be reckoned with – you do an amazing job in spreading the word about new books and I really do appreciate the time you take to comment, read and write reviews.

Anna Collins is not only a wonderful friend but a great source of medical information – any inaccuracies are mine. Mike Adams was very kind to share his knowledge of life in the navy in the sixties – thanks to Harriet Benge for facilitating it. I'd also like to thank Lisa Timoney who generously offered a wealth of personal details about her own adoption.

I've had great support from my family – immediate and extended. Thank you – I'm looking forward to not peering at you over a laptop lid for a few weeks!

Finally – a huge thank you to all the readers who buy, review and recommend my books – and especially anyone who takes the time to contact me personally. Those messages never fail to lift my day.

Made in the USA
Middletown, DE
16 July 2019